THE SALBINE SISTERS

SARAH ETTRITCH

NORN PUBLISHING
TORONTO, CANADA

Library and Archives Canada Cataloguing in Publication

Ettritch, Sarah, 1963–
The Salbine Sisters / Sarah Ettritch.

ISBN 978-0-9813320-2-4

I. Title.

PS8609.T77S24 2010   C813'.6   C2010-906294-9

Editing by Marg Gilks
Cover design by Boulevard Photografica/Patty G. Henderson

Printed in the USA
v1

Published by Norn Publishing
www.NornPublishing.com

For Kath and Jim

Acknowledgements

My thanks to Jennifer Brinkman for always believing in me, which makes all the difference. Thanks also to Marg Gilks, a true Mistress of Editing. Finally, to Patty Henderson: you worked on the cover during a difficult time in your life, yet you were attentive and went the extra mile to please. For that, you have my gratitude and respect.

Chapter One

MADDY RAN HER HAND UP LILLIAN'S arm, her fingertips skimming along the pale, damp skin. "I can't wait for our next lesson." She gently pressed her lips against Lillian's shoulder and then her ear.

Lillian rolled onto her back and threw her arm over her head, her chest still heaving. "I'm supposed to be teaching you how to draw and control fire," she said breathlessly.

Maddy laughed. "If the point was to generate heat, I'd say you succeeded." She quickly smoothed her expression when Lillian glared at her.

"Your examination is next month and you can barely light a bloody candle!"

"I guess extra lessons are in order." Somehow she managed to say that with a straight face. All her lessons except the first had followed a similar route: first the training room, then Maddy's chambers.

A gust of wind blew one of the shutters against the wall with a *thwack* that drowned out Lillian's words, but her bulging eyes and pinched mouth clearly conveyed her response. Maddy could understand why one stern look from Lillian always sent the other initiates into a bobbing fit. She might have become immune to Lillian's powers of intimidation, but she didn't want to disappoint her. "I'll try harder," she murmured as she leaned over and traced one of the lines near the corner of Lillian's eye. "I know I can do it."

"I'm sure you can." Lillian's face softened. "But you have to focus. We both have to focus."

Suddenly feeling like the inexperienced initiate she was, Maddy snuggled into Lillian and buried her face in the other woman's shoulder. Not for the first time, she wondered what they were doing and where it would lead. An initiate and a mistress? And not just any mistress—Mistress Lillian.

The wind carried a chill and the fire had long-since died. Shivering, Maddy reached for the blanket heaped at their feet and pulled it to their shoulders. They lay quietly for a while, the only sounds their quiet breathing and the echoing footsteps of the defenders patrolling the courtyard below.

Maddy almost asked if Lillian would care to take tea together one day. But Lillian had never approached her outside of their scheduled lessons, had never asked her to go for a walk or to share a meal. Maybe Lillian's interest didn't extend beyond Maddy's bedchamber. Maddy would only ruin it if she asked for more, and she must remember her place. Even so, curiosity pushed her to pry. "What do you usually do after early morning prayers?"

"Nothing important," Lillian said.

"Oh." She searched for something else to say, then jumped when Lillian threw the blanket aside, doused the kerosene lamp sitting on the table near the bed, and stood. "Where are you going?" Maddy asked, hoping her curiosity hadn't driven Lillian to return to her own chambers.

"Nowhere." The moonlight silhouetted her as she pulled the window shut. When she closed the shutters she disappeared in enveloping darkness. The bed creaked. Maddy pressed her body against Lillian's, to warm her.

"What—what will you be doing tomorrow?" Lillian asked.

"I have a history lesson, and my embroidery time," Maddy said, thrilled by Lillian's interest. "Oh, and my lute lesson." Though she planned to give that up; her ears agreed too often with Sister Edith's pained expression.

"It's been a long time since I sat through a lesson. Can't say I miss them." Lillian rolled away. "Anyway, I have to be up for early morning prayers."

Disappointed, Maddy closed her eyes when Lillian's lips brushed her cheek, then smiled when Lillian's hand bumped into hers. "Good night," Lillian murmured, holding Maddy's hand.

"Good night, Lillian."

It didn't take her long to drift off.

HER EYES FLEW open; she shot upright, ears attuned to the foreign voice. A man, in the Initiates Tower! She blinked and wondered why the shutters were open, then saw Lillian, already in her shift, stepping into her rough leather shoes. The muffled male voice came again, followed by a shriek. Maddy swung her legs off the bed, adrenaline coursing through her.

Lillian pulled on her robe and quickly buttoned it. "Stay here."

Maddy nodded. Lillian unbolted the door and grasped its iron ring to pull it open. The moment she stepped over the threshold, Maddy slipped into her shift, wrapped herself in the blanket, and padded after her.

Now that the door was open, she could make out the man's words: "Come on, darlin'. Give us a kiss."

Maddy stayed in the shadows just inside her chambers. In the early morning light, she recognized Conrad, the Duke of Merrin, pawing at Gwendolyn.

"Get off her!" Abigail shouted, pulling on his elbow.

"Let her go!" Lillian snapped. When Merrin turned toward Lillian, Gwendolyn seized the opportunity to duck away from him. "Go back to your chambers," Lillian said, her eyes still on Merrin.

Gwendolyn darted into an open door across the hall and quickly swung it shut. Abigail scampered away. A moment later, Maddy heard the thud of another door closing. Where was Nora? Her chambers were also across from Maddy's. Surely she wouldn't be sleeping through this racket. Maddy was tempted to step across to check Nora's door, but she didn't want Lillian to see her.

Merrin squinted bleary eyes at Lillian. "Now, who have we here?" He staggered toward her. Maddy's nose wrinkled—the man reeked of ale. "I prefer lamb, love, but I suppose a bit of mutton wouldn't hurt." He leered at Lillian.

The hairs on the back of Maddy's neck warned her. She stepped back.

"Come to me, darlin'," Merrin slurred, reaching for Lillian.

Lillian thrust out her right hand. Merrin flew back and slammed against the wall, narrowly missing Gwendolyn's door. He slid to the floor, his mouth hanging open. Then he clamped it shut and his eyes cleared. "You bitch!" he spat, leaping to his feet. "You f—" His eyes bulged. He sank to his knees.

"I don't like it when people are rude," Lillian murmured, her taut hands and the veins prominent near her temples the only visible signs that she was drawing an element.

Merrin's mouth moved, but only a squeak came out. He clawed at his throat, tears streaming down his red face.

Maddy was more interested in how Lillian was preventing air from reaching Merrin's lungs than in his discomfort. Forgetting herself, she moved into the hall, closer to Lillian. The duke wasn't turning blue—Lillian wasn't completely starving him of air.

A voice cracked out: "Lillian!" Abbess Sophia and her consort, Mistress Elizabeth, emerged from the stairwell with Barnabus and Nora on their heels. "Enough!"

Annoyance flashed across Lillian's face, but she relaxed and turned away from the duke. Still on his knees, Merrin supported himself with one hand while his other clutched his throat. He gulped in air as if he were hyperventilating.

Mistress Elizabeth raised the lamp that had illuminated the stairwell, casting more light on the situation. Barnabus stepped to Lillian's side, the glowing lamplight flickering along his polished gold breastplate. The clink of armour announced the imminent arrival of more defenders. The two newcomers stopped next to the abbess and her consort.

"I told you," Nora said to the abbess.

"Yes, thank you, Sister." Abbess Sophia adjusted the position of her spectacles and peered at Merrin.

"Apparently he's mistaken us for tavern whores," Lillian said as Merrin struggled to his feet and stood swaying. He managed to keep his balance—barely.

The abbess looked to the heavens and shook her head. "You're not supposed to be here, Your Grace. The defenders will escort you out."

He pointed at Lillian. "I want her punished," he said hoarsely.

Lillian's eyes widened. "Me, punished? You're the one trespassing. You're the one who tried to force yourself on sisters when the whores didn't want you."

Merrin lunged at Lillian, then raised his hands and backed away, three swords at his throat.

"Get him out of here," the abbess murmured.

The three defenders slid their swords back into their scabbards. Two of them grasped Merrin by the arms and half led, half supported him into the stairwell. Barnabus dropped to one knee in front of the abbess and bowed his head. "Forgive me."

"You'll have my forgiveness when you find out how he got through the gates," the abbess said. "And how did he make it up the hill in his state? Where are his men?"

"I'll find the answers you seek, Abbess."

"And have Stephen tell him to stick to the whores next time," Mistress Elizabeth added. "All that ale must be addling his brain."

"Yes, do," the abbess agreed, nodding. "The fool!"

"As you wish, Abbess." Barnabus rose and nodded, then marched away.

"Sister Nora, Sister Maddy, return to your chambers," the abbess said.

Maddy bobbed a curtsey along with Nora, then winced when Lillian turned to her in surprise. She should have ducked back inside before Lillian noticed her.

"Lillian, my study, half an hour," the abbess barked as Maddy pushed her door shut. Did the abbess want to discuss Lillian's handling of Merrin, or her presence in the Initiates Tower at this hour? Maddy leaned against the door in dismay. If the abbess ended her lessons with Lillian, what followed them would likely end too, dashing Maddy's hope for more.

"MERRIN IS A vacuous, useless, self-absorbed, lazy pig!" Lillian spat. "Did you expect me to just stand there and watch him paw at the initiates?"

Sophia lifted the teapot from the silver tray and raised her eyebrows at Lillian, who shook her head. "No, I didn't expect you to just stand there," she said, holding the teapot's lid in place with one hand as she poured tea into a flowered teacup. "But he is the duke."

"Everyone knows Stephen runs the county."

"Well, we all wish Stephen had been born two minutes earlier." Sophia set the teapot on the tray. She lifted the cup to her lips and took a sip, then blew on its contents and returned it to its saucer. "But he wasn't. And as much as I loathe Merrin, we have to be careful not to antagonize him. He comes up with enough reasons to resent us on his own. Did you have to suffocate him?"

"I didn't suffocate him. I made sure he could breathe."

"Barely."

Lillian folded her arms. "I'm not apologizing, to you or to him. He got exactly what he deserved."

"And now I'll have to soothe any hurt feelings," Sophia said, shaking her head at the bother. "He might insist I punish you."

"And will you?"

"No. But only because he had no business being in the Initiates Tower, or on monastery grounds, for that matter. I hope Barnabus gets to the bottom of it." Sophia pointed a warning forefinger at Lillian. "But that doesn't mean I'm not upset with you. If you need to, um, deal with him again, show some restraint—for me."

"Very well," Lillian muttered, feeling a smidgen of regret that Sophia would have to make a grand show of smoothing Merrin's wounded ego. Better Sophia than her; there was a reason she'd never coveted Sophia's position. "Is that it, then? Can I go now?"

"Not just yet," Sophia murmured. She took another sip of her tea.

Annoyed, Lillian shifted in her chair and stifled a sigh. *Would Sophia please get on with it!* She wanted to check an experiment before early morning prayers.

Sophia set her cup down. "I was just wondering when you're planning to let everyone in on the amazing discovery you've made."

"What amazing discovery?" Lillian snapped, wondering exactly what was in Sophia's tea.

"Why, the ability to teleport, of course," Sophia said lightly. "It didn't take long for me and Elizabeth to rouse ourselves when Nora banged on our door. She waited for us in the hall, and a minute later, we were on our way to the Initiates Tower. The door to your chambers is in full view of mine, yet Nora didn't mention anything about you leaving your chambers. Barnabus met us when we were halfway down the east steps, and he didn't mention seeing you either. Yet there you were, fully robed, when we arrived." Her brow furrowed. "I guess you must have developed psychic abilities too, since you knew exactly where Merrin was without anyone telling you."

This time she didn't bother to stifle a sigh. "If you want to ask me something, ask! Why must you always drag everything out instead of saying what you want to say?"

"If that's what you want. Who were you with, Lillian?"

"I don't think that's any of your affair."

"It is my affair if there's going to be drama in the Initiates Tower," Sophia said harshly. "Now, there are only four chambers on that floor, so if I have to summon four sisters here, I will. Though I presume I can eliminate Nora, because you wouldn't have sent her for me. So who is it?"

Lillian blew out some air and studied her fingernails. The last thing she wanted was Sophia questioning everyone about her bed partners. "Maddy."

"Maddy?"

Lillian snapped her head up. "Yes, Maddy! Can I go now?"

"Maddy is, what, twenty-four?" Sophia said, ignoring Lillian's question. "And you are . . ." She stared at Lillian.

"Forty-one. And a half." Sophia continued to stare at her. "Three-quarters?" Sophia's eyes narrowed. "All right, forty-two next month." Much to Lillian's dismay, her face had grown hot. "And before you tell me I'm making a fool of myself, I know she probably has a different sister in her bed every night."

"Would it bother you if she did?"

Terribly. She'd admitted as much to herself last week, when she'd had trouble working out a potion formula because thoughts of Maddy had continually broken her concentration. But admitting that to Sophia . . .

Her silence answered for her. Sophia's forehead creased. "Oh, Lillian," she said softly. "I've hoped you might find a reason to emerge from that claustrophobic old laboratory of yours every once in a while, but I thought perhaps another mistress might catch your eye. Dorothy shares your love of alchemy."

Well, good for Dorothy.

"She's been alone since Winifred went to Salbine last year."

"Sophia, I'm perfectly happy on my own, all right?"

"You *were* perfectly happy." Sophia peered at Lillian through her spectacles. "Why Maddy?"

She'd asked herself the same question many times. "I don't know."

"And you don't seem bothered that you can't explain it. Oh dear."

"What's wrong with Maddy?"

"Nothing. It's just that Maddy's . . . not like you. She doesn't question, she simply believes."

"Are you going to forbid me from seeing her?" Lillian asked, wanting to end a conversation that had quickly become uncomfortable.

"Of course not. You're both of age. But where do you see it going? I hope . . ." She swallowed. "I hope she's not another Caroline."

Rage forced Lillian to her feet. "She isn't!" she shouted. Needing to move, she crossed to a window and stood with her shaking hands shoved into her robe's pockets.

A chair scraped across stone; a moment later, Lillian felt Sophia's hand on her back. "I'm sorry, but I had to say it," Sophia murmured. "I don't want to see you hurt like that again."

And it had hurt, and still did. After all this time, it still hurt as if it had happened yesterday, not almost twenty years ago.

"Maddy's young. She's not much older than Caroline was when she left."

"Maddy isn't Caroline," Lillian said quietly. "Perhaps she does see me as nothing more than a bit of amusement, but she's never been cruel."

"Perhaps not, but if she sees you as nothing more than a bed partner, you'll be hurt nonetheless. Because you don't see her that way, do you?"

She took her time answering. "No." Even though they'd never spent time together outside Maddy's bedchamber—apart from the training room, but that didn't count.

"Have you told her how you feel?"

No, because she was afraid Maddy might tell her she was too old to be more than a bed warmer. As Sophia had pointed out, Maddy was only twenty-four; she'd likely grow bored with the monastery's loner once the novelty had worn off, especially since she spent most of her time with fresh-faced initiates. And if Lillian were to voice her feelings to Maddy, she could no longer pretend that Maddy didn't matter. She'd be vulnerable, and she hated being vulnerable.

"You do talk, don't you?" Sophia asked.

"Not about . . . whatever it is we're doing," she said, glad that Sophia couldn't see her face.

"Oh dear." Sophia stepped to Lillian's side and slipped an arm around her shoulders. "Talk to her, Lillian. You might not like what she says, but at least you'll know."

She rested her head on Sophia's shoulder. "Do you think I'm making a fool of myself?" she asked faintly.

Sophia squeezed her. "I don't know. Only Maddy can answer that. So talk to her."

The prayer bell sounded. Lillian tutted. "I wanted to check an experiment."

"No time now." Sophia dashed to her desk and gulped down the remains of her tea. "You can do it after prayers."

When Lillian had nothing in particular to say to Salbine, which happened often, she took advantage of early morning prayers to plan her day. But she knew what she'd beseech Salbine for today: courage.

MADDY PLUNKED HER bowl onto the wooden table and squeezed herself onto the bench between Nora and Rose. She stirred her porridge, hardly able to hear her spoon scraping the bowl over the spirited chatter that filled the communal dining hall.

Gwendolyn and Abigail eyed her from across the table. "We got the shock of our lives last night," Gwendolyn said over the din.

Maddy nodded. "I couldn't believe it when I saw Merrin. What on earth did he think he was doing?"

"Oh, well, that was shocking too, but I wasn't referring to that."

Maddy paused her spoon. "Oh?"

"I meant Mistress Lillian coming out of your chambers," Gwendolyn said, her eyes bright.

Those around Maddy grew quiet. "You spent the night with Mistress Lillian?" Rose said around a mouthful of porridge.

"I didn't know you'd taken up the study of ancient artifacts," Nora said, prompting gales of laughter.

Maddy hunched her shoulders and quickly lifted a spoonful of porridge to her mouth. The sooner she finished eating, the sooner she could escape.

"I'm sure there are easier ways to pass your fire exam," Gwendolyn said.

"What are you implying?" Maddy snapped, more offended on Lillian's behalf than her own.

"Don't be crude, Gwendolyn," Rose said.

"All right, maybe she was with the mistress because she misses her ma," Gwendolyn said, provoking a chorus of groans.

"Thank you very much," Abigail shouted, rising from the bench. "I have a hard enough time choking down this slop every morning without you saying things that make me want to bring it back up. Salbine preserve me." She grabbed her bowl and stomped off to another table.

Gwendolyn rolled her eyes. "She's always cranky when she hasn't had enough sleep."

"Or maybe you're not as funny as you think you are," Rose said.

Maddy silently thanked her friend. She should stand up for herself and Lillian, but Gwendolyn would only twist anything she said to show off her so-called wit.

Gwendolyn threw Rose a dirty look. "If Maddy wasn't so quiet, we wouldn't have to speculate. So come on, Maddy, enlighten us. What's the attraction?"

Maddy dropped her spoon into her porridge. If Gwendolyn thought she'd defend or explain herself, she could think again! "I'm sure you were shocked when you realized Mistress Lillian was in my chambers," she said, bristling. "But not half as shocked as I would have been to see *anyone* come out of yours."

When everyone snickered, Maddy felt ashamed to have sunk to Gwendolyn's level. Her anger shifted from Gwendolyn to herself. If she continued to see Lillian, she'd have to get used to the teasing and the barbs, learn to brush them off.

Gwendolyn glared at her. "Perhaps I'm more discreet than you," she said with a sniff, then drained her mug of milk and slammed it down on the table. "And I can assure you that if you ever do see someone come out of my chambers, she'll be my age!" She rose and flung "See you all at morning prayers" over her shoulder as she strode off in a huff.

With Gwendolyn gone, everyone seemed content to let the subject drop, at least until Maddy had finished breakfast. She was on her way to feed the squirrels, her pockets stuffed with the nuts one of the cooks always put aside, when Rose caught up with her. She slipped her arm through Maddy's as they neared a copse popular with the squirrels in the monastery's western grounds. "Now that we're alone, tell me everything!" she squealed. "How did you end up with Mistress Lillian?"

Maddy had entered the monastery a month after Rose, and they'd become fast friends. They usually told each other everything. Rose wouldn't give her any peace if she refused to divulge details. "It started during my second fire lesson," she said as she dug a handful of nuts from her pocket and scattered them on the ground. Trying to coax that one shy squirrel to take a nut from her hand would have to wait; even the brave ones were still in the trees, suspicious of the stranger.

"You mean last night wasn't the first time?" Rose exclaimed, elbowing Maddy in the ribs. "Why haven't you said anything?"

"Because I wasn't sure if Lil—the mistress wanted anyone to know." They'd always managed to make it to her chambers without running into anyone on her floor. And since Lillian attended early morning prayers, she was always gone by the time Maddy and the other initiates woke. Maddy had wondered what Lillian would do if she wasn't expected at the chapel, if she would still slip out early, regardless.

"So what happened at your second lesson?"

She'd literally fallen into Lillian's arms. "I drew fire for the first time."

"Right, I remember you telling me. I didn't want to say anything at the time, but I was surprised that you waited until your second lesson. I did it during my first lesson, and so did Abigail and Grace."

Perhaps she would have done the same, if Lillian hadn't been her tutor. As a rule, Lillian didn't accept students. Horror had rippled through the assembled initiates when Mistress Ivy announced that because Mistress Clarissa was away tending to her ailing ma, Mistress Lillian had agreed to teach one student about the basics of drawing fire. The same thought had run through everyone's mind: please, don't let it be me! To the initiates, Lillian was an intimidating figure, a powerful mage who cared little for people and was easily annoyed. She spent most of her time preparing poisons in a secret laboratory—at least that was the rumour. Aloof, impatient, unforgiving, and in possession of a supply of poisons—who'd want someone like that for a tutor?

Maddy couldn't have been more dismayed when Mistress Ivy announced that Lillian would be her tutor. Everyone patted her arm in sympathy, relief in their eyes. By the time she arrived at the training room for her first lesson at the unusual time of eight in the evening—when Lillian could "fit her in"—she was terrified of making a mistake or of failing to quickly grasp a concept, sure that Lillian would eagerly pounce on her. Nothing could have been further from the truth. If anything, Lillian was bored, valiantly trying to appear engaged while wishing she were somewhere else. Still, Maddy was too nervous to draw fire during that first lesson. When she'd tried and failed, Lillian hadn't pushed her. "Next lesson," she'd said as she'd dashed off to wherever she'd rather have been for the past hour.

"Well, I didn't try until my second lesson," she said to Rose, not wanting to admit to her failures, "and the mistress warned me not to draw too quickly or I might feel nauseous or light-headed."

Rose nodded. "I swayed a little."

Maddy snorted as she pulled Rose away from the trees and up the path that led to the inner courtyard. She'd visit her other spots later; she preferred to be alone when she fed her furry friends. "I did more than sway." Fortunately Lillian had been prepared. "I almost fainted, and would have ended up on the floor if the mistress hadn't caught me."

"Did she get angry?" Rose asked, her eyes wide.

"No. I grabbed onto her to steady myself." Lillian's rough robe had scratched her hands. "And I looked up at her, and she looked at me, and I don't know why, but . . . I kissed her. Or she kissed me. Or we kissed each other. I don't know, we just kissed."

"Mistress Lillian!"

"Yes." And they hadn't stopped at one kiss. The lesson, the training room, everything had faded away as they'd melted into each other. They'd briefly come to their senses when they'd started to unbutton their robes and remembered where they were. "We ended up in my bedchamber, and that's where we've ended up after every lesson since."

"Mistress Lillian?"

"Will you stop saying that, please?"

"Sorry," Rose murmured. "You've certainly kept it quiet."

"As I said, I wasn't sure what the mistress wanted."

"You, obviously." Rose grinned, then yelped when Maddy playfully slapped her arm. "Though are you sure you're not part of some experiment?"

She hoped not.

"I didn't think Mistress Lillian had," Rose lowered her voice, "those sorts of needs."

Maddy could personally vouch that she did.

"But she does like to do experiments, or so I've heard," Rose added.

"Maybe she does." She'd heard the same, and wished she could hear it from Lillian herself. "But I'm not part of an experiment."

Rose grunted, looking unconvinced. "What do you think will happen, now that everyone knows?"

"I don't know." She paused. "I hope she'll still see me."

Rose stopped and faced her. "You like her! As more than a friend, I mean."

Maddy nodded. "But I don't know how she feels." She bit her lip. "Do you think I'm foolish?"

"No. You can't control who you like in that way."

"Oh, so if I could control it, then you'd think I'm foolish," Maddy said ruefully.

"I didn't say that," Rose said with a laugh, slipping her arm through Maddy's again. "I just hope the mistress likes you in the same way you like her."

She fervently hoped so, too. Her next lesson should be interesting—though it could turn out to be disappointing and humiliating if Lillian made it clear that she'd return to her own chambers when it finished.

Rose frowned. "We'll be a bit early if we go to the chapel now."

"Let's go to my chambers so I can empty my pockets."

"Tell me about what happened with Merrin," Rose said as they wandered toward the Initiates Tower. "I wish I'd been there."

"Somehow he got past the defenders at the—"

"Maddy, look!"

She followed Rose's gaze, and her breath caught in her throat. Lillian stood near the Initiates Tower's main entrance. When they approached her, she crooked a finger. "Sister Maddy, a word, please."

"I'll see you at chapel." Rose let go of Maddy's arm and bobbed a curtsey to Lillian. "Mistress."

"Yes, run along, Sister—um . . ." Lillian screwed up her face. "Rose! Yes, Sister Rose."

With an amused smirk, Rose strolled away.

"I didn't mean to interrupt," Lillian said as soon as Rose was out of earshot. "I should have waited until your next lesson. We can talk then."

"You didn't interrupt anything," Maddy said quickly. Waiting until her lesson would be excruciating. "We were just on our way to my chambers, so I can empty my pockets before morning prayers."

Lillian looked down at Maddy's bulging pockets. "Oh."

"What would you like to talk to me about?" Maddy asked, hoping Lillian wouldn't rush off.

"Talk . . . Yes, talk." Lillian scratched her head. "Let's go in. I don't want to be interrupted." Without waiting for a reply, she pushed open the door and disappeared inside.

Maddy followed, in time to see Lillian knock on one of the first floor study room doors and open it a crack. She closed it and moved on to the next one. "In here," she said, waving Maddy inside. She shut the door behind Maddy. They remained standing, ignoring the four chairs around a square table. Lillian stared at Maddy and gulped.

"Was the abbess upset about Merrin?" Maddy asked, then kicked herself. She wasn't supposed to know about Lillian seeing the abbess.

"No," Lillian said. "Well, not really."

"Good."

"She wanted to know who I was with last night."

Maddy's heart sank. "Oh."

"Talking to the abbess helped clarify things for me. About you."

No wonder Lillian seemed nervous. Telling someone you'd no longer share her bed was never easy, regardless of how much or little you cared for her. Maddy braced herself.

"I realized . . ." Lillian swallowed. "I realized that I'd like to know more about you, more than how well you draw fire and . . . and how you like to be touched. I'd like to spend time with you outside your bedchamber." She crossed her arms against her chest and gripped her robe. "But that's probably not what you want. And that's all right. I understand." She turned to the door. "I won't keep you."

"Wait! Please don't go, Lillian. I want the same thing you do," Maddy blurted, elated.

Lillian became very still. "You do?"

"Yes, very much. I've wanted to ask to see you, but I didn't know if that's what you want." She longed to touch Lillian, but Lillian's posture dissuaded her.

"It is," Lillian said, turning to Maddy and slowly lowering her arms.

They stared at each other. "Would you like to meet tonight, after evening prayers?" Maddy asked, sensing that Lillian's nerve had run its course. She'd already learned that a shy woman hid beneath the bluster.

"Yes, I would." Lillian's face fell. "Oh, but I have to go to my laboratory, to prepare something for Mistress Meredith. I'd do it earlier, but I'm helping Thomas all day. It has to be tonight. She needs it."

So the laboratory did exist. But what would Mistress Meredith want with poison? "Would you like company?"

Lillian hesitated, then nodded.

"Where is it?"

"What?"

"Your laboratory."

"Oh. Why don't you meet me outside the chapel after the service?"

"All right."

Lillian cleared her throat. "Well, then." She looked down at Maddy's pockets. "What's in your pockets?"

"Nuts."

"Nuts?" Lillian's brow furrowed. "All for you?"

The morning prayer bell sounded. Maddy couldn't resist the urge to touch Lillian any longer. She took Lillian's hand and rubbed her thumb along the red markings on its back, markings that matched those on her own hands. Warmth flooded through her when she felt Lillian's fingers curl around hers. "No, not for me. I'll tell you later."

Lillian nodded and squeezed Maddy's hand. "Later, then." She turned to leave the room, but not before Maddy caught her smile.

Chapter Two

MADDY FOLLOWED ROSE TO THE CHAPEL'S leftmost aisle, resisting the urge to glance at the bench where Lillian usually sat. She was already disappointed with herself for staring at Lillian's back throughout the service, instead of focusing during prayers.

Rose gripped her arm as they entered the chapel's vestibule. "You all right?" she asked.

"Just a little nervous," Maddy admitted, feeling excited, sick, and silly. She'd lain with Lillian numerous times over the past several weeks, so the prospect of holding an extended conversation with the woman shouldn't petrify her.

Outside, she pulled Rose over to one of the torches lighting the path, to make it easier for Lillian to spot her. "Maybe this wasn't such a good idea," she murmured.

"I thought it's what you want," Rose said.

"It is. But—"

"She's coming," Rose hissed. "Good luck! I want to hear all about it later—or maybe tomorrow," she said with a glint in her eye.

Maddy turned as Rose hurried off, and took a deep breath, trying to look at ease.

"Come with me," Lillian said, briefly meeting Maddy's eyes but not breaking stride. "Lovely night, isn't it?" she said when Maddy fell into step with her. "Though it feels like rain is on the way."

"Yes," Maddy said, "though I hope it stays away. Tomorrow's market day."

Lillian glanced at her. "You go to the market?"

She nodded. Every two weeks she wound her way down the hill to Merrin's market after morning prayers with a group of sisters and defenders, and several mules. She didn't actually trade for any goods; the defenders did all the haggling for the herbs, textiles, glass, and other items the monastery required. They didn't have to go every two weeks, especially since the monastery cultivated its own crops, had plentiful stores, and tradesmen devoted to Salbine lived within its walls. But while the defenders honed their bargaining skills, the sisters mingled with the townsfolk and noted their concerns, particularly those for which they could offer help or that might spell trouble for the monastery. Maddy loved to wander among the stalls with their brightly-coloured awnings, listening to the peddlers shouting entice-ments to browse their wares, ruffling the hair of the wide-eyed chil-dren who bobbed before her, and offering an encouraging word or a promise of aid to those who approached her and confided their worries.

"You've never come with us," she said to Lillian at the same time she realized it. On average, about ten sisters visited the market. Six, like Maddy, were regulars; the rest tagged along so they could personally choose an item, or to spend a day outside the monastery.

Lillian shrugged. "The defenders always know what I want. No need for me to go myself."

"Don't you ever feel like a day out?"

"Not to the market, no."

"Where would you go?"

"Somewhere quiet," Lillian said with a hint of exasperation.

Not wanting to annoy Lillian further, Maddy dropped the subject and resolved to remain silent until Lillian next spoke. She looked along the line of burning torches lighting the path, and realized it led to the library. She'd thought they were going to Lillian's labora-tory. She was about to ask where they were going when Lillian cut in front of her and turned onto a dark path. Maddy leaned over to take an unlit torch from the bucket standing near the path, but then a ball of fire appeared in Lillian's left hand. Lillian made it look so effortless; Maddy hadn't even sensed her draw fire. Perhaps the more capable the mage, the less "noisy" the drawing, and nobody was more capable than Lillian.

Not wanting to offend her, Maddy left the torch and fell into step with her again. The fire burning an inch above Lillian's hand threw only enough light to see a foot or two ahead. They walked in silence, the rustling of their robes and their footsteps sounding unnaturally loud. "Your laboratory is in the catacombs?" Maddy blurted when she remembered where this path led.

"Yes," Lillian said. "All the laboratories are. Nobody there cares when you brew a noxious potion or have a little accident."

"Accident?" she asked in a shriller voice than she would have liked.

"Working out a formula involves trial and error, Maddy. Some errors are . . . er, more spectacular than others."

She swallowed. "Oh."

"Don't worry. I won't be brewing anything tonight."

"What does Mistress Meredith need?" Maddy asked, wondering again what Mistress Meredith would want with poison.

"That's Mistress Meredith's affair," Lillian said.

Maddy made a mental note to be more careful around Mistress Meredith from now on. She refocused on her surroundings, squinting at two torches flickering in the gloom ahead.

Once again, Lillian ignored the bucket of torches standing at the catacomb's entrance. She descended the stone steps, pushed open the door, and led Maddy down more steps to a lower passage. Maddy resisted the urge to grab the back of Lillian's robe so she wouldn't lose her only light source. Her heart pounded as she imagined herself wandering the maze of passages in the dark, hopelessly lost, her cries falling on the deaf ears of long-dead sisters. She wasn't claustrophobic, but the narrow passage and the shadows dancing on its walls unsettled her.

"Why didn't you take one of the torches?" Lillian asked when Maddy, determined to stay right behind Lillian, bumped into her.

"Because you're lighting the way," Maddy said. "And I didn't think you wanted me to," she added faintly.

She was close enough to feel as well as hear Lillian's chuckle. "Well, we're almost there," was all Lillian said. A minute later, she stopped in front of a door and pulled an iron key from her robe pocket. "I need both hands for this," she murmured. The ball of fire disappeared, plunging them into darkness. "Why don't you try holding fire? It's not much different than lighting a candle. You want to focus on the point just above your hand."

"What do you do when you're alone?" Maddy asked, her insides fluttering. What if the fire touched her hand? What if she couldn't do it?

"I stick the torch in the sconce next to the door," Lillian said.

So Lillian normally used a torch? She'd been showing off! Elation chased away Maddy's nervousness. She wanted to kiss Lillian, but since she couldn't see her, she'd probably end up planting one on her nose or an eyebrow.

"A ball of fire, please," Lillian ordered.

"All right." Maddy closed her eyes, turned inward, and reached for Salbine's raging fire. She could sense it, feel it, smell it, but she couldn't draw it, no matter how hard she tried. Frustration threatened her concentration. She felt the same way she did when a word on the tip of her tongue eluded her. Fire swirled around her, taunting her; why wouldn't fire flow *through* her? Her hands clenched; her lips compressed. *Salbine, aid me, I beseech You!*

She felt light-headed and reached out to steady herself. Her fingers collided with stone; she gasped, then doubled over when pain stabbed through her.

A steadying hand touched her elbow. "Are you all right?" Lillian asked.

Maddy lifted her head. Lillian's concerned face swam before her, illuminated by the fire that once again flickered above her hand. "I—I don't know," she stammered, then grimaced as a wave of nausea washed over her.

"Let me take you back to your chambers."

"No! I tried too hard, that's all."

Lillian's brows drew together. "Are you sure? Because I didn't sense anything."

"I'm sure!" she snapped. "I must be doing something wrong. I'm sorry."

"No, I'm sorry." Lillian let go of Maddy's elbow. "I shouldn't have asked you to try something new, not tonight. Because . . . well, we're not here as tutor and pupil, are we?"

"I didn't think so," Maddy said quietly. Now that her physical discomfort had passed, humiliation was setting in. "But I obviously have a lot of work to do to pass my examination." If the other initiates learning fire were telling the truth, they were already lighting fireplaces and hurling fireballs around the training room. Rose had triumphantly declared that she'd lit all the candles around the room's perimeter in under a minute. Maddy was still struggling to light one. She should pay more attention to the lessons and less to the tutor. "I have to admit, I haven't been as focused during our lessons as I should be," she said.

"And I haven't pushed you as hard as I might have pushed someone else. I've also been distracted," Lillian replied, colouring slightly. "We'll work on holding fire at your next lesson. Are you sure you don't want to go back to your chambers?"

Cutting her night with Lillian short was the last thing she wanted, and it was completely unnecessary. The pain had subsided and her stomach had already settled. "I'm fine, really. I want to stay here." She forced herself to meet Lillian's eyes. "With you."

Lillian blinked and stepped forward, then frowned at the fire she sustained. She pulled the key from her robe pocket again and handed it to Maddy. "Why don't you open the door?"

Maddy set her shoulders and slipped the key into the keyhole. Had anyone else ever prayed to Salbine that a lock wouldn't jam, or would she be the first? *Please, Salbine, don't let me botch this up too.* Fortunately the key turned with an easy *click*. She removed it, pushed the door open, and stepped aside, holding the key out, so Lillian could enter first. Lillian accepted the key and tucked it into her pocket as she moved past.

Maddy followed her through the doorway, but stopped just inside as the fireplace ignited and three torches burst to life—with Lillian's help, no doubt. Bunches of herbs hung from the ceiling above a round table piled with paper, parchments, and curling scrolls. Glass jars, both full and empty, labelled and unlabelled, were neatly arranged on a set of shelves. Crucibles, a mortar and pestle, scales, filters, and other items Maddy didn't recognize covered a rectangular table.

"Come in and shut the door," Lillian said, no longer holding fire. "You can sit over there." She nodded toward a wooden chair not far from the rectangular table, then moved to the shelves as Maddy pushed the door closed and sat. "Shouldn't take long." Lillian scanned the jars. "Ah, here we are." She set a jar filled to the brim with black liquid on the table. Bits of . . . something . . . floated around inside. When Lillian started to remove the sealing wax from around the jar's lid, Maddy leaned away.

Lillian stopped and looked at her. "What are you doing?"

"I'm just, um . . ."

Lillian put a hand on her hip. "Don't tell me that poison rumour is still going around. Would you like to see my thrall, too?"

"Your what?"

"My thrall."

Maddy gave her a blank look. She had no idea what Lillian was talking about.

"So *that* rumour finally died. Good. I never liked that one." Lillian bent to work on the jar again. "Effective rumours have to sound halfway plausible. I can understand the poison one, but the thrall one never made sense. If I had a thrall, why would I keep it down here? I'd want it in my chambers, dusting and lighting the fire in the morning and making my tea. It would only be a nuisance in here, getting in my way and knocking things over. Honestly," she finished in exasperation.

When the lid came free, a stench burst into the air that reminded Maddy of unwashed, sweaty feet. Grimacing, she covered her nose with her hands. Lillian's nose wrinkled, but otherwise she seemed unaffected. Amusement flashed across her face when she noticed Maddy's discomfort. "Don't worry, it's perfectly harmless. Oh, I suppose there's no harm in telling you what it is. It's a valerian root tincture. Mistress Meredith sometimes has trouble sleeping. A bit of this in her tea before bed does the trick." She fetched an empty jar, then spread a piece of muslin over the jar's mouth. "She always leaves it until the last minute to tell me she's about to run out," Lillian said as she poured the tincture through the muslin. Her voice took on a snide, lilting tone. "No need to warn Lillian in advance. Lillian doesn't have anything better to do than to make my tincture. No matter when I ask, Lillian will do it." She wrapped the muslin around the solids it had trapped and wrung it over the jar. "And Lillian does, because if Mistress Meredith isn't getting enough sleep, we all suffer, believe you me."

Maddy grinned.

"So, no poisons here." Lillian dropped the muslin and its contents into a bucket and wiped her hands on a piece of cloth. "Tinctures, salves, oils, various other aids. That's all."

"A sister and the healing arts seems an odd combination," Maddy said in surprise.

"Granted, Salbine's gifts are of a more destructive nature, but I don't limit myself to Salbine's gifts. Anyway, I don't know why you're surprised. The people come to us with their aches and boils and we do what we can."

Which usually wasn't much. "You mean you're the one who supplies the adepts?"

"I am." Lillian frowned at her. "Where did you think their supplies were coming from? You don't trade for them at the market."

Maddy hadn't thought about it when she'd occasionally helped the adepts minister to the poor souls looking for relief from various physical ailments. The outer courtyard was always busy on Monday afternoons, the line-up sometimes snaking through the monastery's main gate and along its southern wall. Few could afford the fees demanded by physicians, who weren't terribly interested in treating callused feet and bad teeth anyway. The adepts aided those they could and prayed for those they couldn't. She'd assumed the medicines they passed out had come from outside the monastery's walls. She would never have guessed that a sister was supplying them, especially Lillian. "I've never seen you with the adepts."

Lillian's face screwed up in distaste. "I don't want to mix with the rabble. No. No, no, I do my work here." She held up the jar. "Half a jar of valerian root tincture," she declared with a satisfied smile, then set it on the table and placed a lid over its mouth. "I don't think I'll seal it. She'll want to use it tonight, so she can seal it herself if she likes. We'll have to be careful when we walk back, though. I don't want to spill any." After moving the dirty jar to a ledge with several others, she returned to those sitting on the shelves. "Would you like to lend me a hand? I have quite a few preparations that need to be shaken."

"Of course." Maddy moved to Lillian's side.

"You start here and I'll start over here," Lillian said, walking to the other end of the shelves. She picked up a jar from the lowest shelf.

"Give it a good shake," she said, demonstrating. Maddy lifted a jar from her end of the shelf, grasped its top and bottom, and shook it. "Are you going to tell me about those nuts?" Lillian asked.

"They're for the squirrels," Maddy said with a grin. "One of the cooks puts some aside for me each morning."

"Don't get too attached to the ones that hang about here," Lillian said. "One foot outside the walls and they'll be on someone's table in no time."

"They have no reason to go outside the walls. They have everything they need here."

"You like animals, then?"

Maddy nodded. She'd always been a bit suspicious of those who didn't. "Do you?" she asked hesitantly, hoping her budding relationship with Lillian wasn't about to come to an abrupt end. "This morning you said you'd spend the day with Thomas."

"I helped him with a couple of new horses. First time they'd felt anyone draw." When Lillian set her jar back on the shelf and picked up the next one, Maddy did the same. "You need absolute control with the new ones. Just a whisper, at first. Had one horse bloody-well near kill me a few years ago. I'd barely drawn air when it reared and charged at me. I should have been more prepared, had a barrier up, but it had never happened before. I didn't have time to throw one up when it panicked, so I did what anyone else would have done and ran for my life. Somehow, in all the ruckus, it managed to kick me in the back before Thomas and the other men calmed it down. Spent a week lying on my stomach."

Maddy stifled a laugh. "Is that how you got that scar on your, um . . ."

"My arse? Yes, that's how. And yes, I do like animals—prefer them to people. That's why I got right back out there once I felt up to it. I work with the new ones, and I'm every horse's final test. Or nightmare, depending. Surprising thing about the horse that charged me was that I was drawing air. It's fire that usually gets them. They don't like fireballs whizzing over their heads." Lillian chuckled. "Can't say I would, either."

Maddy vividly remembered the first time she'd seen Lillian test a horse. She'd just started to help out at the stables and had been mucking out a stall on a beautiful, sunny afternoon. A loud thunderclap had made her drop the pitchfork and race from the stable in confusion. Having only arrived at the monastery two weeks earlier, she'd never seen such a display. She stood transfixed as the mage rode the horse around the yard, drawing fire, air, earth, and water. Neither the horse nor the stable hands seemed afraid, and when Maddy screamed at a fireball heading straight for her, the men looked her way in amusement. "It's all right, there's a shield," one shouted, which explained why the fireball exploded into nothingness before it reached her. She wondered later whether Lillian had deliberately thrown it at her.

Though the horse was inside the barrier, it trotted around as if it hadn't a care in the world. She later learned of the intense desensitization to the elements all Salbine horses underwent. Now she barely noticed when mages were working with horses, but she'd never forget that day. When Lillian had completed her test, she'd walked by a shaken Maddy with hardly a glance. Maddy had stared after her in awe—and fear.

"Your horse must be deaf and blind," she said to Lillian, still not quite accepting that a horse could endure a display of prowess from a mage as strong as Lillian for long.

Lillian's lips pressed into a thin line. "He most certainly isn't! He's very brave, and I love him. I ride him as often as I can. We like to go up to the river and watch the currents. I can give him a good workout there. If the weather's good, sometimes we pack a lunch, spend the whole day."

We? "Who's we?"

"Me and Baxter."

"Baxter?"

"The horse! I like to ride alone. Though . . . maybe you'll come with us, sometime?"

"I'd like that very much," Maddy said, warmed by Lillian's invitation.

They finished shaking their last jars and looked at each other. "Well, that's that," Lillian murmured. "Time to take Mistress Meredith her tincture."

"You know, we could have arranged to meet later, after you'd finished here," Maddy said. "I thought we'd be here all night."

Lillian nodded sheepishly. "I know. I realized that afterward. I . . . You surprised me, when you said you wanted the same thing I do. I didn't think you'd want to see me at all."

She reached for Lillian, and sighed contentedly when Lillian leaned into her.

"What are we doing?" Lillian whispered.

"I don't know. I just know I like being with you."

"Me too. I mean, with you."

"Then let's be together. We'll eventually figure out what we're doing."

"Take an empirical approach, you mean? I can certainly agree with that."

Maddy chuckled and drew back, her arms looped around Lillian's neck. She moved in and gently touched her lips to Lillian's. "For someone with such a gruff exterior, you have the softest lips," she murmured.

Lillian arched an eyebrow.

"I wasn't ready for you to take me to my chambers when you suggested it earlier, but I am now."

"And I'll be happy to oblige. We do have to make a stop along the way, though." Lillian hesitated, then pressed her palm against Maddy's cheek. "Do you think it'll be different, now that . . ."

"Now that we're not pretending we don't really care?"

Lillian swallowed. "Yes."

She turned toward Lillian's hand and kissed it. "Let's go find out."

"Here, carry this." Lillian slid a torch from its sconce and handed it to Maddy with a wink.

"Thank you."

"You have the torch, so I suppose you'd better lead." Lillian strode to the door and turned around. "You coming?"

"Aren't you forgetting something?"

"Oh, yes." Lillian waved her right hand, and the fire and the two torches still hanging on the wall flickered out.

Maddy struggled to keep a straight face. "Very impressive. But that's not what I meant."

Lillian's brow furrowed. "What, then?"

"The tincture."

"Right." Red-faced, Lillian collected the jar from the table and cleared her throat. "Lead the way."

In the passage, Maddy held the tincture while Lillian closed and locked the door. "You'll have to direct me," she said as she handed the jar back.

"Go left."

Maddy set off, smiling when Lillian grasped her free hand. "I don't want to lose you," Lillian murmured.

Aware that Lillian was only trying to make her feel useful, Maddy squeezed her hand. "You won't."

Only later did she realize that she hadn't sensed Lillian drawing fire in the laboratory—at all.

Chapter Three

LILLIAN SHIFTED IMPATIENTLY, WAITING FOR MADDY to emerge from the lower common room in the Initiates Tower. Maddy had said they'd finish about three, and it must be past that by now. A passing sister slowed her pace and bobbed. Lillian nodded absently, not registering who it was and not caring, either. *Ah, the door's opening.* She reminded herself not to appear too enthusiastic when Maddy came out. She had to show restraint, not embarrass herself by behaving like an infatuated girl.

Sisters spilled into the hallway, chattering to each other. "Mistress," said one, bobbing to Lillian. That led to a chorus of greetings and much knee-bending. Lillian resisted the urge to roll her eyes and remained focused on the door. To her dismay, a smile spread across her face when she spotted Maddy. *Restraint! Restraint!* She tried to smooth her features, but Maddy had already witnessed her pleasure and was smiling in return.

Lillian's heart skipped a beat when Maddy stopped in front of her, but then she read confusion in Maddy's eyes. With a start, she realized that Maddy was wondering whether to curtsey. "Don't," Lillian quickly murmured, then felt the blood rush to her face when Maddy pecked her on the cheek. The sisters around them grew quiet and stared. She surveyed them in horror. "Don't you all have somewhere else to go?" she bellowed. "Move!" They scurried away, whispering.

Maddy studied Lillian and bit her lip. "You know, if we were to go to your laboratory now, we wouldn't need a torch or fire. Your face would light the way."

"Oh, hush!" Lillian snapped. It was easy for Maddy to make light of it; nobody thought she was a foolish old woman who'd end up hurt and alone. Maddy's friends and fellow initiates were probably wondering what Maddy was doing. "Have the other initiates said anything to you? About me?"

"Just a bit of teasing, nothing I can't handle."

"I don't want to cause you any distress, Maddy."

"Not seeing you would cause me more distress," Maddy said, "and since everyone knows about us now, there's no point acting as if we don't matter to each other. Do you want to see what we're working on?" she asked, effectively changing the subject.

"Yes." Embroidery didn't interest her, but Maddy did.

Maddy led Lillian into the common room, where a line of embroidery frames and accompanying stools stretched its length. She moved to a frame in the middle of the room. "This is mine."

Lillian leaned in for a closer look at Maddy's part of what would ultimately become a tapestry, once all the pieces were sewn together. "Lina, receiving the gift of water from Salbine." Based on the images Lillian had glimpsed as she followed Maddy, she'd already deduced that the tapestry told the story of Lina's banishment and survival. She peered at the gold-robed figure standing in the shadow of a red tree, a silver goblet lying on its side near her feet. Lina's right arm was raised, her head tipped back; water flowed from her hand to her open mouth. Yes, to draw the elements was to drink the raw power, and refine it as it flowed within—reshaping, redirecting, and releasing it.

Lillian formed a fist with her right hand and held it over the tapestry. "You did the branches well," she murmured, comparing the red branch on the back of her hand to those of the red tree. "Look at that exquisite stitching," she added, not having a clue if the stitching was any good, but wanting to offer praise. "Exquisite," she repeated solemnly. "Exquisite."

"You think so?" Maddy said brightly.

"Oh, yes," Lillian said, lowering her hand. "Wonderful."

"You haven't embroidered a thing in your life, have you."

"What?"

"I was a bit sloppy here." Maddy touched two of the branches. "I said to Mistress Bertha that the first thing I'll have to do next time is pull out those stitches and do them again. I wasn't paying attention. I was too busy chatting to Nora."

"I have to admit, I'm not an expert at embroidery," Lillian said, hoping Maddy would never ask to embroider with her. "But your panel is certainly better than the one over there."

"Where?" Maddy asked, then nodded when Lillian pointed to Lina receiving the gift of earth. "That's Sister Gail's. I don't know why she volunteered for this. All she ever does is moan and groan about how bored she is. Here." She grabbed Lillian's hand and pulled her back to the frame nearest the door. "Lina telling the villagers about her vision of Salbine, just before they sentenced her to death. That's Rose's. And here's Lina bound to the tree, surrounded by wild animals. Sister Pearl's." They moved to the next frame. "Salbine granting Lina the gift of fire. Sister Catherine's." Lillian noted the now red tree and the ring of fire keeping the animals at bay. "Lina receiving the gift of earth. Sister Gail's. And then the gift of air. Sister Ivy's. Then mine. Salbine's command to establish the Order. Nora's. The villagers the next morning, surprised to find her alive. Sister Amelia's."

"She should have burned the lot of them," Lillian said.

"I think Salbine wanted Lina to tell them about Her gifts. Wasn't that the point? To show them that Lina's vision was true, that Salbine came to her and gave her what she needed to survive."

"I'm sure they would have quickly grasped that point if she'd set them on fire."

"But what would that have accomplished?" Maddy asked, moving to the next frame without waiting for an answer. She pointed to the half-embroidered figures sitting at Lina's feet. "And finally, Lina establishes the Order and teaches those marked by Salbine how to use Salbine's gifts. Sister Sadie's."

"As I said, I'm no expert at embroidery, but I do think your panel outshines the others."

"Well, people do tell me I'm good at it," Maddy said, her face flushed with pleasure, "and I do enjoy it. I've been asked to work on the cassock for the abbess's fifth anniversary. I'm not completely hopeless, you know."

"I didn't think you were."

"I've only been here for the last three years of the abbess's tenure, so I was quite pleased when Mistress Bertha put forward my name for the cassock."

Lillian couldn't believe Sophia had already been abbess for five years. She remembered when they'd first arrived at the monastery gates and gazed at the chapel in awe, relieved that their perilous journey was finally at an end. Their hunger and exhaustion hadn't dampened their excitement; they'd raced onto the grounds and accosted poor Mistress Agnes, the first sister they encountered. That had led to a meeting with Abbess Margaret, a soft-spoken yet imposing woman who'd wrinkled her nose and ordered them to bathe. Neither guessed then that Sophia would become the next abbess, when Margaret went to Salbine twenty years later.

"Like you, the abbess joined the Order late," she said. "She was twenty-five. You were—what, twenty-one?" *Twenty-one! What am I doing?* Whatever it was, she didn't want to stop. "Most arrive around seventeen, eighteen. Was something holding you back?"

Maddy slipped her arm through Lillian's. "Let's talk outside. I only have about twenty minutes before my history lesson, and I want some fresh air."

Not caring where they were as long as they were together, Lillian readily agreed, and they were soon strolling along one of the grounds' numerous paths. "It wasn't something that held me back," Maddy said, picking up their conversation. "It was someone."

"Oh." Lillian hoped Maddy wouldn't stop there.

"I would have come earlier, if not for her. As soon as I was sure I was marked and that Salbine was calling me, I wanted to join the Order."

"But she didn't?"

"No."

Lillian had never understood those who chose to remain on the outside. Here, those marked by Salbine could not only receive Her gifts, but learn to read and study history, art, music, alchemy—just about anything that tickled one's fancy. And all in the company of women dedicated to Salbine, if one desired such company. Why would anyone choose to remain illiterate and ignorant? "Why didn't she want to join?"

Maddy took her time answering. "She didn't feel called. And you do give up certain freedoms when you join the Order."

"What do you give up?" Lillian retorted. "You can do anything here."

"Yes, here, at the monastery. Where you answer to those above you. Where your relationships are limited to sisters. Where you exist to serve Salbine."

"You'd rather be out there, waiting tables in some smelly tavern or hocking your wares at the market, or slaving away on a farm?"

"I grew up on a farm, Lillian."

"Oh. Give me a moment to remove my foot."

Maddy chuckled. "Joanna valued her independence."

Joanna. Jealousy surged through Lillian. Silly, since Maddy was on *her* arm, but she couldn't help it.

"I hoped that Salbine would call her, but She didn't. I tried to tell myself that I could serve Salbine outside the Order, but Salbine's call grew stronger." Maddy paused. "Along with my unhappiness."

"Did you love her?" Lillian asked, silently cursing the catch in her voice.

"Yes, I did, and leaving her wasn't easy. The first few months here were rough. I missed her terribly and sometimes wondered if I'd made a mistake. But that tempered with time. I don't wonder anymore. My place is here."

"She might show up here one day."

"She won't," Maddy said firmly. "She had absolutely no interest in joining the Order. If anything, she was dead set against it. And after I'd been here a year, I thought I'd write to her. Well, not to *her*, I sent it to the local tax collector so he could read it to her. Sounds silly now, but I wanted to let her know I wasn't coming back, in case she was wondering."

"That doesn't sound silly," Lillian said.

"It felt silly when I received her reply about her new lover," Maddy said wryly.

"Oh."

"To be honest, it was a bit of a relief. I could stop feeling guilty." Maddy pulled on Lillian's arm. "But what about you?" she said, her voice lifting.

Lillian swallowed. "What about me?"

"Has there ever been anyone special?"

She didn't want to talk about Caroline, but if she said no, Maddy would wonder why someone her age had never had a relationship. Ha! Relationship! Could she call what she'd had with Caroline a relationship? She'd thought so, until time and the advantage of hindsight had forced her to face the truth. "There was someone, a long time ago."

"What happened? Did you break her heart?"

What heart? "She left. For another monastery." Lillian blinked back tears. Why, why did it still hurt so much? She'd meant nothing to Caroline. Nothing! Looking back on that part of her life filled her with sorrow, humiliation, and regret. When Caroline had breezed out the monastery gates without a backward glance, Lillian had realized how stupid she'd been and had promised herself that she'd never let anyone do that to her again. Yet here she was, acting like a lovesick girl with someone almost half her age. She must be bloody insane!

"I'm sorry, Lillian. I didn't mean to pry."

Lillian shook herself. Maybe she was making an arse of herself, but not because Maddy was using her. They'd agreed to be together, to see where their fledgling relationship led. She wouldn't let Caroline poison this for her, too. "It's all right," she said, patting Maddy's arm. "But if you don't mind, I'd rather drop this subject."

"Of course." They walked in amiable silence, the birds twittering around them in the afternoon sun. "I suppose I should think about making my way to my lesson," Maddy murmured.

"And I need to pop over to my laboratory. Then I think I'll read a bit, save my energy for our lesson."

"Will you be saving it for our lesson, or for what comes after?" Maddy said impishly.

Lillian grinned. "Don't be cheeky!" She effortlessly formed a ball of fire in her left hand. "Look, we have to focus tonight. We're not going to your chambers until you can do this."

"What?"

"This."

Maddy stopped walking and turned to look.

"You'll be able to do it," Lillian said, frowning at the concern etched on Maddy's face. "You just need to apply yourself." She broke the flow; the fireball winked out.

"I'll try." Maddy looped her hands around Lillian's neck. "But it's difficult to concentrate when you're wondering if the tutor will end up in your chambers afterwards."

"Well, you won't have any excuses tonight, then, will you?" Lillian closed her eyes when Maddy's lips touched hers.

"MADDY!" A FAMILIAR voice called as she left the dining hall. She glanced over her shoulder, then stopped and waited until Rose caught up to her. "Are you all right? You were awfully quiet during supper."

"I'm just trying to work something out."

"What?"

Maddy's first instinct was to say nothing, but maybe Rose could help put her mind at ease. "Listen, do you sense it when your tutor draws fire?"

Rose's brows lifted. "Of course! Don't you? And not just with Mistress Dorothy, with everyone. I sense it all the time now."

"So do I. That's why I'm asking," Maddy said, lying through her teeth as her heart sank. "I wasn't sure if I was supposed to."

"What do you and Mistress Lillian talk about during your lessons?" Rose said with a laugh. "Or should I ask? Mistress Dorothy warned me that once I was fully open to the elements, I'd sense when others drew nearby. Hasn't Mistress Lillian said anything about it?"

"She might have said something early on, and I forgot." Maddy's mind raced. Lillian had spoken about it, and Maddy had sensed Lillian during her lessons and when she'd drawn air to subdue Merrin. But earlier, on the path, the sight of the fireball in Lillian's hand had taken her completely by surprise. Lillian had drawn fire right next to her, but Maddy hadn't sensed a thing! She hadn't sensed anything that night in Lillian's laboratory, either.

"At first, sensing everyone was terribly distracting in the training room. But I'm used to it now. I hardly notice it." Rose squeezed Maddy's arm. "Talk to the mistress. I'm sure she'll explain it again."

Maybe she *should* talk to Lillian. She'd failed miserably when trying to draw fire outside Lillian's laboratory, making herself dizzy and nauseous in the process. Drawing the elements shouldn't be that difficult—it didn't seem to be for anyone else. Salbine knew she'd been distracted during her lessons; maybe she'd misunderstood a key concept or technique. She smiled weakly. "I will. Thank you."

But later, on the way to the training room, her resolve to discuss her concerns with Lillian crumbled. Lillian would only be disappointed, or worse, blame herself for Maddy's ineptitude. They'd both been distracted. Tonight, now that their relationship wasn't tied so closely to Maddy's lessons, things would be different. Lillian had already said they'd remain in the training room until Maddy could hold fire, so they'd both be motivated to focus and succeed.

Lillian was waiting for her. "Oh good, you're here," she said, smiling.

Despite her anxiety, Maddy returned her smile and pecked Lillian on the lips.

"Now, now, none of that," Lillian said, her cheeks reddening. "Not until you've held fire." She gestured at the unlit candle standing in a tall candlestick in the middle of the room. "Let's start with that, to warm up. No pun intended."

Maddy stared at the candle, then closed her eyes and reached within herself for Salbine's fire. Yes, she could feel it, now she just had to draw it. Yes, yes! It was flowing through— Sharp pain, in her chest. Her eyes snapped open; her stomach roiled.

"Maddy?" Lillian peered anxiously at her.

She took a deep breath. "I'm fine. Let me try again." Determined not to let Lillian down, she squeezed her eyes shut, reached for the fire, gritted her teeth, pulled, pulled . . . yes, here it came; now to direct it to the candle, to the— Scorching pain ripped through her. She doubled over and her knees buckled. The fire burned, consuming her.

"Maddy? Maddy, what's wrong? What's wrong?"

Flames, everywhere! Searing heat, from the top of her head to the tips of her toes. "I'm on fire!" She stared at her hands in horror as they withered within the engulfing flames. Skin and muscle melted away, leaving behind dead, skeletal hands. "No!" She flailed around, danced, screamed. The stench of burning flesh filled her nostrils. *Salbine, help me! Help me!* "I'm on fire! I'm on fire!" she sobbed. "Help me! Oh, Salbine, please help me!"

"Maddy, stop drawing! Maddy, stop. *Stop!*"

The world went black.

Chapter Four

MADDY OPENED HER EYES AND BLINKED into the dim light. Something cool was pressed against her forehead. She slowly turned her head and recognized the robe hanging over the back of a chair. She was in her chambers, in her bed. Licking her lips, she reached up and touched the damp cloth lying above her eyes.

A shadow fell across her: Rose, hovering anxiously. "Maddy? Oh, thank Salbine, you're awake!" Then she was gone. Footsteps, followed by the door creaking open. Murmuring voices. The door thumped shut.

Maddy tried to sit up, but the room spun. Uh-oh. "I'm going to be sick." She grabbed the cloth from her forehead and held it over her mouth.

"Hang on!" Rose rushed over and lifted a bucket sitting near the bed.

Maddy hung her head over it just in time. Her throat burned. "I'm sorry," she croaked, then wiped her mouth with the cloth and handed it to Rose. When she lifted her head, fire raged within. *I'm on fire! I'm on fire!* Maddy gasped and clawed at her face. Her skin . . . it felt smooth, cool. It wasn't burned. She held her hands out in front of her, flipped them over and looked at her palms. "They're whole. They weren't burned," she whispered.

Rose's eyes filled with tears. "Oh, Maddy," she moaned, her lips trembling.

Maddy looked at her. "I don't understand. What happened?"

"I don't know." Rose avoided Maddy's eyes. "I've only heard snatches here and there. The abbess should be here soon, a defender is fetching her from the chapel. Everyone's there, praying."

"Praying? For what?"

"For you!"

"For me," Maddy breathed.

"Lie back down." Rose pushed gently on Maddy's shoulder. "You're sweating." She turned away and dipped another cloth into a bucket of water sitting on the table, next to the lamp.

Maddy lay still as Rose dabbed at her forehead; the slightest movement induced a wave of nausea. "Did Lillian bring me here?" she asked, suddenly wondering where Lillian was.

"Barnabus brought you." Rose sank onto the chair beside the bed. "The mistress is probably in the chapel. I'd be in the chapel too, if I wasn't here." She rested her hand on Maddy's shoulder. "But I wanted to be here," she said softly, "so when I heard them say they needed someone to stay and tend to you, I said I'd do it." She bit her lip. "You've had me so worried. They said you'd probably wake in two or three hours, but it's gone past three."

"Three in the morning?" Maddy exclaimed. Rose nodded.

Someone rapped at the door, then pushed it open. The abbess bustled in. Rose stood and bobbed a curtsey. Maddy started to push herself upright, but the abbess held out her hand. "No, it's all right." She gratefully sank back, swallowing bile.

"Would you give us a moment, Sister?" the abbess said to Rose.

"Of course." Rose hung the cloth over the side of the bucket and turned to leave.

"Rose?" Maddy called. Rose looked over her shoulder. "Thank you." The pity she glimpsed in Rose's eyes frightened her.

Abbess Sophia sat in the chair Rose had previously occupied. She pushed her spectacles up her nose and studied Maddy. "How are you feeling?"

Maddy swallowed. "Confused. Nauseous. What's wrong with—" She gagged. "Oh no, I have to—"

The abbess quickly lifted the bucket. "It's all right, this will eventually pass," she murmured, patting Maddy's back. Maddy's retching subsided and the abbess plucked a rag from the pile on the table and handed it to her, then dipped the cloth Rose had left into the water.

Maddy held onto the rag this time, embarrassed and mortified. "Do you know what's wrong with me?"

"Yes."

She closed her eyes as the abbess dabbed at her forehead. "Am I dying?" she whispered.

"No, you're not dying. You'll be all right."

"Then what's wrong with me?" she asked, opening her eyes. "What happened in the training room?"

The abbess wrung the cloth over the bucket before turning back to Maddy. She sighed. "You're what we call malflowed. For reasons we don't understand, the elements don't flow through you as they should." Her face softened. She gently touched Maddy's cheek. "It means you can't draw the elements."

No. Salbine wouldn't do this to her. "But I can! I've lit a candle."

"With great difficulty, according to Lillian. And that's not surprising. You see, you'd never know you're malflowed unless you draw the elements. From what we've observed, when a malflowed sister first draws the elements, there's no indication that she's malflowed. Drawing the elements somehow provokes the condition, brings it to the surface. It becomes more difficult to draw, and then what's drawn is distorted. Around the same time, the malflowed stops sensing when others draw."

Oh, Salbine. Oh, no. "Why would Salbine deny me Her gifts? Why?" She blinked back tears, but one escaped and rolled down her cheek. "Why would She turn Her back on me? I must have done something wrong, offended Her in some way." Maddy couldn't hold it in any longer. She covered her face with her hands and wept. Salbine had called her. Maddy had left everything behind to serve. Why this?

The abbess stroked Maddy's hair. "We don't understand why it happens, but we're sure it's not a form of punishment."

It bloody-well felt like one! "I've drawn fire." She peeked at the abbess through a gap between her hands. "Maybe if I worked at it hard enough—"

The abbess shook her head. "No. I know this is difficult for you, but you must accept it. If you try to draw and an element does flow, it would be dangerous for you, Maddy. You'll experience a similar episode to what happened earlier. But I doubt you can still draw. In the few cases we know about, an episode like the one tonight always rendered the malflowed incapable of drawing. The elements are closed to you now."

"You tested me! I passed the Test of Salbine. I am marked by Salbine."

"When you undergo the test, you're not the one drawing the elements," the abbess reminded her. "And at that point, the elements would have flowed freely through you, undistorted."

"I *am* marked!"

The abbess nodded. "Nobody doubts that," she said evenly. "And nobody doubts that Salbine called you to the Order."

Maddy did. How could she be a Salbine Sister when she couldn't draw the elements? She was as useless as a smith who couldn't shape metal or a potter who couldn't mould clay. "When will I have to leave the monastery?" she asked, her voice tremulous.

"You don't!" the abbess exclaimed. "Look at me. Give me your hands."

She reluctantly lifted them from her face. The abbess grasped them. "You see the branches on their backs? We welcomed you into the Order, claimed you as ours, the moment you took your vows. You're marked by Salbine and you want to serve—you are serving. That's all we require. Your place is still here, with us. It always will be."

But she couldn't draw the elements. She'd be the perpetual initiate, the odd one out, the sister on the outside, looking in. "Maybe I shouldn't feel this way, but it'll be embarrassing when I'm twice the age of the other initiates."

The abbess's forehead creased and she squeezed Maddy's hands. "You won't be. Granted, a sister's title usually relates in some way to her competence with the elements, but it doesn't have to. I want you to take it easy for a few days. Then we'll have a chat about how you can best serve within the Order. We'll find something in which you can become the resident expert, perhaps even the Order's expert."

But she couldn't draw the elements! Whatever else she studied wouldn't feel as important; she'd always know its sole purpose was to make her feel useful. But what was the alternative? To return to her farm and village and tell everyone she'd been mistaken, that Salbine hadn't called her after all? She'd been so sure. "What do other sisters like me study?"

Abbess Sophia took her time answering. "There aren't any others. Not alive, anyway. You'll have to go to the library to learn about others like yourself."

Why, Salbine? Why?

"How's your belly?"

Maddy lifted her head. The motion still made her gag. "Still queasy." Her head still throbbed, too.

"Lillian's brewed something to help. She didn't want to pray with us, she said she'd rather do something practical." The abbess looked amused, not annoyed. "I sent a defender for her when they told me you'd awakened. She's probably waiting outside."

Lillian. The most powerful mage alive. Her estimation of Maddy must have plummeted. "So she knows?"

"Yes, she knows."

"What does she think about . . . my condition?"

The abbess leaned over and touched her lips to Maddy's forehead. "I think that's a question for Lillian," she murmured. "I'll drop in tomorrow to see how you are."

She left before Maddy could reply. Maddy heard her speaking to someone outside her door, but couldn't make out the words. The door thumped shut again. Lillian towered over her.

"I hope you don't think this forward, but I'm staying with you tonight. I've brought a clean shift in case you throw up on me and I have to change." Lillian indicated the shift folded over her arm with a glance, then lifted a jar filled with a dark yellowish liquid. "But if you drink this, you probably won't."

Maddy eyed the jar suspiciously. "What is it?"

"An extremely complex concoction I've spent hours slaving over, commonly referred to as ginger tea. It will help your head, too."

Despite her headache, Maddy smiled.

"I'll just warm it a bit." Lillian tossed the shift onto the end of the bed and moved toward the fire. "Can you sit up?" she asked.

"Sitting up will be risky, though I'd be surprised if there's anything left to come up."

"There's always something." Lillian returned and reached for the bucket on the floor. "Let's get it over with."

Maddy slowly raised her head, waited until the room slowed down, then sat up. "I think I'm ok—" She twisted and retched over the bucket, one hand over her nose to block both the smell and the sight of the bucket's contents.

"Done?" Lillian asked when Maddy straightened, groaning.

"I think so."

"Good." Lillian returned to the fire. A minute later she was back to settle on the side of Maddy's bed. "Drink."

The warm liquid soothed her throat. Maddy gave it a moment to settle, then lay back. Her head pounded. "I just want to close my eyes a minute," she murmured, letting her eyelids sag.

When she opened them, the light had changed. Morning. Past eight, she guessed. Memories of the previous night came rushing back. She rubbed her forehead; her head felt fuzzy, but she didn't need to reach for a bucket. She still ached, though—ached with sorrow at Salbine's rejection.

Lillian stirred next to her. Lillian! She rolled over and shook her shoulder. "Lillian. Lillian!"

Lillian's eyes flew open. "What?"

"You missed early morning prayers."

"No, I told Sophia I wouldn't be there today." She rubbed her left eye. "I had to tell her, otherwise they would have rushed to my chambers to see if I'd expired. I'll go to morning prayers with you, if you feel up to it."

"I don't know," Maddy said. "The abbess said to take it easy for the next few days." And what would be the point of going to morning prayers? What would she pray for? Guidance? *Salbine, I'm a sister who can't draw the elements. What does my life mean now?* Salbine's laughter would ring in her ears. Tears welled. She lay back and threw her arm across her forehead. How would she face everyone? Would they all look at her in pity, as Rose had?

The bed creaked as Lillian pushed up on one elbow to study Maddy's face. "You gave me a terrible fright last night."

"I must have looked a right arse, running around the training room, screaming and flailing about. But I thought I was on fire." She felt for Lillian's hand. "I could feel it, smell it—see it!" Her grip tightened.

"I wanted to help, but I didn't know what to do. I'd never seen anything like it. All I could do was shout at you to stop drawing." Lillian briefly closed her eyes. "And then you collapsed, just fell to the floor like a sack of oats."

"Then what happened?"

"I couldn't wake you," Lillian said, breathing rapidly. "So I sent for the abbess. She arrived with several mistresses in tow. Fortunately Mistress Averill was with them. She remembered reading about a sister who'd sat motionless and in tears, convinced her body was encased in ice despite everyone's efforts to dissuade her of the notion. Sophia sent her to fetch the tome. One tome led to another, and by the time Barnabus carried you in here, we understood what had happened."

"You knew I was malformed."

Lillian's mouth twitched. "Malflowed. Trust me, you're not malformed." Her face clouded. "Why didn't you talk to me? Why didn't you tell me you couldn't sense others drawing?"

Maddy looked at her in surprise. "How did you—"

"Your friend, er . . ."

"Rose?"

"Yes, Rose. She said you'd talked to her about it. Or rather, lied to her about it, from the sound of it. Why did you talk to her? Why didn't you talk to me? I am your tutor."

Was. And Lillian had always been more than her tutor. "I didn't want to disappoint you."

Lillian frowned. "You wouldn't have." Her frown deepened when Maddy snorted. "I would have wondered why, investigated, maybe prevented what happened last night."

"By telling me I'd never be a mage so our lessons were a waste of time?"

Lillian tipped her head from side to side. "Not in those words, but yes."

"And you expect me to believe that you wouldn't have been disappointed? That you aren't disappointed?" Maddy swallowed. "In me?"

"It doesn't matter."

"That's easy for you to say. You flick your pinkie and we're suddenly in the middle of a blizzard."

"I can't help that I'm not malflowed, any more than you can help that you are!" Lillian shouted. She slowly inhaled, then blew out some air. "My estimation of someone doesn't hinge on how well they draw the elements. Are you telling me yours does? Is that why I'm here?"

"No!"

"Then stop talking nonsense. If you want to berate yourself for being malflowed, fine, but leave me out of it. You've never been able to draw the elements, the whole time we've . . ." her face screwed up ". . . been together."

"Yes, I have!"

"Barely." Her voice softened. "And yet I'm drawn to you and enjoy your company immensely. You being malflowed . . . it doesn't matter."

"Yes, it does." Maddy sighed. "Why would Salbine do this to me? Why would She turn Her back on me?"

"Why do you think She's turned Her back on you?"

"Lillian, I can't draw the elements. She's denied me Her gifts."

"The ability to draw the elements isn't a measure of Salbine's favour."

"Of course it is! What's the point of being a Salbine Sister if you can't draw the elements? What am I supposed to do? The abbess said we'll discuss what I can contribute, but what's the point?"

Lillian's mouth pressed into a thin line. "The point is that you are marked by Salbine and She called you here."

"To make a mockery of me!"

"Maddy, you've been a contributing member of this community for three years without drawing the elements. I can't do what you do. I don't help the adepts with the afflicted. I don't go to the market and mix with the people. I don't offer them comfort and listen to their concerns."

"Anybody can do that!" Maddy snapped, annoyed by Lillian's patronizing attitude. "You don't need to be a sister to do that."

"Look at your beautiful embroidery."

"Oh, please!"

"What about those marked by Salbine who don't join the Order? Are you saying that Salbine doesn't care about them?"

Maddy sat up and glared at Lillian. "They weren't called, and maybe I wasn't either. Because there's no difference between me and them. They'll never draw the elements, and neither will I. So what am I doing here?"

Lillian sat up. She brushed Maddy's hair out of her eyes and gazed at her. "You were called here to serve Salbine. Nothing's changed, Maddy. You'll see that in time."

No, everything had changed. Everything. She couldn't draw the elements. Lillian could blather on all she wanted about her other talents, but they didn't matter. Salbine Sisters drew the elements. Salbine Sisters protected the people by using the elements. What would she do during a conflict, while the mages manipulated the elements to repel hostile forces? Make everyone's tea?

She'd left everything behind and come to the monastery because she'd believed that Salbine had called her. She'd thrown herself into monastery life with the expectation that she'd eventually serve Salbine as a competent mage. Every other sister could draw the elements, so why couldn't she? Had she offended Salbine, or deluded herself? What did her life mean now? Yesterday morning her life had brimmed with purpose; now it felt hollow. She no longer understood her place in the world. Perhaps she never had.

Chapter Five

MADDY SLOWED AS SHE APPROACHED THE dining hall in the Community Tower and the chatter inside reached her ears. She'd spent the better part of the last four days hiding in her chambers, venturing out only to empty her chamber pot, fetch water, and nip to the kitchen to see what the cooks could spare. Lillian had managed to coax her out for an afternoon walk the day before last and had visited most evenings, and several others had dropped in, Rose and the abbess among them; otherwise Maddy had kept to herself.

Today she was to meet with the abbess in her study, so she'd decided it was time to emerge from her sanctuary and face everyone. But now that she was here . . .

Footsteps behind her heralded Rose's arrival; she squeezed Maddy's arm and said cheerfully, "Glad to see you didn't back out."

"And I'm glad you're here," Maddy said, bolstered by Rose's presence. She talked a little too much as they stood in line for their porridge, and fought the urge to cling to Rose when they reached their usual table. Abigail and Nora looked up from their bowls. Maddy searched their faces for pity, but found only curiosity.

Nora's mouth turned up at the corners. "We've missed you at embroidery." She moved over slightly so Grace could squeeze onto the bench. "Sister Gail threatened to work on your panel, but I managed to hold her off."

"Thank you," Maddy said as she and Rose sat down across from them. She lifted the pitcher from the middle of the table and filled a mug with milk. "I would have spent the entire next session pulling out her stitches."

"So you'll be there tomorrow?" Nora asked.

Maddy nodded. Someone sat down on her right. She turned to look, then quickly faced forward in dismay. Gwendolyn.

"And I guess you'll be starting on the abbess's cassock soon, won't you?" Rose said brightly.

"I guess so," Maddy mumbled, embarrassed. Nobody cared about her embroidery; it wasn't as important as their training with the elements.

"It's good to know you'll have plenty to keep yourself busy while we're all in the training rooms," Gwendolyn said. Those across from Maddy stared at their porridge. "In fact, I think we all have lessons this afternoon," Gwendolyn continued, her voice rising. "What will you be doing? Mucking out the stables? Helping the cooks peel potatoes? Oh, but your lessons were always in the evenings, weren't they." She snickered. "Your 'lessons'—right. Now I understand why you've latched onto the mistress. One way to make yourself useful, I suppose."

Maddy shot up as those around her gasped. She yanked Gwendolyn's spoon from her porridge bowl, picked up the bowl, and tipped it over Gwendolyn's head.

Gwendolyn's eyes bulged. "You bitch!" she screeched, leaping to her feet, the bowl balanced on her head and porridge running down her face. The spoon in Maddy's hand burst into flame. She yelped and dropped it to the table. Abigail quickly doused the fire with milk.

Everyone else was on their feet. "You're not supposed to draw outside the training room," Grace hissed.

"What is going on?" a voice cracked out. Mistress Phyllis bustled forward and surveyed the mess in horror. "Who drew fire?" she asked as others in the dining hall crowded around.

The initiates glanced uncertainly at each other. "You can eliminate Sister Maddy," Gwendolyn said with a sneer.

Mistress Phyllis's mouth tightened. "Since nobody wants to own up, I'll take a wild guess and assume it was the one with the bowl on her head." Everyone except Gwendolyn burst into laughter. "Clean up this mess, Sister Gwendolyn. I shall have a word with your tutor about your inappropriate use of the elements. And take that blasted bowl off your head!"

Gwendolyn lifted the bowl as Mistress Phyllis turned to leave, revealing bits of porridge pasted into her hair. "What about Maddy? She dumped my porridge over me!"

An exasperated sigh escaped Mistress Phyllis's lips. "I don't want to see you in the chapel looking like that. Sister Maddy, fetch water and heat it for Sister Gwendolyn. She'll be bathing before morning prayers."

"Fill one of the tubs in our tower. And be quick about it!" Gwendolyn snapped when Mistress Phyllis was out of earshot. "I want my water waiting for me when I get there!" As those who'd rushed over to see the show trickled away, she plucked at the oatmeal on her robe, groaning, "Oh, look at this mess."

"The bowl suited you," Rose murmured when Gwendolyn passed her, presumably on her way to get a rag.

"You're as pathetic as your crippled friend," Gwendolyn retorted without breaking stride.

Crippled. Was that how everyone saw her? "I'd better start on the water." Maddy downed her milk and picked up her bowl.

Rose touched Maddy's arm. "Finish your breakfast first. Don't rush yourself for Gwendolyn."

No. She'd not only lost her temper, but her appetite too. Plus she wanted to see her squirrels. They were capable of taking care of themselves and probably hadn't missed her, but she'd missed them. "I'm not."

"See you at morning prayers?"

Maddy nodded, though she'd prefer to skip them. Her presence might offend Salbine. Uninvited guests were always an intrusion.

MADDY MURMURED HER thanks as she accepted a cup of tea from the abbess. She took a tentative sip. Lemon. Not her favourite, but she hadn't wanted to refuse it.

Abbess Sophia blew on her tea. "It was nice to see you in the chapel this morning."

It had been horrible. The sun filtering through the stained glass, the sculpture of Lina in the vestibule, the sisters' voices rising to Salbine, the tapestry illustrating the founding of the Merrin monastery—everything that normally exhilarated and humbled had left her cold. And when it had come time to pray . . . she'd pressed her palms together, bowed her head, and quietly despaired.

"I heard about what happened in the dining hall, but I don't know why it happened." The abbess eyed Maddy over the rim of her cup.

"I'm sorry." With the heat of the moment long past, her behaviour that morning disappointed and shamed her. "Sister Gwendolyn started going on about how everyone would be busy training except me."

"And that bothered you enough to dump porridge over her head?"

"It wasn't just that. She said something about me . . . and Mistress Lillian. That's when I dumped the porridge over her head."

"I see." The abbess set her cup on its saucer. "What did she say?"

Suddenly grateful for the tea she held, Maddy sipped it to give herself time to think. "She implied that my interest in the mistress isn't genuine, that I spend time with her for other reasons." Specifically, that she lay with Lillian for other reasons.

"Is that true?"

"No!" Maddy exclaimed, offended that the abbess had to ask. Lillian was the one bright spot in her life, the only light in the oppressive gloom that had hung over her since she'd learned of her condition. Their relationship was as much a surprise to her as it seemed to be to everyone else. A wonderful surprise, one she'd thank Salbine for every day—if Salbine cared. "I spend time with the mistress because I like her." That felt inadequate; she liked Rose, and Thomas. "I care about her." In a different way than she did for Rose, but that explanation would have to do.

"Since Lillian is a mistress and you're an initiate, some sisters are bound to draw the wrong conclusions," the abbess said. "You'll have to learn to brush them off."

Or some sisters, like Gwendolyn, were just cruel and ignorant. "I know, and I have. I guess it got to me this time because . . ." She swallowed. "The other things she said, about what I'll do while they're all training. Well, what *am* I supposed to do?"

The abbess smiled. "That's why we're here. To talk about potential areas of study."

"But should I even be here?" Her teacup rattled against its saucer. She looked around for somewhere to set her tea, then carefully lowered her cup and saucer onto the small round table next to her chair that seemed to be there for that very purpose.

"What do you mean?" the abbess asked, frowning.

"Here, at the monastery."

"We've talked about this already, but perhaps you don't remember. It was just after you came around. You're marked by Salbine and you're serving Her. That's all we require."

"But how am I different from a cook or a stable hand? Why isn't Dora a sister, or Penelope?"

The abbess folded her hands on her desk. "By serving us, they serve Salbine, but they're not marked by Salbine. Only those marked by Salbine can be sisters. And only those who answer Her call become sisters. You answered Her call, Maddy. You left your family and your village to come to us."

But had Salbine's call been an excuse to escape farm life and a relationship that had become routine? She hadn't thought so. Her decision to leave Joanna had been heart-wrenching, and she'd always enjoyed her chores around the farm. She would have happily stayed, if not for Salbine's call, the pull she'd felt ever since she'd discovered she was marked. Had it all been a delusion? Every other sister had her decision to answer the call affirmed when she learned to draw the elements. Every other sister could say with certainty that she belonged, that Salbine wanted her service. "I can't draw the elements, Abbess. If Salbine called me, why would She deny me Her gifts? Why would She set me apart?" *Why would She cripple me?*

"I don't know. Perhaps She has something else in mind for you and doesn't want you distracted. Perhaps drawing the elements could be dangerous to you in some way and She's protecting you. Or perhaps She's simply not all that concerned with who can draw the elements and who can't."

Or perhaps only those She'd called could draw the elements. Often the most obvious explanation was the truth.

"You're not the first malflowed sister, Maddy. We've turned away women who claimed to be marked but failed the Test of Salbine, and women whose desire to serve Salbine wasn't genuine. We've never turned away a woman because she can't draw the elements. In fact, we claimed you long before you entered a training room. You're marked.

You've served Salbine admirably during your time here. You're a sister. Nothing has changed."

Everything had changed. Last week she'd felt part of a community, imagined herself becoming competent at drawing the elements and eventually becoming a mistress. She'd harboured no doubts about her chosen path, or about Salbine's love for her. Now she felt like an outsider, with nothing of value to contribute, and wondered if she deserved to be at the monastery. "I have to be honest—I can't help but wonder if I belong. Nothing sets me apart from those outside. Anything I might contribute, they could too."

The abbess blinked at her. "Yet Salbine didn't call them. She called you, and you answered that call."

Maddy had once believed that; now she wasn't sure.

"I was going to discuss your interests and afterward speak to the mistresses, but I've changed my mind. I'd like you to spend some time researching other sisters who were malflowed. We can discuss other potential areas of study later." The abbess stood, drained her teacup, and set it back in its saucer on her desk. "Let's go see Mistress Averill. She can tell you where to start, help you draw up a study plan."

"Yes, Abbess." Maddy rose and followed her to the door. When they spoke with Mistress Averill, she wouldn't have to feign enthusiasm. She wanted to read about the other malflowed sisters, to see if any of them had eventually regained Salbine's favour and overcome the malflowed condition.

SOPHIA ROTATED THE sealing wax over the candle, then smeared it onto the folded paper in front of her. She picked up her seal, licked it, and pressed it into the wax. Seconds later, she lifted the seal and grunted in satisfaction.

The door to her study creaked open. Elizabeth bounced in and pushed the door shut. "You've been busy," she said, taking in Sophia's stained fingers and the pile of sealed messages at her elbow.

"I've written to the other monasteries, requesting that they send any material they have on the subject of malflowed sisters. I've asked Maddy to learn about others like her, but we don't have much in our library. Averill suggested I check with the others."

"How did your meeting with Maddy go?" Elizabeth sank into the chair Maddy had occupied earlier.

"Not well." Sophia moved the letter aside and clasped her hands on the desk. "When was the last time you drew the elements? Outside the training rooms, I mean."

"I tested that newcomer a couple of weeks ago, the one that failed."

"*Outside* the training rooms, Elizabeth."

"Oh. Well, um, there was that time last month, when that piece of stone fell from the east archway. It would have hit poor Jacob if I hadn't been passing by."

"And before then?"

Elizabeth grimaced. "Oh dear . . . I did help with a horse—when was it, February? No, March. Thomas was desperate."

"So over six months ago."

"Yes. Oh, I did help take care of some bandits, but that must have been almost ten years ago."

"And when was the last time you sensed someone draw the elements outside the training rooms?"

"Is there a purpose to this?" Elizabeth asked, grinning.

Sophia smiled indulgently. "Yes, there is."

Elizabeth folded her arms. "All right, then. I wasn't near the dining hall this morning, but I heard about what happened."

"Gwendolyn doesn't count. She broke a rule."

"Okay, then. Lillian's been drawing lately."

Sophia snorted. "Lillian's been showing off, and she's stopped now. She was already tapering off before we found out that Maddy's malflowed."

"Well, I don't know, then. Just when sisters have been working with the horses, I guess."

"Exactly."

Elizabeth's brow furrowed.

"Drawing the elements is such a small part of our life here. But try telling that to Maddy. She's convinced that since she's malflowed, she doesn't belong here, that Salbine has turned Her back on her."

"That's nonsense!"

"Of course it is. The initiates don't know this yet, but unless there's a conflict, they're drawing the elements now more than they ever will.

The only difference between Maddy and the rest of us is that she won't have to spend time in a training room every once in a while."

"And that we *can* draw the elements and she can't," Elizabeth pointed out, "though that likely won't ever matter in practice. Anyway, I thought we were going to find Maddy an area of study, something to focus on while the others are training."

"And which, ironically, will probably lead to her being a more valuable resource than many other sisters. But she doesn't see it that way. No matter what we find her to do, she'll feel as if we're patting her on the head and telling her to go out and play while the adults get down to the important business." She gazed out the window, watched the clouds float by. "I'm worried about her. She seems so lost. And then there's Lillian."

"What about Lillian?" Elizabeth rose and rounded the desk.

Sophia closed her eyes when Elizabeth gently touched her shoulders and worked her fingers into them. "After all this time she finally risks another relationship. I was starting to think it would never happen, that Caroline had done so much damage that she'd never take a chance again. And then all of a sudden she's with Maddy. Not who I would have guessed and it's early days, but they seem to enjoy each other's company."

"But?"

"Even before we discovered that Maddy's malflowed, I wondered where it would end up. Maddy's so young."

"That doesn't mean they're incompatible," Elizabeth said.

"No, but realistically, what's going to happen? Almost eighteen years separates them. Will they accept each other as consorts?"

"Consorts!" Elizabeth blurted. "They've only just started to see each other."

"I know, but I'm thinking ahead." She reached up and patted Elizabeth's hand. "I can't help it. After what happened with Caroline . . ." Her eyes welled with tears. She pulled a handkerchief from the desk drawer and dabbed at them. "It's so silly. I've wanted so much for Lillian to find someone, and now that she has, I'm afraid for her. What if Maddy leaves, as Caroline did?"

Elizabeth's fingers stopped moving. "Why would Maddy go to another monastery, especially now?"

"Not leave for another monastery. Leave the Order."

"But she can't! The rules forbid it. Not only has Salbine marked her, but we have, too." Elizabeth reached over Sophia's shoulder and held her hand in front of Sophia's face, as if she needed reminding.

"I know we have, but sisters are bound to the Order because they can draw the elements. That's the agreement. You forfeit your freedom to learn how to draw. Maddy will never be a threat to anyone. If she doesn't feel she belongs here, if she's miserable and wants to leave, who am I to deny her request?"

"Her abbess. Someone who sees what she doesn't see and has faith that she'll eventually see it."

"She has to be the one to have faith, Elizabeth. And what if she never sees it?" Sophia rubbed her temples. "If I had been abbess when Caroline was here, I would have searched for a reason to kick her sorry arse out the gates."

"Lillian would never have forgiven you," Elizabeth murmured.

"I know, but I would have done it anyway, sent Caroline to another monastery the moment I realized how much she was hurting her. Do you know how dreadful it was to watch and not be able to do anything? Oh, I tried talking to Lillian, but she didn't want to know. So yes, if I could have prevented Caroline from harming her, I would have, and suffered Lillian's wrath." Sophia drew a shuddering breath. "And now I wish I could stop Maddy from leaving, but I don't think I can, not in good conscience."

Elizabeth hugged her from behind, pressing her cheek against Sophia's. "I know how much you love Lillian," she said softly. "I love her too. But we can't prevent her from being hurt. All we can do is be there for her."

"That's another thing. I don't think Lillian's told Maddy about me. I wish she would. Maddy brought her up during our conversation, and I felt dishonest. I don't feel comfortable discussing Lillian with her, not when she doesn't know."

"Maybe she does. She could have heard it from someone else."

"I doubt it. Not many know, and those who do wouldn't tell her." And if Maddy knew, her demeanour while talking about Lillian would have been different. "No, I'm sure she doesn't know."

"Why don't you talk to Lillian, ask her to tell Maddy?"

Sophia shook her head. "I don't want her to think I'm interfering. And don't you say anything, either." She felt Elizabeth's smile against her cheek.

"I won't," Elizabeth said. "I learned a long time ago not to get in the middle of you two. But I can say something to you, and I think you should stop worrying and see what happens. Maddy's only just found out she's malflowed. Give her time to adjust. As for her relationship with Lillian, it's too early to tell where it's going. For all we know, Lillian could be the one to end it. So stop worrying."

But she was supposed to worry. She was the abbess. And Lillian's big sister.

Chapter Six

MADDY CLOSED THE THICK TOME WITH a thud and lugged it back to the bookshelf. Its pages hadn't provided enlightenment, only disappointment. A malflowed sister mentioned in passing, among passage upon dry passage that described new discoveries related to reshaping and redirecting the elements. So far, her month in the library had given her the overwhelming impression that malflowed sisters had always been on the periphery, their accomplishments, if any, not worth recording. Hardly encouraging.

"We've received another two responses from the other monasteries," Mistress Averill said cheerfully, making Maddy jump. "Brettony's librarian said she'll copy the few references she's found and send them to us." The mistress pursed her lips. "I expect we'll receive the material in about a month's time." Her voice lifted. "But the more exciting response is from Heath. Apparently they had quite the prolific malflowed sister in their service. She left behind journals, and she's mentioned quite frequently in their history tomes."

Maddy wanted to leap into the air with joy. "That's wonderful!"

"Yes, but unfortunately they value the material too much to part with it."

Her heart sank. "Can't they do what Brettony will do and copy it?"

"Apparently there's so much of it, it would take months. They've invited us to send a sister, someone to sort through the material and decide what's important to us. Their scribes will then copy her selections, and she can bring the copies back to us."

Why should another sister decide what was important? Maddy should be the one to go—but only those who'd achieved the title of adept were permitted to travel.

"You can't go, of course," the mistress said, perhaps deducing Maddy's thoughts from her expression. "But the abbess has asked me to speak to our scribes, to see if anyone is interested. If we send a scribe, she can help their scribes, come back to us sooner." She pressed her finger against her chin. "Sister Clara's seemed a bit bored lately. Maybe she'd like to go. I'll speak to her this afternoon."

"Thank you," Maddy murmured, though she wished she could go herself. "May I leave now? I've finished with the Ivers tome, and I don't have much left to go through until more material arrives." Plus, she wanted to finish embroidering a cushion cover for Lillian's birthday, now only two days away.

Mistress Averill nodded. "I don't see much point in spending hours here each day if you'll only run out of material. I'll see you in the chapel later."

Maddy bobbed and left the library.

Excited voices turned her head as she crossed the inner courtyard. Several initiates were on their way to the training rooms, probably chattering about the fire examinations that had begun yesterday and would continue for the next two days. Initiates were examined in front of their peers and the adepts. Mistress Ivy, who oversaw all training, had invited Maddy to attend, but she'd declined. Watching her friends draw fire would be like pouring salt on an open wound, and her presence would only put a damper on things. Everyone was in a celebratory mood, looking forward to moving on to air. She didn't want them to feel sorry for her, or to minimize their achievements to spare her feelings.

She'd had Nora hide the cushion and the cover she was working on in her chambers, so Lillian wouldn't stumble across them. Maddy pulled the cover from its hiding place in Nora's chest and sank into a chair, but had only just started to stitch when someone rapped loudly on a door—perhaps hers. She put the cover down and opened Nora's door a crack. "Lillian!" she said, stepping into the hallway and pulling the door shut. "I was just returning something I'd borrowed from Nora."

Lillian's face lit up. "There you are! I went to the library first, but Averill said you'd left."

"I needed a break. And I'm running out of material. But," she pulled Lillian into a hug, "a malflowed sister at the Heath monastery kept journals. They won't send them to us, but they've invited us to send someone to copy them."

"You can't go," Lillian said, drawing back and frowning at Maddy.

"Mistress Averill plans to send a scribe. Probably Sister Clara."

Lillian nodded. "I don't know much about her, but I'm sure she'll apply herself to the task with enthusiasm."

Maddy hoped Sister Clara would focus on how the malflowed sister had reconciled her condition with serving in the Order—or better yet, how she'd overcome her condition.

"It sounds to me like you're free until evening prayers. The sun is shining, the birds are singing, and the trees are still. Why don't we go down to the kitchen, pack a lunch, and go for a nice long stroll?"

"That sounds lovely."

"Come on, then." Lillian started for the stairwell. Maddy smiled and grabbed her hand. The cushion cover could wait. Since Nora had been with Maddy the last time Lillian had unexpectedly shown up, she'd guess what had happened when she saw Maddy's things all over her table.

Two hours later they lounged under the shade of a grand oak tree, sighing contentedly, their bellies full. Maddy snuggled into Lillian, who sat propped against the tree's trunk, and rested her head on Lillian's shoulder, feeling the now familiar scratch of Lillian's rough robe against her cheek. Perhaps she should have made her a robe instead of a cushion cover—a bright, soft robe, in contrast to the dark, rough robes Lillian habitually wore. But would Lillian wear such a robe? And how would Maddy have measured her? They were about the same height, but Lillian had more meat on her bones; some would describe her as plump. Maybe she could have sneaked out of bed one night after Lillian had fallen asleep and measured one of her robes. An idea to tuck away for another time.

"Would you like to do something on your birthday?" she murmured, her eyes half closed. "I can cook supper for you if you like. We can have it in my chambers." Or would Lillian finally invite Maddy to hers? Maddy was starting to wonder if Lillian's chambers were in a shambles, or if she had a pastime or habit she didn't want Maddy to know about. She'd almost knocked on Lillian's door once when she'd been in the Mistresses Tower for another reason, but had lost her nerve and been grateful for it later. Better to wait for an invitation than to force the issue.

"I usually dine with the abbess and Elizabeth, and this year will be no exception," Lillian said.

"Oh." She hadn't been aware that the abbess hosted suppers for mistresses on their birthdays.

"But I'd like it very much if you would join us," Lillian continued.

Maddy stifled a snort. "I doubt the abbess would want me there."

"Actually, she suggested it."

She lifted her head from Lillian's shoulder. "She did?"

"Yes. But there's a condition."

"What? What do I have to do?"

"No, I have to do something. I have to tell you something." Lillian grimaced and scratched her head.

"What?" Maddy asked, bursting with curiosity.

"The abbess and I . . . we came to the monastery together. Joined the Order together."

"You came together?" Shock stabbed through her as she suddenly understood. Maddy gasped in disbelief. "You mean you and the abbess, you used to be together?"

Lillian barked a laugh. "No! No, no, no. We're sisters."

"Sisters," Maddy repeated, momentarily confused. Of course they were sisters. "Oh, you mean *sisters*, not sisters." When Lillian looked confused, she elaborated. "You're sisters in the sense that you have the same parents, not in the sense that you both belong to the Order."

"That's what I bloody-well said! You don't have to explain it to me!" Lillian bellowed.

"You're sisters!" Maddy exclaimed, now that it was sinking in. She shifted to face Lillian and sat cross-legged. "Why didn't you tell me before?" she asked as she frantically reviewed everything she'd ever said to the abbess about Lillian.

Lillian bit her lip. "I didn't want to scare you off."

"You wouldn't have, you silly goose," Maddy said with a grin. She slipped her hand into Lillian's. "I'm surprised nobody's mentioned it to me."

"Few know, and they wouldn't say anything. I suppose we've always kept it quiet so that everyone would think of us independently, not in the same breath."

Maddy studied Lillian's face. "I can't say I see much of a resemblance. Maybe a little around the eyes and mouth." And their temperaments were so different. "You must be the younger one."

"By almost ten years."

"That would make the abbess . . . fifty-one?"

"Yes."

"Didn't you say the abbess arrived at the monastery when she was twenty-five?" Maddy asked, recalling a conversation they'd had some time ago. "So that would mean you were sixteen." The minimum age for admittance to the monastery.

Lillian nodded. "We set out when I was fifteen. We knew I'd be sixteen by the time we reached the gates. Sophia was about fourteen when she knew she was called. She would have arrived here at sixteen, if not for me."

"What do you mean?"

"My ma died in childbirth, when she had me."

Maddy squeezed her hand. "I'm sorry."

"So that left my pa and Sophia, and a newborn. Apparently I had two older brothers, but they didn't see their first birthdays." Lillian took a deep breath and slowly exhaled. "Our pa remarried and started a family with bride number two. He and Mildred didn't have much time for us, so Sophia watched over me. She yearned to come here when she turned sixteen, but she didn't want to bugger off and leave me behind. When I was old enough to understand, I told her to go, but she wouldn't. She said she would when I could take care of myself."

"She never did leave you behind, so what does that mean?" Maddy asked, trying to keep a straight face, but failing.

Lillian's eyes narrowed. "Don't be cheeky. I was perfectly capable of taking care of myself when I was old enough to understand her dilemma." She looked at her lap. "I suspect it was more that she didn't want to leave me behind without anyone who cared," she said softly.

Regretting her joke, Maddy leaned in to hug Lillian, and closed her eyes when Lillian rubbed her back. "You both must have thought it a miracle when you were called too," she murmured into Lillian's neck. Lillian's hand stopped moving. Maddy lifted her head. "What?"

"Well, I wasn't exactly called," Lillian said slowly.

"What do you mean?" Maddy asked, her voice sounding shrill to her ears.

Lillian shrugged. "When I realized I was marked by Salbine too, I told Sophia I'd go to the monastery with her. It was the perfect resolution to her dilemma. She could come here without leaving me behind."

Maddy stared at her, open-mouthed. "So you're telling me you weren't called. You just decided to join the Order. Why? Why would you join if you're not called?"

"To learn. To grow. To serve. And to live among women who honour Salbine."

"But you weren't called," Maddy said, still bewildered. Were there other sisters like Lillian—here by their own choice, not Salbine's? "Does the abbess know?"

"Of course she knows. I didn't lie to her."

"And she doesn't care?"

"Maddy, I'm marked by Salbine and I serve Her. I belong here as much as the next sister."

Maddy leaped to her feet. "But you weren't drawn here, didn't feel it was your destiny. You just . . . just . . . tagged along with someone else!" she shouted, throwing up her arms.

Lillian frowned and struggled to her feet. "Why are you so upset?"

"Look at you! You freely admit you weren't called by Salbine, yet you can draw the elements better than any sister here, perhaps any sister anywhere." Her agitation forced Maddy to pace. "Why can't I draw them? I was called. I left my family to come here, left everything I knew behind. And Salbine denies me Her gifts?"

"As I've said before, I don't believe how well someone can draw the elements is a measure of Salbine's favour."

"Maybe not, or you'd be up there with bloody Lina herself, wouldn't you?" Maddy pointed at the sky. "And that wouldn't make sense, since you weren't even called. You must have a good laugh every time some poor deluded woman shows up at the gates because Salbine called her. No wonder you keep to yourself. You don't want to mix with the simpletons who think Salbine has a say in what goes on around here."

"Don't be so bloody immature," Lillian said, rolling her eyes.

"Oh, so now you're throwing my age in my face."

Lillian heaved a sigh. "I'd say the same thing if you were eighty-five. Stop acting like a child!"

She clenched her hands. "And now I'm a child. Fine. I'll go take my nap." Whirling, Maddy marched away.

"Maddy!"

No, she wouldn't look over her shoulder. Hot, angry tears stung her eyes. She was tired of everyone saying that being malflowed didn't matter. It would matter if it were them! They wouldn't be so dismissive if they couldn't draw the elements. If she were to ask those at the market to name the first two things that came to mind when they saw a sister, everyone's answer would be the same: Salbine and the elements. Not embroidery, art, or research. The elements. So would everyone please stop trying to convince her that she was as much a sister as they were? Nobody outside the monastery would believe that, so why should she?

Lillian, especially, was in no position to advise her. She'd joined the Order for her sister, not for Salbine. If the abbess hadn't been called, Lillian wouldn't be here. Did she even care about Salbine? Probably not, and yet drawing the elements was second nature to her. Nothing made sense anymore. Nothing!

Half an hour later she threw herself onto her bed, her anger spent. She'd acted like a right arse, and had probably driven away the one person who'd kept her from going mad since she'd learned she was malflowed. Faced with losing Lillian, she suddenly understood how much she'd drawn on their relationship to bolster herself. Lillian still wanted her, so she must be worth something, right? Maddy no longer felt as if she belonged, but she didn't feel alone. Lillian was here. Lillian cared. Lillian still valued her company. And how had Maddy rewarded her when she'd opened up about her reason for joining the Order? She'd lashed out at her for something that wasn't her fault.

Lillian was right, she was a child. If her behaviour had frightened Lillian off, she couldn't blame her. And she had nerve, throwing a tantrum because Lillian hadn't felt called. Lately her prayers had been empty and her attentiveness to Salbine minimal. She'd once awakened every day with a sense of purpose; now she drifted from day to day, struggling to find meaning where it used to abound and wondering if her relationship with Lillian was the only thing holding her to the monastery. She might soon find out.

At least Lillian was honest. Maddy felt as if she were living a lie. Or perhaps 'trapped in a lie' would be more apt. She couldn't leave the monastery. The branches were on her hands, her fate sealed. *Trapped.*

Someone rapped at the door. "Maddy?"

Lillian! She pulled a handkerchief from her robe's pocket and quickly wiped her eyes, though she knew the action was futile. "Come in," she called, pushing herself to a sitting position. Lillian opened the door and stepped into the room. "Are you still talking to me?" Maddy asked, not caring that her voice quavered.

"I think the more pertinent question is whether you're still talking to me," Lillian said wryly. She pushed the door shut and met Maddy's eyes. "Now, I know I'm not here for reasons you consider acceptable, but I've served at this monastery for almost twenty-six years. I value this community, and I do honour Salbine. In those twenty-six years, I've missed early morning prayers only three times—twice when I was ill, and once when someone I care about found out she's malflowed. And in those twenty-six years, my right to be here has been questioned once." She held up her index finger. "Only once."

Maddy couldn't remember when she'd last felt so humbled and ashamed. She swung her legs off the bed and sighed. "I'm sorry. I'm questioning my own right to be here, and I guess that's making me question everyone else's." She twisted the handkerchief. "I know you don't think Salbine has deliberately done this to me, but I can't help but think that She has. And it hurts, Lillian. It hurts." She hung her head.

The bed creaked when Lillian sat next to her. "I have to confess, I didn't understand until today how much it is hurting you," Lillian murmured. "I thought you were all right, that you were adjusting. You haven't said anything when you've told me about the few interesting bits you've come across in the library."

Maddy hadn't wanted to bore her by constantly talking about her condition. But keeping it bottled inside had probably contributed to her infantile behaviour and ruined a pleasant afternoon with a woman she cared for deeply. "I'm struggling, Lillian." She shoved the handkerchief back into her pocket. "I've lost my way. I used to be so sure of everything. But now everything I believed with all my heart has been snatched away, taking with it my purpose."

"The only thing that's changed is that you can't draw the elements. Why has that taken away your purpose?" Lillian took Maddy's hand. "Didn't you join the Order to serve? You can still do that—you are doing it. Why do you believe that only drawing the elements counts?"

"It's what makes us different, Lillian. Don't we refer to the elements as Salbine's gifts? Look at Lina's story. She received the gifts and then founded the Order so she could teach others to draw the elements."

"She had many reasons for founding the Order."

"But surely that was one of the primary ones. I wonder what she would have thought of malflowed sisters. Right now, I'm apparently the only sister who can't draw the elements, and that has me doubting everything I believed about my life." Maddy turned her head toward Lillian and gently pressed her lips against Lillian's cheek. "If you woke up tomorrow and could no longer draw the elements, wouldn't you think Salbine was displeased with you in some way?"

Lillian was silent for a moment. "I suppose I might wonder, and it would be a bit of a shock, but I'd still have my laboratory, and I'd still be at early morning prayers every day. I'd miss my work with the horses, though," she said with a frown. "I rather enjoy that."

"Don't take this the wrong way, but maybe you wouldn't be upset because you never felt called."

"I didn't say I wouldn't be upset!" Lillian snapped. "I probably would be. But my life would still have purpose. This would still be my home and exactly where I'm supposed to be."

"I used to think the same." Maddy wouldn't have left everyone she loved if she hadn't been certain. "I truly believed Salbine had called me. Maybe you don't believe that, but I did."

"I believe you, Maddy. I have no reason to disbelieve or disrespect sisters who believe they were called. But I'm not one of them."

"Maybe you just didn't delude yourself about the reasons you came here."

"It doesn't sound like you did, either. You've said several times that you left behind everyone and everything you knew. It couldn't have been easy. If you weren't called, why did you do it?"

She'd asked herself the same question numerous times over the past month. It *had* been difficult to leave. How many times had she said to her parents that she'd happily live out her life on the farm, if not for Salbine's call? How many times had she lain awake at night, torn between her love for Joanna and her desire to serve Salbine? How many times had she cried herself to sleep during those first months at the monastery, homesick, missing Joanna, and wondering if she'd made a terrible mistake? She hadn't wanted to get away. Her life hadn't been perfect, but she'd felt blessed. What possible reason would she have had for convincing herself that Salbine had called her? "I don't understand why She would call me and then deny me," she said, not having an answer to Lillian's question.

A horrible thought struck her. Maybe the malflowed sister who'd served at Heath was like Lillian. Maybe she hadn't been called. Maybe she'd never expected to draw the elements, hadn't suffered the same crushing sense of disillusionment that dogged Maddy from the moment she opened her eyes in the morning till the moment she closed them at night.

"Perhaps Salbine has other plans for you." Lillian blew out an exasperated sigh. "I wish I could help, find the right words to show you that your life still has purpose and that you belong here."

Maddy kissed her cheek again. "Lillian, you're the one bright spot in my life. You're helping by being here, and I'm so sorry about how I behaved earlier. I hope I haven't discouraged you from telling me more about yourself."

"Oh dear," Lillian said, flustered. "I've already told you the exciting bits."

She doubted that. Lillian had once mentioned a former relationship. Maddy hoped to hear more about it one day, when Lillian was ready to tell her.

"My twenty-six years here have been fairly uneventful." Lillian's eyes brightened. "Well, apart from the last couple of months. Those have been rather interesting."

"They have, have they?" For one glorious moment, the sun burst through the dark clouds. "And twenty-six years. . ." She slipped her arms around Lillian's neck. "You were here before I was born. You've been here all my life."

Lillian arched an eyebrow. "Thank you very much for pointing that out to me." The amusement in her eyes faded. "I am here for you, Maddy. Maybe you feel you have to put on a show for everyone, but you don't for me."

She tightened her arms around Lillian and fiercely hugged her, warmed, and a bit frightened. Her feelings for Lillian were intensifying to the point that she was starting to imagine them together in the future. Lillian would be horrified if she knew. And was it prudent to grow closer to a Salbine Sister when everything else associated with Salbine was slipping away from her?

"You never said if you'd come to my birthday supper," Lillian said, her breath tickling Maddy's ear.

"Do you still want me to?"

"Of course."

"Then I'll be happy to attend." Though the thought of dining with the abbess and Mistress Elizabeth intimidated her. She hoped she wouldn't say anything that would make Lillian regret her invitation. "Now, if I promise to behave like an adult, can we continue our afternoon together? I was enjoying myself until I lost my senses."

"We certainly can. We have to go collect our rubbish, for one thing."

"You mean you left everything there?" Maddy asked in surprise.

"You're more important than rubbish."

Maddy laughed. "More romantic words have never been spoken." She looped her arm through Lillian's and pulled her toward the door.

Chapter Seven

Pleased that she hadn't made a fool of herself at Lillian's birthday supper, Maddy slowly climbed the steps to her floor in the Initiates Tower. Lillian had loved the cushion, had seemed deeply touched that Maddy had embroidered the cover for her. Maddy had suggested that Lillian put it on the chair in her laboratory, but Lillian had declared it too nice for her bottom and had said she'd rather have it in her chambers. Unfortunately an invitation to her chambers hadn't followed, the only disappointment of an otherwise lovely evening. Lillian had allowed Maddy into her laboratory; perhaps she wanted their relationship to have more time behind it before she invited Maddy into her home. After all, she'd waited two months to tell Maddy the abbess was her sister, and might have taken longer if not for her birthday.

A cacophony of excited voices broke into Maddy's thoughts as she neared her floor's landing. It sounded like a celebration, an impression that was confirmed when she saw Gwendolyn's open door, and several sisters from a gathering taking place inside who had apparently spilled out into the hall.

When Rose spotted Maddy, she waved and came over to her, a tankard of ale in her hand. "Our examinations are finished," she said brightly. "Mistress Ivy said we could have one drink to celebrate, and we all ended up here. We knocked on your door, before I remembered you wouldn't be in. Do you want to join us?"

"Yes, come on, Maddy," Grace called, raising her tankard. "Someone pour Maddy an ale."

Before she knew it, a tankard had been pressed into her hand and she was swept into Gwendolyn's chambers. "How did supper go?" Rose asked. "I'm surprised to see you, actually. I thought you and the mistress were," she lowered her voice, "having a romantic evening."

"No, no, just a nice supper in her chambers." Maddy sipped her ale and hoped Rose would drop the subject. Lying to her didn't sit well, but telling the truth would lead to questions she couldn't answer without revealing Lillian's relationship to the abbess.

Fortunately Nora chose that moment to throw her arm around Rose and grin at her. "Did you tell Maddy that you won the time competition?"

"Time competition?" Maddy repeated.

Nora nodded. "She lit all the candles and the fireplace in the least amount of time."

"It was just a silly game, to break the tension before the final test," Rose said, almost apologetically. "Hardly worth mentioning."

"Hardly worth mentioning?" Nora repeated incredulously. "You beat Abigail by almost half a minute. Abigail came in second," she told Maddy.

"Yes, I did," Abigail said, peering over Nora's shoulder. "We asked Mistress Beatrice which mistress would win, and she said Mistress Lillian would light everything simultaneously. Can you imagine?"

Nora's eyes lit up. "Maddy, does Mistress Lillian draw the elements when you're, uh, you know . . ." She burst into laughter.

"Oh, be quiet, you," Rose said primly as Abigail doubled over and almost spilled her ale. Not minding a bit of friendly teasing, Maddy couldn't help but laugh along with them. When everyone had composed themselves, Rose continued. "As I said, it was just a silly game."

Maddy forced a smile. "No, that's quite the accomplishment, beating everyone else. You must be pleased."

"Well, I am, I suppose," Rose said hesitantly. "Thank you."

Rose's reluctance to share her triumph dismayed Maddy. More than likely Rose was only trying to spare Maddy's feelings, but Maddy would prefer that Rose treat her like everyone else. Up to that point, Rose had. She touched Rose's arm, then grasped her sleeve and pulled her away from the others. "I'm glad I found out about the competition and you winning. I want to hear about things like that, and your training."

"And I want to tell you." Rose's face scrunched up. "It's just that I can see it hurts sometimes."

"It will hurt more if you treat me differently," Maddy said. "Don't worry about me. I'll get over it." Eventually. She hoped. Or was that the second lie she'd told Rose in the past five minutes?

"So this is where you all got to," a voice thundered from the hall. "What's going on here?" Mistress Ivy pushed her way into Gwendolyn's chambers. "I said one ale. From the looks of it, some of you can't count."

"We did have one ale, Mistress." Gwendolyn lifted an empty pail from the floor. "This was mine." She giggled, swaying, and the swinging pail narrowly missed Grace's head. "Oops."

Mistress Ivy eyed the four other pails sitting on the floor and frowned. "I don't want you all moaning at the assembly tomorrow, so the celebration's over." She swept her arms toward the door. "Come on, now. Back to your chambers." Everyone groaned. "Oh, save it. Come on—out! And don't forget to return your tankards to the dining hall tomorrow." Shaking her head, Mistress Ivy surveyed the group. "Sister Nora, Sister Grace, you don't look like you're swaying. Help me with these pails."

Maddy shuffled out with the others. "What assembly?" she whispered to Rose.

"Air assignments," Rose whispered back. "I'll see you at breakfast."

"Good night," Maddy said as she slipped into her chambers, then closed the door with a sigh. Why shouldn't Rose and the others treat her differently? She *was* different. And no matter how much they tried to include her, she'd always feel as if she was on the outside looking in. All the initiates would be at the air assembly—except her. She understood why Mistress Ivy hadn't invited her and was relieved that she wouldn't have to attend. What possible purpose would attending the meeting serve, other than to make her feel worse about her condition? Having to listen to everyone chatter about their assigned tutors and their upcoming air lessons would be bad enough. She did want to hear about her friends' training, but Rose was right. It often hurt. Terribly.

She disrobed, recited a short prayer that sounded empty, and climbed into bed, only to lie awake, wishing Lillian was with her. But they'd spent the last two nights together. Maddy wouldn't mind falling asleep next to Lillian every night, but they weren't consorts and so didn't share chambers. Acting as if they did would raise eyebrows. Maybe that was why she'd never seen the inside of Lillian's chambers—maybe an initiate in a mistress's chambers was worse than a mistress in an initiate's. Or maybe Lillian didn't want to share that part of her life yet.

Maddy rolled onto her side and closed her eyes, but sleep eluded her, as it often had in the past month. Gone were the days when she lay her head on her pillow with a feeling of contentment, secure in the knowledge that she was serving Salbine and looking forward to the next day with enthusiasm. Now she felt as if she were biding her time until she figured out what to do with her life. Her chambers felt less like home. Her sisters in the Order were sharing experiences she'd never share with them. She no longer belonged.

Tears prickled at her eyelashes. She wiped them away, pulled the blanket up to her shoulders, and said a silent prayer. *Please Salbine, if I'm supposed to be here, can you give me some type of sign? I don't know where I belong anymore. Please, Salbine.* She opened her eyes and stared into the darkness. She hadn't really expected to receive a vision or hear a voice, so she wasn't disappointed by the same old stony silence that had greeted her cries for enlightenment since she'd learned of her condition.

She woke the next morning in a gloomy mood. The hollowness and detachment she felt at morning prayers only worsened it. By the time she arrived at the library, the prospect of skimming a dusty tome all morning depressed her further. What did she hope to find? Words that would suddenly make everything all right?

Despite her suspicion that such words didn't exist, she carried one of the remaining tomes Mistress Averill had set aside to the podium and began to read. Sister Clara bustled into the library, breaking Maddy's fragile concentration. "You'll have much more to read when I return from Heath," she said. "I'm setting off in a few days."

"How long do you expect to be away?" Maddy asked.

"Oh dear . . ." Sister Clara pursed her lips. "According to Mistress Averill, there's quite a bit of material. I can't possibly review it all in one visit, or I'll be away for years. I plan to focus on material that offers insight into the genesis of the malflowed condition, if there is any. Observations recorded by the malflowed sister's contemporaries will also be useful, of course."

"What about her personal observations? Mistress Averill said she left behind journals."

"I'll have a look at them, but they'll probably have to wait for another visit."

Maddy swallowed. "But I was hoping to learn more about the sister herself, about how she learned of her condition and lived with it."

"I know that would be helpful to you, but I have to consider what would be helpful to the monastery at large. Mistress Averill says I'm to record information that will help us further our understanding of the malflowed condition, and that's what I intend to do."

"Reading the sister's journals may help us to understand."

"I doubt it. You're malflowed, and you don't know anything more about it than we do, do you? And it's not all about you, Maddy. You'll come to appreciate that in time." Sister Clara's face brightened and she placed her hands against her chest. "Oh, but listen to me, lecturing an initiate. It wasn't long ago that I was in the Initiates Tower. I'll tell you what, I'll sneak in a few passages from the journals, just for you. It'll be our secret." She patted Maddy's arm. "I have to see the mistress. I'll see you later."

Maddy stared after her in disbelief. Sister Clara would sneak in a few passages from the journals? A few bloody passages? And yes, Sister Clara's journey *was* all about Maddy, as a matter of fact—at least, it was supposed to be. Why else did she think she was going? If not for Maddy's condition, there wouldn't be a visit to Heath.

She sighed and turned back to the tome, but her mind was in turmoil. She should be going to Heath. She should review the material and decide what was important—for her! She couldn't care less about what was important for the monastery at large. Perhaps she should, but honestly, she didn't. Had the malflowed sister at Heath lived out her life at the monastery in quiet despair, or had she somehow reconnected with Salbine, found meaning without the elements, understood her place in the world again? Maybe her journals would be disappointing, an account of her daily activities with no reflection or insights into her condition. Maddy would rather know that right away, than pin her hopes on a second visit to Heath, whenever that might happen.

She hadn't realized until now how important the Heath material was to her, how she desperately hoped it would provide her with the catalyst that would reinvigorate her spiritual life. Those journals had to contain something that would help her. They had to! But now she wouldn't know, not for a long time.

An hour later she gave up on the tome, having spent most of that time staring at the same passage. Mistress Averill was nowhere to be seen. Maddy left, not caring that the mistress might consider her impertinent. She didn't care about much at all, actually. Everything seemed so bloody pointless.

Walking with her head down, she almost bumped into Mistress Clarissa on the path outside. "Watch where you're going!" the mistress snapped. "And why are you heading in that direction? The assembly is in the main hall in the Training Tower."

Maddy lifted her head. "I'm not going to the assembly."

"Of course you are! Mistress Ivy is handing out air assignments today."

She peered at Mistress Clarissa in confusion, then remembered that the mistress had been away, tending to her ma. "You haven't heard?"

"Heard what? I only got back last night."

"I can't draw the elements."

The mistress tutted and rolled her eyes. "Give me strength. You're not the first initiate to fail her fire exam. You'll get another chance, but now it's time for air. Get to that assembly and apply yourself this time."

"No, you don't understand," Maddy said, mentally adding *you old bat!* "I didn't fail my fire exam. I didn't even take it. I can't draw the elements." She kept her voice even with great difficulty. "I'm what's called malflowed. The elements are closed to me."

Mistress Clarissa was silent for a moment, then she snorted. "You mean you can't draw the elements *at all*? That's the silliest thing I've ever heard in my life."

"Well, I'm glad you find my condition so amusing. If there's any-thing else I can do to entertain you, let me know." Maddy hitched up her robe and stomped off. If the mistress thought she'd bob, she could think again!

"Come back here, you rude little so-and-so," the mistress called. Then, when Maddy ignored her, she added, "The abbess will hear about this, I assure you."

At one time, the mistress's threat to report her to the abbess would have horrified Maddy, struck the fear of Salbine Herself into her. But now she didn't care, not one bit. She couldn't disappoint the abbess any further. After all, she couldn't draw the elements. How silly!

Without giving herself time to think, she strode to the Mistresses Tower and climbed to the second floor. The door to the abbess's study stood ajar. Maddy knocked on it and waited, trying to slow her breathing.

"Come in," the abbess called.

She pushed the door open. "May I speak with you?"

"Of course." The abbess set down a document and indicated a chair before her desk. "Sit down."

"If you don't mind, I'll stand." Wanting privacy, Maddy shut the door, then faced the abbess. "I want to go to Heath. I want you to consider sending me instead of Sister Clara. Please."

The abbess pulled off her spectacles. She reached for a cloth on her desk, cleaned the lenses, and popped the spectacles back onto her nose. "Sister Clara is a scribe. She can help the Heath sisters copy the material."

"But she doesn't know what's important. What she copies may not be useful to me." Maddy started to pace. "Understanding the malflowed condition on a scholarly basis is important, but understand-ing how the sister dealt with the condition is even more important to me. I need to know if she reconciled her condition with Salbine." She stopped in front of the abbess's desk and forced out the words that would lay her bare. "I need to know if she lost her connection to Salbine. If her life lacked meaning."

"Does yours?" Abbess Sophia asked impassively.

Now Maddy sank into a chair. "I don't know." Was the part of her that used to feel so alive and imbued with purpose depressed, or dead? "I don't know anything, that's the problem. I just . . ." Too many thoughts competed for her attention, frustrating her. She took a moment to sort through them, wanting to get to the crux of the matter so she wouldn't try the abbess's patience. "I'm alone in this. Nobody else is in my position. Someone once was, and I need to know how she dealt with it on a personal level."

The abbess nodded. "Heath said there are journals. But they may not hold what you're hoping for."

"But at least if I go, see what's there for myself, I'll know for sure. I won't wonder if something could have helped me, but Sister Clara didn't recognize its importance. She said it's not about me, but isn't it? If I wasn't malflowed, nobody would be travelling to Heath. And you said if I wanted to find sisters like me, I would have to read about them. Well, there isn't much to read here, but we know there's plenty to read at Heath. I'd like to get to know Heath's malflowed sister myself, not through someone else."

The abbess leaned forward, rested her elbows on the desk, and sighed into her hands. "Normally only those who've reached adept are allowed away from the monastery for extended periods."

"I thought that was because they're able to defend themselves," Maddy said, a glimmer of hope rising within her. "We both know I'll never be able to use the elements to defend myself."

"As I've tried to tell you, you're a sister, just like all the others. I can't bend rules for you because you're malflowed. I didn't think you'd want me to."

In this case, she desperately did. "I don't think I can be happy here, not unless I sort this out."

"And you're hoping the material at Heath will help you."

Maddy nodded.

Abbess Sophia sat back, pressing her palms against the desktop. "You're sure you can't sort it out here?"

Not when reminders of her condition were everywhere she looked. Everything that usually inspired now inflicted pain. The same might happen at Heath, but at least she'd have a purpose there, albeit a temporary one. "I need to get away. Sometimes I almost forget that I'm malflowed, start to believe that perhaps I do belong here and that I can be happy." Maddy lifted her hands and let them fall to her lap.

"And then I'll see my friends on their way to training, or feel empty during prayers. It's as if I've burned my hand and just as it's starting to heal, I burn it again. Here, the fire is all around me. It's just—I need to get away."

The abbess frowned. "You would be going to another monastery. Though I suppose the journey could prove beneficial. Perhaps you'll have sorted things out before you arrive at Heath."

If that turned out to be true, nobody would be happier than Maddy.

"I could send you with Sister Clara, instead of in her place. Though I suppose the point of sending you is so you can look at all the material yourself."

Exactly. Sister Clara would only be extra baggage. And it sounded as if the abbess would grant her permission to go!

"Have you spoken to Lillian about this?" the abbess asked.

Maddy's burst of excitement instantly fizzled. "Not yet. I thought it best to see if you'd grant me permission first." Actually, she hadn't thought at all. She'd rushed here in a fit of anger and frustration. She didn't regret it—she needed to go to Heath—but leaving Lillian behind would be difficult. "Lillian is the one bright spot in my life. I don't want to leave her, but I have to sort this out. I'll never be happy if I don't." She hesitated, then spoke to Lillian's sister. "I know we haven't been seeing each other for long, but I care about Lillian very much. I don't know where our relationship will go, but I do know that I'll find it difficult to be happy with someone if I'm not happy with myself, with my life."

Now the hard part. "And I want to be sure I'm with Lillian for the right reasons, not because I'm leaning on her, or because I want a reason to remain at the monastery that doesn't involve Salbine." Her daydreams of a future with Lillian, of becoming Lillian's consort and sharing chambers with her, had made Maddy wonder, given the newness of their relationship. On the other hand, didn't wondering mean that she wasn't fooling herself, that she wanted a future with Lillian for the right reasons? Or was that part of her self-deception, fed by her desperation to find a reason to call the monastery home again? "I believe I'm with Lillian for Lillian, but everything is so intertwined that I can't say so with certainty."

"So you wouldn't want Lillian to go with you?" the abbess said. "I can ask her to accompany you, but she doesn't like to leave the monastery, so she might refuse."

"No, I don't want her with me," Maddy said firmly. She already knew Lillian was most comfortable inside the walls and would never ask her to venture outside on a journey that could be futile. And what if they fell out? They could fall out here, but they could avoid each other here, too. Up until a few months ago she'd rarely seen Lillian outside of evening prayers, where Maddy had become familiar with her back. And having Lillian along would only distract her and perhaps hinder her healing process, if there was one. "I have to go on my own." Sorting things out included sorting out her feelings for Lillian. If Maddy quickly forgot about her, she'd have her answer.

The chapel bells rang the noon hour. The abbess stared stonily into space until long after they'd fallen silent. "I'll let you go," she finally said, then lifted a finger. "If you promise me you'll come back."

"Of course I'll come back," Maddy exclaimed, shocked that the abbess would raise the possibility that she wouldn't. "I took my vows. I know I can't leave."

Abbess Sophia lifted an eyebrow. "Can't you? As you pointed out, adepts are allowed to travel because they can use the elements to defend themselves. Along the same lines, sisters can't leave the Order because a sister who's turned her back on Salbine may use the elements against others. You'll never be a threat in that sense."

Maddy hadn't turned her back on Salbine either. Salbine had been the one to turn Her back.

"Having said that, I would hate to see you leave the Order. It would greatly disappoint me," the abbess continued. "But as you said, you are alone in this. Nobody else is malflowed. If you were to ask me to release you from your vows, I would reluctantly consider it, even though I think you'd be committing a grave error."

"I'm not asking for that." Yet. While the prospect of leaving the Order frightened her, Maddy couldn't deny a smidgen of relief. Perhaps she wasn't trapped after all. But what of Lillian? "I promise I'll return." She'd at least want to say good-bye.

Abbess Sophia blinked at her. "Then you have my permission to go. Though Sister Clara will probably be upset," she added with a sigh. "I'll have to come up with something else for her, make sure she gets her journey."

Maddy closed her eyes. "Thank you, Abbess. Thank you."

"But you're not going alone."

Maddy's eyes snapped open.

"I'm sending a defender with you." The abbess held up her hand. "Not because you're malflowed. Sisters always travel with defenders, so I was sending one with Sister Clara, too. Even if that wasn't the custom, I would always send a defender. I value every sister here. Every single one."

A lump formed in Maddy's throat.

"Sister Clara planned to leave on Thursday. Will you be ready to leave by then?"

"Yes."

"Good." The abbess scratched her nose. "Now, I don't want you to mention this to anyone until I've spoken to Mistress Averill and Sister Clara. Except Lillian. You will leave this study and go directly to Lillian and tell her, do you understand?"

"Yes."

"She's probably in her laboratory."

"I don't know the way," Maddy admitted. "I've only been a couple of times."

"Remember this: left, right, right, left, right."

"Once I've entered the catacombs?"

The abbess nodded. "After you've seen her, come to the library. I'll be there by then." She paused. "I do hope you find what you need," she said softly.

Me too.

"Off you go, then."

Maddy stood and bobbed. "Thank you, Abbess." She left the study, elated that she'd go to Heath but dreading Lillian's reaction.

LILLIAN SQUINTED AT the parchment and moved it farther away from her until the words came into focus. Sophia had suggested it was time for spectacles, but Lillian's eyes were perfectly fine. She only ever had a problem reading in the laboratory, where there wasn't much light. And when reading tiny script, like Mistress Meredith's. And the odd tome challenged her, but that was all. She had no idea why spectacles had entered Sophia's mind.

It didn't help that she was distracted. How long had she stared at this formula, while brooding over inviting Maddy to her chambers? She should have extended an invitation long before now, but her chambers in the Adepts Tower had tortured her for months after Caroline left. Everywhere she'd turned, a reminder. If the memories had been bittersweet, they would have been easier to bear. Instead they'd mocked her, berated her, reminded her of her stupidity and filled her with regret. She didn't want to repeat the experience with Maddy.

But barring Maddy from her chambers for Caroline's transgressions was unfair. It was time. When Maddy left her—and she would—it wouldn't be the same as when Caroline had left. Her relationship with Maddy was healthy and positive; it bore no resemblance to the sick, life-leeching association with Caroline she wished had never happened. This time, the memories would be bittersweet. The knowledge that Maddy had genuinely cared would temper the sadness over losing her.

Lillian refocused on the parchment. Once she understood the formula, she'd find Maddy and invite her to drop in for a hot cider. And perhaps stay the night? She'd see how she felt.

"Good, you're here."

Lillian jumped and twisted toward the door. Maddy stood in the doorway, illuminated by the torch she held. "What a nice surprise," Lillian said, setting the parchment down on the table. "I was just thinking about you."

Maddy came closer, and Lillian's delight faded when she saw her grim face. "Are you all right? You look a little tense."

"I've just come from the abbess," Maddy said.

"Is something wrong?"

Maddy sighed and slid the torch into an empty sconce. She turned to Lillian. "I don't know how to say this, so I might as well just come out with it. I'm going to Heath, instead of Sister Clara. I leave in a few days."

The shock that reverberated through her made Lillian's voice shake. "Why is she sending you instead of Sister Clara?"

"I asked her to," Maddy said softly.

She'd asked her to. She was leaving. Lillian hadn't expected this moment to arrive so soon, or to be so dramatic. She'd imagined Maddy gently severing their relationship when she'd grown bored or was ready to take a consort, not an abrupt and final end that had her leaving the monastery.

"I need to go to Heath, need to sort through the material myself." Maddy reached out to touch Lillian's face.

Lillian drew back. She picked up the parchment and focused on it. "Thank you for telling me," she said stiffly.

"Lillian, please look at me. Please."

Why, so Maddy could see her pain laid bare and smile smugly, as Caroline always had?

"I don't have much time. I have to meet the abbess in the library."

"You'd better get going, then." Lillian swallowed when she felt Maddy's hand on her arm. Why wouldn't she just leave?

"We have to talk about this. Why don't you come to my chambers in about an hour?"

"I don't see the point, Maddy. You'll be gone for longer than we've been seeing each other."

"But—"

"If you still want to, we can talk when you get back from Heath." If Maddy returned.

"Lillian, please." Maddy's voice was filled with sorrow.

"I have work to do," Lillian said, her eyes still on the parchment.

A moment later, Maddy's hand left Lillian's arm. From the corner of her eye, Lillian glimpsed her sliding the torch from the sconce, then she could see her no longer. Maddy's footsteps stopped when she neared the doorway. One part of Lillian hoped Maddy would turn back and press her to talk; the other wanted to be alone and to never see her again. The footsteps resumed, and then Maddy was gone, leaving a dimmer laboratory behind.

Once again Lillian had trouble reading the script on the parchment, but this time the tears in her eyes caused the blur.

Chapter Eight

SOPHIA STOPPED OUTSIDE LILLIAN'S LABORATORY AND peered through the doorway. Her heart ached. Lillian sat motionless, hunched over the table. "Maddy said you were here," she said loudly, pretending not to notice when Lillian grabbed a piece of parchment and held it in front of her face.

"Not another visitor," Lillian said with an exasperated sigh. "I come down here to be alone. I might as well be sitting in the middle of the bloody courtyard!"

"I've come to see how you are." Sophia glanced around for an empty sconce and slid her torch into the nearest one. "Maddy said you were here."

"And I suppose Maddy told you I'm not pleased that she's leaving," Lillian said, her voice even. She couldn't relax the tautness in her face, though, and Sophia read her inner turmoil.

"Maddy didn't tell me anything. She didn't have to. Her long face told the story, just as yours does."

Lillian let the parchment drop to the table. "Well, I'm fine, so you can go. But before you do, is there anyone you'd like me to pretend to be interested in so they'll flee the monastery? Or is driving one sister away every twenty years good enough?" Her mouth tightened; she propped her elbows on the table and dropped her head into her hands.

"Caroline didn't leave because of you. And Maddy isn't, either." Sophia slipped her arm around Lillian's stiff shoulders and squeezed her. "She cares about you."

"But not enough to stay," Lillian said quietly.

"It's not about you. It's about her, about being malflowed."

"It doesn't matter that she's malflowed!"

"It matters to her, Lillian. It matters to her."

Sophia narrowly dodged the chair when Lillian suddenly pushed it back and stood. "I should never have gotten involved with her," Lillian said, pacing. "I was content, Sophia. Content." She stopped in front of the table and stabbed it with her finger for emphasis. "And then Maddy happened."

"Things rarely just happen with you, Lillian," Sophia said, her sympathy deepening at the sight of Lillian's red eyes.

Lillian stared at her, then swung away to pace again. "Maddy did." She threw up her arms. "Oh, and I suppose you and Elizabeth have been snickering at what a foolish cow I am, falling for a sister almost half my age."

"We've done nothing of the sort!" Sophia exhaled sharply and reminded herself that Lillian was hurting. "I'll admit that I was skeptical at first. But at the same time, I was pleased. I was starting to worry that you'd never risk a relationship again."

"Well, I did, and look how it turned out." Lillian stopped pacing and stared into space. "I don't think I'm meant to be in a relationship. They're for other people, not me."

"I suspect Maddy would disagree. It's clear to me and to everyone who's seen you together that she cares about you very much. And you obviously care for her. I was starting to think . . ." She hesitated.

"What?"

"I was starting to think that perhaps you might end up as consorts."

Lillian gaped. "Consorts? Have you lost your mind? Maddy would never take me as a consort."

"Why not?" Sophia asked, noting with interest that Lillian hadn't said *she* wouldn't take Maddy as a consort.

"Look at me!" Lillian slapped her chest with both hands. "One day Maddy will wake up and realize how old I am."

Sophia smiled gently. "I think she knows how old you are. Unless I dreamed it, she dined with us on your birthday."

"No, Sophia, I mean really realize it—when she starts playing the 'how old will Lillian be when I'm this old?' game. When she's ready to take a consort, she'll want someone her own age. Someone to grow old with, not someone who'll drop dead tomorrow."

Sophia tutted. "You're as healthy as an ox, you have years ahead of you. And nobody knows when Salbine will take them, Lillian. Too often, age has nothing to do with it."

"Why would you even think we'd be consorts?" Lillian's hands went to her hips. "You never once raised the possibility of consorts when I was seeing Caroline. I've been with Maddy five minutes and you already have us on our knees at the front of the chapel."

Sophia didn't have to betray her conversation with Maddy to answer. "Caroline would never have taken you as a consort. She didn't care about you. She was using you." If not for the table acting as a barrier between her and Lillian, Sophia wouldn't have been so blunt. "I know you loved her and perhaps hoped it would go that way, but it never would have happened, Lillian. Never." She winced at the pain that flashed across Lillian's face. So time and a new relationship hadn't healed the wound once and for all. Would Lillian ever put Caroline behind her?

"I'm not sure I loved her." Lillian dropped her hands to her sides. "I thought I did, but now I'm not sure."

"Because of your relationship with Maddy?" Sophia asked, hopeful and surprised. Perhaps the wound was healing after all. She stepped back when Lillian rounded the table, then relaxed when her sister sank back into the chair, her shoulders slumped; the fight had apparently left her. But Lillian didn't answer the question. Sophia moved closer, lightly touched her arm. "I know it's early days with Maddy, but I have a good feeling about the two of you. When we dined together, I could see you as consorts. You're comfortable with each other, and you seem to enjoy each other's company."

Lillian snorted. "Comfortable. How exciting! I bet that's just what Maddy wants in a consort."

"It had better be what she wants. Once that initial burst of lust and excitement and novelty has worn off, there had better be a genuine friendship left in its wake, one that allows you to be yourselves with each other. That's what will see you through to the end. And that's another reason I never saw you and Caroline as consorts." When Lillian didn't say anything, Sophia continued. "Don't make the mistake of equating comfortable with boring. Anyway, if you're convinced that Maddy will never accept you as a consort, why are you with her?

I wouldn't ask if your relationship with her was a casual one, but it obviously isn't." When Lillian didn't respond, Sophia started to ask the question again. It was too important for Lillian to ignore. "Why are—"

"Maybe when I'm dying and looking back over my life, I want to be able to say that someone cared once, even if for a short time. That someone chose to be with me in that way for a little while. That—" Lillian broke off and rubbed at her eye.

Sophia blinked; Lillian's eyes weren't the only ones holding tears.

Lillian drew a shuddering breath. "I don't mind being on my own, not really. Sometimes I look at you and Elizabeth and wonder, but I'm set in my ways now. If I wanted a consort, I'd have taken one years ago."

"No, you wouldn't have! You've been too hung up on what happened with Caroline."

Lillian smashed her fist onto the table. An empty jar tipped over but didn't break.

"I think you have a chance with Maddy," Sophia pressed, "but let's say you don't. There are a number of sisters around your age who have yet to take consorts, or whose consorts have gone to Salbine."

"Then go find consorts for them! I don't need one. And I doubt anyone would want me, if I did."

Sophia couldn't resist putting her arm around Lillian's shoulders again. She pressed her cheek against Lillian's. "I think there might be an initiate who'd consider taking you on, in time." Maddy had to sort out her own life, first. By understanding that, the woman had demonstrated a maturity beyond her years and raised Sophia's estimation of her.

"Will you please stop forcing Maddy on me?" Lillian said, though she didn't pull away. "I've spoiled everything anyway."

"How?"

"She wanted me to see her later, to talk. I told her no. I said I'd talk to her when she gets back from Heath."

Sophia smiled. "You're allowed to change your mind. I doubt she'll mind if you do."

Lillian sighed loudly. "What's the point?"

"Do you care about her?" After a moment, Sophia felt Lillian nod. "Then send her on her way with your blessing. I know you don't want her to leave and perhaps don't understand why she has to go. But if you care about her, you'll put yourself aside and give her what she needs from you right now. Sometimes you have to do that when you care about someone. And it will be better for you, too. You'll regret that you didn't, once she's gone."

Lillian swallowed. "I'm afraid she won't come back."

"She's promised me she will," Sophia said, despite sharing Lillian's fear. "And thank you."

"For what?" Lillian asked, turning to Sophia.

"For not shouting at me for giving her permission to go. I had to say yes. If she doesn't come to terms with being malflowed, we might all lose her for good."

"The material at Heath might not help her."

"If so, she'll at least have seen it with her own eyes and know for sure."

Lillian grunted. "You're her abbess, Sophia. You can't keep her here for me, and I suppose I wouldn't want you to."

"That may be, but it was a difficult decision all the same, knowing how it would affect you." It was the first time her duties as abbess had clashed with her love for her sister. Sophia squeezed Lillian's shoulders and straightened. "I'll let you get back to that parchment. Or perhaps you'll go see Maddy?" She didn't expect a reply. "You know where I am. And Elizabeth."

She patted Lillian's arm and slid the torch from the sconce. At the doorway, she stopped to glance over her shoulder. Lillian didn't notice. She appeared deep in thought, hopefully trying to persuade herself to swallow her pride and talk to Maddy.

MADDY LIFTED THE lid of the small chest one of the defenders had carried up and peered inside. There wasn't much room, but she didn't have much, and the less they took with them, the sooner they'd arrive at Heath. She planned to take a few shifts, a couple of robes, an extra pair of shoes, and her sewing and embroidery tools—she needed something to occupy her when she wasn't in Heath's library. Oh, and paper, sealing wax, quills, and ink. She'd write to Lillian, even if Lillian didn't come around before she left. The packhorse wouldn't carry the chest; it was for the convenience of the defender who'd be carrying her things to the stables, where he'd bundle her items into a pack, perhaps two, to sling over the horse.

She closed the lid with a sigh and pushed herself up from her knees. Supper would be served soon, but she had no appetite. Lillian's reaction had left her despondent, not only because Maddy was afraid she'd lost her, but because the despair she'd felt since then had made it clear that Lillian was her only source of joy at the monastery.

Her journey to Heath had taken on a new urgency that frightened her. What if the malflowed sister hadn't left anything behind to help Maddy deal with her condition? What if she had, but it didn't help, didn't rekindle Maddy's relationship with Salbine or point her to a next step? Now that she knew the abbess wouldn't stand in her way if she decided to leave the Order, the temptation would be great. Perhaps it would have been better to not know, to feel trapped and so never give up, to keep searching until she drew her last breath.

She studied the branches on her hands that no longer reflected her inner spirit. They weren't bare and dry and withered, nor turning to dust that a wind would eventually scatter, leaving no trace of the lush leaves formerly nourished by the knowledge that Salbine had chosen her to serve. *Why, Salbine? Why?*

Someone rapped at the door. Probably Rose, wondering if Maddy wanted to head to the dining hall. Maddy grasped the door's iron ring and pulled it open, ready with an excuse to put Rose off. "Lillian!" she blurted.

"Would you still like to talk?"

"Yes! Come in." She stood aside.

Lillian strode in and gazed at the chest sitting on the floor. "I wish you weren't going, but I know you have to. I told you once that I was involved with someone who left the monastery."

"Yes," Maddy said from behind her. Sensing that Lillian didn't want to speak to her directly, she remained where she was.

"When you told me you're going to Heath, I felt as if I was being abandoned again. I wanted to protect myself. But I've since realized that you leaving has nothing to do with me."

Actually, it partly did, but not in the way Lillian feared.

"I'll miss you very much."

"I'll miss you, too, more than I can express," Maddy said, but didn't go to her. "What was her name?" she asked, hoping Lillian would remain open to the subject.

Lillian's shoulders hunched. "Caroline."

"And she left the monastery because of you?"

"No."

Maddy tipped her head, confused.

"I thought she had, but later I realized that she hadn't considered me at all in her decision to leave. Our relationship meant a lot more to me than it did to her. I'm not sure she even saw it as a relationship. But I did."

"What do you mean?"

"I thought I was special to her." Lillian's head bowed. "But I was just a plaything."

Maddy reached for her, but the instant she touched Lillian's back, Lillian moved to sit on the bed. "Have you finished packing your chest?"

The sudden change in topic disappointed Maddy, but she wouldn't push Lillian to reveal more about Caroline when she obviously wasn't ready to talk about her. "I haven't started. I was just thinking about what I'll take." An idea formed. "Would you wear a red robe?"

"No, I wouldn't. I'd stick out like a bloody peacock!"

Smiling, Maddy sat at Lillian's feet and gazed up at her. "All right. Would you wear one made with a finer wool, perhaps broadcloth?" she asked, fingering Lillian's rough robe. "I thought I might make you one while I'm away."

Lillian arched a brow. "If you make me a robe, I suppose you'll have to come back, to give it to me."

"I suppose I will. And I'll expect you to wear it." She took Lillian's hand, squeezed her fingers. "And I'll write to you as much as I can. Every time we reach a town, the first thing I'll do is find a messenger."

"Who's going with you?" Lillian asked, her face clouding.

"Jonathan. He was going with Sister Clara. Now he's going with me."

Lillian scowled. "If he doesn't bring you back in one piece, he'll have me to deal with."

Maddy rested her head in Lillian's lap and closed her eyes when Lillian gently touched her hair. "We'll be fine, so don't worry." Though she had to admit, Lillian's concern for her welfare pleased her.

Given her inner turmoil, Maddy couldn't make any promises, but she didn't want to leave without telling Lillian how much she cared about her. "My decision to go to Heath . . . I'd be happier about it, if not for you. Not your reaction to it," she quickly added when Lillian drew breath, "but because it means leaving you. I wish I didn't have to, but I'll never be happy here unless I find my purpose again."

"And if Heath doesn't offer an answer?" Lillian asked softly.

"Then I'll keep searching," Maddy said, despite suspecting she'd be crushed, disheartened, and fighting the temptation to leave the Order. Until proven otherwise, she'd prefer to believe that her journey to Heath wouldn't be a waste of time, that she'd return to the monastery intending to live out her days as a sister, or at least prepared to step onto the path toward that destination. "When I'm away, you'll always be in my thoughts. And when I return, I hope to see even more of you than I do now." She lifted her head and met Lillian's eyes. "You grow more precious to me with each passing day."

Lillian swallowed. "Just before you came to the laboratory, I was thinking of inviting you to my chambers for cider." She caressed Maddy's cheek with trembling fingers.

Maddy smiled inside. "Let's save that for when I get back. It'll give me another reason to work hard and not tarry at Heath. I'll return all the sooner."

"Even if you were to return the day after you left, it wouldn't be soon enough," Lillian murmured. She leaned forward and gently kissed Maddy's lips.

Warmth mingled with worry. The material at Heath had better hold the answer, or a signpost, because Lillian would always be behind monastery walls. Maddy desperately needed a reason to remain behind those walls, with the woman she loved.

MADDY HUNCHED HER shoulders against the nip in the morning air and pulled the collar of her travelling cloak up around her ears as she left the chapel. She'd feel the chill more as she rode, but vanity prevented her from pulling the cloak's hood over her head. She wanted Lillian to see more than her eyes and red, cold nose when she bid her good-bye, especially since the service to send her and Jonathan on their way had already left her eyes red-rimmed. For the first time in ages, a service had touched Maddy, though not for the usual reason. Her bond with her fellow sisters was still there, albeit a bit strained. Her bond with Salbine . . .

Thomas stood near the gates with three magnificent Salbine horses. Maddy had stupidly asked him why they'd need trained Salbine horses, since she was malflowed. "Those at Heath aren't, Sister," he'd replied. "And we'll have to train a horse for you, one you'll call your own. You'll be riding with mages, more often than not." But not today. Jonathan was already at the gates, his breath forming misty clouds in the air as he checked that the weight of their baggage was evenly distributed across the packhorse's back. His breastplate lacked a crest, and Maddy's cloak was plain. When travelling, sisters and defenders didn't avoid drawing attention, but they didn't seek it, either.

Maddy drew a deep breath. Now the part that had kept her awake last night. She turned around to face those who had followed her in silence from the chapel to the gates. Most sisters had wished her well in the chapel's vestibule. Those before her were her friends. She forced a smile that probably looked sickly.

Rose stepped forward and hugged her. "Hurry back, all right?" she said, her voice quavering. Next it was Nora's turn, then Grace came forward, then Abigail. The faces became a blur. Even Gwendolyn appeared sorry to see her go.

"Safe journey, Maddy," Mistress Elizabeth said. "And a safe return." She grasped Maddy's shoulders and kissed her cheek.

The abbess swam into view. "Remember, you don't have to study the material while you're there," she said. "Put the scribes to work as soon as you find something that might be interesting and then move on to the next item." She took both of Maddy's hands and squeezed them. "Come back to us."

"I will," she whispered, then sank to one knee and felt the abbess's hand on her head.

"May Salbine guide you. May Salbine provide for you. May Salbine keep you." Usually the blessing ended there, but the abbess's hand didn't move. "May Salbine enlighten you. May Salbine return you to us." She lifted her hand.

"Salbine's will be done," Maddy said, rising in time to see those gathered raising their heads.

The abbess nodded. "We'll leave you now. Next time we see you, I hope you have the answers you seek." She turned to the others. "Let's return to our duties, sisters."

Maddy acknowledged shouts of "Safe Journey!" and "Salbine preserve you!" with a wave as she watched the sisters trail away. All except one. She swallowed; she was already shaking. A sombre Lillian stood before her. Maddy reached for her, held her tight, rubbed her chin on Lillian's rough robe. "I'll send letters as often as I can."

"I won't be able to reply until you're at Heath," Lillian said against Maddy's ear. "Then you'll likely get a barrage of letters from me."

Maddy smiled through her tears. "I hope so." She drew back, took Lillian's face in her hands. "The first thing I'll do when I come back is find you."

"I'll have my work in the laboratory to keep me busy while you're gone," Lillian said briskly.

"You'd better churn out those tinctures and salves and whatever else you concoct down there, because when I come back, I fully intend to monopolize your time for a bit."

"Not everything will keep for long," Lillian said, her chin trembling. "But I'll do what I can. And I might start training a horse for you. Thomas said you've shown interest in the dappled mare."

"Oh, she's a cracker, that one," Maddy said. "I'd love to claim her as mine."

"Then I'd best get started, so she's on her way when you get back," Lillian said hoarsely. "I don't normally train them from start to finish, but I will for yours."

Ignoring the wetness on her own face, Maddy used her thumbs to wipe away Lillian's tears. "Thank you." They stared at each other. It was time to go. Maddy embraced Lillian again, wanting to hold her once more. She dreaded letting her go. But she had to, for both of them. "I'll see you soon," she whispered, then pulled back and kissed her. But the gesture felt empty, and her lips, dead. Passion would have to wait for a better time; it would have its day when she fell into Lillian's arms upon her return, hopefully rejuvenated and looking forward to living out the rest of her life as a sister.

She pulled her riding gloves from her cloak pocket and allowed Jonathan to boost her onto her horse.

"I'll feed the squirrels," Lillian said.

Maddy managed to smile at her. "You can try." She drew a shuddering breath and gazed at Lillian one last time. "Salbine keep you, Lillian. Salbine keep you." After nodding to Jonathan, she nudged the horse forward. They passed through the monastery's gates. Maddy didn't look back.

A BEAD OF sweat formed on Lillian's temple as she worked the pestle against the dried sage in the mortar. The hours used to pass quickly when she worked, but now they dragged. Maddy always hovered in the back of her mind. She wouldn't even be halfway to Heath yet, and would likely spend several months reviewing material and waiting for scribes to complete their work. It would be months before she returned. If she returned.

Lillian had hoped the ache would subside with time, but it still gnawed at her. She gained pleasure from her work, but the feeling that something—or rather, someone—was missing prevented her spirit from soaring.

"This is the first dry day we've had all week, but of course, you're down here," Sophia said from the doorway.

"Where did you expect me to be?" Lillian asked without looking up. "Running through the fields, singing?"

Sophia chuckled. "No, that would mean Salbine had blessed us with a miracle. But you might consider a walk later, get some sun."

Lillian grunted.

"Several letters were delivered earlier today," Sophia said, moving closer. "One's for you."

"For me?" She wiped her hands on a cloth before accepting a folded paper from Sophia. The seal was intact; Sophia hadn't peeked. Lillian wasn't familiar with Maddy's script, but it had to be from her. "She actually wrote, then? She meant it when she said she would?"

"Yes," Sophia said, smiling broadly.

"Then maybe she meant it when she said she'd come back."

"I think she just might have. Are you going to read it?"

"No, no, not until I've finished preparing this tincture," Lillian said, setting the message on the table, out of harm's way.

"I'll let you get back to work, then. And do go for a walk. Put some colour in your cheeks!"

"Out!" Lillian bellowed, shooing Sophia away. She picked up the pestle and resumed grinding. As soon as Sophia's footsteps faded, Lillian rushed to the door and listened. When she was certain that Sophia wouldn't return, she pushed the door shut and returned to the table. She wanted to grab the message and rip it open, but forced herself to carefully break the seal and unfold the paper.

My dearest Lillian, the letter began.

Oh. Dearest. Well, that was a good start, wasn't it?

I hope this letter finds you well. We'll arrive at the town of Leaton tomorrow, and I hope to find a messenger there. Fingers crossed. We've passed through several lovely and friendly villages, but not a single messenger to be found, and none due for days.

She'd obviously found one, if not in Leaton, then soon afterward.

Our journey so far has been a pleasant one, with only one wet afternoon. Everyone along the way has greeted us warmly, and though we vigorously protest, we often leave a village with our poor packhorse carrying a heavier load. I'm looking forward to sleeping in a bed in Leaton. Jonathan will try to find us a quiet and clean inn, and if it's not too much trouble, I might soak in a tub, try to get all the dust out of my hair.

I think about you all the time, always wonder what you'd think of a village and its people. Yesterday we passed a travelling merchant selling herbs, and I thought of you in your laboratory, hunched over your table. I say good night to you every night. I know it's silly, but I do.

Lillian smiled. It might be silly, but it warmed her more than any fire ever had.

I pray with Jonathan every morning and evening. The ritual comforts me, but not the prayer itself. But I don't feel I'm an intruder when I pray under the sun and stars, as I did in the chapel.

Then perhaps she'd been right, and had a better chance of coming to terms with her condition away from the monastery.

I'm running out of room. Lillian, I miss you more than I can express. I can't wait to see you again, and I promise that I'll send another letter as soon as I can.

Yours with the deepest affection,
Maddy

Lillian read the letter once more, then refolded it and turned it over in her hands. She'd always treasure it, knew she'd reread it umpteen times over the coming months. And whenever she needed a boost, it would be there to remind her that someone had cared, had sent a message to "dearest Lillian" and ended it "with the deepest affection." Perhaps others received letters like this all the time, but this was her first.

As soon as Maddy reached Heath, Lillian would send her a reply. In the meantime, she'd look forward to more letters! Maddy had promised to send another, and Lillian couldn't wait for it to arrive.

It never came.

Chapter Nine

MADDY SPOONED THE LAST OF THE thick stew into her mouth and leaned back in her chair with a satisfied sigh. Jonathan was still working his way through a second bowl. While she waited for him to finish, she glanced around the tidy and mercifully quiet common room. Despite the early evening hour, a raucous gathering had been in full swing at the first inn they'd tried. Maddy had left with the impression that it wasn't the most reputable establishment in Garryglen. The many buxom women hanging off the men, their breasts spilling out of their dresses, had been the first clue.

A kindly gentleman outside had suggested several more suitable alternatives, and so here they were, finishing a nourishing and relaxing supper. In addition to themselves and the innkeeper, two merchants stood in conversation near the fire, and three young boys sat with their parents around a nearby table, their ma keeping them on a tight leash. Maddy's eyes were starting to droop, but she'd already asked for hot water, wanting to wash away the accumulated dust and dirt of the last three weeks' travel. She'd bathed several times in springs and lakes they'd passed along the way, but that wasn't the same as a good, hot soak.

"The innkeep says we're sure to find a messenger if we head to the main market square, Sister," Jonathan said. "Always messengers looking for work there. Might not carry our letters all the way to Merrin, but I'd imagine most will go to Leaton and pass them on."

In anticipation of entering Garryglen, Maddy had written a letter to Lillian the previous evening. She missed her more than she'd expected, and hoped Lillian hadn't grown impatient waiting for her next letter. She hadn't known there wouldn't be an opportunity to send another one until three weeks after they'd left Leaton. Jonathan had thought one of the larger villages along the way would see a messenger regularly ride through, but every time they'd asked, the consensus had been that hiring one in Garryglen would be just as quick as waiting for a messenger to arrive, if not quicker.

"How far away is the square?" she asked.

"Innkeep said it's about fifteen minutes at a brisk walk. I think we should stop there on our way out, rather than walk there and back."

"I agree." Travelling was starting to wear thin, and Heath was still two weeks away. The sooner they arrived there, the better. They planned to pay a visit to Garryglen's lay chapel in the morning, so they wouldn't have time to walk to the market square if they hoped to leave Garryglen before lunch.

Jonathan pushed his bowl away and picked at his teeth with his thumbnail. Maddy slid her chair away from the table. "I'm going to my room. The girl should have finished filling the tub by now. I'll meet you—"

The inn's wooden door smashed open. A wild-eyed man burst in. "Frank's place is on fire. He's trapped inside. We need help on the line!" he shouted, then whirled and rushed out.

Jonathan was already on his feet and buckling on his sword. The two merchants brushed by him; the boys at the nearby table clung to their ma as their pa followed the merchants out the door.

"Pray on your own tonight, Sister. I'll see you in the morning," Jonathan murmured.

Smoke wafted into the common room through the open door. The innkeeper coughed into his hand and motioned for Jonathan to hurry, wanting to shut the door. Then his eyes fell on Maddy and he stepped outside. "Wait!" he bellowed. "There's a sister here. She can put out the fire."

No, she couldn't!

Jonathan backtracked. "Go upstairs, Sister. Now!" But it was too late. Several townsfolk ran into the inn and rushed toward her table. Maddy stood and instinctively backed away.

"Help us, Sister!" a woman cried.

Someone grabbed Maddy's sleeve.

"Frank's in there," shrieked another.

Maddy's back hit the wall; she pressed herself against it. People crowded around her and Jonathan.

"Please, Sister, come right now. He doesn't—"

A loud crash from outside, then screams, drowned out the words.

"Where's that sister?" a man shouted from the doorway. "The roof's just collapsed and the fire's spreading to the shop next door. We need her now!"

A high-pitched wail sent shivers up Maddy's spine. "He's dead, isn't he? He's dead!" a woman moaned. She collapsed into the arms of the woman next to her.

"Whether he's dead or not, we need to put out that fire before it spreads," the man said. "Come on, Sister." He beckoned for Maddy to follow him.

She swallowed. "I can't put out the fire."

He didn't hear her. "Come on."

"I can't," she said, louder.

Shocked faces stared at her.

"You won't help?" the man said incredulously.

"You're just going to stand there and watch the town burn?" someone cried on Maddy's right.

"We not good enough for you?" someone else yelled.

"No! I can't put out the fire," Maddy said, her heart pounding. "I can't draw the—"

The crowd grew ugly. Shouts rang out. Jonathan slid his sword from its scabbard and jabbed it toward anyone who lunged at Maddy. She raised her hands and shrank back, trembling with fright. "I can't draw the elements," she screamed, but the din swallowed her words. People were grabbing at her from all sides. Jonathan moved in front of her but the crowd closed in.

"Stop!" a commanding voice roared.

Everyone froze.

"What are you all doing in here? Get out there and help on the line. Anyone who isn't out of my sight within thirty seconds will answer to the magistrate!"

The crowd quickly dispersed, leaving two town guardsmen in its wake—and two women weeping in each other's arms. One pointed at Maddy. "She refused to help, and now my Frank's dead," she sobbed.

"Evelyn speaks the truth, Captain Wheeler" the innkeeper said to the sandy-haired guard, leaving his place behind the bar. "Everyone begged her for help, but she denied them."

The guardsmen turned their attention to Maddy. "Is this true?" asked Wheeler, his eyes glittering in the torchlight as he examined her and Jonathan.

"I would have helped, if I could," Maddy said quietly. "But I can't. I can't draw water."

"Fraud!" shouted Evelyn's companion. "I saw your overloaded packhorse when you arrived at the inn. How much do you demand for Salbine's blessing? How much bread have you taken off people's tables?"

"I haven't demanded anything," Maddy said, knowing she wouldn't sway the condemnation and conviction in their eyes.

Jonathan slid his sword into its scabbard. "The sister is malflowed. She can't draw the elements."

The guardsmen glanced at each other. "You ever heard of a malflowed sister, Park?" Wheeler asked.

"Can't say that I have," the other guardsman muttered.

Evelyn launched herself at Maddy, shrieking, "You killed my Frank!" She grabbed the front of Maddy's robe and pulled her forward. "You killed him!" She slapped at Maddy, scratching her cheek. Maddy tried to push her away, but Evelyn refused to let go of her robe and slapped Maddy again. Jonathan pushed between them to separate them.

"Stand back!" Wheeler ordered.

"You're not a sister!" Evelyn hissed as Park moved behind her and dragged her away from Maddy.

"Fraud!" Evelyn's companion spat at Maddy. "Impersonating a sister. You can't get any lower!"

"She is a sister," Jonathan said as Maddy wiped spittle off her nose.

"I think that'll be a matter for the magistrate to decide," Wheeler said. "Something isn't right here."

"We have documents that prove who we are." Maddy's blood ran cold. They may have documents from Merrin, but none included a mention of her condition.

"If you are a sister, then you're a murderer, you cold-hearted bitch!" Evelyn shouted.

Park winced. "Simmer down." He tightened his arms around Evelyn's waist when she struggled to break free.

"She'd better get what's coming to her, or I'll take care of her myself, you mark my words!" Evelyn screamed, swinging at Maddy from a distance.

Wheeler turned to Jonathan. "Your sword, please." Jonathan stared at him. "Your sword," he repeated firmly.

Jonathan glanced at Maddy, then unbuckled his belt and dropped it to the floor.

"Evelyn, Park's going to let you go. If you try to harm . . . the sister, I'll cut you down. Do you understand?"

Evelyn's eyes bulged. "Cut me down? Why are you protecting her? Can you believe these two, Fran?" she said to her companion, whose mouth pressed into a disapproving line. "If she turns out to be a sister, you'll let her go, won't you?" Evelyn shrieked. "Always a different type of justice for the high and mighty, eh? Which means no justice for us poor folk who've been wronged."

"The magistrate will listen to both sides," Wheeler said with a sigh. He kicked Jonathan's sword underneath the table, well out of Evelyn's reach. "Now, are you going to behave yourself?"

"I suppose I'll have to, or I'll be the one punished, even though she's the guilty one." She shook her fist at Maddy. "Salbine curse you!"

Fran's hands went to her hips. "Ha! Salbine! I bet you don't know a thing about Her, do you, except how to use Her name to fill your pockets." She glared at Maddy.

Despite knowing she was innocent of all accusations, Maddy felt her face burn. She probably looked guilty, perhaps because she felt guilty. If she could have put out the fire, she would have, without hesitation. But she was crippled. Crippled!

Wheeler rested his hand on his sword's hilt and nodded to Park, who let go of Evelyn's waist and stood back. Evelyn's eyes bored into Maddy. "Don't think you'll get away with this. If the magistrate doesn't take care of you, I will. We have our own brand of justice. You won't leave this town alive!" She jerked her head toward the door, "Let's go, Fran. Let's make sure everyone knows what's happening." Her lips trembled. "And then I'll take care of my Frank." She marched from the inn, Fran on her heels.

Moments later, Maddy heard Evelyn shouting over the commotion outside. Park raised his eyebrows at Wheeler. "I think we'll need more guardsmen to escort them to the town hall," Wheeler said. "Have Jenkins round up a few, then find the magistrate and tell him he's needed. Oh, and take his sword with you."

Wheeler shut the door behind Park and barred it. He studied Jonathan and Maddy while they waited. The innkeeper had apparently slipped away when Evelyn held everyone's attention. He was probably outside, helping her whip the crowd into a frenzy. "I don't know what would be better for you," Wheeler said. "If you're a fraud using Salbine's name for your own gain, then you're a despicable piece of rubbish, but can't be blamed for not helping. If you're not a fraud . . . I hope Salbine has mercy on your soul. Not sure what the magistrate will do, since you're not obligated to help, but by golly . . . I have a lot of respect for the Salbine Sisters, the ones I've met have always been right helpful. It was probably too late to save Frank, but you could have stopped the fire from spreading." He shook his head. "No, you must be a fraud. I can't see any sister turning her back like you did."

"I'm not a fraud," Maddy said miserably. What was the point? "And I wasn't lying when I said I can't draw the elements."

"We're on our way to a monastery in Heath, to find out more about the sister's condition," Jonathan added.

"All sounds a bit far-fetched and convenient to me," Wheeler said.

"We have documents," Maddy said, in case he'd forgotten about them.

Jonathan nodded. "They're in the travel bag in my room. Second door on the left."

"But they don't mention my condition." The abbess had probably thought it unnecessary, if she'd thought about it at all. She didn't have any experience with travelling malflowed sisters, so how could she have anticipated the situation in which Maddy and Jonathan were embroiled?

Wheeler snorted. "Of course they don't." He looked past Maddy, disgust written all over his face. He didn't speak again until he'd opened the door to let more guardsmen into the common room.

"Crowd wants blood," one said, eyeing Maddy up and down.

"We have to make sure they don't get it," Wheeler said. "Robinson, go upstairs, second door on the left. Get the travel bag." Robinson clunked up the stairs.

"Stand here," Wheeler barked to Maddy and Jonathan, pointing to a spot on the floor. They did as they were told. The guardsmen formed up around them. "Is that it?" he asked Jonathan when Robinson returned and held up a bag. Jonathan nodded. "Then let's deliver these two safely to the town hall."

Acrid smoke filled Maddy's nostrils the instant she left the inn, surrounded by guardsmen. She glimpsed one of the lines stretching from a nearby well; there were likely others. The fire burned up ahead, its glow lighting up the sky.

"There she is!"

The guardsman nearest Maddy bumped into her, then pushed away the man who'd lunged at them. Jonathan grasped her arm and pulled her closer to him. He wouldn't be a match for the hostile mob, but he'd die trying to protect her. She forced herself to be brave and not shrink into him.

"Fraud!"

"Murderer!"

"Salbine curse you! Salbine curse you!"

"Out of the way! Move!" shouted the guardsmen in front, forcing their way past those blocking their path.

"Help with the fire!" Wheeler yelled.

They turned off the road before they reached the fire. Maddy realized with shock that they'd only moved to a point just past the inn, but the crowd seemed to be thinning, allowing them to move faster. A glance over her shoulder killed the hope that a glimpse of her would satisfy the curiosity of most. There weren't many obstructing the guards in front, but behind them, the road was packed. The shouts had stopped, but she could sense the hostility seething through the crowd. Would they accept the magistrate's ruling, or would the mob tear her apart when she left the town hall?

Maddy had no idea how much time had passed when the guardsmen finally escorted her into a large meeting room with observation balconies running around its perimeter. A guardsman pushed her down into a chair at the front and took the seat to her left. Jonathan was forced into the chair to her right. As townspeople poured into the room, she tried to calm herself, but the noise fed her anxiety. The seats behind Maddy quickly filled; soon the balconies were crowded to bursting, as well. Everywhere she looked, people were staring, pointing, sneering.

She didn't look behind her when a loud commotion erupted near the doorway, the result of the guardsmen turning away a group of newcomers. Every seat was taken, and the balconies would collapse if more squeezed onto them. They were all here to see the fraud, the one with the audacity to impersonate a Salbine Sister. Based on overheard snatches of conversation, that seemed to be the prevailing view.

A robed man entered the room through a side entrance at the front and stopped just inside the doorway. A ripple of excitement ran through the assembly. Wheeler emerged from the same doorway and set two rolled documents on the desk at the front of the room—their Salbine documents, Maddy suspected. He stood to the right of the desk, stepped forward, and smartly saluted. "His Grace, Lord Jameson Hayes Collin Maxwell Langston the Fourth, of Garryglen," he intoned.

The robed man, presumably the magistrate, strode to the desk and surveyed those gathered. He reeked of power and self-importance. Maddy glanced at Jonathan, saw the resignation in his eyes. The magistrate knew the people wanted a show, and he'd give it to them, while basking in the attention. Langston raised his hand with a flourish, signalling for silence. The multitude of voices slowly faded to the odd cough and clearing of a throat. With a satisfied nod, Langston pulled the chair from under the desk and carefully lowered himself into it, then lifted the bell sitting on the desk and rang it. "This meeting is now in session. I understand that I'm here to determine whether we have a brazen imposter in our midst. Captain Wheeler, if you'd be so kind as to describe the events that took place earlier this evening."

Wheeler cleared his throat. "A fire broke out in the lower southwest quarter. Swordsman Park and myself were in the area and went to help on the lines. When we arrived, a rowdy crowd was gathered outside The Traveller's Rest. We were told that a Salbine Sister was inside, but refused to help battle the fire. We pushed our way inside and found her surrounded by more townsfolk. We ordered everyone but the sister and her companion to leave and asked why she wouldn't help us. She claims she can't draw the elements."

Catcalls and shouts filled the air. "Who ever heard of a sister who can't draw the elements?"

"Liar!"

"Fraud!"

Maddy stared straight ahead, cursing her hot face.

Langston rang the bell. "Silence!" When several still shouted, he rang the bell again, and continued to ring it until they'd simmered down. He turned to Wheeler. "You questioned her. You were at the inn. What do you think?"

"Before I answer, you should know that we've managed to get the fire under control, but not before it spread to a neighbouring shop. A man has also perished in the flames."

"Yeah, my Frank!" Evelyn shouted from behind Maddy. "So either she murdered him, or she's a lying, thieving bitch, posing as a sister so she can fill her pockets."

"Now, now, murder is a bit strong, um, Madam," Langston said.

"She stood by and did nothing while my Frank burned. Maybe that's not murder to you, but she murdered him as sure as if she'd set him on fire herself."

"Which she didn't do, because apparently she can't draw the elements," Langston said, to raucous laughter. Clearly pleased with himself, he turned his attention back to Wheeler. "You didn't answer my question."

Wheeler shifted his weight. "I believe she's an imposter, My Lord. I've never met a sister who can't draw the elements, and I find it hard to believe that someone in Salbine's service could be so devoid of morality and humanity that she wouldn't at least try to save a man's life. She must be an imposter."

Langston grunted. "You said she and her companion carried documents?"

"Yes, My Lord." Wheeler picked up the two documents and set them down directly in front of Langston. Langston unrolled one and read it, then did the same with the other. He slid open a desk drawer and rummaged inside it. "Hold it flat for me, will you?" he said to Wheeler as he pulled out a magnifying glass. The spectators fidgeted as he bent over and examined each document in turn, moving the magnifying glass slowly from one side to the other. "The seals look authentic," he said to Wheeler. "But someone brazen enough to pose as a sister would know where to find a good forger, no doubt. And I don't see any mention of the sister's inability to draw the elements."

He moved the documents away and returned the magnifying glass to the drawer. "So, we're apparently in the presence of one Sister Maddy and the Defender Jonathan. Would the sister rise?"

Maddy swallowed and stood.

"Murderer!" Evelyn screamed over the whispers.

Langston looked past Maddy. "Sit down, Madam. If you can't remain silent, I'll have you removed." His eyes settled on Maddy again. "Who are you?"

"I am Sister Maddy, of Merrin."

The crowd erupted into boos and catcalls; those above banged on the balcony railings.

"Silence!" Langston shouted, ringing the bell, though it could hardly be heard over the din. "Silence!" He heaved a sigh and set the bell down. "Can you explain to us, Sister Maddy, why you refused to aid the townsfolk in putting out the fire?"

"Especially when a man was trapped inside, you cold-hearted cow!" Evelyn shrieked.

Langston winced and nodded to Wheeler, who in turn motioned to two guardsmen. "Oy!" Evelyn cried. "Get your hands off me!" Maddy didn't look behind her, but could hear scuffling and banging. "I'll be waiting for you outside, you murderer! Or is it fraud?" Evelyn's voice grew more distant. "Giving false hope to those in need. You'll get what's coming . . ."

"Remain at the door," Langston said to the guardsmen when they returned. "We don't want her back in here." He shook his head. "Sister Maddy, explain yourself, please."

"I would have helped, if I could. But I'm what's called malflowed. I can't draw the elements."

The assembly rumbled in disbelief.

"I've never met a sister who can't draw the elements," Langston said, "and as part of my duties, I've met quite a few. I've also never heard mention of this . . . malflowed?"

"It's rare. As far as we know, I'm the only malflowed sister alive."

Langston raised his brows and glanced at Wheeler. "You may sit." He waited for Maddy to take her seat. "When Captain Wheeler's colleague informed me of the basic facts of this, uh, dispute, I sent for two women who might help us sort out this mess." He cleared his throat. "Would Mrs. Dickerson come forward, please?"

Whispers mixed with the rustle of skirts and nervous coughs as the audience watched Mrs. Dickerson hobble forward, hunched over her cane. A gentleman in the front row stood and held her elbow as she lowered herself into his former chair.

"Mrs. Dickerson, you are the leader of the Salbine lay chapel here in Garryglen, correct?" Langston asked.

"Yes, My Lord," she said in a quavering voice.

"How many years have you served as leader?"

Dickerson had to think about it. "Almost forty, My Lord."

"Forty. I'd imagine you've hosted many sisters during that time."

"Yes, My Lord. When sisters pass through town, they often visit our chapel to pray, since we don't have a monastery here. Oh, we've asked for one. I've lost track of how many letters I've sent over the years. Linbrock's half our size, but it has one. Our girls have to—"

"If we could focus on the matter at hand, Mrs. Dickerson."

"Yes, My Lord," Dickerson said with a sigh.

"Have you met any sisters who couldn't draw the elements?"

Dickerson snickered. "No, My Lord."

"And have any sisters ever mentioned others who couldn't draw the elements, or this, uh, malflowed condition?"

"No, My Lord."

"Thank you, Mrs. Dickerson. I see that Mr. Smithson took your former seat, so you can remain where you are. I'd now like to ask Miss Clarke to come forward." A woman who looked to be in her late teens strode to the front. "Miss Clarke, you recently spent several months at the Linbrock monastery, correct?"

"Yes, My Lord. I entered the monastery as a novice, but decided not to take my vows."

"You've heard the proceedings so far?"

"Yes, My Lord."

"What are your thoughts on the matter?"

"I believe she's a fraud, My Lord."

A few claps accompanied the murmurs of agreement.

"Why do you believe that, Miss Clarke?"

Clarke sneered. "While she certainly looks the part with her robe and marked hands, I can't believe that a sister would refuse to save a man's life. I've also never heard of this condition she claims to suffer from, nor did anyone ever mention it at Linbrock."

Langston leaned forward. "Can you draw the elements, Miss Clarke?"

"No. Only those who take their vows are taught, and not right away. But the novices talked about drawing the elements all the time. Everyone looked forward to their training. After all, that's when they'd start down the path to becoming true sisters."

Maddy bitterly remembered those conversations—everyone wondering how it would feel to draw; everyone marvelling that Salbine had called them to receive Her gifts.

"Perhaps this sister hasn't learned to draw the elements yet," Langston said.

Clarke shook her head. "If so, she would have said, instead of making up some cockamamie story. And not only was I a novice for a little while, but one of my great-aunts lived and died a sister. Sisters aren't allowed to travel until they're skilled at drawing the elements."

Langston stroked his chin. "Thank you, Miss Clarke. You may go."

She curtsied and returned to her seat.

"What do you have to say for yourself now?" Langston asked Maddy, his mind apparently made up, since he no longer addressed her as sister.

Maddy suspected that whatever she said from this point forward would fall on deaf ears, but she stood and collected her thoughts. All she could do was speak the truth. "As I said before, my condition is rare. Even the sisters at my own monastery were unaware of it until I started my training." And failed. "Miss Clarke was correct when she said that sisters must become adepts before they can travel, but that's because they can then defend themselves. I'll never be able to defend myself using the elements. That's why the abbess at Merrin made an exception in my case. We're going to the monastery at Heath, to study materials left behind by another malflowed sister."

"'We' meaning you and your companion?"

"Yes. Defender Jonathan."

"Or perhaps your lover."

"That's preposterous!" Jonathan shouted, leaping to his feet. "How dare you insult the sister in that manner! I am the Defender, Jonathan, pledged to protect the Salbine Sisters with my life."

"Sit down!" Langston barked. Two guardsmen approached and pushed Jonathan down onto his chair.

Langston leaned back and folded his arms. "My, the two of you put on a good act."

"This isn't an act!" Maddy cried. "What about our documents?"

"It wouldn't surprise me if the real Sister Maddy and the Defender Jonathan met with an unfortunate accident. You had to get the robe and documents somewhere, and anyone could have marked your hands."

Maddy was struck speechless. He actually believed she and Jonathan had murdered!

"And the documents make no mention of any condition, which isn't surprising. You say you're a sister, but you can't draw the elements. As Miss Clarke said, drawing the elements is what makes one a sister."

"I can't draw the elements, but I am still a sister," Maddy said. "I took my vows. I serve Salbine. I am a Salbine Sister." But she could hear the lack of conviction in her voice, and so would everyone else. How could she convince them of something she herself doubted?

"No," Langston said, shaking his head. "You can either draw the elements, or you're a fraud. I don't believe this condition you speak of exists. I think you're a fraud, that you make promises in Salbine's name in exchange for food and goods. Though I suppose there's an off chance that you can draw the elements, but you are a miserable human being. Perhaps you thought denying aid would go unchallenged. But we're decent folk, here in Garryglen. We help each other, and we don't take kindly to those who turn their backs on people in need." He had to pause when the crowd erupted into applause and cheers. "I bet you're not used to being challenged, sister or no. Otherwise you might have had a better story prepared to explain your wickedness, whether that be turning your back or stealing in Salbine's name." He pointed to the floor in front of his desk. "Stand there."

When Maddy hesitated, the guardsman next to her grasped her arm and pulled her forward, to the delight of the assembly. She stood before Langston, exposed and humiliated.

"We'll settle this now," Langston said. "Captain, put out one of those torches and bring it here."

Wheeler used a snuffer to extinguish a nearby torch, slid it from its sconce, and returned to his place at the side of the desk.

"Good." Langston gazed at Maddy, his face grim. "Now, you're going to light that torch from over there. If you succeed, then you are a disgrace to your Order, but unfortunately you didn't commit a crime. In that case, my guardsmen will escort you and your companion from Garryglen and you'd be wise to never set foot here again. I shall also write a letter to your abbess, expressing my shock and disappointment that someone as callous as you was accepted into the Salbine Order, and suggesting that she reconsider sheltering one of such heinous character." His eyes narrowed. "If you don't light the torch, then you are a wicked, wicked woman, using Salbine's name to steal from those who don't have anything to spare. You are despicable, have sunk as low as a human being can sink, and I will make an example of you. If you don't light that torch, you will hang."

The assembly roared; shouts and jeers assaulted Maddy's ears and shook the floor under her feet. Those above her pounded on the balcony railings and called for her execution.

"Silence!" Langston shouted, his bell swaying from side to side but drowned out by the ruckus. "Silence!"

Maddy dared not glance over her shoulder at Jonathan. He'd hang too, no doubt; both their lives depended on her lighting that torch.

Langston's face shone with triumph. He swept his arm toward the torch. "If you would." His words evoked an epidemic of coughs and shuffling. Then the room fell into an unnatural stillness fraught with tension.

Maddy eyed the torch. She hadn't tried to draw the elements since that terrible episode in the training room. The abbess had said the elements would be closed to her, but how could she be certain? They knew so little about the malflowed condition. *If you try to draw and an element does flow, it would be dangerous for you, Maddy.* But if she didn't try, they'd hang her, and probably Jonathan. Could this be a test of faith? Had Salbine deliberately brought her to this point? If Maddy trusted Her and tried to draw, would She bestow Her gifts?

Maddy lowered her head and ignored the titters from those who presumed she was play-acting. *Salbine, I don't know why You've denied me Your gifts. Perhaps I was mistaken. Perhaps You never called me, yet I entered Your home and robed myself. If I die now, I'll never know what I did to offend You, never be able to make amends. I want to continue my journey in Your realm, Salbine, not in the realm of the godless. Please, let me draw, just this once. You know I am innocent. Please help me. Please, Salbine. Help me.*

She raised her head, drew a deep breath, and reached inside herself. To her surprise, she sensed fire—the elements weren't closed to her! She beckoned to it, reached for it, touched—pain! The most intense pain she'd ever felt ripped through her, driving her to her knees. She doubled over, hugged herself. "Salbine," she gasped, "Salbine, have mercy." Then every inch of her body was on fire, from the top of her head to the tips of her toes. Maddy threw back her head and opened her mouth to scream.

Flame shot from her lips.

From somewhere far away came screams and shouts of "Salbine preserve us!" and "It's the judgement of Salbine!" Shadows moved through the haze of pain; the ground under Maddy vibrated, every jolt intensifying her agony. She fell onto her side, rolled back and forth, tried to put out the fire. "Salbine, have mercy, have mercy," she sobbed. "I'm sorry, I'm sorry!" She clawed at her face; her fingers sank into charred flesh.

Lillian's voice rang in her memory. *Maddy, stop drawing! Maddy, stop. STOP!* Yes, perhaps pushing back fire would end her pain, but how? The fire was out of control. Or was it? She gritted her teeth, tried to calm herself so she could think through the agony. Hadn't she emerged whole the last time? The fire had felt as real as it did now, but it had all been in her mind, like that sister who'd thought she was encased in ice. She wasn't on fire! It wasn't raging out of control! Perhaps simply cutting the flow as Lillian had taught her would end it.

Struggling to concentrate, she clenched her jaw, turned inward, and pushed the fire back to its source—the inner fire, not the imaginary fire that consumed her body. Suddenly the pain stopped. The meeting room swam into focus. The nausea hit and her body convulsed. She tried to choke back the bile, but then forced herself to a sitting position and turned to her side so she wouldn't soil herself. When the heaving stopped, she raised her head. The room was in pandemonium, shouts ringing out as townsfolk fearing for their lives crowded the doorway, desperate to get out. Dizziness forced her back to a prone position.

Wheeler cautiously approached and nudged her with his foot. "She's alive." Langston hovered a short distance behind him. The clink of armour alerted her to the other guardsmen curiously peering at her, along with a couple of brave townsfolk.

"Have you ever seen anything like that?" Langston said. "Salbine Herself passed judgement." He lowered his head and murmured under his breath.

"He's gone!" someone shouted. "The bastard's gone!"

Langston and Wheeler turned toward the voice, brows raised in query.

"Jonathan, or whatever his name really was. Must have slipped away during the commotion."

Still on the floor, Maddy turned her head to look, then curled up as a wave of nausea roiled through her. *Run, Jonathan. Make it back to Merrin and tell Lillian what happened, that I didn't abandon her.* She should have told Lillian that she loved her. Now Lillian would never know.

"Park, go outside and look for him. Get the folk to help you. They'll want his blood. And send someone to let the other guardsmen know. I want him found!" Wheeler leaned over Maddy, his rapid breaths whistling through his nostrils. "What should we do with her?"

Langston spoke, sounding closer than he had before. "Salbine punished her, but spared her life. I won't go against Her will." He snapped his fingers. "On your feet!"

It took Maddy a moment to realize he was talking to her. She slowly uncurled, tried to push herself up, but nausea racked her and she started to heave.

"What a mess," Langston muttered. "You two, get her on her feet!"

Guardsmen gripped her arms and hauled her upright. She hung between them, unable to lift her head. If they let her go, she'd drop to the floor.

"Look at me!" Langston ordered. When she didn't comply, someone grasped her hair from behind and pulled her head back. Langston towered over her, his face moving in and out of focus. "I would have hanged you, but Salbine is merciful. Instead, you will have the rest of your life to contemplate your wickedness. From here, you will be taken to Dunmurk Prison, where you will live out the rest of your days. Salbine have mercy on you."

Her nausea and pounding head prevented Maddy from caring. She closed her eyes and swallowed bile.

"Bring round the wagon and fetch the irons," Wheeler barked, presumably to another guardsman.

It felt as if an eternity had passed by the time a guardsman grabbed one of her hands and pulled her arm forward, his gauntlet scratching her palm. He clamped an iron around her wrist, then did the same to her other wrist. The chain connecting the two irons slapped against her stomach. "Get her out of my sight," Langston said.

Wheeler took the lead. The two guardsmen supporting Maddy dragged her forward. "Walk, you stupid bitch!" one growled, delivering a sharp kick to the back of her leg for encouragement. She tried, but her legs were jelly, likely hindering more than helping her mobility.

Wheeler threw open the town hall's doors. A tremendous roar set Maddy's heart racing.

"She's alive!"

"Salbine preserve us!"

Townsfolk jostled for a closer look as the guardsmen dragged Maddy through the mob.

"She should be hanged!" someone screeched.

"Murderer!"

Spittle hit Maddy's cheek. "Hey, watch your aim!" the guardsman on her left shouted.

Someone lunged, grabbed the chain connecting the irons and tried to pull her into the throng. Wheeler turned and pushed the man away. "Almost there, boys," he said.

More guardsmen waited near the wagon. They formed a barrier as the two who'd supported Maddy lifted her inside and dropped her onto the bench, not minding how she landed. Pain stabbed through her left leg, momentarily overwhelming the nausea. Armour clinked next to her as guardsmen sat. The door thudded shut. A guardsman pounded on the wagon's roof.

Maddy's stomach lurched along with the wagon when it moved forward. She covered her ears to block out the shouts and the incessant banging on the wagon's heavy wooden sides.

"Murderer!"

"The bitch should hang!"

"Salbine has forsaken you! Salbine has forsaken you!"

Salbine has forsaken you!

She passed out.

Chapter Ten

MADDY OPENED HER EYES AND BLINKED into the sun, confused and . . . wet? A shadow fell over her; another blast of ice cold water full in the face left her gasping and shivering. "Awake yet?" a voice rumbled.

A man, not a guardsman, peered down at her. He grabbed one of her hands. "What's this? She's marked. A sister."

The guardsman holding the pail snorted. "That's why she's here, gov. She's been pretending to be a sister, collecting goods and the like from folk who don't know better. Even had a so-called defender with her. He ran away when he thought she was done-for. That should tell you something."

The governor shook his head. "I don't know, this doesn't seem right to me. You'd have to be mad to impersonate a sister. If they ever found out . . ."

"Reckon she's lucky she ended up here. Anyway, she's your problem now."

The governor scowled. "Aye." He straightened. "Madison, Graves, over here."

Maddy pushed herself to a sitting position in time to see two men whose armour bore an unfamiliar crest clink over to the governor's side. She felt light-headed, probably from lack of nourishment. She vaguely recalled drinking water, but to her knowledge, hadn't eaten during the journey to the prison. At least the world had stopped spinning.

"We've got another prisoner I don't know what to do with," the governor said to Madison and Graves. "Blasted nobles, playing their games. If they got off their arses and put in an honest day's work like the rest of us, they wouldn't have the bloody time." Madison and Graves nodded. The governor sighed. "Oh well. On the off chance she's actually a sister, we'd better take care of her, in case other sisters come looking for her. Put her in with the master thief."

They all laughed raucously. "The master thief," Graves repeated, wiping a tear from his eye.

Master thief? Maddy didn't like the sound of that.

"Stand up," Madison said. When he saw that she was trying but didn't have the strength, he grasped her elbow and helped her.

"When did you last eat?" the governor asked.

"I don't know," she mumbled, not feeling so great now that she was upright.

"Get her to the cell and then bring her a bit of broth," the governor said to Graves before he strode off.

Maddy was barely aware of her surroundings as they dragged her through the prison, but the stench! Urine, excrement, blood, sweat . . . thank goodness her stomach was already empty. Occasionally the resident of a cell moaned or screamed, frightening her. She kept her head down, afraid of what she'd see if she glimpsed a face at a cell window. Madison slapped away the hands of any who reached for them through the bars.

Ahead of them, Graves turned a key in a lock. The door scraped open. "In here," Madison murmured. Mercifully he didn't push her inside, because she would have ended up flat on her face. He stepped into the cell with her and lowered her to the floor. "I'll be back with your broth." The thick wooden door thudded shut; the key turned in the lock again.

She lay down, resting her head on her arm rather than on the cold, stone floor. Would she ever feel all right again? The abbess had said that drawing the elements could be dangerous for her. Doing so hadn't killed her, but she was taking much longer to recover this time. The lack of food didn't help. She wrapped her free arm around her stomach and groaned.

"Are you all right, Miss?"

The high-pitched voice startled her and irritated her aching head.

"You're not going to throw up, are you, Miss? It'll be days before they get rid of it."

Maddy started to turn toward the voice, but stopped when she felt nauseous.

"You don't look well, Miss."

"Give me a minute, please," Maddy murmured, determined to roll over once the wave of nausea subsided.

"All right." Then, after a brief silence, "Has it been a minute yet, Miss?"

"No, it hasn't!" Maddy hissed. Exasperation propelled her onto her other side. Her mouth fell open. "How old are you?" she blurted.

The girl—at least Maddy thought it was a girl; it was difficult to tell under all the muck—blinked at her. She held up all the fingers on her right hand and three on her left. "Eight. How old are *you*?"

"I suppose that was a bit rude, wasn't it?" Maddy said. "I'm twenty-four. What's your name?"

The girl, sitting on the grimy floor a few feet from Maddy, scratched at her matted hair and hugged her thin legs to her chest, her elbows poking through the holes in the worn rags clinging to her skin. "Emmey, Miss."

"I'm pleased to meet you, Emmey. I'm Maddy." She pressed her hand against her chest, then winced when sharp pain stabbed through the right side of her head.

"Are you all right, Miss?" Emmey asked, keeping her distance.

"I'll be all right." She hoped.

"I'd give you some water, but I already drank it all."

"Maybe they'll bring some with the broth."

Emmey frowned. "Might be a while before you get that, Miss."

"You can call me Maddy. You don't have to address me as Miss." Talking to Emmey helped distract Maddy from her physical discomfort. "Why are you here, Emmey?"

"I nicked something I shouldn't have."

Maddy managed a small smile. "As opposed to something you should have?"

Emmey shrugged.

So this was the master thief? "I didn't think they put little girls in prison."

"I'm not a little girl!" Emmey shouted. "I don't need nobody. I can take care of myself!"

Maddy's head pounded. She closed her eyes and groaned.

"Oh, I'm sorry, Miss. I didn't mean to hurt you."

"It's all right," Maddy murmured. She opened her eyes when she felt a gentle pressure on her arm. Her nose wrinkled, but she didn't draw back.

Emmey leaned over her. "You don't have a plague, do you, Miss? We had one here, not long back. Carried them out day and night. I could hear them groaning. Don't know what happened to them."

"Don't worry, you can't catch what I have," Maddy said. "How long have you been here?"

"I dunno. Just know I'll be here until I die."

It didn't make sense. What could Emmey have stolen that would prompt them to throw a child into this place and throw away the key? "What did you steal, Emmey?"

"Huh?"

"Nick. What did you nick?"

"Someone's purse, Miss."

Maddy didn't approve, but it sounded like a typical theft, not one that would condemn an eight-year-old to life imprisonment.

"What did you do, Miss? Must have been very bad, whatever it was."

Maddy opened her mouth to tell Emmey to drop the "Miss" and use her name, then decided it didn't matter. "Why do you say that?"

Emmey sat on her heels and studied Maddy, a keen intelligence in her eyes. "Your hands, Miss. I saw one of you once, when I was with my ma. She pulled me away, told me you could hurt me. But you don't look like you could hurt no one."

She couldn't, but other sisters certainly could.

"My ma said people like you belong to Salbine."

"Do you know who Salbine is?"

Emmey let Maddy know that she considered the question condescending by rolling her eyes and sighing loudly.

"Well, your ma was right." And where was her ma now? "I belong to the Salbine Order."

"You mean you live in one of them mono—monetaries?" Emmey said, wide-eyed.

"Monasteries. Yes, I do."

"Never seen one, just heard of them. How did you end up here, then?"

"Do you know anything about the sisters in the monasteries?" Maddy asked, wondering where to start.

Emmey's mouth formed an O. "My ma said you can make fire!" she breathed. "Is that why you're in here? You hurt someone?"

"No, I—"

"Oh, and you like ladies!"

Maddy laughed. Her head hurt, but her mood lightened.

Emmey scratched her leg. "So why you in here, then?"

How to explain? "You're right, the Salbine Sisters can make fire. But we call it drawing the elements. What usually happens is that a little while after we've, uh, decided to live at the monastery for the rest of our lives, we learn how to draw them." She paused to see if Emmey was already bored or confused, then went on. "When I started to learn, I had problems. It turns out I can't draw the elements. If I try to, I get sick."

"So they put you in here?"

"The other sisters? No, they didn't. But we don't know much about sisters . . . like me. I was on my way to a monastery to learn about another sister like me when someone wanted me to draw the elements. When I said I couldn't, they accused me of not being a sister and told me that if I didn't draw the elements, uh, something bad would happen to me. So I tried, and I failed. That's how I ended up here."

Emmey rocked on her heels. "And that's why you're not well? Because you tried to do it?"

"Yes. But as I said, it'll pass."

"But are you really a sister, Miss?"

Maddy wished she knew the answer, though when she asked herself the question, she meant in Salbine's eyes. Was she a sister to other sisters? Apparently. To those outside the monasteries? Apparently not. But she'd taken her vows. She belonged to the Salbine Order. That was how Emmey meant the question. "Yes, I am," she said, not offended that Emmey had asked.

Emmey seemed to believe her. "You shouldn't be in here, then."

"No, I shouldn't. But it could be a while before the sisters find out I'm here and come for me."

"You mean you think you'll leave?" Emmey's eyes filled with sorrow, and she shook her head. "No, Miss. Nobody ever leaves here, not walking."

A key turned in the lock. Madison stepped into the cell and took a quick look around, then beckoned to someone outside. Graves entered, carrying a tray. Emmey stood up. "Out of the way, child," Graves muttered. He nudged Maddy with his foot. "Sit up, if you want this."

Her arms trembled as she pushed herself upright. A small hand helped steady her. "Sit against the wall, Miss," Emmey whispered, pushing Maddy's arm in the direction she should move. Maddy dragged herself backward and leaned against the wall, already exhausted. Graves set the tray on the floor next to her, then left the cell with Madison. A moment later, a blanket flew through the open doorway and landed on the floor near Emmey. The cell door thudded shut.

"I guess this is yours, Miss," Emmey said, examining it. "It's not as worn as mine." She dropped the blanket and turned to the tray. "Only one bowl and pitcher," she said with a sigh.

"We'll share." Maddy twisted toward the tray, not sure she had the strength to lift it.

Emmey skirted around her. "I'll get it for you." She set the tray on Maddy's lap and held its sides.

Maddy dipped the spoon into the broth and brought it to her mouth. When she sniffed at it, her stomach didn't recoil. Warm, not hot, it soothed her on its way down. "Your turn," she said, holding the spoon out to Emmey.

Emmey shook her head. "You need it more than I do, Miss," she said, her eyes on the broth.

"How about I'll have two spoonfuls and you have one, then? Would that be all right?"

"If you don't mind," Emmey said, after a moment. "But you drink all the water. I don't need it."

"All right." Maddy swallowed her second spoonful and handed the spoon to Emmey, who quickly spooned broth into her mouth and handed the spoon back.

"We should get supper later," Emmey said, "and if Evans brings it, we might get extra."

"Oh, why is that?" Maddy asked, pausing between her two spoon-fuls.

"Because he likes me! He said it won't be long now before he'll visit me and bring me things, because I'll be his special friend."

Maddy covered her mouth and willed the broth to stay down.

Emmey peered at her. "Are you all right, Miss?"

"I will be in a moment," Maddy said hoarsely. "This Evans, he hasn't . . . hurt you, has he?"

"No, he likes me! He wouldn't hurt me."

He eventually would, but not while Maddy was here. She'd have to intercede on Emmey's behalf once she was freed, get Emmey out before the lout got his hands on her. This was no place for a child, especially one who'd committed common thievery. There must be more to the story. And where was Emmey's family? Was her ma still alive? Maddy forced down her second spoonful and handed the spoon to Emmey.

They finished their meal in silence, handing the spoon back and forth until they'd scraped out every last drop. Maddy sipped the water, not wanting to drink it too quickly. Now that she had something in her stomach, she paid more attention to her surroundings. It looked like the stone floor would be her bed and her hands her pillow, since the nights would be too cool to bundle the blanket under her head. She'd relieve herself using the hole in one corner. The odours emanating from that area told her the waste wasn't landing in water running underneath the prison, unfortunately. One thing was for certain—she and Emmey would come to know each other in ways they'd rather not.

Hopefully she wouldn't have to wait long before someone arrived from Merrin. *If* someone arrived from Merrin, she realized with a start. If the Garryglen guard hadn't recaptured Jonathan, he could meet with misfortune on his way back to the monastery. Even if he made it back safely, he'd escaped without knowing her fate. They might assume she'd died with a noose around her neck. Would they send someone to Garryglen to find out what had happened? If Jonathan didn't return, would they retrace Maddy and Jonathan's journey in an attempt to discover their fate? Surely they'd want to confirm Maddy's death before a defender delivered the sad news to her parents. If not,

Emmey would be right; Maddy wouldn't leave the prison until they carried out her lifeless body and threw it onto the common pyre.

LILLIAN PUSHED OPEN Sophia's study door, strode inside, and stopped in front of the desk. "Have any messengers been through today?"

Sophia heaved her shoulders. She set her quill down on the desk and looked at Lillian. "Why, hello, Lillian. Yes, do come in." She shook her head. "No, no, I'm not busy. I can spare a few moments. You don't have to apologize for barging in and interrupting."

Lillian folded her arms. "Are you finished?"

"Yes."

"Good. Have any messengers been through today?"

Sophia glared at her. "Yes. One." She picked up her quill and poised it over the paper.

"Sophia!"

The quill went down again. "Nothing for you."

Still no word from Maddy? "I should have heard from her by now."

Sophia's face softened. "Maybe she hasn't had time to write."

"Or decided she no longer wants to." Deflated, Lillian sank into a chair.

"No," Sophia said with a curt shake of her head.

"You sound certain about that."

Sophia remained silent, arousing Lillian's suspicion. "What aren't you telling me?" she asked. When Sophia squared her shoulders, Lillian prepared to tell her not to be stubborn.

"Barnabus is a bit worried," Sophia said, clasping her hands on top of the desk. "Jonathan promised to send regular reports about their progress, but Barnabus hasn't heard from him since Leaton."

Lillian sucked in her breath. "Why haven't you said anything?"

"Because I didn't want you to worry."

"So instead you let me think she just wasn't bothering to write?" Lillian leaped to her feet and started to pace. It had taken her ages to swallow her pride, to come right out and ask about messages. She'd hoped Sophia had forgotten to pass one along to her. "Something's wrong. Why haven't we heard from them?"

"I don't know. But Barnabus thinks it's time we found out, and I agree. We could send messages to the tax collectors along their route, but we've decided to send a couple of defenders, instead. If they've run into trouble, and I'm not saying they have, I don't want to waste time sending messages back and forth. I'd rather we have someone right there to help them. I'm meeting with Barnabus after evening prayers, to decide which defenders will retrace their route."

"But what sort of trouble could they have run into? If they can't even send a message . . ." Were they dead? She could hardly bear the thought, let alone verbalize it.

"It's possible they're perfectly fine, Lillian," Sophia said, though her face betrayed her reassuring words. "They may have been delayed by—"

The clink of armour and the ring of boots on stone drew their attention to the doorway. Barnabus tapped on the open door, his face ashen. Christopher, another defender, stood behind him. "May we speak with you, Abbess?"

Sophia nodded. "Yes, of course."

Lillian moved to the side of Sophia's desk to make room for the defenders. When Christopher followed Barnabus into the study, her breath caught in her throat. A third defender was behind Christopher, leaning against his back for support.

Jonathan staggered over to Sophia and fell to his knees. He looked like a beggar, not a Salbine Defender. His hair and beard were matted and dirty, his boots were caked in mud, and he wasn't armed or armoured. The stench of stale sweat filled Lillian's nostrils. "Abbess," he said hoarsely. "Forgive me." His voice broke and he bowed his head. "Salbine, forgive me. I am so sorry."

Sophia's face flushed. She rose from her chair. "What's happened?"

More importantly, "Where's Sister Maddy?" Lillian glanced toward the doorway, blind hope overriding sense.

"Allow me to tell the tale, Abbess," Barnabus said. "Jonathan barely had the strength to climb the tower steps."

"Jonathan, do sit," Sophia said, at the same time Lillian noticed his trembling hands and legs. Jonathan grasped the arm of the nearby chair and used it for support as he lowered himself into it. "Christopher, fetch him a drink of water. No, bring him brandy."

Christopher inclined his head. "As you wish, Abbess." He strode from the room.

Sophia looked at Barnabus. "What's happened?"

"First, I must tell you that Jonathan is a wanted criminal in Garryglen."

Sophia's eyes bulged. "What? Are they pursuing him? Should we prepare to meet them at the gates?"

"I believe I slipped away unnoticed," Jonathan murmured. "And this is the last place they'll look for me, even if they believe me to be in Merrin."

"He's wanted for impersonating a Salbine Defender, Abbess," Barnabus said.

Lillian gaped at him. "Start from the beginning," Sophia said, her expression mirroring Lillian's.

"Jonathan and Sister Maddy were supping at a Garryglen inn when a fire broke out nearby. The townsfolk asked Sister Maddy for aid. When she said she couldn't aid them, that she's unable to draw the elements, they turned on her, accused her of presenting herself as a Salbine Sister for personal gain. They called her a fraud."

Icy fear gripped Lillian's heart. "What did they do to her?"

Barnabus hesitated.

"What did they do to her?" Lillian roared, blood pounding in her ears. She heard the rustling of Sophia's robe, felt Sophia's hand on her arm, but her eyes remained on Barnabus.

"They hauled her before the town's magistrate. He didn't accept her explanation that she's malflowed."

"What about your documents?" Sophia asked.

She'd posed the question to Jonathan, but Barnabus answered. "He judged them forgeries."

"They didn't include mention of her condition," Jonathan added.

Sophia pressed her lips together and shook her head. "So what happened?"

"The magistrate said she was either a sister who'd refused aid, or a fraud. If she was a sister, he'd let her go and expect us to deal with her. If she was a fraud—" Barnabus swallowed "—she'd hang."

And she wasn't here, so . . . Lillian closed her eyes and lowered her head. She felt numb, but grief had to be written all over her face.

"Did they hang her?" Sophia asked in a hushed tone.

"I don't know," Jonathan said quietly.

"What do you mean, you don't know?" Lillian bellowed, her eyes now wide open. "What are you doing here, if you don't know? Did she hang?"

Barnabus rested his hand on Jonathan's shoulder. "The magistrate brought out a torch, asked Sister Maddy to light it. He said she'd hang if she couldn't."

Sophia sighed. "And she tried?"

Barnabus nodded.

"She fell to the ground, Abbess," Jonathan said, to Lillian's dismay. "They thought Salbine was passing judgement on her. Everyone started screaming and running for the doors. I took that opportunity to get away, and I had to escape Garryglen as quickly as I could. I couldn't stay around to see what happened. The guardsmen and townsfolk were all looking for me."

Red hot anger coursed through Lillian. "You just left her?" Her fingernails dug into her palms as she fought the urge to draw fire and set him alight. "You ran away and left her?"

"Mistress, I had no weapon. I was surrounded by hostile townsfolk and guards. If I'd stayed, they would have hung me. If I'd fought them, they would have defeated me. I thought it best to escape when I had the chance, so I could return here and tell you of Sister Maddy's fate."

"Or maybe you're just a coward!" Lillian spat.

"Lillian, enough!" Sophia's voice cracked out.

"It's all right, Abbess," Jonathan said. "I've . . . ever since that night, I've asked myself if I am, if my motives for escaping were truly noble." His face screwed up in anguish. "I'm sorry, Mistress. I know I was supposed to protect her. I'm sorry I couldn't."

The misery in his eyes touched Lillian, but she couldn't bring herself to forgive him.

"I must point out that Jonathan's death would have served no purpose and been a terrible waste," Barnabus said, patting Jonathan's shoulder. "He couldn't save Sister Maddy, so he decided to bring important information to us, information that will save us time. I believe he made the right decision."

Perhaps, but Maddy had died alone as a common criminal, her body unrecoverable—or so Lillian's mind said. The rest of her railed against it, refusing to accept something so terrible. Maddy couldn't be dead, not Maddy. Since Jonathan hadn't witnessed her hanging, she could be alive. Lillian wouldn't recite the Prayer of Deliverance to Salbine's Realm for Maddy just yet.

Christopher returned and handed Jonathan a glass. "Thank you," Jonathan murmured before downing the brandy and handing back the empty glass.

"Now we know exactly where to go," Barnabus continued.

Sophia gripped Lillian's arm and squeezed it in warning. "I agree. We were planning to send out defenders tomorrow to search for Jonathan and the sister. Now we'll send them straight to Garryglen. And we'll send Sister Lucille with them. I don't want anyone to doubt who they are."

"No," Lillian said.

Sophia turned to her. "I beg your pardon."

"I'm going."

Sophia's brows shot up. "What?"

"I'm going," Lillian said firmly.

Sophia stared at her, then returned to her chair and sat down. "Christopher, walk with Jonathan to the barracks and then ask one of the cooks to prepare him a meal."

"Yes, Abbess."

"And Jonathan, you did well. When you're feeling better, I'd like to hear a more detailed account of what took place in Garryglen."

"Of course, Abbess." Jonathan bowed his head and slowly rose to follow Christopher from the study.

"Will you wait outside for a moment, Barnabus? And close the door." As soon as it was shut, Sophia glared at Lillian. "I know you're upset, but don't undermine me like that in front of others again."

"I didn't like what you were proposing."

"Then try, Sophia, I have a suggestion."

"Fine. Sophia, I have a suggestion. Send me."

"You're not the right sister to go."

Lillian's hands went to her hips. "Why not? Because it's me?"

"No, because this journey will likely require diplomacy."

"I can be diplomatic."

Sophia arched an eyebrow. "How long has it been since you last left the monastery? And I don't mean ventured just outside the walls. I mean went on a journey."

She hadn't embarked on a journey since she'd arrived, as Sophia bloody-well knew.

"Do you even know how to speak to the folk outside our walls?"

"You mean the rabble?"

"Yes, Lillian. The rabble."

"If Maddy's alive, she'll want to see me, not Sister bloody Lucille!"

"Lillian . . ." Sophia heaved a sigh. "She's probably dead, if not from the hangman's noose, then from trying to draw the elements. And don't blame Jonathan. Blame me. I should never have let her go. But she was so troubled."

"And still is. I'm not giving up on her until I know for sure." Lillian slipped her right hand into her robe pocket to finger the letter she'd read so many times. *Please, Salbine, don't let this be all I have left of her.*

"If I were in your shoes, I suppose I'd feel the same way," Sophia said.

"And you'd want to go. If it was Elizabeth, would you be content to sit here while Sister Lucille went to sort it out?"

Sophia removed her spectacles and rubbed her eyes. "No."

"Then let me go. I'll go mad here, waiting for news."

"You're not going alone."

"Sophia, I'm worth twenty defenders. Nothing will happen to me."

"You can certainly defend yourself, and prove that you're a Salbine Sister, if need be. But that's not my concern. As I said, this journey will require diplomacy. And that's not, uh, one of your strong points. So you either agree to take a defender with you, or you're not going."

"Oh, very well! He'd better not slow me down." A thought struck her. "We could meet Maddy on the way. If they didn't hang her, they could have let her go."

"Why would they let her go?" Sophia asked softly. "They obviously believed her guilty of fraud, of impersonating a sister, and her failure to draw the elements would only have supported that belief. You heard what Jonathan said. They believed Salbine was judging her. The best we can hope for is that they're still holding her, but the chances of that are slim." She bit her lip. "I am sorry, Lillian. I truly am."

Lillian's eyes filled. She swallowed the lump in her throat. "Save it until we know for sure."

Sophia nodded. "But prepare yourself, just in case. Don't get your hopes up too high." She rose, came around the desk and reached for Lillian.

"Get off me! I don't need you fussing," Lillian said, but Sophia knew her too well and held her anyway. Lillian gratefully clung to her. "I don't think I'll be able to bear it if she's dead."

"Yes, you will. You'll come back here, to those who love you. We'll take care of you until time does."

She snorted. "I'm sure everyone will be concerned."

"Yes, everyone will be," Sophia murmured into her ear. "You don't appreciate the affection everyone has for you. We leave you alone because you want it that way, not because we don't care."

Lillian drew a shuddering breath, then stepped back and let Sophia go. Sophia, her own eyes moist, smiled weakly and dabbed at Lillian's. "I'll bring Barnabus back in now, all right?"

She nodded and wiped her eyes more vigorously. Sophia opened the door and motioned for Barnabus to enter. "I've decided to send the mistress to Garryglen," she said, gesturing toward Lillian as she lowered herself into her chair. She lifted her spectacles from the desk. "I want you to go with her."

Surprise flickered across Barnabus's face. "Yes, Abbess."

"Find out what happened. If, by Salbine's grace, the sister is still alive, bring her back here."

"Back here?" Lillian said. "But she'll probably want to continue on to Heath." She glanced at Barnabus. "Or go home, to the farm." She hoped Maddy wouldn't want to leave the Order, and would desperately try to dissuade her of the notion, if necessary.

"No. Before this, I would have granted her request to leave the Order, if she'd asked. But not anymore. Sisters who aren't malflowed have to remain in the Order because they're a threat to others. Maddy has to remain because others are a threat to her. She was—is—marked. And she was right. Those outside our walls equate drawing the elements with being a sister. They're wrong, but that doesn't change things." She leaned back in her chair. "She'll go to Heath, but with a full contingent of sisters and defenders." Sophia's face clouded with guilt. "And with documents that describe her condition. How foolish of me not to mention it."

"You couldn't have foreseen what might happen, Abbess," Barnabus said.

Or known that Garryglen's folk and magistrate were imbeciles, Lillian added mentally.

Sophia squared her shoulders. "I'll write a new set of documents immediately."

"I want to leave as soon as possible," Lillian said.

Barnabus nodded. "We'll leave tomorrow, Mistress, at first light."

"We should take Maddy's horse. She's not fully trained yet, but ready enough." She met Sophia's eyes, willed her not to disagree. Maddy was alive until proven otherwise.

Barnabus stepped in. "Taking the sister's horse will probably slow us down."

"Garryglen has three of our horses, remember," Sophia said. "Get them back, if you can. At the very least, demand compensation, but I'd prefer the horses. If you don't get them back, purchase a new one for the sister."

Barnabus nodded. "Yes, Abbess."

"Now, find out what happened, and without a fuss." Sophia looked at Lillian. "I don't want to hear stories about towns burning, do you understand? We, ourselves, didn't know about the malflowed condition until recently. So watch your temper and let Barnabus do the talking. Don't make me regret sending you."

"All I care about is finding Maddy and bringing her back," Lillian said. "If I have to hold my tongue while I listen to simpletons spew nonsense, I will."

Sophia shot Barnabus a wry look. "Now you see why I'm sending you with her."

He caught Lillian's eye and cleared his throat. "I'll bring her back in one piece, Abbess."

"Oh, I'm not worried about *her*. I'm worried about everyone else." Sophia nodded wearily. "But yes, do bring her back in one piece. And try not to let her offend everyone between here and Garryglen."

Lillian silently fumed. They sounded like two parents talking about a recalcitrant child.

"I should go make preparations, Abbess. With your permission."

"Of course."

Barnabus bowed his head and strode from the study.

Sophia shifted her attention to Lillian. "Will you dine with Elizabeth and me tonight?"

"I won't be good company."

"I don't care if you don't say a word. I just want you with us."

Bloody Sophia, getting all sentimental! Lillian didn't need that, not when she was struggling to hold herself together. "All right." She jerked her thumb over her shoulder. "I should go. I have to see Dorothy, see if she'll take over a few things for me in the laboratory."

"If she protests, tell her to see me. But I doubt she will."

Lillian nodded, anxious to get away. "I'll see you later, then." Her mind in a jumble, she left the study. So much to do, which was a blessing. She wouldn't have time to think about Maddy, not until she lay her head on her pillow and stared into the darkness. Then the torment would begin.

Chapter Eleven

MADDY WAITED PATIENTLY WHILE EMMEY, HER face screwed up in concentration, stared at the letters traced into the smear of sand they'd persuaded one of the guards to dump into a corner. "This one's hard, Miss. There's too many letters."

"Just do exactly what you did when we worked on two letters. Sound it out."

"All right. Um . . . c, ca—t." Her eyes widened. "Cat!" she squealed. "It's cat!" She leaped to her feet and ran around the cell.

Maddy didn't know where Emmey got the energy. "Careful, Emmey. You don't want to hurt yourself." Emmey's bony elbows would bruise easily if she bumped them against the cell walls.

Emmey stopped several feet from Maddy and twirled around.

"All right." Maddy scratched her arm, then smoothed the sand and traced a new word into it. "Come try this one."

"Dog," Emmey said, still twirling.

"How do you know it's dog?" Maddy asked, perturbed. "You haven't even looked at it!"

"Everyone always talks about cats and dogs at the same time, Miss." She came over to look at the letters.

"There's no point now." Maddy rubbed her hand over *dog* to erase it. "We'll try that one another time, when you don't already know what it is. Hmm." She traced *egg* into the sand. "Try this one."

Emmey studied it. "E—g—g. Egug?"

"Egg."

"No, egug. There are two *g*'s, Miss."

"Yes, but the second one is silent, meaning you don't say it."

Emmey threw up her arms. "How am I supposed to know?"

"You learn through experience. When two of the same letters come right after the other, one of them usually isn't spoken. And if you sound out a word and it doesn't mean anything to you, try it another way. Here's another funny rule." She rubbed out *egg* and traced *fin*. "Read this."

Emmey sighed. "F—in. Fin!"

"Right!" Maddy added the letter *e* to the end. "Now try this."

"Mmm. Fineh? No."

"See, this is another funny rule. Remember when I taught you how to pronounce *a*, *e*, *i*, *o*, and *u*? The vowels?"

Emmey nodded.

"If a word ends with an *e*, then sometimes—but not all the time—that changes the sound of the vowel that came before it."

Emmey blew out some air. "This is stupid."

"No, it's not," Maddy said, though she agreed that the rules should be more consistent. "Most of the time, when a word ends with an *e*, the *e* is silent and you say the previous vowel differently. It sounds like the letter. So in this case, you'd say the letter *i*. Now try it."

"All right." Emmey fixed her eyes on the sand."F—eye—n. Fine!"

Maddy smiled. "Right! But, as usual, sometimes when you use that rule, the word won't make sense. Now, don't be frightened, but try this one." She traced *Salbine* into the sand.

Emmey's eyes bulged.

"It's not as hard as you think. Just sound it out."

"I don't know, Miss. I'll try." Emmey clenched her fists and gazed at the letters. "Sal . . . b—eye—n. No. Oh, but I know what it sounds like, Miss! There's no word like Salbineh, so it must be Salbin!"

"Right! That's one case where the last *e* is silent, but it doesn't change the sound of the vowel that came before it."

Emmey rolled her eyes. "Whoever made up these rules is stupid. Sometimes they do, sometimes they don't. It's dumb, Miss. But I'm learning how to read, right?"

Maddy patted Emmey's back. "Yes, you are."

"Don't know why," the girl muttered.

Maddy wanted to tell Emmey that she would get out of this cell one day, but she wouldn't make promises she wasn't sure she could keep. "It helps to pass the time, doesn't it? And once you know how to read, you'll be able to write. You can make up your own sentences, write your—"

They both twisted toward the door as the key turned in the lock. Maddy frowned; it was too early for the slop that passed for supper. Graves stepped into the cell and beckoned to Maddy. "Come with me."

"Is someone here for me?" she asked, her spirit soaring.

He guffawed. "No, but the gov seems to think there will be eventually, so he wants you to have a bath." He sniffed the air and grimaced. "I can understand why. Come on."

Her shoulders slumped. "What about Emmey? She could use a bath."

Graves shook his head. "Gov didn't say anything about her."

"Surely he wouldn't mind if she bathed. What harm would it do?"

Graves hesitated. "I suppose it doesn't make much sense, you having one and then putting you back into a cell with a filthy pig."

Maddy's jaw clenched. "She's not a filthy pig," she said through gritted teeth. "She just needs a bath, like I do."

Graves shrugged. "Suit yourself. But if she tries anything, you'll be the one in trouble."

She pushed herself to her feet and reached for Emmey's hand. "Come on, Emmey."

They followed Graves from the cell. Another guard waiting outside fell in behind them, but his presence was unnecessary. Even if Maddy weren't weak and fatigued, she wouldn't attempt an escape that was bound to fail. A prisoner shrieked, but Maddy barely noticed; she'd grown so used to the screams and groans that she could sleep soundly through them. But Emmey's grip tightened on Maddy's hand and she leaned into Maddy's leg. "It's all right," Maddy murmured, giving Emmey a reassuring smile.

"In here." Graves ushered them into a small cell containing a tub of water. "There's soap and a pail, and some linens. None for the girl, though." He paused in the doorway. "Bang on the door when you're finished. Don't take all day." He stepped out and swung the windowless door shut, then locked it.

"Let's get you in first," Maddy said to Emmey. "If I go first, they might rush us out before you're finished." She eyed Emmey's rags.

Emmey's body was probably holding them together, and once they were off, Maddy couldn't see Emmey wanting to put them back on. She certainly wouldn't, if it were her. She smiled. "Off with your . . . clothes, then."

While Emmey undressed, Maddy examined the linens: a rough shift, a skirt, and a shirt. All looked a little big, but anything would be better than her dirty shift and robe.

"I'm ready, Miss."

Maddy moved over and lifted Emmey into the tub. "It's not too hot, is it?"

"No."

"Here." She handed Emmey the soap, wincing at the girl's prominent ribs. "I'll do your back and hair when you've finished with the rest of you."

She turned back to the linens. If only she had a needle, thread, and a pair of scissors. She could wash her robe in the bathwater, then try to fashion a dress from it for Emmey. Or perhaps she could alter her shift? It wasn't as bulky as her robe. She could shorten it and roll up the sleeves. The end result wouldn't look pretty and would hang off Emmey's thin frame, but it would do.

"You can do my back now, Miss."

"You're not finished already!" Maddy exclaimed. "Come on, give yourself a good scrub." She unbuttoned her robe and removed it, then knelt next to the tub and dipped the pail into the water. "I'll start on your hair, though. Close your eyes." She poured water over Emmey's head. "Give me the soap for a minute." When she'd worked up a good lather, she handed the soap back to Emmey and washed the girl's hair, her fingers working the soap down to Emmey's scalp.

"You're blonde!" Maddy breathed as the dirt fell away. "I thought your hair was brown." She ignored the lice, but seeing them made her want to scratch her ears, even though she'd grown used to the persistent itch. Sister Garnet handed out oils to those who came to the adepts because they had lice. Simple soap wouldn't get rid of the pests. She rinsed Emmey's hair and rubbed it dry with one of the rags Graves had failed to mention. "I'll do your back now," she said, taking the soap.

"My ma never did my back," Emmey said.

"No?" Maddy soaped up Emmey's back. "Do your ma and pa know you're in here?" she asked, wondering if Emmey would answer. She'd tried numerous times to find out if Emmey's parents were alive, but Emmey had always changed the subject. Not this time. "I don't got no pa."

"Oh. Well, what about your ma?"

"She knows I'm here, Miss."

The poor woman must be going out of her mind. Likely a commoner, she'd be powerless to help Emmey. "Does she live close by?"

"Dunno."

"Where does your ma live?" Maddy pressed.

"Pinewood."

That wasn't too far from Leaton, but if she'd understood a guard correctly, it was quite far from the prison, which was apparently about a day's ride from Garryglen. How had Emmey ended up here? "Were you visiting someone when you nicked that purse?"

"Are you done with my back, Miss? I want to get out."

At least Maddy had gleaned a bit of information this time. "All right, out you come, then." She helped Emmey out of the tub and handed her one of the larger rags. "Dry yourself with this."

Forget about altering this so Emmey can wear it, Maddy thought as she pulled her filthy shift over her head and smelled its pungent odour. It was beyond salvaging, especially using dirty tub water. They lived barely above the level of animals, so she'd do fine with just a skirt and shirt. "Don't put those clothes back on," she said quickly when Emmey reached for her dirty rags. "Wrap yourself in that clean shift over there."

"But it's yours, Miss."

"No, when we get back to our cell, I'll try to alter it for you." Shivering, Maddy lowered herself into the tub. The water was dirty and lukewarm, but she didn't care.

Emmey leaned over the tub's side. "You're starting to look like me, Miss."

Maddy looked down at herself, hardly recognizing her emaciated body. Her insides weren't faring any better. She still experienced bouts of nausea and didn't feel quite right within herself. Was it because of her living conditions and the lack of nourishing food, or had she suffered permanent damage when she'd tried to draw the elements? Doing so hadn't killed her, but she was sure the next time would. She could never try it again, no matter what was at stake. The elements were truly closed to her. And there was no point trying to figure out what her life meant, whether her place was still within the Order, if she was going to die within these prison walls.

Was there anyone on the way from Merrin, or had they assumed she was dead, mourned, and carried on with their lives? Since she had no idea how long she'd been imprisoned, she didn't know if someone should have arrived by now. When she'd first explored her and Emmey's cell, she'd found a series of marks a former prisoner had scratched into a stone. He or she must have been counting the days; without marking their passage, they all blended together. Maddy had bled once, but didn't know how much time had passed since then. If Jonathan hadn't made it to Merrin, had the abbess realized they were missing, or was she still waiting for word from them? If he had, what had he told the abbess about Maddy's fate?

And what about Lillian? Maddy tried not to think about her; the resulting loneliness and longing was almost impossible to bear. Wouldn't Lillian be wondering why she hadn't received another letter, or would she think Maddy had forgotten about her? Maddy never would, but Lillian had sometimes seemed insecure about their relationship, as if she'd expected Maddy to call it off at a moment's notice. She might be quick to jump to the wrong conclusion. It could be months before someone arrived at the prison—if someone arrived.

"I can do your back, Miss, and your hair," Emmey said, bringing Maddy back to her surroundings.

"You can do my back, but I can wash my hair."

"Oh, but can I pour the water over your head, Miss?"

Maddy chuckled. "Yes, you can pour the water. But give me a moment to soak." She leaned back against the tub and closed her eyes, wanting the illusion of luxury for just a minute. Then she'd open her eyes and face the harsh reality of her life, and smile at the brave little girl who shared it with her.

LILLIAN HANDED BAXTER's reins to the inn's stable hand and hobbled after Barnabus, who was already on his way to make arrangements with the innkeeper. His easy stride mocked her—his inner thighs obviously weren't as sore as hers. And did she still have an arse? She slipped one hand behind her and felt for it. Still there, and still numb. At least she'd sleep in a real bed tonight, not in a roll in some accommodating farmer's barn. And, mercifully, there wasn't a crop in sight. If she had to murmur a few words of blessing over one more field, she'd scream. Did they actually think Salbine cared about their bloody crops? That was more Turena's domain.

But conversing with farmers along the way hadn't been a complete waste of time. Several had spoken to Maddy; one had hosted her and Jonathan in the same barn as Lillian and Barnabus. He'd marvelled that two sisters had graced his farm within such a short period of time, regarding it as a sign that his fields would be bountiful that season. Everyone spoke highly of the sister who'd patiently chatted with them, commiserating with their worries and offering encouraging words.

Lillian must have disappointed in comparison, but reaching out to folk came naturally to Maddy, a strength she unfortunately didn't appreciate. Maddy could listen to the same complaint a hundred times and sincerely empathize again and again. Idle chatter didn't bore her—or perhaps she was adept at not letting her boredom show. Lillian was always ready to strangle someone after a minute of it, to put both her and the chatterer out of their misery. Thank Salbine for Barnabus. He picked up her slack and didn't try to pretend they were close friends. She could understand why Sophia held him in such high esteem.

Barnabus had waited for her by the inn's entrance. He held the door open for her and she nodded her thanks as she stepped past him into a noisy common room. The stables had appeared almost full, with barely enough room for Baxter, Barnabus's horse Griffin, and their packhorse, Ticky. Considering this was the first inn they'd encountered along the road in three days, it wasn't surprising that many travellers had decided to stop here for a meal and a roof for the night. Nobody took much notice of Lillian in her nondescript brown travelling cloak.

Barnabus strolled over to the man tending the bar. "We're looking for lodging," he said cheerfully.

The man stopped wiping a tankard and glanced at Lillian. "A room for you and the wife?"

Lillian bit her tongue. Hard.

"No, two rooms," Barnabus said, unruffled. "We're not man and wife. I'm a Salbine Defender, and this is Mistress Lillian, from the Merrin monastery."

Lillian removed her riding gloves. The grovelling usually started at this point, but the innkeeper suspiciously eyed her and Barnabus up and down, taking particular interest in Lillian's hands. "We had a sister through here not long ago," he said. "Or what we thought was a sister. Turned out she wasn't. A wicked woman, she was, using Salbine's name to steal."

If this kept up, Lillian's tongue would bleed. Barnabus had reiterated several times that they weren't to defend Maddy or to become embroiled in arguments about her. They were to find out what happened and then worry about restoring Maddy's reputation.

"Hadn't seen a sister through here in ages, and now all of a sudden two—or supposedly two—appear on my doorstep barely months apart." His voice had risen; those sitting nearby grew quiet. "This some new racket making the rounds? You should have tried somewhere else."

"I assure you that we are who we say we are," Barnabus said stiffly.

"And that's supposed to be good enough?"

Barnabus reached for his travel bag.

"Oh, don't bother with documents, I can't read them." His eyes narrowed. "And don't think you'll get away with waving them in my face. Your documents mean nothing, not after that other sister. Might be best if you carried on your way."

Enough of this nonsense! Lillian drew air.

The innkeeper's eyes bulged when his feet left the floor. He flailed about as he rose to the ceiling; the rag he held dropped from his fingers. Gasps rose behind Lillian. "Salbine preserve me," the innkeeper wailed, his arms and legs dangling. All eyes were on the innkeeper; several travellers had risen to their feet, their mouths open.

"Since he doesn't want to host us, I suppose we'll have to find another inn," she said to Barnabus. They turned and walked away.

"No! Please, let me down! I'm sorry, Sister. Please!"

For a moment Lillian considered abruptly cutting the flow and unceremoniously dumping him to the floor. But he might hurt himself, and that would mean a fuss, and more wailing, and probably her supper would be late. Her stomach grumbled, underscoring that last point. With a sigh, she gently lowered the innkeeper to the floor.

"Oh Sister, forgive me," he cried, throwing himself at her feet and grabbing her cloak. "What can I do to make it up to you?"

He could get his grimy hands off her cloak, for a start. She stepped back. When he still clung to her, she took another step back and fought the urge to give him an encouraging kick. He finally let go.

"We've had travellers through here from Garryglen, see," he said, gazing up at her. "They had a bit of trouble there, with someone posing as a sister, the very sister who stayed here not long ago. Warned us there could be more about, asking for handouts." His brow furrowed. "Is that why you're here? You're on your way to Garryglen to see if there are more?"

She ignored his question. "Did any of these travellers mention what happened to the sister?"

"The one posing as a sister, you mean? Aye. Salbine took her."

Lillian's breath caught in her throat. No.

The innkeeper rose hesitantly, then straightened when Lillian didn't react. "Salbine swooped right out of the sky, She did. Taller than all the trees, with flames shooting out of Her eyes. Reduced the poser to a pile of ash. Nothing left of her, I hear."

Oh, for Lina's sake!

A nearby traveller found his voice. "It's true, Sister. One of the guards told me."

One who hadn't been present when Maddy had been dragged before the magistrate, no doubt. "Can you show us our rooms?" she said.

The innkeeper stared at her.

"Our rooms," Barnabus repeated.

Comprehension dawned in his eyes. "Ness!" he bellowed. A barmaid who looked no older than fourteen approached the bar, her eyes downcast. "Take them to the two rooms at the end of the hall. And if there's anything you want, Sister—"

"Bring me a bowl of stew and a tankard of cider, as soon as you can." She looked at Barnabus.

"Make mine ale." He drew several coins from his purse and dropped them into the innkeeper's hand.

"Of course," the innkeeper said, bowing.

Barnabus turned to Lillian as they followed Ness up the stairs. "It's not surprising that they've heard of the sister's trouble," he whispered. "We're within a week of Garryglen now."

"Yes, and the tale grows taller with each passing mile," Lillian murmured.

"I'll fetch what we need from the stables," he said, no longer whispering.

Lillian nodded. Not long now until she found out if Maddy lived. If she didn't, it would take every ounce of willpower Lillian had to keep herself from incinerating the magistrate and anyone else involved, on the spot. She wasn't taller than all the trees and didn't have flames shooting from her eyes, but reducing morons to piles of ashes—that she could do! But she wouldn't. Not only would she disappoint Sophia and face her wrath, but she wasn't sure Maddy would approve. Lillian snorted. Her love for Maddy was turning her soft! A love that would never die, even if Maddy had.

Chapter Twelve

*A*ND, AS ALWAYS, *I'LL TRUST THAT You know what's best for me. Your will be done.* Maddy lifted her head. That last part of her prayer was growing more difficult to say as the days dragged on. If her malflowed condition hadn't already made her question Salbine's guiding hand, she'd certainly be questioning it now.

Behind her, Emmey shifted position for the fifth or sixth time. She'd learned to remain quiet through Maddy's morning and evening prayer time, but it wasn't easy for her. Maddy stretched, signalling that she was done, and Emmey instantly spoke. "Who's the abbess, Miss?"

Certain that she'd never mentioned the abbess, Maddy turned to Emmey in surprise.

"The abbess," Emmey repeated, interpreting Maddy's expression as confusion. "Sometimes you say that when you're praying."

"I didn't realize I was praying out loud."

"You don't do it all the time, Miss. But sometimes you do. Sometimes I have to move closer to you before I can hear anything."

Part of Maddy smiled. The other part wanted to say it wasn't polite to eavesdrop on others' prayers, but given their circumstances, that part lost. "The abbess is the head of a monastery."

"You mean she's the leader?"

"I suppose she is, yes. Though she doesn't order us around very often."

"Who's Rose?"

Anticipating a lengthy conversation, Maddy sat cross-legged. "Rose is a sister, and a friend. We joined the Order around the same time. She's a bit younger than I am, though. I joined later than most sisters do."

Emmey's face scrunched up. "Why?"

"I didn't want to leave my family." Well, it was half true.

"Who's Lillian?"

"She's also a sister," Maddy said, hoping her answer would satisfy Emmey.

"You say her name a lot, like you're worried about her." Emmey turned her attention to furiously scratching her feet.

Maddy was grateful for that; her face felt hot. But Emmey was a bright girl; why not tell her the truth? "You know what it means to be marked by Salbine?" she asked, stalling a bit. Based on her very first conversation with Emmey, she already knew the answer.

"Uh-huh," Emmey said, still scratching. "Oh!" Her head jerked up, her eyes wide. "Is Lillian . . . is she . . . ?"

"Yes, she is," Maddy said. "And yes, I'm worried about her. I promised I'd write to her, but I obviously haven't. She's probably worried about me." At least Maddy hoped she was.

"Is she pretty?"

"I wouldn't say she's pretty," Maddy said slowly.

Emmey pondered Maddy's answer. "If she's not pretty, how come you like her?"

"When I said she's not pretty, I meant that's not a word people would use to describe her, not that she isn't appealing. She's appealing to me."

"Did she join at the same time you did, Miss?"

Maddy shook her head. "Lillian's older than I am. Quite a bit older. She joined the Order a long time ago."

"You must miss her."

More than she could express.

"Maybe she'll be the one that comes to get you!" Emmey said excitedly.

"I doubt it."

"Why, Miss? She'd want to come get you. Because she misses you!"

If only it were that simple. "Lillian doesn't like to leave the monastery, and she's not . . . um, very good with people. Most people either bore or irritate her."

"You don't, Miss."

Maddy couldn't help but smile. "You're right. Apparently, I don't." And she sometimes wondered why. "Even if Lillian wanted to come, I'm not sure the abbess would let her."

"Why?"

"Because Lillian is the opposite of me. Remember I told you I can't draw the elements? Well, she can, and she's very powerful."

Emmey nodded knowingly. "Makes sense, Miss."

"Does it?" Emmey's confident response surprised Maddy. Surely Emmey couldn't have some insight into Salbine's mind that Maddy didn't have.

"There's gotta be a reason you like her. She's not pretty and she's old, and she don't like nobody."

"Older, not old."

Emmey's expression clearly conveyed that she considered "older" and "old" one and the same. She sat back on her heels. "I'll miss you when you're gone."

"No, you won't," Maddy said firmly.

"I will, Miss!" Emmey cried. "I will!" She stared fiercely at Maddy, defiance in her eyes.

"You won't miss me because I'm not leaving without you," Maddy said, patting Emmey's knee.

"No, I'm never leaving, Miss," Emmey said, shaking her head. "I have to stay in here."

"Why? You told me you nicked a purse. Is that all you did? Nicking a purse was wrong and you shouldn't have done it. But you don't deserve to be in here for the rest of your life, if that's all you did."

Emmey scratched her ear. "I didn't do nothing else."

"Just nicked a purse?"

Emmey nodded.

It didn't make sense. "Whose purse did you nick?" Maddy vaguely recalled the governor making a remark about nobles, though she might have dreamed it.

"It don't matter whose purse I nicked. Nobody can get me out of here, Miss."

"The Salbine Sisters have influence. When they come for me, you're leaving too." If they came. "And once we're out, I'll take you home. That's a promise." She'd expected to boost Emmey's spirits, but Emmey remained sombre.

The key turned in the lock and the cell door swung open. Maddy's skin crawled when Evans stepped into the cell. He glanced around, distaste plain on his face. "Quite thick in here, isn't it?" he said as his hungry eyes settled on Emmey.

In her weakened state, Maddy would be no match for him. Brawny and over six feet tall, he'd easily overcome her, even if she were healthy. That wouldn't stop her from fighting him if he laid a hand on Emmey, though. So far her presence alone had kept him at bay, and today was no exception.

"Gov says it's time for another bath, and I have to agree with him," he said. Madison poked his head into the cell and wrinkled his nose.

Her heart sank. Had that much time passed already? Was anyone from the monastery on her way? Maddy slowly pushed herself to her feet and shuffled after Evans, barely aware of Emmey's hand clutching hers. Irritated by her slow gait, Madison pushed her forward and she picked up her pace.

"Can I watch?" Evans said with a leer when they reached the same cell they'd bathed in previously.

Madison groaned. "That's sick, that is. What if the gov's right and she's a real sister?"

Evans caught Maddy's eye. They both knew he wasn't interested in her. She tugged on Emmey's hand. "Come on," she murmured, trusting Madison to ensure that Evans remained on the other side of the cell door. She examined the pile of clothing near the tub and held up a shift and simple dress that looked roughly Emmey's size. The governor must have special-ordered it from a seamstress. Maddy would remember his kindness in her evening prayer.

Emmey chattered away as she bathed. Physically and mentally weary, Maddy only half listened, and by the time she lowered herself into the water, her mood had darkened. It was becoming increasingly difficult to remain positive, to keep hoping, to reassure herself that one day the cell door would swing open and she'd be led to a sister waiting in the governor's office. Had Salbine utterly abandoned her? Was it not enough that she couldn't draw the elements? She had nothing more to lose—but then she felt Emmey rub soap on her back and realized she did. Without Emmey, she'd go mad. Apparently she was already saying her prayers out loud. How had Emmey survived alone?

As she dried off, she noticed the silence and cursed herself. Emmey must have sensed her mood. Maddy slipped into her clean clothes and lifted Emmey's dress from the table. She forced a smile. She must never allow her despair and resignation to show, no matter how down she felt. "Let's get you into this dress."

After helping Emmey into it, Maddy stepped back and studied the girl, her hands on her hips. "That's a much better fit than the tent you've been wearing, isn't it?" she said, smiling when Emmey giggled. "Mine looks like a—"

The cell door smashed open. "Out! Now!" Madison barked, gesturing furiously.

Her heart pounding, Maddy grabbed Emmey's hand. When she stepped out of the cell, the smoke curling up the passageway stung her eyes and clogged her nostrils. "What's happening?" she gasped. He didn't answer. "Don't let go of my hand, do you understand?" she said to Emmey. "Keep holding my hand." She covered her mouth and tried not to lose sight of Madison.

The smoke thickened. It seemed to be billowing into the passageway from ahead of them. Madison turned, motioned for Maddy to go in the opposite direction. Somewhere distant, a bell was ringing.

"Help!" someone shouted. "Let me out!" A prisoner reached through the bars into the passageway. *Salbine have mercy.* The prisoners would die unless they were released!

"We have to keep moving," Madison said hoarsely. "If we stop to let them out, we'll die."

She opened her mouth to demand his keys, then wheezed when smoke filled her lungs. Madison pushed her forward. She turned to check on Emmey. Emmey held a hand over her nose, but the smoke wasn't as thick near her face. Maddy crouched and sucked in air. A loud shout from behind set her trembling. She glanced over her shoulder.

A figure emerged from the gloom, followed by another. "Bastard!" the first prisoner yelled, swinging a mace into Madison's helmet. Madison staggered and fell to his knees. The prisoner smashed the mace into Madison's face. "Stupid bastard!"

Maddy tugged Emmey forward, hoping to escape unnoticed, but the second prisoner had already spotted them. "What have we here?" He lunged at Maddy, waving a flaming piece of wood.

"No!" Emmey screamed, leaping at him. He swung the wood at her.

"Emmey!" Maddy thrust out her arm to block the makeshift torch, then grabbed it. Searing pain made her drop it; she stared in horror at her right hand, now aflame. For a moment she didn't think it was real, thought she'd unconsciously drawn fire. Emmey's screams brought her to her senses. Maddy shook her hand and beat it against the stone wall, but it continued to burn, encouraged by the oil she'd picked up from the wood.

"Bitch is on fire!" the prisoner shrieked; hysterical laughter rang in her ears. "Watch the fire burn. Ha-ha! Watch it burn!"

All the shaking and beating finally extinguished the flames. Wisps of smoke rose from her trembling hand. She pressed it against herself, but felt little pain. "Miss!" Emmey cried, and Maddy turned.

The prisoner with the mace stepped toward her. "Your turn!"

Her mouth opened as he drew back his arm, but smoke stifled her scream. Then his eyes widened and he pitched forward, slamming into her, driving her head and back into the wall. She glimpsed the guards behind him, then she passed out.

MADDY OPENED HER eyes, then quickly closed them, not used to the light.

"Her eyes flickered!" Emmey exclaimed. "Miss?"

She turned her head toward Emmey's voice. The horror in the passageway came flooding back. Her hand and lower arm felt sore, but not overly so. She opened her eyes again and lifted her right hand. The moment she saw it, she knew.

"Does it hurt, Miss?" Emmey was kneeling at the side of the bed, her elbows propped on its edge.

Bed? They weren't in their cell, then. "Part of it hurts," she said, managing a smile. The red edges around the charred areas smarted.

"A healer came to see you, Miss. She's with the gobernor."

"Governor," Maddy said reflexively. "Where are we?"

Before Emmey could answer, the governor and a woman Maddy presumed was the healer stepped into the room. "Thought I heard voices," the governor said gruffly.

The healer approached the bed and peered down at Maddy. "Go with the governor, child. I have to . . . tend to your friend."

Emmey frowned.

"Do what she says, Emmey," Maddy murmured.

Emmey's shoulders slumped. "All right."

"You can come back in as soon as I'm finished," the healer said as the governor ushered Emmey from the room and shut the door. She turned to Maddy. "Have you ever seen burns like yours before?"

"Yes. I used to help tend the sick." And those with burns like hers were in the group that received prayers, not aid. They rarely returned.

"Then you'll know there's nothing to be done for you," the healer said briskly, though her eyes were kind. "Are you hurting much?"

"Not much, no."

The healer nodded. "I've left a few teas with the governor, to help when the inner fire starts. If it gets really bad . . . if you're feeling you'd rather pass to another realm . . ." The healer swallowed. "I've left a special tea with the governor. Just ask him for the special tea. He'll know which one you mean."

"Thank you." Maddy hoped she'd have the courage not to use it, but knowing she had the option could help her endure whatever she faced before she passed.

"I'll let you rest, then. If you need anything else, ask the governor to send for me. I'll come."

"You're very kind. Would you do me one favour?"

"If it's something I can do, yes."

"Would you stay with the girl outside while I speak privately to the governor for a minute?"

"Aye." She patted Maddy's shoulder. "Salbine keep you."

"And you."

The healer left the room. Moments later, the governor came in and shut the door. "Mazie says you want to talk to me."

"I do."

"If you're wanting somewhere more comfortable, I can probably find a place for you in Reedwick, the town just down the hill. I have friends there who'll help. I'd like to help." He wrung his hands. "Because you're a real sister, aren't you?"

She met his eyes. "Yes, I am."

He dropped to one knee beside the bed. "I suspected. I would have got a message out, but I can't write, you see. And those that brought you, they made it clear that you were to stay, that if you got out, the folk would tear you apart. I couldn't risk involving anyone else. The guards . . . most thought you guilty. We're only a day from Garryglen. We'd all heard about what happened at the town hall. The guards would have reported any special treatment. I couldn't risk it. I have a wife and kids."

"Why did you believe me?"

"If you were guilty, you would have screamed about your innocence at the top of your lungs, day and night. The number of times I've seen that, I tell you . . ." He rolled his eyes. "And the way you've cared for the child . . . Nay, the longer you were here, the more I knew. I kept hoping someone would come for you. I'm sorry I couldn't offer you more than a tub now and then." He bowed his head.

"You did what you could, and you're showing me great kindness now," she said, wanting to ease the sorrow and regret evident in his voice.

"Let me move you somewhere more comfortable." He lifted his head. "Please!"

"You'd find yourself in the same trouble as you would have if you'd helped me before. This bed is as good a deathbed as any." A hay pile would have been luxurious, compared to the cell's stone floor.

"I can maybe try to get a message out."

"No. I don't want you to put yourself at risk, not when it's too late. But you can do something else for me."

"What? Anything."

"Let Emmey go."

His eyes moistened. He shook his head. "I can't."

"Why not? What's she doing here?"

"A very powerful man put her here, Sister. If he ever found out I let her go—"

"Who is he?"

The governor remained silent.

"Has he checked on her since she arrived?" Maddy pressed.

He hesitated, then shook his head.

"Then let her go. If anyone asks, she perished in the—" She was going to say fire, but what exactly had happened? "Was it an uprising?"

"Nay. A couple of new prisoners overpowered the two numbskulls who brought them in and used their weapons to kill a guard and get his keys. The lucky few they released rampaged and set fires wherever they could." He lowered his voice. "Several guards died, and only a few prisoners survived. Most died in their cells—the smoke. Many of them were destined for the gallows, but you can't help but feel sorry for the poor sods."

"And poor Emmey died in her cell, too. Those friends you said would help . . . get them to help her. Because it would be wrong to keep her here, you know that."

"I do know of a lady who keeps her eye on the urchins," he said slowly. "Doesn't give them a roof, but makes sure they get a bit to eat every day."

It wasn't much, but it would have to do. At least Emmey would be free and have a chance at a life. "Then take Emmey to her. Today. The less people who've seen her here after the fire, the better. Can the healer be trusted?"

"Aye. And I'll do what you ask, Sister. Reckon I owe you that much. I'll take her right now."

"Can you bring her in first?" A lump formed in Maddy's throat. "I'd like to say good-bye."

He pushed to his feet. "I'll get her."

"Wait." Maddy struggled to a sitting position and covered her right hand with the blanket. The governor adjusted the pillow behind her. "Thank you," Maddy said. "You can bring her in now."

As soon as he opened the door, Emmey rushed into the room. "Did the healer make you better, Miss?" she asked, plopping down next to the bed again.

"Call for me. I'll be right outside," the governor said to Maddy, then he nodded sadly and closed the door.

Maddy patted the bed with her left hand. "Why don't you come up here and sit with me for a minute?"

Emmey scrambled eagerly onto the bed and sat next to her.

"I want you to go with the governor to Reedwick," Maddy said, her forced cheerfulness making her voice shrill. "He's decided to let you go. He knows someone who'll watch out for you."

"What about you, Miss?"

"I have to stay here. I'm not well enough to leave."

"I'm not going without you, Miss." Emmey's mouth pressed into a thin line.

"You have to go now, Emmey. If the man who put you in here comes looking for you, the governor will pretend you died in the fire. He won't be able to do that if you stay here and everyone sees you." Some already had, but that couldn't be helped. It probably wouldn't matter. Maddy suspected this mysterious man had left Emmey to rot and forgotten about her.

"Then I'll just stay in here, with you. Nobody will see me." Emmey's face brightened. "And then, when you're better, we can leave," she squealed. Her words tumbled out. "Because he'll let you go too, right, Miss? He knows you're a sister now. And then you'll take me home."

Maddy wished it could be so. Emmey's shining face hurt her more than any physical injury ever could. Lying to her was wrong. In some ways, Maddy was closer to Emmey than she was to anyone else; their shared ordeal had forged a tight bond. Emmey understood what it felt like to be a caged animal. She'd earned Maddy's respect and admiration, and deserved the truth, no matter how grave. "Emmey," Maddy said quietly, "I won't be leaving."

Emmey gave her an incredulous look. "Yes, you will! I heard the gobernor say to the healer that you're a sister. He knows, Miss. He'll let you go. Why would he let me go and not you?"

"Because I'm not going to get better."

Emmey blinked. "What?"

"The burns on my hand—they're bad, Emmey. They won't get better, and they'll make me sick. I'll . . ." She faltered when Emmey's face tightened and her chin trembled. "I'll soon leave this realm."

"No! You'll get better!"

Maddy shook her head. "No, I won't." Her voice was barely a whisper. She drew a deep breath. "Very few survive burns like mine. Even if I were stronger, the chances would be slim. So you need to go, Emmey. There's no reason for you to stay here."

A tear rolled down Emmey's cheek. "You're here, Miss. You shouldn't . . ." She swallowed. "You shouldn't die on your own."

"I won't be alone. The governor will be here, and the guards."

"But they don't love you, Miss," Emmey said, the tears coming faster and her nose running. "You should be with someone who loves you."

Oh, no, she couldn't cry, not in front of Emmey. She reached for Emmey with her left arm and hugged her close to her chest. "It's because I love you, Emmey, that I want you to go. I want you to be free, to have a chance to eventually find your way home. I'm sorry I can't take you myself. I promised I would."

"Don't feel bad, Miss," Emmey said between sniffles. "I know you would, if you could. But why can't I stay with you until . . . until you're gone?"

"I've already explained why you can't stay. And it would help me to know that you're away from here, that you won't be thrown back into a cell."

"You mean it would make you happy?"

Maddy nodded. "It would, indeed. So I want you to go with the governor. And I want you to stick close to the lady who'll care for you. From what I understand, she won't have a bed for you, so see where the other children sleep. They might know of a friendly stable or another safe place."

"All right, Miss."

Maddy comforted Emmey a bit longer—or was Emmey comforting her? When Emmey's sniffles subsided, Maddy tapped her back. "You'd better get going, Emmey."

Emmey wiped her red eyes, where more tears lurked. "Do you need help with anything before I go, Miss?"

"No. But I want you to remember something for me and maybe do something later."

"What?"

"If you ever see a woman with markings like mine on her hands, I want you to tell her what happened to me. Do you think you can do that?"

Emmey nodded.

"You'll need to tell her my name. Can you remember this? Sister Maddy, from Merrin. Say it."

"Sister Maddy, from . . ."

"Merrin."

"Sister Maddy, from Merrin."

"That's it."

"Sister Maddy, from Merrin!" Sorrow quickly replaced Emmey's triumphant smile. "I wish I didn't have to go, Miss."

"Me too. But it'll be better this way, for both of us."

Emmey leaned in and hugged her fiercely. "I'll never forget you, Miss."

Fighting tears, Maddy couldn't reply. Assuming that since her right hand was useless, her left hand would be acceptable to Salbine, she placed it on Emmey's head. "May Salbine guide you. May Salbine provide for you. May Salbine keep you." Her voice trembled. "And may you find your way home, and have a long and wonderful life." Her composure threatening to flee completely, Maddy held Emmey against her and called for the governor.

"It's time for her to go," she said to him.

"Come on, lass." When Emmey didn't budge, he gently pulled her away. Maddy was grateful when he lifted Emmey into his arms and held her face against his shoulder. "I'll be back soon. There's a guard outside, if you need anything. He's a good man. The one on tonight will do right by you, too," he said over Emmey's loud sobs.

"Thank you."

His forehead creased. "Best be off, then."

"Good-bye, Miss," Emmey said, his shoulder muffling her words.

"Good-bye, Emmey."

The governor closed the door behind them, but Maddy could still hear Emmey crying. When Emmey's wailing had faded and Maddy was certain she wouldn't return, she lay on her stomach and wept into her pillow, her sobs racking her frail body.

Chapter Thirteen

Lillian slowed Baxter to a walk and stopped next to Barnabus and Ticky. They eyed Garryglen's west gate. "So you don't like my idea of setting the first person who asks me to prove I'm a sister on fire?"

"The abbess made herself clear," Barnabus said.

"The abbess said she didn't want to hear about towns burning. She didn't say anything about individual people. If I set the first one who asks on fire, the news will quickly spread. Nobody else will dare ask me."

"You might be giving the townsfolk too much credit, Mistress."

Lillian was sure she was. "Well then, I'll set the first one who asks on fire, and then the next one, and then the one after that. I'll be doing Garryglen a service by culling its idiots."

Barnabus gave her a sidelong look. "Sometimes I can't tell if you're being serious or pulling my leg," he said stiffly.

Right now she was delaying them from passing through the gate ahead. Her stomach hurt and her hands felt clammy. She'd cursed the length of the journey to Garryglen, but at the same time, had dreaded this day. Hope would either become certainty, or be banished. She wasn't ready to learn which would prevail, but she never would be, so stalling was pointless. "What did Jonathan say the name of the inn was, where it all started?"

"The Traveller's Rest."

"Let's stay clear of it, and the surrounding area."

Barnabus nodded. "Not only will it be hostile, but that's where we'll find the tallest tales. I'll ask these guards about the sister. If they don't know, let's try the nearest market that's away from the inn. Once we know more, we'll decide who to see from there."

Lillian tightened her hold on the reins. "We're seeing that magistrate no matter what we find out. He made a mockery of a Salbine Sister." And if he'd hanged Maddy, he'd bloody-well pay!

"I agree, Mistress. But the more we know when we see him, the better. Shall we?"

In response, she nudged Baxter forward. Barnabus hailed the guards at the gate. Lillian remained silent while he exchanged pleasantries and obtained directions to the market and The Traveller's Rest. "We heard you had a bit of trouble with a sister that came through here," he said.

"No," the guard standing to the left of the gate said.

"We've heard stories on the road about a woman who impersonated a sister."

"Oh, that. Happened a while ago, that did."

"Any chance we'll run into her?"

"No. We took care of her."

Lillian's throat tightened.

"Sent her to prison. She won't be getting out."

Prison? Then she was alive!

The guard to the right shook his head. "No, we didn't. We hung her."

"No, we sent her to prison!"

"Don't know where you got your information from, Cliff. I just know it's wrong. We hung her."

"Were either of you there when she was sentenced?" Barnabus asked.

They both shook their heads.

Lillian wanted to scream. So, Maddy might have hung, she might be in prison, or she might have sprouted wings and flown away! What a waste of time!

Barnabus thanked them. "Sounds like the nearest market is about fifteen minutes away," he murmured as they trotted through the gate. The knot in Lillian's stomach tightened. She focused on following Barnabus, wishing she'd learn of Maddy's fate privately, not in the middle of a bustling market.

Too soon, she was securing Baxter and Ticky to a post and surveying the chaos of haphazardly arranged wooden stalls and gaily-coloured tents. Smoke from cooking fires tickled Lillian's nose, and she quickly stepped out of the way as three children tore past her, oblivious to those around them. "Do you mind if I wait with the horses?" she said to Barnabus. "I'd rather hear what's happened from you, not in the middle of that." She jerked her chin toward the market where townsfolk thronged, examining textiles, haggling for better prices, and gossiping. "You'll do all the talking, anyway."

"Of course, Mistress. I'll return as soon as I know." He disappeared into the crowd, his hand on his purse.

Lillian patted Baxter's side. "Not long now." She scowled. "I don't know why anyone would enjoy the market. Look at it! All those townsfolk. You're probably smarter than most of them." She moved to where he could see her and wagged her finger at him. "And you won't be able to complain anymore that we don't go on long rides, not after this. Oh no, no, no. And we're having quite the ride, aren't we? I just wish it was under—"

Two children were staring at her, snickering.

"Bugger off!" she roared.

Wide-eyed, they raced away. Children! Why couldn't they all be locked away until they were at least twelve? Yet another benefit to living behind a monastery's walls.

The minutes passed, and she grew restless. Given the performance at the west gate, Barnabus would have to hear the same tale from numerous folk before he trusted one over another. She could be in for a long wait, and there was nowhere nearby to sit. But she didn't have to remain rooted to this very spot. As long as she could see the horses, she'd see Barnabus when he returned. As she scanned the benches outside several of the shops ringing the market, she spotted Barnabus striding toward her. Surely he couldn't know what had happened already.

Her heart sank when he drew closer. His face was grim. "Salbine smiled on me, Mistress. I ran into a guard who was not only there that night, but carried out the sister's sentence."

"What happened?" she croaked.

"They spared her. She was sent to prison. The guard I spoke to rode in the wagon with her."

If not for Barnabus's face, she would have felt light-headed with relief. "Then what's wrong?"

"They've had a bit of trouble at the prison, just recently. A couple of prisoners overpowered the guards and set fires." He hesitated, cleared his throat. "Many of the prisoners died. They were trapped in their cells."

Lillian couldn't believe it. "So we're back to she's probably dead." It was too much to bear. She turned away from Barnabus and hugged Baxter, pressing her cheek against his. If only they'd arrived last week . . .

"I'm sorry, Mistress," Barnabus said.

She held onto Baxter a little longer, then let go of him, keeping her back to Barnabus. "There's still a chance she's alive. How far away is the prison?"

"About a day's journey." He paused. "The guard also gave me the name of the magistrate and where we can find him. I suggest we go and see him now, to secure the document we'll need to free the sister, if she's alive. We can also ask for our horses. We can set off for the prison first thing tomorrow."

No! Her inner voice urged her to leave for the prison immediately. Lillian trusted it implicitly; it had never been wrong. Sometimes she wondered if it was the voice of Salbine Herself. She turned to Barnabus. "It's only just gone midday and the horses are still fresh. Let's ride on. I want to reach the prison as soon as possible. We can rest along the way and be there by midday tomorrow."

"But if the sister's alive—"

"If she's alive and they insist on a pardon, you can return here and get it. We leave now."

Barnabus bowed. "Yes, Mistress."

By the time they trotted through Garryglen's southern gate, she felt an overpowering urgency to reach the prison. Perhaps it was her way of distracting herself from the real possibility that Maddy was dead, but she didn't think so. That inner voice had never lied. Maddy was alive, but in trouble. This time, Lillian was determined not to arrive too late.

MADDY CAREFULLY SIGNED her name and read over her letter in dismay. Two hours of struggling to write with her left hand, for this?

The scrawled letters, barely legible, reminded her of when she'd learned to write, though her novice efforts had been much better than the mess in front of her. Lillian wouldn't be able to read it!

The governor, whom she now knew as Arthur, peered into the room. "Are you ready for the wax yet?"

"Just a minute." She carefully wrote *I love you.* If that was all Lillian could read, it would have to be enough. She laid the quill on the tray. "I'm ready now."

"Wish I could have written it for you," Arthur said as he folded the paper and sealed it. He lifted the tray from her lap. "And it's for Mistress Lillian, of Merrin?"

"Yes. But you can give it to any sister. Any one will see that the mistress gets it."

"Sisters don't pass this way as a rule, with Reedwick being off the main trade route and no reason for them to come to the prison. But if a sister comes for you, I'll give it to her. If not, then in a few months' time, when . . ." he gulped " . . . when everyone knows you're gone, I'll send it. Can't imagine I'll get into trouble then."

"Thank you." She wiped her brow. "And thank you for finding me the supplies I needed to write it."

"The thanks belong to those in town willing to lend them. Would you like some more tea?"

"Yes, please." It didn't quell her inner fire and only slightly eased the pain in her hand and arm, but it emotionally soothed her.

"I'll go brew it." He left with the tray and letter, probably relieved to be away from the foul smell for a few minutes. She'd grown used to it. Arthur sometimes held a handkerchief over his nose, but he hadn't today.

Maddy lay down, trying not to look at the monstrosity that used to be her right hand, or at how far the sickness had crept up her arm. She'd accepted that she'd die here, and nobody except Arthur would notice. If there was a lesson to be learned from all this—being malflowed, falsely accused, rotting in prison, and burned—she didn't see it, despite lying in this bed for hours on end, searching for one. She was as far from understanding Salbine's will as she had been when she'd set out for Heath, all those months ago. She could only hope that it would be Salbine's realm she entered and not the realm of the godless, though she had a difficult time believing that Salbine hadn't forsaken her, and no reason to believe that any of the other gods had claimed her.

At least Emmey was free, and hopefully well. In her worst moments, Maddy clung to that one bright spot. It hadn't all been for nothing. In every prayer, she beseeched Salbine to guide Emmey safely home. Maddy also prayed earnestly for Lillian. If she could only see her one last time, she could die at peace. So much in her life felt unfinished.

She struggled to sit up when Arthur returned. He set the tray on her lap again. A cup of tea had replaced the quill, ink, and paper. "I'll stay here and hold it for you," he said, lowering himself into the chair next to the bed and grasping the edge of the tray with one hand.

"I'd appreciate your company." Someone always held the tray for her when she ate, too. When she could no longer feed herself, she'd ask for the special tea, though she might lose her appetite before then.

They chatted while Maddy sipped her tea. She asked after Arthur's family and listened to him recount the antics of his youngest son. "I told my Jill that he'll make a right good smith when he—"

A guard rapped at the open door. "You'd better come out, gov. A couple of folk are here to see you."

"Will you be all right with the tray?" he asked Maddy.

"You can take the tray. I'll hang onto the tea."

He did as she'd suggested. Maddy tightened her fingers around the cup's handle and closed her eyes. She was definitely growing weaker, and her head constantly ached. The limbs she could feel were heavy, and moving them took effort. Her inner fire raged. She didn't think it would be long now, no more than a few days.

Voices broke into her thoughts and grew louder as their owners approached her room. Maddy's eyes snapped open. The illness must be affecting her mind. One sounded like—no, it couldn't be. She turned toward the door anyway. "Lillian!" she gasped.

Lillian strode to the side of the bed and bit her lip. "Oh, Maddy. I want to hug you, but I don't want to hurt you." If the smell bothered her, she didn't show it.

"It's my right hand and arm," Maddy said, still wondering whether Lillian was real or the sickness had touched her mind. She needed to feel her. "Take this cup off me and come sit on the edge of the bed. And take off your cloak. I want to feel your robe."

"I'm not robed." Lillian set the teacup on the chair and removed her cloak, revealing her riding clothes. She threw her cloak over the back of the chair and sat next to Maddy. "Why would you—"

Maddy touched Lillian's cheek, then her lips. She ran her hand along Lillian's shoulder and down her arm, then met her eyes. "It's really you, isn't it? Oh, Salbine, thank you." She buried her face in Lillian's shoulder and cried. "Thank you, Salbine," she sobbed again and again.

Lillian held Maddy and rubbed her back. "I'm sorry it took me so long to get here," she murmured. "We left as soon as we knew you'd met with trouble."

"You're here now," Maddy managed to say between sniffles. "That's all that matters." She hadn't realized it, but she'd given up, accepted her fate with a shrug. Her primary concern had been not to burden others by dragging out her demise. Now that Lillian was here, she'd fight for every second, every last breath. She'd still die, but she wouldn't go meekly. Arthur wouldn't brew that special tea. Lillian would bolster her courage, and hold her hand as she drew her last breath and left this realm naturally.

Maddy drew back, smiled through her tears, and wiped away Lillian's. "How did you find out I was here?"

"Jonathan made it back to the monastery." Lillian leaned over to the chair to pull a handkerchief from her cloak pocket. She wiped Maddy's eyes. "So we knew to go to Garryglen." Her voice wavered. "But we didn't know if they'd hanged you. We only found out yesterday that they hadn't."

"I thought someone would come eventually, but I didn't expect it to be you."

"Do you know who Sophia wanted to send? Sister bloody Lucille! Is that who you'd want here right now?" Lillian asked incredulously. "Sister bloody Lucille?"

For the first time in days, Maddy laughed. "I've missed you," she said, resting her head on Lillian's shoulder.

Lillian touched Maddy's cheek. "You feel hot. Can I have a look at your hand?"

Maddy stiffened. "There's nothing to be done, Lillian."

"I can tell by the odour that it's bad, but I'd still like to have a look. Please?"

"All right." She lifted her head from Lillian's shoulder and pulled down the blanket, revealing her right hand and lower arm.

Lillian looked down at it. She clutched her shirt and gagged. "I'm sorry." She gagged again, then held out her hand, as if to balance herself. "I think I'll be all right now." Her gaze travelled up Maddy's arm.

"I told you there's nothing to be done."

"You're hot," Lillian murmured, shifting her attention to Maddy's face, "but your eyes are clear. Are you still eating?"

Maddy nodded.

"You're awfully thin."

"Imprisonment did that to me, not the burn."

Lillian stared at her, then through her.

"Lillian?" Maddy said after a minute had passed.

"I wish we had more time." Lillian's eyes refocused on Maddy. "I want to hear all about it. About what happened when you tried to draw the elements again." She swept out her arm. "About your time here. How you were burned. Everything. But we don't have time."

Panic made it difficult for Maddy to breathe. "You're not leaving?" she managed to say.

"Of course not." Lillian pulled the blanket over Maddy's hand, then looked at her. "There may be a way to save you."

"The healer said there's no remedy. And I've seen burns like this at the monastery. They don't get better, especially once they've gone gangrenous."

"There is a treatment," Lillian said quietly. "But it kills more than it saves. That's why it's rarely performed. With it, you'll probably die. Without it, you'll definitely die."

She appreciated Lillian's honesty. "Can you make this treatment?" she asked, assuming Lillian must be referring to a medicine.

"I've read about it, but I've never done it, which means you'll have even less of a chance of surviving. And we'll have to do it soon. That's why we don't have much time to talk. If you agree to it, I'll make preparations." Lillian held up her finger when Maddy drew breath. "Before you make a decision, let me tell you what it will involve." She grimaced. "I want to cut off your hand."

"What?"

"I want to cut off your hand."

"Not 'what' as in I didn't hear you, 'what' as in are you out of your mind?"

"It's your only chance, Maddy. This," she gestured at the lump under the blanket, "is poisoning you. We have to get rid of it. Otherwise you'll die. I'd like a chance at more time with you." She sighed, then reached out and touched Maddy's cheek. "But it's your decision."

So it was a choice between definitely dying in a few days and probably dying in a few hours, and the latter would probably involve a great deal of pain.

"I'll have to cut off your arm, too," Lillian said. "But only part of it."

Well, that made all the difference! "Lillian, I haven't been able to use my right hand since it was burned. I can't write. I need help when I eat, though I could probably eat all right at a table. I'd probably struggle to dress myself. I can no longer sew, embroider, do anything that requires two hands. I've gone from sort of useless to absolutely bloody useless!"

"You'll adapt."

"How? All the folk I know with missing limbs are at the market. Do you know what they do? Sit near the stalls, hoping pity will bring them coin."

"You're a Salbine Sister. You won't become a beggar."

"I'll feel like one. Everyone said, 'Don't worry about being mal-flowed, you have other talents. You can still contribute to the community.' That won't be true anymore, will it?"

Lillian sighed. "We can waste time talking about this, but let's not. I have to make preparations."

"I haven't said yes yet."

"Yes, you have. If it was no, you wouldn't be thinking about what life will be like for you afterward. If you survive. We have to be realistic."

"Probably won't survive is better than definitely won't survive."

Lillian nodded. "That's my thinking, too." She started to rise, but Maddy grabbed her shirt. "Two more minutes, Lillian. I have a couple of things I want to say to you." She was grateful that Lillian didn't insult her by insisting they'd have time to talk later, after her hand was gone. She met Lillian's eyes. "I want you to talk to the governor about a girl named Emmey. I want you to help her get home. Will you do that for me? He'll tell you where she is."

"Who is she?"

"We shared a cell. She's only eight."

"Eight?" Lillian frowned. "I'm not very good with children."

"I just want you to help her get home, that's all. You don't have to take her yourself."

"This girl is important to you?"

"Yes."

Lillian pursed her lips. "I suppose I could hire someone to escort her."

"It would put my mind at rest."

"Then that's what I'll do."

"Promise me."

"I promise," Lillian said. "In Salbine's name, I promise."

"Thank you. Now, listen." She pressed her palm against Lillian's cheek. "If I don't survive this, I don't want you to blame yourself. I would have died anyway."

Lillian's cheek trembled under Maddy's hand. "I'll try not to, but I can't promise." She reached up and covered Maddy's hand with hers. "I wish we had more time."

"So do I." Maddy swallowed. "I love you, Lillian."

Lillian gulped. "That's the sickness talking."

"No, it isn't. It's me. And I love you. Never forget that." She slipped her hand from under Lillian's. "Go make those preparations." She wasn't at all offended when Lillian left without reciprocating her declaration of love. Lillian had said *I love you* the moment she'd walked into the room.

HER HEART POUNDING, Lillian closed the door to Maddy's sickroom and leaned against it. Barnabus and the governor turned to her. "Are you all right, Mistress?" Barnabus asked.

No, she wasn't, but she'd better pull herself together, and quickly. Otherwise Maddy wouldn't have even the tiniest chance of pulling through.

Concern creased Barnabus's face. "How is she?"

"Not good. Terrible."

"The healer . . . she left me a tea that will help her pass to another realm," the governor said.

"That was kind of her, but the sister won't be needing it. We have one chance to save her, albeit a slim one. She's agreed to let us try. If we fail, she'll pass quickly on her own." Lillian met the eyes of each man in turn. "I say 'we' because I'll need your help."

"Of course, Mistress. What do we have to do?" Barnabus asked.

"We're going to cut off her hand."

Barnabus merely blinked. The governor paled, then swayed and steadied himself with a hand to the wall.

"She'll probably die, but we'll do it anyway." Though the governor would likely faint and be of no use. "We'll need a room with a table long enough to hold the sister," she said to him, then cast her mind back to the description she'd read of the procedure. If only she had the tome with her. Hopefully her memory was sound. "And I'll need the following tools: a knife and a saw or axe—sharp!—a pry-bar, a—"

"Begging your pardon, Sister," the governor said, slightly green. "I've heard there's a physician in Reedwick. Just passing through, he was, so I don't know if he's still there."

"Why didn't you bring him here to see the sister?"

"I just found out about him this morning," he mumbled. "And Mazie—the healer—she said there's nothing to be done."

Lillian bit her tongue and hoped the physician was still in Reedwick. Even if he'd never performed the procedure, he'd be a great help. An hour or two's delay wouldn't make much of a difference to Maddy's chances of survival. "Do you know where he's staying?"

"Aye, but as I said, he might be gone."

"If he hasn't left, I want him here. Barnabus."

"Can one of your men take me to him?" Barnabus asked the governor.

"Aye. And then I'll show you a room I think'll be all right." He gestured for them to follow him.

"And have your men gather the tools I need." She would finish listing them for him after Barnabus set off.

"I will, Sister."

"Good." Everything was in motion. *Maddy loves me.* No, she couldn't think of Maddy. If she did, she'd lose her nerve. For now she had to remain aloof. Later, she'd weep at Maddy's bedside, or at her funeral pyre.

Chapter Fourteen

As LILLIAN EXAMINED SEVERAL CLOTHS AND chose the one she thought would be the best fit, Barnabus strode into the kitchen with a smartly dressed man at his side. "The governor told us we'd find you here, Mistress. I present to you Mr. Crandall. And this," he said to Crandall, "is Mistress Lillian, of Merrin."

Crandall dropped his bag to the floor and bowed. "It's always an honour to meet one marked by the gods."

"And to meet a learned man," Lillian responded. "I presume Barnabus has told you what we intend to do."

"Yes," Crandall said, his face grave. "I've never performed the procedure, but I have observed it on several occasions. I must be blunt: of the five I've observed, only one survived."

"We know the odds we face, but we still want to try. I've read about the procedure, but never performed it. Do you think you can do it?"

"Yes."

His confidence bolstered Lillian's spirits. When they were in that room cutting through Maddy's arm, it was important that everyone believe that the procedure could succeed, even if they were deluding themselves. "I'd like to apply a poultice to the wound when we're finished. I've prepared the herbs, but I can't mix the paste and spread it onto the cloth until we're almost ready for it. It has to be warm."

"I assume this will promote healing?" Crandall said.

Lillian nodded. "And help to preserve her lifeblood."

"At the last procedure I observed, the lifeblood was preserved by tying off the vessels that carry it."

"Oh? That wasn't mentioned in the tome I read," Lillian said with interest.

Crandall nodded. "It's a new development. But you have to be quick, and this being my first time . . . In the others, heat was applied to the wound by way of a hot iron."

Both Lillian and Barnabus shuddered. "You mean they burned everything shut?" Lillian exclaimed. "Wouldn't that just inflict another wound?"

Crandall's mouth turned up at the corners. "Guess which of the five survived? But we might have to consider it. As I said, because of my inexperience, I might not be able to tie quickly enough. We may need to use heat."

"Forget the hot iron. We'll focus the heat only on the vessels, and only if we have to."

"And how do you propose we do that?"

Lillian lifted an eyebrow.

Crandall's brows shot up. "Of course! Can you be that precise?"

"Yes, I can. But I'm surprised the tome didn't mention anything about tying or irons. Well, it did mention tying, but only in reference to a strip of cloth above where you plan to cut. Tied tightly."

Crandall scratched his chin. "I've not seen that, but I don't see what harm it could do. As for your poultice, its healing properties will be beneficial regardless of how we preserve her lifeblood. You should have time to prepare it while I'm covering the wound."

"Covering the wound?"

"With her skin. I'll cut the bone at a higher point than the skin, so I can use the skin to close the wound."

"I would have just cut it all at the same place," Lillian said, making a chopping motion with her hand. "We're very fortunate that you're here."

"And lucky. I was planning to leave today. Another couple of hours and I would have been gone."

She and Barnabus exchanged a glance. "Well, I suppose we should get on with it."

Crandall picked up his bag and she led him to the room the governor had prepared, one the guards used for meals. Two tables had been pushed together, and the tools Lillian had requested lay on a smaller table against the wall. Crandall crossed to the table and examined each tool in turn. He tested the edge of the saw with his thumb, then did the same with the knife. "I'll use my own knife," he said, opening his bag.

The governor hesitantly stepped into the room and raised a bottle of ale. "Thought you might be wanting this. Might knock her out."

"We certainly don't want her to drink the entire bottle," Crandall said, "but a nip or two might help calm her. Do you have anything stronger? Rum, perhaps?"

"Aye, if that's what you want. I'll fetch a bottle from the cellar." The governor glanced at the tools. "I don't have to be here, do I, when you're . . . cutting?"

"No, you don't," Lillian said quickly. "If you'd like to help, you can go to the kitchen once we've started and boil the pot of water we'll need over the fire. Keep it simmering until I come for it."

He brightened. "It'll be simmering, Sister, I promise you that."

"And we'll need your three strongest guards. Can you fetch them now?" Crandall said.

The governor rolled his eyes. "The sister isn't a prisoner anymore, and is too weak to escape, even if she was."

"I'm not worrying about her escaping. I need the men to hold her down."

"I see." The governor set the ale on the table with a trembling hand. "I'll fetch the men and the rum."

"Do we have everything we need, then?" Lillian asked Crandall.

He nodded. "I'd like to see the sister, look at her hand and arm, before we bring her here."

"Barnabus, will you take him to Sister Maddy and then wait there for me? I'd like a moment with her alone before we start."

"Yes, Mistress."

Lillian covered the tools with a cloth before leaving the room so Maddy wouldn't see them, then went to the prison's main gate, where they'd left their horses. She pulled a robe from one of Ticky's saddlebags and took a moment to breathe. The sun warmed her face and the clear blue sky settled her nerves. *Maddy can't die, not on such a beautiful day.* But people did all the time. Lillian patted Baxter's side and steeled herself, determined not to have another reason to spend all her days in her laboratory, out of the sun.

Barnabus and Crandall were waiting outside Maddy's room. "She's already weak," Crandall said. "But her lower arm definitely has to go. I'll do my best for her."

"That's all we can ask." Lillian sighed. "I'll be out in a minute."

Maddy's eyes were closed when Lillian entered the room. She peeled off her travelling clothes and stepped into her robe. When she'd finished buttoning it, she knelt next to the bed and stroked Maddy's hair. Maddy's eyes opened. "We're ready for you," Lillian murmured.

"You're robed." Maddy inched over, rested her cheek on Lillian's shoulder. "It's rough. I said I'd make you a new one."

"You might still have the opportunity."

"Not with one hand. Though I suppose one hand is better than dead."

Lillian managed a smile. "That's the spirit."

Maddy lifted her head. "Will you pray with me?"

"Yes." She took Maddy's hand, bowed her head. *Salbine, I don't talk to You very often, so when I do, You know it's important. I firmly believe You brought me here in time to help Maddy. So help us. Help me, help Crandall, help Maddy. She thinks she's malflowed because she's lost Your favour. But she hasn't, has she? Otherwise You wouldn't have rushed me here. If You still have work for her to do, if there's a reason she's malflowed, then guide me. Guide Crandall.*

That inner voice spoke. *"So you want Me to save Maddy for Me and not for you? Lillian, if you're going to ask Me for something, at least be honest about why you want it."*

And . . . and if You won't save her for You, save her for me. I love her. I don't want to lose her when I've just found her. Please, Salbine, consider my plea. At the very least, welcome Maddy into Your realm. She deserves at least that.

Your will be done.

Lillian raised her head.

"It will be all right, Lillian," Maddy said softly. "No matter what happens, it will be all right."

Embarrassed, Lillian wiped moist eyes. "I should be comforting *you*."

"Whatever happens will touch both of us."

"What you said before . . . about loving me . . ." Her face crumpled. *Blast it! What's wrong with me? I'm a mess!*

"I know." Maddy's hand tightened around Lillian's arm. "Salbine keep you, Lillian."

Taking her lead from Maddy, Lillian composed herself and leaned over to kiss Maddy's forehead, then her lips. "And you."

It was time. She gave her face one last wipe with her sleeve and hoped she looked all right, then rose and opened the door. "Barnabus."

He nodded grimly and entered.

"Barnabus!" Maddy said, smiling at him as he approached the bed. "It's so good to see you." Lillian realized he must have remained outside while Crandall examined her arm.

Barnabus bowed. "And you, Sister."

Lillian pulled back the blanket and tried not to wince at Maddy's emaciated body. Barnabus's jaw tightened; he caught Lillian's eye as he slipped his arms under Maddy and lifted her from the bed. Crandall led the way back to what Maddy would likely view as a torture chamber. Walking behind Barnabus, Lillian could only see Maddy's thin legs dangling over his arms.

"Gently," Crandall murmured as Barnabus lowered Maddy onto the tables. He uncorked the rum bottle and handed it to Lillian.

She helped Maddy to a sitting position and supported her back. "Drink a bit of this." Maddy gulped some down. Barnabus and the guards positioned themselves around her, sweat beading on their brows and fear in their eyes. "Hold her tightly," Crandall said.

Lillian stood near Maddy's head. Once Crandall started to work, she'd try to disassociate herself from the fact that it was Maddy lying on the table and observe him, but for now, Maddy was all that mattered. She gazed at her, hoping her terror didn't show. Maddy blinked at Lillian, then closed her eyes. Her lips started to move. The room went quiet, save for Maddy's whispering. Lillian caught the word "Salbine" over and over again.

Maddy jumped and whimpered when Crandall touched her arm. Dismayed, Lillian rested her hand on Maddy's clammy forehead. "He's just tying a piece of cloth around it," she said quietly.

Crandall tightened the strip of cloth, then straightened. He drew aside the cloth covering the tools and lifted his knife. The guards tightened their grips. As if sensing what was coming, Maddy's body trembled. Her whispers resumed, the words running into each other. Lillian forced herself to turn toward Crandall and watched him touch the knife to Maddy's skin. He cut.

Maddy's whispers rose to agonized screams.

MADDY TURNED TOWARD the light visible in her peripheral vision, saw Lillian bent over a nearby table, her quill scratching the paper in front of her. "I'm alive!" she breathed.

Lillian twisted around. "Try not to sound so surprised." She set down the quill and wiped her fingers on a cloth. "Let's have a look at you."

"Did you cut it off?" They must have. Maddy remembered the searing bite of pain before she passed out.

"We did."

"I still feel like I have my hand."

Lillian pressed her palm against Maddy's forehead. "Do you mean you feel pain there?"

"Yes. And it's painful here." She went to touch the area that hurt, but stopped, afraid of what she'd feel.

"That's where we cut. Crandall said you would be in pain, but with proper care, the pain should subside. How do you feel in general?"

"Tired."

"Do you want to look? You're bandaged, so you won't see much, but—"

She shook her head. She wanted to, but didn't want to. "Not yet."

"I'll brew a tea. It'll help with the pain and soothe you to sleep."

"I don't need it to sleep." She could already feel herself dropping off. "But I could use it for the pain."

Lillian stroked Maddy's hair. "I'll be right back."

Maddy closed her eyes. Her hand was gone, along with part of her arm. Forever. Not only could she not draw the elements, but she was less capable than the average child. What would she do with her life? She was—had been—right-handed. She was useless! Absolutely bloody useless! Yet she'd decided to put herself into this state, rather than die.

The decision must have come from her soul, because her mind didn't understand it. Her previous struggle to accept her place in the

Order would pale in comparison to the one she'd face now. Was Lillian the reason she'd clung to life? Would Lillian still want her? And if Maddy couldn't reconcile her broken life with Salbine, would it be right to remain in the Order primarily because she loved a sister? Would it be right . . .

When Lillian was suddenly there with the tea, Maddy realized she must have dozed off. They both held the cup as Maddy lifted her head and drank down its contents. The silence and the dim light in the room told Maddy it was the middle of the night, yet Lillian had been awake, and the dark half-moons under her eyes suggested that she probably hadn't slept since the procedure. "You look exhausted," she said when Lillian took away the cup. "Get some sleep."

"I have to change your bandages and apply a fresh poultice in about an hour. I'll sleep after that."

"Does it . . . look bad?"

Lillian shrugged. "No worse than other wounds. And Crandall used your own skin to cover it."

"That was lucky, him being in Reedwick."

"Luck had nothing to do with it," Lillian said firmly.

Maddy's eyes slid shut as the tea took effect. Next time she opened them, light was streaming into the room. Lillian wasn't at Maddy's bedside, but Maddy could see her talking with Barnabus in the room across the hall. Lillian glanced over her shoulder and immediately broke off her conversation with Barnabus to come over to Maddy.

"Did you get any sleep?" Maddy asked.

"I certainly did. And you've been out for almost twelve hours."

Twelve hours?

"How do you feel?"

Hungry! "I'd like something to eat."

"And the pain?"

"Still there, but the tea did help."

Lillian felt Maddy's forehead. "How's your head?"

"It feels a bit better than it did last time I woke."

"Good. Let me change your bandages, and then we'll see about getting you something to eat."

Maddy stared straight ahead as Lillian worked on her arm, or what was left of it. "You'll have to look sometime," Lillian murmured.

"I'll look when you've finished."

Barnabus came in bearing a tray, but it didn't hold food; it was a fresh poultice. Lillian accepted the tray with a nod of thanks and dismissed him, then finished dressing Maddy's wound. "Let me capture my observations before I forget them." She returned to the table and dipped a quill into the ink.

"You're keeping notes?"

"Who knows, we might need them someday. Averill can add them to our collection."

Thank goodness Maddy hadn't imagined that Lillian was capturing her emotions or writing a love letter. She would have been crushed. Of course, she hadn't imagined it because that wouldn't have been Lillian.

While Lillian was preoccupied, Maddy forced her eyes to her right arm. She felt no emotion as she stared at the stump, but her stomach roiled, and she gave in to the compulsion to reach over with her left hand and feel where her right hand and lower arm would be. Then the panic started. It was gone—really gone. She couldn't change her mind and get it back. Her body was irreversibly, fundamentally different, and so was her life.

"Are you all right?" Lillian asked quietly from the table.

"I don't know." Maddy started to lift her right arm, then covered her face with her left hand. "It'll take some getting used to."

"Of course it will."

"Lillian, I know you're trying to help, but I like it better when you're being honest."

Lillian rose and came over to peer down at Maddy. "I am being honest. It will take some getting used to."

"Maybe it's the way you said it, then, as if you know how this feels," Maddy said, still resentful. "You don't know what it feels like to look down and see half your arm gone. You sounded as if you were patting me on the head and telling me it'll be all right in the morning. Don't treat me like a child."

Lillian folded her arms. "If you think I plan to coddle you, you can forget it. Enjoy your time in bed today, because tomorrow I'll be walking you around this room."

Maddy had always managed to use the chamber pot, but it was right next to the bed. She hadn't walked much since she'd been burned. "Do you think I'll be able to?"

"We didn't cut off your legs!" Lillian exclaimed. "And I want you out of here as soon as possible. You've spent enough time in this prison already. Barnabus has found us temporary lodging in Reedwick. You'll recuperate there. I'm hoping you'll use the time to practice writing with your left hand. You'll also want to learn to dress yourself." She dropped her arms to her sides with an exasperated sigh. "Now, what do you want to eat?"

Duly humbled, Maddy drew the blanket up to her chin. "I think I can handle a bit of broth and bread. And some more of your tea, please. I feel a bit better than I did earlier, but I still need the tea."

Lillian's face softened and she knelt next to the bed. "Look at me, shouting at you. I'm sorry. I have to admit, yesterday was quite the experience. I don't think I've quite settled down from it yet."

"You did a brave thing," Maddy said.

"I wasn't the brave one. You were."

"We both were, in different ways."

"Sometimes you're too kind, Maddy." Lillian stared down at her hands.

"And you're too hard on yourself." Maddy wanted to touch her, but didn't want to roll onto what was left of her right arm. "I'm afraid that saving me means you'll have a love-struck sister on your hands, now," she said, wanting to lighten the mood. "A one-armed, love-struck sister."

"One and a half armed." Lillian lifted her head. "And I certainly hope so."

They smiled.

"Oh, I talked to the governor about the child and sent Barnabus after her," Lillian said. "I'll let him tell you about it while I prepare your tea and broth." She gently touched Maddy's cheek, then used the bed to push herself to her feet.

A minute later, Barnabus towered over her. "How are you today, Sister?"

"On the mend, thanks to you and everyone else."

He nodded. "The mistress says you'd like to hear about the child. I went to see the lady the governor told us about, but the girl wasn't there. After the governor dropped her off, she returned for one meal, but hasn't been seen since."

Maddy's heart sank. She never would have sent Emmey away if she'd known that Lillian was so close! "She has to be in Reedwick." And hopefully hadn't met with trouble.

"If the lady sees the girl again, she's promised to tell her that we're looking for her."

Realizing he must have visited the woman soon after the procedure, before knowing if Maddy would survive the night, she asked, "Who will she say is looking?"

"Friends of Sister Maddy."

"Thank you, Barnabus. Would you mind shutting the door on your way out?"

"Not at all. I'll visit with you later, Sister."

"I'll look forward to it."

After he'd gone, she threw the blanket aside and struggled to sit up, then drew a deep breath and swung her legs off the bed. Good, the pot was still nearby. Though her head floated and her legs trembled, she managed to reach and use it. Lillian just might walk her around this room tomorrow, especially since Maddy was determined to get back onto her feet as soon as possible. The sooner they moved to Reedwick, the sooner she could search for Emmey.

She'd just pulled the blanket over her legs when Lillian returned. "You're sitting up!" Lillian exclaimed. "Good." She set the tray on Maddy's lap and turned to her notes.

"Lillian?"

"What?"

"Can you hold the tray for me? Otherwise it might slide."

"Oh." Lillian moved the chair to the bedside and held the tray. "When your, uh—" She gestured at Maddy's right arm.

"Stump?"

"Yes. Perhaps when it's healed, you'll be able to use it to hold things in place."

"Perhaps." Right now, she didn't even like to look at it; she hoped her revulsion would pass. That thing hanging next to her was still her arm. "Thank you for helping," she said as she dipped the spoon into the broth, burning with shame. It hadn't bothered her when Arthur and others helped her, but for some reason Lillian's aid made her feel small and inadequate. She'd always been less capable than Lillian, and now the situation had worsened. Lillian might say she wanted a one and a half-armed sister following her around, but would that hold true when she realized that Maddy was a malflowed cripple half her age?

Did it matter? Her relationship with Lillian should be the least of her worries.

"Maddy, I have to tell you something," Lillian said, her tone sombre.

She lowered the spoon. "What is it?"

"Sophia wants you back at Merrin. You'll still go to Heath, but with a group."

"I wasn't expecting to carry on to Heath. She wouldn't want you and Barnabus away for so long." Maddy didn't add that she wanted to find Emmey and take her home, which would have them travelling away from Heath anyway.

"There's more." Lillian met her eyes. "She said you have to remain in the Order, for your protection."

Maddy rested the spoon in the bowl. "So I'm to leave one prison for another."

"Is that how you see the monastery?" Lillian asked sadly.

Was it? Before her imprisonment, Maddy had wondered how she'd offended Salbine. Now that she'd lost her hand, she could no longer afford to spend time and energy trying to fathom the unfathomable, not if she hoped to adapt. From this point forward, she was either a sister, or she wasn't. She'd left her home, joined the Order, and served in good faith. She didn't understand why she was malflowed, or why she'd spent months in a cell and literally lost part of herself. Events since leaving Merrin had only deepened her initial confusion around her relationship with Salbine.

But through it all, she'd still prayed. She'd still desired Salbine's approval. Despite her doubt, she'd still affirmed that she was a sister, when asked. She'd entertained the notion of leaving the Order, but had never truly seen herself outside it. The issue had never been that she didn't want to serve, but that she didn't know if Salbine wanted her service, or how to serve Her, if She did—an even greater problem now. If Maddy hoped to find her way, she had to start by accepting her place in the Order, despite doubting it. The word "faith" had always come easily, but she'd never understood what it demanded, until now. She closed her eyes.

Salbine, I can't spend time wondering anymore, so I'll just have to believe. You called me, and I came. I am a Salbine Sister. I'm Yours. I will discover how I'm to serve You, if it takes me the rest of my life.

Your will be done.

Maddy meant every word of her prayer. She wouldn't rest until she discovered how to serve Salbine in her condition. The same key to that answer would unlock her purpose, the reason Salbine had called her to the Order but denied her the elements. There had to be a reason. There had to be.

She opened her eyes and picked up the spoon. "I'd like to find Emmey and take her home," she said, ignoring Lillian's question.

"The child could be anywhere."

"She has to be in Reedwick."

"If we find her, we'll hire someone to take her home."

"No. I promised I'd do it." And Maddy wouldn't be satisfied that Emmey had made it home unless she was with her. "She lives in Pinewood. That's not too far out of our way."

"Sophia was clear. She wants you back in Merrin."

"Lillian, I made a promise, and I intend to keep it. If you're not comfortable making a small detour, then don't. Go back to Merrin. I'll meet you there."

Lillian barked a laugh. "If you honestly expect me to let you out of my sight before you're back behind the monastery's walls, you can forget it."

"Then you'll either come with me and Emmey, or you'll have to sling me over your horse and listen to me whine the entire way home."

"Home," Lillian echoed. "Do you mean that?"

"I certainly do." She put the spoon down and took a deep breath. "I can't take Emmey by myself. I don't even know if I can ride. I don't have a horse, for that matter. Or coin. I need your help. With everything." The enormity of what lay ahead overwhelmed her. She motioned for Lillian to take the tray and covered her eyes with her hand. When Lillian sat on the edge of the bed and pulled Maddy toward her, Maddy didn't protest.

"We're in this together," Lillian murmured, rubbing Maddy's back. "I'll be here to push and cheer you along, whether you like it or not."

"I wouldn't have it any other way." Maddy's eyes slid shut. She drifted off to sleep in Lillian's arms.

Chapter Fifteen

"HERE YOU ARE," LILLIAN SAID, BUSTLING in with a short shift, a shirt, a riding skirt, and a pair of sandals. "Arthur gave me these."

Wrapped in a blanket and perched on the edge of the bed, Maddy lifted her head. "I thought you said you'd brought me clothes from Merrin."

"Just a robe and a shift."

"I'm a sister. I should be robed." But all those buttons! "Will you robe me? I can try the buttons, but we'll be here all day. I think I can handle the shift on my own, though. I'll wear that one."

"You can't ride in your robe. Put these on for now. I'll robe you when we go out for a walk later."

"To look for Emmey?"

Lillian nodded and dropped the clothes onto the bed.

"All right." Acutely aware that Lillian was watching, Maddy stood. Since the shift didn't have buttons, she expected it to be easy, but she was mistaken. Her stump only mildly complained when Lillian helped guide it into a sleeve. Lillian had stopped applying the poultice days ago, so the bandages covering it were dry.

Maddy no longer turned away when Lillian changed the dressing. By the time she'd finally forced herself to look, her stump couldn't live up to the hideous monstrosity her imagination had created. Impatience was now her primary adversary. She wanted to learn how to do everything herself—right now!

Next, the riding skirt. It took Maddy less than a minute to drop it onto the floor, step into it, and pull it to her waist over the shift.

She turned her attention to the shirt, eyeing its buttons with trepidation. "No!" she snapped when Lillian reached for the first button. "Let me try." Five minutes later, she was still struggling to fasten the button. "Every time I'm just about to thread it in, it slips!" she said with exasperation.

"Do you want me to do it?" Lillian had already stepped toward her several times.

"I have to do at least one." She tried a new tack, pushing the buttonhole toward the button. "Ugh! That's worse than before."

"It might be easier if it fit you better."

Maddy nodded. A moment later she raised her arms to clap when the button finally went through the buttonhole and stayed. At the last moment, she lifted her left hand above her head.

"What was that?" Lillian asked, amused.

"A half-cheer. I was going to clap," Maddy said wryly, then sighed. "You might as well do the rest." She'd dress herself, in time.

Lillian made fast work of the buttons, then wrapped her travelling cloak around Maddy's shoulders and buttoned its collar. "You need it more than I do. Are you feeling all right?"

"Not perfect, but better than I have in a long time." She slipped into the pair of sandals; they were a bit big for her.

Lillian studied her. "You've put on a bit of weight, but your robe will probably dwarf you." She smiled. "We'll see how it looks. Are you ready?"

More than ready. Glad to leave the room behind, Maddy didn't stop for one last look around.

Arthur and Barnabus were waiting in the hall. "The horses are ready. You'll ride Griffin," Barnabus said to Maddy. "I'll lead him."

"What about you?"

"It's only an hour's walk to Reedwick, Sister."

"One of my friends has agreed to lend you a mare to get you to Garryglen," Arthur said to Maddy.

"Thank you, again," Barnabus said. "I promise we'll leave her with the guardsman you mentioned."

"It's the least I can do." Arthur turned to Lillian. "May I have a word with Sister Maddy alone? I can walk her to the horses."

"We'll meet you outside, then." Lillian strolled away with Barnabus.

"Reckon you'll be wanting this." Arthur led Maddy into the room across the hall from her former sickroom and pulled open a desk drawer. He handed her the letter to Lillian she'd entrusted to him. "I was under the impression it was meant to be given because you'd gone to Salbine. Since you didn't, I thought I'd hang onto it, let you deliver it yourself."

"Thank you. You did right." The sappy sentiments it contained would probably have Lillian kicking Baxter into a gallop so she could get away from Maddy as quickly as possible!

Arthur motioned for her to leave his office before him. "It'll be odd, not having you here, but I'm glad to see you go. It was a disgrace having you here in the first place, and it cost you dearly. I can't say how sorry I am."

"It wasn't your fault, Arthur. You didn't send me here."

"If another sister ever passes through this prison's gates, I'll protest loudly."

Every other sister could demonstrate her connection to Salbine. And deterred by the risk to himself and his family, Arthur would probably handle the situation in the same manner, should a sister find her way here regardless. She couldn't blame him. "I might pass through these gates again, as a visitor." The prison was only a couple of days' detour from the route to Heath. "I hope you'll receive me warmly, if I do."

"I'd welcome a visit from you, Sister." They stepped into the morning sun. "Can you let me know if you find Emmey?"

"I'll send a message through the guard."

"It'll put my mind at ease, knowing the lass is all right."

Hers too. They joined Lillian and Barnabus. Maddy nodded to Arthur. "Good-bye, Arthur."

"Good-bye, Sister." His Adam's apple bobbed. He blinked, then dropped to one knee.

After a brief moment of confusion, Maddy rested her hand on his head. She hadn't thought of blessing him. For her, their recent caretaker-and-patient relationship hadn't erased their initial one as governor and prisoner, but she didn't resent him and wished him well. "May Salbine guide you. May Salbine provide for you. May Salbine keep you."

He lifted his head. "Thank you, Sister."

Barnabus boosted her onto Griffin as Lillian mounted Baxter. From the hill where the prison rested, Maddy could see Reedwick below them. She watched its details gradually emerge as they walked down the dirt path.

"Can you slow down a bit?" she said to Barnabus when they passed a group of children playing among the travellers' tents lining the road into town. No sign of Emmey. Alert for any sign of her young friend, Maddy glanced up every alleyway and checked every doorway, until they stopped in front of a two-storey stone house not far from the market.

"A bit noisy, but it was the best I could do on short notice," Barnabus said as he reached for Maddy.

"I think I can dismount myself." She almost managed it, but lost her balance when she tried to steady herself with a right hand that wasn't there. Barnabus caught her and didn't let go until both her feet were planted firmly on the ground. "The things I do without thinking are the things that give me the most trouble," Maddy murmured, more to herself than anyone else.

"You'll have to change the way you automatically do them," Lillian said as she glanced around.

"We have to use the stables of a nearby inn, Mistress. I've already arranged it with the innkeeper. I thought we'd drop you here, so Sister Maddy can rest." Barnabus took Baxter's reins from Lillian. "I'll take the horses over."

"I don't want to rest, I want to look for Emmey," Maddy said.

Lillian frowned. "Are you sure?"

"Yes," she insisted, unwilling to admit that she did indeed need a nap.

"All right, then." Lillian unhooked a bag from Ticky's saddle, accepted a key from Barnabus, and unlocked the door. "I would have preferred no steps," she said over her shoulder as they entered the common room, "but since we needed somewhere on such short notice, we couldn't be choosy. At least it's furnished."

Maddy eyed the staircase rising to the second floor with dismay. If she climbed those steps to the bedchamber, she'd definitely need a lie-down. "Why don't you robe me here?"

Lillian set the bag on a table, then opened it and pulled out a deep red robe with billowy sleeves. "It's a bit creased, but it'll smooth out."

"Undoing buttons is much easier than doing them up," Maddy said as she unbuttoned the shirt. She stepped into the robe and let Lillian lift it to her shoulders. This time she didn't need help with the sleeves, and stood patiently while Lillian fastened the robe's buttons.

Lillian stood back. A smile spread across her face. "It's a bit big on you now, but you look wonderful. A Salbine robe suits you."

Maddy looked down at herself. A lump formed in her throat. "I'll grow into it again."

"I'm sure you will," Lillian said quietly. She tossed a pair of sandals to the floor. "These are yours, so they'll fit you better."

Maddy stepped into them, tutting when the movement made the robe's right sleeve flop. It looked silly. "Can we pin the sleeve to the robe?"

Lillian grimaced. "If we do, you won't be able to move your right arm very much."

"Can we pin it up?"

"Let me put a quick stitch in it," Lillian said, turning to rummage in the bag. She shook her head. "The needle and thread are in another bag. So are the pins."

"We'll do it later, then," Maddy said, anxious to continue her search for Emmey. "Let's go."

"We have to wait for Barnabus. He won't be long." Lillian slipped her arm around Maddy's shoulders and squeezed her. "And don't overdo it. I know you want to find this girl, but you won't be much use to her if you make yourself ill."

Unfortunately Lillian was to Maddy's right. Maddy tentatively pressed her arm against Lillian's lower back. "Can you feel that?"

"Of course I can. Most of your arm's still there."

True. They'd cut below her elbow. "If you want to hold my hand, you'll have to make sure you're on my left."

"This is fine," Lillian said firmly. "More than fine."

They dropped their arms when Barnabus walked in with their remaining bags. Maddy barely gave him enough time to set the bags next to the door before she urged him and Lillian out onto the road.

An hour later, discouraged and tired, she reluctantly agreed to return to the house.

"Everyone nearby is looking out for her now," Lillian said.

"But she could be anywhere," Maddy said, grateful for Lillian's steadying hand as she slowly climbed the steps. She sighed. "I suppose it was stupid of me to expect to spot her the moment I rode into Reedwick." Now she worried they'd never find Emmey at all.

"You're tired. You'll feel more optimistic after a rest."

Lillian lowered Maddy into a chair in the upstairs hallway before popping into all the rooms. "Four bedchambers," she declared. "Barnabus outdid himself. Here, we'll put you into the nearest one."

Exhausted, Maddy lay on the bed without disrobing. "There's enough room here for you," she said to Lillian. "Why don't you have a nap with me?"

"I'm not really tired, but I'll lie with you for a bit."

Eyes closed, Maddy heard the door shut. She opened them when the bed creaked to see Lillian staring at the ceiling. The empty inches between them worried her. "If a bard was telling our tale, we'd share a passionate afternoon together now," she said, hoping to break the tension.

Lillian grinned. "If a bard was telling our tale, we would have been rolling around while your arm was still bandaged with the poultice."

Maddy burst into laughter, and couldn't stop. Lillian laughed along with her, both women clutching their stomachs. When she'd calmed down and wiped the tears from her eyes, Maddy turned to Lillian. "I hope there's a passionate afternoon or evening in our future, when I'm feeling more myself," she said softly.

Lillian drew back in mock astonishment. "Only one?" She eyed Maddy's arm, then inched toward it and leaned gently in to Maddy. "That doesn't hurt, does it?"

"No. I like you on that side, too. My hand's free."

"Oh, yes, your left hand." Lillian's eyes glinted mischievously. "It'll have to learn to do what your right hand used to do in the bedchamber. I'm looking forward to that. I want you to know that, when you're ready, I'll make myself available so you can practice. It's the least I can do."

"You will, will you?" Maddy playfully slapped Lillian's shoulder. "So you'll be there to cheer me on when I light the lamp, and make the bed, and stoke the fire?"

Lillian arched an eyebrow.

"I know there are four bedchambers, but why don't we share this one? I'm sure Barnabus won't be scandalized."

"Barnabus?" Lillian snorted. "Of course he won't. He's been a defender too many years to be scandalized. He probably knew about us not long after we did."

Us. Maddy liked the sound of that.

"And I'm sure he knows much more than we'd ever want to know about the nocturnal comings and goings at the monastery."

"It's settled, then." She met Lillian's eyes. "I'm feeling stronger every day. I'll soon be myself."

Lillian brushed Maddy's lips with hers. "Don't push yourself on my account. We have plenty of time." She swallowed. "I hope?"

Maddy smiled. "We do."

Lillian returned her smile, then lay back. Maddy carefully rolled onto her right arm and snuggled into her. She drifted off, content to be with Lillian but worried about Emmey.

"I THINK WE should go back," Lillian said, noting Maddy's drawn face and the perspiration on her brow. The increasing weight Maddy put on Lillian's supporting right arm over the last fifteen minutes had tipped her off.

A child ran up and smiled at Barnabus. He reached into his purse and handed her a coin.

Maddy shook her head. "No."

Lillian inwardly sighed. Barnabus had come up with the idea of handing coins to children. Word had quickly spread about the kind man with the two sisters, and children now approached them wherever they went. But no Emmey, despite searching for over a week and losing count of the number of children who'd raced away with coins clutched in their dirty fists.

Maddy didn't tire as quickly as she had and her colour had returned. Barring a setback, she'd be ready for the journey to Merrin in a few days' time. But would she be willing to go? They couldn't search forever. The child might have left Reedwick—or worse.

"Let's try around Lila's again tonight," Maddy suggested, referring to the governor's friend who cared for orphans. "We could have just missed her last time."

"All right." Lillian caught Barnabus's eye; his thoughts probably matched hers. "And since we'll do that, we should really go back now and have supper."

Barnabus nodded. "I'll pick up a couple of pies from the baker on the corner."

"Oh yes, please!" Maddy said, her enthusiasm pleasing Lillian.

They returned to where they'd tied the horses and trotted them back to the stables near their temporary lodging. "Barnabus, I just want to nip to the market to see if I can trade for some herbs," Lillian said.

"I can get what you need, Mistress."

"No, I don't want to delay supper. I'd prefer that you pick up the pies."

"I don't think I can face the market," Maddy said as Barnabus filled the tiny purse Lillian pulled from her pocket.

"Come with me to the baker, Sister. It will only take a minute and then we'll get you settled by the fire, "Barnabus said.

"Do that, Maddy. I won't be long." Especially since she hoped to avoid speaking to anyone but the merchant with the herbs she wanted. If her stomach wasn't grumbling and Maddy didn't look so worn out, she would have sent Barnabus.

The market was only around the corner. Lillian spotted a stall with dried herbs close to the road and made a beeline for it. "Fresh herbs," the toothless merchant shouted, sweeping his arm above a selection of flowers and plants native to the area and recently harvested.

"Actually, I'm interested in dried herbs. Do you have any chamomile?" A nice hot cup of chamomile tea would hit the spot before bed. "And how about sage? Valerian root? Horsetail?"

"You're in luck!" the merchant exclaimed, pointing above him. Wanting to complete her business with him as quickly as possible, Lillian didn't bother to haggle and soon had several bunches dangling from her fingers.

"Excuse me," a little voice said, just as Lillian reached the road. She glanced around, then down. The scruffiest, skinniest wisp of a child stared up at her. "I have to tell you something," the girl said.

"You do, do you?" Lillian transferred two herb bunches from her right hand to her left and dug into her pocket for a loose coin. This couldn't be the child Maddy was seeking; she was too small to be eight and had brown hair. "Here you go, child." She forced the coin into the girl's hand. Where was Barnabus when she needed him? "Now run along."

"I don't want your coin!" the child screeched, giving Lillian such a start that she almost dropped the herbs. "I have to tell you something."

"What do you have to tell me?" Lillian said, wondering what the child was after. If a bunch of riffraff thought to rob her while she was distracted, they were in for quite the shock.

"It's about Sister Maddy, of Merrin."

Lillian's breath caught in her throat. She studied the girl with renewed interest. Her hair *might* be blonde, under all the muck. Was this Emmey, or had the child overheard someone mention Maddy? They'd roamed the streets for over a week and identified themselves to numerous folk.

The girl pointed to Lillian's hands. "I promised that if I saw someone with hands like yours, I'd tell what happened to her."

"Very well. I'm listening."

"I was in the prison, and the Miss, she was put in the same cell as me because they didn't believe she was a sister, even though she was," the girl said, twisting her ripped dress with one hand while holding the coin in the other.

"The Miss?"

The child rolled her eyes. "The sister! And then we were in the cell for a long time. And then one day we were having a bath, and Madison told us to get out. And when we left, there was smoke. And then a man was going to hit me. The Miss stopped him, but she burned her hand."

Strange. When Maddy had recounted how she'd received the burns, she hadn't mentioned saving the child. She'd said only that a prisoner had attacked her.

The girl lowered her head. Her shoulders shook. "And then . . . she got sick." Lillian had to strain to hear her. "And she died. The Miss died."

To Lillian's astonishment, the child, who had to be Emmey, collapsed onto the stones and sobbed. "I wanted to be with her when she died, but she sent me away. I miss her."

Unable to remain indifferent in the face of the child's distress, Lillian bent over. "You must be Emmey."

Emmey's hands went to her mouth. "How do you know my name?" she asked, wide-eyed.

"Sister Maddy told me."

"You saw her before she died?"

"She didn't die. She's looking for you." Lillian thought the child's eyes couldn't open any wider, but eyes as wide as saucers stared back at her. "The Miss isn't dead? Where is she, you have to take me to her!"

"Not far. Come on." Lillian straightened and started to walk.

"I told her they'd let her go." Emmey leaped to her feet and scampered after Lillian. "But she said she'd die. She wouldn't lie to me." She gasped. "Did they let her go because you came for her, and she decided she didn't want to die in the prison, and so you brought her here and she'll die soon?"

"No. She's not going to die." Lillian glanced at her right hand, wondering what kept bumping into it. Her jaw tightened. Emmey wanted to hold her hand. Lillian grasped one of her fingers, all she was willing to do.

"Are you from Merrin too, because your hands are the same as the Miss's and it would make sense that you'd come for her, if you're from Merrin."

"Yes, I'm from Merrin," Lillian said tersely, quickening her pace.

"Are you like the Miss, or can you, um . . . do elements?"

"I can draw the elements." In fact, she could feel a fireball coming on right now.

"Because the Miss, she couldn't, and that's why they put her in the cell with me. They thought she was a liar. But she wasn't."

Mercifully, they'd reached the house. When Lillian stepped over the threshold, Maddy was sitting in front of the fire, her back to the door, and Barnabus was setting the table. He turned toward Lillian and raised his eyebrows.

"I've brought a guest," Lillian announced.

Maddy looked over her shoulder. Her mouth dropped open and she shot to her feet. "Emmey!"

Emmey squealed and ran toward her, but then stopped dead.

Maddy frowned. "What's the matter?"

"You look different."

"Oh. You mean my arm."

"Your clothes, Miss."

"My robe? You've seen me in a robe before."

"It was dirty. That one's pretty," Emmey said solemnly.

"Why, thank you." Maddy crouched and held out her arms. "Come here."

Emmey didn't need further encouragement. She leaped into Maddy, making Lillian wince. "It's so good to see you," Maddy said, tightening her arms around Emmey.

Lillian didn't know how Maddy could stand to hold the girl. Now that they were inside, she could smell Emmey all the way over at the door. And Maddy's robe! It was probably filthy now.

Maddy sat back on her haunches and smiled at Emmey. "We've been looking for you. Where did you go? Why didn't you stay with Lila?"

"Because they wanted me to nick."

"Who?"

"The others."

"The other children?"

Emmey nodded. "I didn't want to do it, and I knew you wouldn't want me to do it, Miss, so I ran away and didn't go back."

"What have you been doing for food?"

"I find scraps, Miss. And sometimes I get a handout. And I found a place to sleep, in an old shed, but then I heard about the sisters. They said one of them was Sister Maddy, but I didn't believe them, because you were dead, except now you aren't. But I remembered what you told me, Miss. It took me a long time to find a sister, but I did, and I told her about you."

"You told Lillian." Maddy looked over Emmey's shoulder and beckoned to Lillian. "Lillian, come over here so I can properly introduce you."

Lillian resisted the urge to roll her eyes. She handed the herbs to Barnabus on her way to Maddy's side.

Maddy winked at her. "Lillian, this is Emmey. Emmey, Lillian."

Emmey stared at her. "So that's Lillian?" She looked at Maddy. "You told me she was old."

Lillian's nostrils flared.

"Old*er*," Maddy said firmly. "I definitely said older."

Maddy had told this . . . scruffy child about her? What else had she said?

"And that's Barnabus," Maddy said, pointing to him.

Barnabus inclined his head. "Most pleased to meet you, Emmey."

Emmey stuck her thumb in her mouth and shyly said hello, then turned her attention back to Maddy. "What's wrong with your arm, Miss? How come your sleeve is sewed up?"

"Well, you remember how badly my hand was burned?"

Emmey's head bobbed. "You said you'd die."

"And I would have, if Lillian and Barnabus hadn't arrived when they did. But the only way to save me was to get rid of what was hurting me."

"You mean you don't got your hand no more?"

"No, I don't, and part of my arm is gone, too."

"Can I feel it?"

In response, Maddy held out her right arm. A coin clanged to the floor when Emmey reached out and opened her fist. She bent down, picked it up, and held it in front of her eyes. "Can I keep this?"

Maddy peered at it. "Where did you get it?"

Emmey pointed to Lillian.

"Well, Lillian, can she keep it?" Maddy asked.

"I suppose so," Lillian muttered, taking a few steps toward the table in the hope that the aroma of the pies would overpower the smell coming from the other direction. She winced when Emmey shrieked and jumped up and down. Forget the chamomile tea; her head would soon be in need of lime flower.

"Do you want me to hang onto it for you?" Maddy asked.

Emmey dropped the coin into Maddy's left hand. "Ooh," she breathed, fingering the sleeve of Maddy's robe. "It's so smooth."

"It's silk."

"So smooth," Emmey whispered again. "Does it hurt?" she asked, moving her hand up to Maddy's stump and rubbing it through the sleeve.

"No, it doesn't." Maddy held up her left hand. "But now I have to learn to do with this hand what I used to do with that hand. Perhaps we can practice our letters together!"

"Your letters? Can she even write?" Lillian asked.

"She can read—can't you, Emmey."

Emmey's answering nod surprised Lillian.

Barnabus cleared his throat. "Begging your pardon, Sister, but the pies are cooling."

"Sorry." When Maddy pushed herself up and almost lost her balance, Lillian grasped her shoulders to steady her. "Thank you," Maddy murmured. She patted Emmey's head. "I bet you're hungry."

"Yes!"

"So am I, but I think we'd better give you a quick bath before we eat."

Lillian silently approved, glad to see that Maddy hadn't completely taken leave of her senses the moment she'd seen the girl.

"Lillian, why don't you and Barnabus eat while I help Emmey bathe? We can warm one of the pies again."

"You'll need help filling the tub," Barnabus said.

"I have a helper." Maddy ruffled Emmey's hair. "And after supper, we'll go to the market and see about some clothes. I'd make some for you, but I can't sew. Not anymore."

"I can help you, Miss."

"So can I," Lillian said, determined not to be outdone. "I can thread the needle for you and hold the cloth."

"That would hardly be me doing it," Maddy said. "But I appreciate the offers. Now, there's a tub in the kitchen and a well out back. We have work to do."

"Will you do my hair, Miss, and my back?"

"I certainly will."

Emmey clapped her hands. "And this time we won't have to go back to a cell."

"No, we won't." Maddy took Emmey's hand and led her into the kitchen.

Feeling left out, Lillian sat at the table and poured herself a glass of cider. As she ate her pie, bursts of chatter from the kitchen announced the arrival and heating of each bucket of water. The splashing, giggling, and incessant prattling started when she was enjoying her after-supper cider. She rubbed her temples. Barnabus refilled his glass, something he rarely did. He sipped the cider and pressed his lips together.

"How hard can we push the horses?" she asked wearily, not looking forward to weeks of travel with a child whose mouth was perpetually in motion.

Barnabus shook his head. "Pushing them too hard will only slow us down in the end."

"Then it will be a long ride to Pinewood."

"Pinewood?"

"That's where the child lives." When he still looked confused, she realized he hadn't been privy to Maddy's desire to see Emmey safely in her ma's arms. "Maddy wants to take the child home."

His face darkened and he set his glass down. "The abbess was clear. We're to return to Merrin. You haven't agreed to her plan?"

So far, she'd avoided committing herself. "No, I haven't."

"It's not that I don't want to help the child home . . ."

Since Lillian shared his feelings on the matter, she silently completed his position for him. *I just don't want to take her myself.* "I agreed to hire someone to escort the child, had Maddy not survived."

Barnabus pounced on that possibility. "We'll easily find someone in Garryglen."

"I'm not sure that will satisfy her. I don't think she'll trust anyone else to do it, now that she can."

"We'll spend the coin and hire a group of men from one of the reputable guilds," Barnabus suggested. "The guild wouldn't dare risk the wrath of the sisters, nor would it want its reputation tarnished. But to ease the sister's mind, we'll insist that the local tax collector must send us a message vouching for the girl's safe return. We'll include it in the contract."

Lillian picked up her glass. "That sounds reasonable." A loud shriek from the kitchen made her jump. Cider spilled onto her sleeve and the tablecloth. Groaning, she dabbed up the mess with a napkin. "I'll broach the subject with Maddy again," she said to Barnabus, then drained her glass and reached for the cider jug.

Chapter Sixteen

Maddy shut the door to her and Lillian's bedchamber and smiled at Lillian. "She's asleep. I had to tell her three stories tonight. I think she's excited about tomorrow."

Lillian had already disrobed and was sitting on the edge of the bed. "I'm glad we'll finally be heading back."

Maddy had mixed feelings about it. "I'm not looking forward to Garryglen. I wish we could go around it."

"We have to find out what happened to the horses. And don't you want to see that magistrate?"

"No, I don't."

Lillian gaped. "You don't want that bastard to see what he did to you?"

"What would that accomplish? It won't give me back my hand, or the time I spent in that cell."

"He owes you an apology. He should get down on his knees in front of all the folk who jeered at you and beg for your forgiveness."

The last thing Maddy wanted was another spectacle. "I can't be angry with him, Lillian. My story sounded so far-fetched that I can't blame him for not believing me. I kept saying folk outside the monastery see sisters and drawing the elements as one and the same, but none of you would listen."

"You don't blame him because you see yourself as less of a sister than everyone else. He was wrong to send you to prison. He should have inquired of Merrin, not judged you guilty and thrown you into a cell to rot."

Still standing, Maddy picked up the cup of chamomile tea Lillian had prepared and sipped it. "I did see myself as less of a sister at the time," she said quietly, "but not now." Now she had to figure out how she could contribute to the community despite being doubly crippled. But she no longer doubted her place in the Order. Leaving it would only have added another regret to turn over in her mind when she was melancholy. What would she have done with herself? Even more rudderless, she would have drifted. The monastery was home. The sisters, her family. There had to be a purpose behind everything that had happened to her; she just had to discover it. And she'd have a much better chance of doing so among those who loved Salbine.

"If I hadn't ended up in that cell, I wouldn't have met Emmey." She wasn't surprised when Lillian's face tightened.

"About Emmey." Lillian clasped her hands on her lap and fidgeted. "Sophia said we're to take you back to Merrin. I know you promised Emmey you'd take her home, but we can hire men to escort her—good, reputable men. We'll spare no expense, hire men from the most reputable guild."

"No," Maddy said flatly.

"Barnabus said we can ask that a message be sent, vouching that she returned home safely. We can make it a condition of the contract."

"No."

"Maddy, we're supposed to take you right back to the monastery."

"That's not what this is about!" Maddy shouted, then lowered her voice, hoping she hadn't awakened Emmey. "You just don't care whether Emmey makes it home or not. So stop pretending you're concerned about the abbess's wishes. She doesn't even know when to expect us. And if she knew about Emmey, I'm sure she wouldn't mind the short detour."

"I think I know her better than you do. She is my sister."

Something Maddy sometimes found bloody hard to believe.

"She was very clear," Lillian added.

"Yes! She wants me back at the monastery, and that's where I'm going. She's always seemed like a caring person to me. I doubt she'll begrudge me a little side trip to take Emmey home. You're the one who'd like us to dump Emmey with strangers in Garryglen and forget she ever existed." With the air so heavy between them, Maddy didn't want to sit next to Lillian. She sank into the chair near the fire, well away from the bed, and glared at her. "Emmey isn't some random child I took pity on. We shared a cell, a wretched existence, for months. She kept me sane. And I care very much about her. I know you can't stand her, but I'd hoped that you'd help me take her home because you care about me."

"Well, that's hardly fair, is it, framing it like that? Doing what you want means I care about you and not doing what you want means I don't. Am I supposed to help you jump off a cliff, too?"

"That's not what I meant."

Lillian folded her arms. "Then what did you mean?"

"That you'd want to support me in this because you understand how important it is to me. I'm not asking you to do anything unreasonable."

"But I don't understand it. How can I? I wasn't in that prison cell with you." Lillian heaved a sigh. "And I don't hate Emmey. I'm not comfortable around children. I don't know what to say to her—not that I'd be able to get a word in edgewise. She never shuts up. And she's always jumping around and asking questions. I don't know how you stand it."

Maddy's shoulders relaxed as the tension drained away. "She's a child, Lillian. She has lots of energy. She's curious. And bright. I see you in her." She stifled a laugh at Lillian's horrified face. "Perhaps you should try talking to her. Whenever she talks to you, you dismiss her."

"No, I don't."

"Yes, you do. You give her one-word answers, and usually while looking like a sourpuss."

"She can't be that bright, because she doesn't seem to get the message," Lillian muttered.

"Or perhaps she keeps trying because she understands that you're special to me," Maddy said, trying not to sound reproachful.

"I don't see how. Since she's arrived, we've barely spent any time together. It's, 'Emmey, let's go to the market. Emmey, let's practice our letters. Emmey, let's hang the wash. Emmey, let's go see the horses.'"

Was that what it was about? Jealousy? Maddy bit back remarks meant to tease; they'd only add oil to the fire. Plus, she'd erred. She'd assumed that Lillian knew she was welcome to join her and Emmey in all their activities. But despite her blustering, Lillian was shy, and her discomfort around children only worsened the situation. Expecting her to take the initiative with Emmey had been a mistake. Lillian wouldn't participate unless invited, and conversing with Emmey might be easier if they were busy, not staring at each other. Maddy wanted Lillian's support, but realized she hadn't been supporting Lillian. "I'm sorry. I know I'm spending a lot of time with her, but I won't be with her for long. You and I . . ." Should she say it? *We have the rest of our lives together.* She chickened out. "I want to spend time with you, as well as Emmey. Next time we practice our letters, would you help us? It will be more fun if you come up with what we should write."

"I suppose I could," Lillian mumbled.

"And will you think about taking Emmey home? You don't have to decide until we're ready to leave Garryglen. I assume we'll stop overnight there."

"Barnabus won't like it."

Maddy sensed victory, but didn't let on. "Well, you think about it. And I am sorry I've been neglecting you. I didn't mean to." When Lillian's face softened, Maddy abandoned the chair to join her on the bed, making sure to sit to her right so she could pat Lillian's leg. "This probably isn't the best time to bring this up, but Emmey has to ride with you to Garryglen."

"Barnabus already mentioned it to me."

She silently thanked Barnabus. "I know I've been practising on the mare and can ride on my own, but I'm not confident enough to have Emmey ride with me." She almost said, *Perhaps when we leave Garryglen*, but stopped herself in time. "I've had a good talk with her, so she knows to behave and not to talk your ear off. No throwing her off Baxter along the way."

Lillian's eyes narrowed. "It would be too easy for you to find her. If I wanted to get rid of her, I'd be much sneakier about it."

Maddy rested her head on Lillian's shoulder. "I know you would. And I know you wouldn't."

"No, I wouldn't. She might drive me around the bend, but I'd never leave her to fend for herself."

Nor would Lillian hire men to take her home. She just hadn't admitted that to herself yet, but she would. Maddy was sure of it.

LILLIAN WAVED TO Maddy and Emmey, surprised to see them waiting outside the inn. Since arriving in Garryglen the previous afternoon, Maddy had refused to leave their rented room. "Sorry we took so long," Lillian said.

Maddy shielded her eyes and looked past Lillian. "That's not ours."

Leading a chestnut horse, Barnabus stepped to Lillian's side. "No, it isn't."

"Bastard didn't have them," Lillian said. "They were long gone from the inn by the time he sent men to retrieve your belongings. Bloody savages must have made off with what they could the moment you and Jonathan were taken from the inn."

"It's fortunate I hadn't brought any sentimental items with me," Maddy said as Emmey reached up to stroke the chestnut's nose.

"He very generously compensated us for them," Barnabus said.

Lillian snorted. "After we'd told him he'd condemned a sister to life in prison and that she's now maimed as a result? He was practically throwing coin at us. The bastard's lucky you didn't want him harmed."

Maddy shook her head. "It wouldn't have accomplished anything. I want to leave it behind, get on with my life."

"I know." If not for Maddy's wishes, the useless bastard's life would have ended today, and no funeral pyre would have been lit for him. They would have swept him up from the floor. "And now you can. Barnabus has a pardon and an apology in his bag."

"Did he give you the horse, too?"

"We traded for him," Barnabus said. "He'll make a fine Salbine horse, but unfortunately he isn't one now. He could throw the sister if you draw, Mistress."

"Yes, well." Lillian pointed to her left. "Maddy, we passed a street vendor, two corners down. He has jellies. Why don't you take Emmey and see if she wants anything?"

Maddy gave Lillian a suspicious look. "You want me to take Emmey—"

"I'd like a word with Barnabus. Alone."

"Oh. I see. Emmey, let's go see this vendor."

Emmey's face lit up. "Can I have a jelly, Miss?"

Maddy took Emmey's hand. "You certainly can. I might have one too." She met Lillian's eyes before heading for the vendor.

When they were out of earshot, Lillian shifted position so she could keep her eye on Maddy while talking to Barnabus. "I'd like you to ride this horse and let Maddy ride Griffin."

"I don't see how that will help. I'm not immune to injury."

"No, but you won't be with us, so you won't have to worry about me drawing."

Barnabus's brow furrowed. "What do you mean, Mistress?"

"I'm going with Maddy to take Emmey home."

His face clouded. "The abbess was clear. I thought we'd hire men."

"Maddy doesn't want that, and she already has too much to worry about without also worrying about the girl. I know we'll be disobeying the abbess, so I'm sending you back to Merrin now. I've prepared a letter for her that explains what we're doing and that we won't be long."

"You want me to carry this letter to the abbess," Barnabus stated flatly.

Lillian nodded.

He blew out some air. "I'll go with you, and face the abbess's wrath later."

"No. The abbess sent you with me so you could," Lillian waved her hand around, "negotiate on our behalf. Maddy can do that. She's good with folk. And we've accomplished what we set out to do. There's no need for you to remain with us and earn the abbess's displeasure." Lillian watched him ponder his path, hoping he'd agree to return to the monastery. Everything she'd said was the truth, but she'd left out one detail: that she wanted to travel with Maddy alone, wanted private time with her before they reached the monastery.

Since leaving the prison, their conversations had rarely gone beyond trivialities and Emmey. It was next to impossible to have a private conversation with Barnabus and Emmey around, and Maddy was usually worn out by the time she came to bed. After they'd returned Emmey to her ma, it would be just the two of them. Lillian yearned to know how Maddy was feeling and how she'd reached the conclusion that her place was in the Order, considering her uncertainty when she'd left Merrin. Perhaps she was selfish, but Lillian wanted Maddy to herself before their former lives at the monastery swallowed them up again.

"I suppose the abbess will start to worry if we don't return soon, though we could send her a message," Barnabus said.

"Or you can simply carry one."

Barnabus still seemed unsure. He stroked his beard. "I suppose you have a point when you say we've completed our task. I believe the abbess mainly sent me to negotiate for the sister's freedom, if she lived."

"If we'd needed to go to that bastard to get her out of prison, I assure you the negotiations would have been very short," Lillian said through clenched teeth. "He would either have immediately signed documents for her release, or whoever took over after his death would have."

Barnabus couldn't keep the amusement out of his face. "I can't say I would have disapproved, Mistress, though I would have advised restraint."

Lillian grunted.

"If I return to Merrin and you and the sister meet misfortune, the abbess will never forgive me."

"You know I can handle any trouble, and would be the one to do so, even if you're with us." The primary role of defenders was to protect the mages as they drew. They also stepped in if the mages tired, though the latter would only occur during lengthy battles—the sort waged during war, not with bandits along country roads.

"You could be injured." The second reason defenders would step in. Again, important during war, not important when dealing with a group of ruffians Lillian could take down in seconds.

"You know that's highly unlikely, Barnabus. The abbess didn't send you to protect me. She sent you to speak for me."

He surrendered. "Very well. We'll pack the horses after lunch and go our separate ways. We could ride together until Leaton, but you'll reach Pinewood sooner if you take the eastern route."

"Yes, we'll do that."

Barnabus tipped his head toward the horse. "I'll take him to the stables."

Lillian nodded and walked toward the vendor's stall she'd suggested to Maddy. She met Maddy and Emmey strolling toward her, devouring a couple of jellies. "You'll have to wash," Maddy was saying to Emmey. "I think most of yours is on your hands and face! Oh look, here's Lillian." She searched Lillian's face. "Everything all right?"

"Barnabus and I were just discussing what time to leave. We'll ride after lunch."

"We're not staying to visit the guilds?" Maddy said slowly.

"No. He's heading back to the monastery to let the abbess know that we're taking Emmey home. We'll head for Pinewood."

Lillian's legs felt like jellies when Maddy beamed at her and murmured, "Thank you." It was a good thing Pinewood was in the general direction of home. Lillian would have followed Maddy to the other end of the world, to see that smile.

Chapter Seventeen

LILLIAN POINTED TO HER LEFT AND shouted over her shoulder, "Lake. Down there." They were all badly in need of a wash. She slowed Baxter to a walk and waited for Maddy to draw even with her. "And under those trees looks inviting."

"I see a stream," Emmey said, twisting around to face Maddy.

Maddy smiled at her. "The horses will like that." She turned to Lillian. "We still have a few more hours of light, but let's stop anyway. I feel as if I have dust underneath my eyelids, and I wouldn't mind a relaxing evening around a fire."

Lillian agreed. Since leaving Garryglen, they'd ridden until last light most days, often laying out their rolls and tumbling into them right after a late supper. They weren't in a hurry to reach Pinewood—at least Maddy wasn't—and they weren't pushing the horses too hard; they trotted more often than not. But the monastery beckoned. Neither of them wanted to test Sophia's patience by meandering back to Merrin. "All right. We'll lay our heads here tonight." They rode to the trees and dismounted.

"Why don't you two go wash up?" Maddy said.

"We can go together."

As Lillian expected, Maddy shook her head. "No, you go ahead. I want to pray."

"Do you need a fire, Miss?"

"Not yet, no. And put shoes on, Emmey. It looks like you'll have to go down a rocky path." Maddy frowned when Emmey groaned, "I know you hate wearing shoes, but you'd hate cutting your feet even more."

"I suppose so," Emmey grumbled.

Lillian pulled her robe from one of Ticky's bags, preferring it to her travel clothes if they were going to lounge around for hours. "We won't be long," she said to Maddy. "Come on, Emmey."

"What are you doing?" Emmey asked when Lillian stopped at the top of the slope above the lake, turned back to the camp, and drew air to shield Maddy.

"Nothing." When she turned to face the lake, her foot sent a stone skittering down the slope. "It looks like Maddy was right. Be careful." She tucked her robe under her arm and didn't protest when Emmey grabbed her hand.

"Why won't the Miss ever come with us?" Emmey asked as they carefully made their way down the path. "She always says no."

"I think she's shy about her arm."

"But we've seen it!"

Not when Maddy was naked. She rarely allowed Lillian to see her in her shift, let alone naked. Lillian hadn't seen her naked since their last morning at the prison.

Emmey frowned up at Lillian. "She's being silly."

"No, she isn't, and don't you dare say that to her. She just needs time to—" Emmey's feet went out from under her. Lillian pulled her up before her arse hit the ground. The soap Emmey had been carrying rolled down the slope and plopped into the water. "Oh dear," Lillian murmured.

"We'll find it," Emmey said, nonplussed.

Lillian tightened her grip on Emmey's hand. "Right, let's watch where we're going, shall we? We're almost there."

They undressed at the bottom of the slope and left their clothes on a large flat rock beside the path. Lillian waded in first and hugged herself. "It's a bit chilly." And deeper than she'd expected, so close to land. "Walk slowly to me, Emmey."

By the time Emmey reached Lillian's side, the water was up to her chin. Lillian nudged her back toward the path, until the water was about chest-level. "You'll have to bathe here. Don't come in any farther."

Her heart leaped into her mouth when Emmey suddenly plunged beneath the water. "Emmey?" She was about to hold her nose and go under when Emmey burst from the lake and triumphantly held up the soap. "Do you think you can warn me next time?" Lillian snapped, her heart pounding.

"I can swim!"

"Famous last words, my dear."

Emmey's brow furrowed.

"Why don't you wash up while I go for a paddle?"

"Will you do my back?"

"You're old enough to do your own back."

"Aw . . . please?"

"No. And don't swim after me. Stay where your head's above water." Lillian turned away and shook her head. Maddy indulged the child too much.

The water felt pleasant now. She leisurely swam in circles, pleased that the lake naturally confined Emmey to the area near the path. Every so often she glanced Emmey's way, to make sure she was all right. Maddy would never forgive her if something happened to the child. When Emmey beckoned to her, Lillian groaned and swam over.

"I'm finished." Emmey handed her the soap. "Do you want me to do your back?"

"No, I don't. The last thing I need is your grubby little hands all over my back."

"They're clean!" Emmey shrieked.

Lillian ignored her and waded away.

"I'm getting out," Emmey called after her.

"Fine, but don't leave without me." As she washed her arms, Lillian checked to see if Emmey had obeyed her. Emmey was sitting next to their clothes on the rock, letting the sun dry her skin. Good. But how would she keep Emmey busy while Maddy was bathing? Have her water the horses, perhaps, or collect twigs for a fire?

She washed her chest, then glanced Emmey's way again. The rock was empty! Emmey was climbing the slope—with Lillian's clothes! That little rascal! Lillian effortlessly did what most mages could only dream of doing: despite already maintaining an air shield, she drew another element and then transformed it. Water gushed from the top of the slope. Emmey turned around and started to head back down. Suddenly the water froze. Her feet slipped from under her. She slid down the path on her behind and fell into the lake with a splash.

There, that will teach her! Lillian regretted that her clothes had also gone under, but no matter. She held her nose and dunked underwater to wet her hair. "You'd better find all my clothes," she shouted when she could breathe again.

No response.

Annoyed, she twisted toward the slope to shout again. Emmey wasn't there! She hadn't surfaced! Adrenaline coursed through Lillian. Blast it, bloody blast it! "Emmey!" She dropped the soap, raced to where Emmey had fallen into the lake, and was just about to dive under when Emmey leaped from the water with Lillian's robe in her hand. "Ta-da!"

"You bugger!" Lillian sputtered.

Emmey covered her mouth. "Oh, I don't think you're supposed to say that word."

"I'll say whatever I bloody-well feel like saying! Do you know how much you frightened me?" Her hands still shook.

"I told you I could swim! I can hold my breath for a long time, too."

"I don't care!" Lillian snatched her robe from Emmey's hand. "Find the rest of my clothes. Now!" She stomped out of the lake and examined her robe. Soaked! And the same would be true of her shift and travelling clothes. How long until Pinewood? Grimacing, she struggled into the wet robe, not wanting to climb the rocky path naked. Fortunately Emmey hadn't taken her shoes. "Hurry up!" she snapped when Emmey handed her a wet shift and riding skirt.

Minutes later, Emmey emerged from the lake with a limp shirt. "We better be careful climbing back up," she said. "Water could come down again."

Lillian looked at her in surprise. "Where do you think the water came from?"

Emmey thought a moment, then shrugged. "There must be a waterfall, but I didn't see one. Doesn't make sense, though. Water would be there all the time."

Lillian started up the slope. "Didn't Maddy tell you about how sisters draw the elements?" When Emmey reached for her hand, she hesitated, then took it.

"Yeah."

"One of those elements is water."

Emmey jerked her head up to look at Lillian. "You mean you did it?"

"Yes, and then I turned the water to ice. That's why you slipped."

"Oh. I didn't know it was ice. I just fell on my bottom and couldn't stop."

"Exactly what I wanted you to do," Lillian said smugly. "Though it would have been nice if you'd thrown the clothes aside."

"I didn't have time!"

Winded, Lillian didn't respond, focusing silently on navigating up the slope to their camp.

Maddy was kneeling on a blanket. "I was just unpacking what we need for supper," she said, carefully unwrapping the bundle that contained the bread and cheese they'd bought from a farmer earlier that afternoon. She smiled up at Lillian. "Can you cut these while I'm bathing?" Her smile faded. She looked at Emmey, then back at Lillian. "Do I want to know? You know that when you bathe, you remove your clothing, right?"

Lillian dropped her soaked clothes and pointed at Emmey. "It was her fault."

"No, it was hers," Emmey said, pointing at Lillian.

"She was running away with my clothes!" Lillian's mouth tightened when Maddy's twitched.

"She made ice and so I slipped and fell in the lake," Emmey countered.

"You drew water?" Maddy said incredulously. "I thought I heard gushing water at one point. That was you?"

Lillian put her hands on her hips. "I told her to stay put! If she'd done what she was told, none of this would have happened. And when she fell in the lake, she pretended she was drowning and scared the life out of me!"

The amusement in Maddy's eyes died. She turned to Emmey. "Did you do that, Emmey?"

"I wasn't trying to scare her, Miss."

"Then what were you trying to do?" Lillian snapped, her temples pulsing.

"You know what? You two sort this out while I bathe." Maddy pushed herself upright. "I want a quiet evening, all right?"

"You're sure you don't want me to come with you?" Lillian asked. "The water's a bit deep. You could slip. I'm a bit jittery, now."

"I can still swim, Lillian. I'd rather you stay here, with Emmey." Maddy heaved a sigh. "Can I have the soap, please?"

Lillian stared at her.

Maddy held out her hand. "The soap?"

"I dropped it in the lake," she admitted sheepishly.

"We don't have any more!"

Lillian jerked her thumb at Emmey. "If she hadn't played her little prank, I wouldn't have dropped it."

"I didn't know you'd drop the soap!" Emmey shouted.

"Right, I'm going." Muttering, Maddy walked away.

Emmey stuck a finger in her mouth. "I think she's mad at us."

"Really? How astute of you!" Lillian picked up her wet clothes and moved them over to the small pile of twigs Maddy had started. Later she'd use steel and flint to light a fire; she'd already frivolously drawn the elements enough for one day.

"I didn't mean to frighten you," Emmey said.

"What on earth possessed you to do it, then?" she asked, motioning for Emmey to follow her to Ticky.

"I wanted to see if you'd rescue me."

"Of course I'd rescue you." For Maddy's sake. Mainly.

"I wasn't sure, so I thought I'd stay under the water and see if you'd come."

Lillian peeled off her robe and handed it to Emmey, then found another blanket and used it to pat herself dry.

"When I saw how fast your legs were moving, I knew I'd be in trouble. But I was also happy because you were coming to rescue me."

Lillian would never understand this child, but could appreciate her curiosity. "I usually support an empirical approach, but not in this case."

"An empiri-what?"

She pulled a shift over her head and stepped into the dry robe. "Learning through observation or experience."

Emmey still looked confused.

Lillian sighed. "Doing something and seeing what happens."

"Oh!" Emmey said, brightening.

"But not when it frightens people." She finished buttoning her robe, stepped into a pair of sandals, and rummaged around in a bag for the cloth-wrapped knife. Emmey followed her back to the blanket, where Lillian knelt to slice the bread and cheese for their supper. "There was no need to test me in this case," Lillian said. "You should have known I'd rescue you."

"I suppose so," Emmey said, making a great show of laying out Lillian's wet clothes. "The Miss would be upset if something happened to me."

Lillian glanced at her. "That's very insightful."

Emmey's face scrunched up. "What?"

"Never mind."

"I didn't think your legs could move that fast."

Lillian stifled a chuckle. "Change your clothes. Those need to dry."

"Are you still mad at me?" Emmey asked a moment later.

"No."

"Because you don't want to upset the Miss?"

"Partly." Let the child puzzle that one out. "Now go change, and then you can help me unload Ticky." When Emmey turned her back, Lillian smiled. Her legs churning through the water must have been quite the sight, and Emmey had meant no harm. Now that she'd calmed down, Lillian could see the humorous side of Emmey's little experiment, but she'd never admit that to Maddy and Emmey.

Your will be done. Maddy lifted her head and pulled the blanket up to Emmey's shoulders, then pushed herself to her feet, heavy with sadness. Sound asleep, Emmey didn't stir. Maddy stared at her, tried to commit every detail to memory. Perhaps seeing Emmey run into her ma's arms would temper Maddy's sense of loss. She'd imagined the joyous reunion several times—Emmey crying out for her ma; her ma crouching and reaching for her, then pulling Emmey into a hug and holding her tightly, tears streaming down her face. If only it would happen next week, and not tomorrow.

They could have pushed on to Pinewood without stopping for the night, but Maddy had wanted one last evening around the fire with Emmey. Lillian hadn't protested, bless her. She must be itching to return to the monastery, but had readily agreed to camp while the sun was still high. "Good night, Emmey," Maddy murmured.

She joined Lillian, who sat near the fire, her legs drawn up to her chest. "I'm a selfish cow," she said as she sat down and leaned into her.

"Why?"

"I should be happy that Emmey will be back with her family tomorrow, but I'm not, not completely."

"That doesn't mean you're selfish."

Tears stung Maddy's eyes. "And now I'm going to have a little cry," she said with a sniffle. "Don't mind me, I'm just being silly."

Lillian put her arm around Maddy and squeezed her. "You're not being silly."

Maddy rested her head on Lillian's shoulder, rubbed her cheek against her robe. "I said I'd make you a robe from softer wool, but I find your rough robes oddly comforting."

"They're very empathic, my robes," Lillian said, making Maddy smile.

"Will you miss her?" Maddy asked, tucking her hand into Lillian's.

"It'll certainly be quieter."

"You won't miss her at all?"

Lillian took her time answering. "I'm not attached to her in the same way you are. You two shared an experience that brought you close. And I don't relate well to children."

"I've seen the two of you talking, certainly more than you did earlier on."

"I feel more comfortable around her, and I wouldn't want anything bad to happen to her. I could grow fond of her, with time. But right now, my affection for her doesn't run as deep as yours. I'll miss her in the sense that it will be strange not having her around." Lillian lifted Maddy's hand to her lips and kissed it. "I have to admit, I'm looking forward to having you to myself for a bit."

Maddy gazed at her. "We're not having much of a romance, are we? You left the monastery to come save me, and ended up with a cripple and a child."

Lillian snorted. "Romance is for the bards. And you're not a cripple. You're managing quite well."

"I can get along, but I don't know what I'll do back in Merrin." She smiled. "And romance isn't just for the bards. I thought it was quite romantic, you galloping after me on Baxter and riding into the prison just in time to save the day."

Lillian's face flushed. "Now you're being silly."

"Perhaps I am. Most folk would run away screaming if someone whispered, 'I'm going to cut your hand off,' into their ear."

"If you want flowery words, you're with the wrong person."

"I don't. And I'm not." Words came so easily and were often empty. Lillian had shown her love umpteen times since arriving at the prison—in saving Maddy's life, searching for Emmey, agreeing to take her home, and putting up with Emmey without losing her temper too often. Maddy had done nothing but take. She'd miss Emmey terribly and wonder about her every day, but it was time to look toward the monastery and the rest of her life, which she hoped to share with Lillian.

"You'll do fine back in Merrin." Lillian said. "To be honest, I was a bit surprised when you agreed to go back so easily. I thought you'd take some convincing, especially after all that had happened to you."

Maddy was silent while she collected her thoughts. "I still don't understand why I'm malflowed. I still feel as if I must have done something wrong. Salbine's will has been a mystery to me ever since that night in the training room, and recent events haven't helped any. But if I'm to find my way again, I need an anchor, something I can hold onto while I venture out in search of answers. That's the Order, the sisters at Merrin." *You.* "I still love Salbine. I still want to serve Her. I've come to accept that my place is in the Order. But I don't know how I'm going to serve."

"We'll have plenty of time to figure that out."

She liked the *We'll*. "I still want to go to Heath."

"And you will, once Sophia's calmed down."

"Do you think we can see Emmey on the way? I'd like to be able to tell her that she'll see us in a few months' time. Well, me."

"I don't care how many sisters and defenders Sophia sends with you, I'm going too." Lillian cleared her throat. "Though when I said Sophia would have to calm down first, I was thinking in terms of years."

Maddy chuckled.

"How are you feeling, physically?" Lillian asked.

"Stronger. I almost feel normal. For the longest time, I was worried that I'd suffered permanent injury, but I just needed decent grub." She steeled herself, then said the words she knew would hurt. "I can never draw the elements again."

"You should never have tried, especially since you knew you'd fail. You're lucky it didn't kill you."

"I had to try! They wouldn't have hanged only me. Jonathan's life would have been forfeit, too. And if I hadn't tried, I would have been hanged. I only ended up in prison because they thought Salbine was judging me." She didn't entirely disagree with them.

"You didn't deserve prison." Lillian lifted a stick from the pile next to her and threw it onto the fire.

"If I hadn't gone to prison, Emmey would still be rotting there—or worse."

Lillian was silent for a moment. "I'm surprised you don't resent Emmey."

Maddy twisted toward her. "Why would I resent her?"

"When she told me your story, she said you were burned saving her."

"She left out an important detail. That prisoner was going for me. He only went for her when she leaped in front of me, to defend me."

"The silly mite," Lillian murmured.

"I'm going to miss that silly mite," Maddy said, tearing up again. "I won't be very good company for a while, I'm afraid."

Lillian's lips brushed against Maddy's ear. "You're always good company."

"Careful. That almost sounded romantic." Her light tone belied her sorrow. Maddy leaned into Lillian again, and quietly wept as they watched the fire dance.

Chapter Eighteen

Maddy clutched Emmey's hand as Lillian tethered the horses. *Remember to smile.* No matter how conflicted she felt when Emmey and her ma reunited, she must smile and wish them well. There would be time to cry later. Poor Lillian. "Are you sure it's near here?" she asked Emmey.

Emmey nodded.

"That was clever of you, remembering the name of the shop nearby." Using that information, several folk had directed them to this spot. Emmey's home should be just around the corner.

"I used to come here all the time, Miss."

Maddy had expected Emmey to be excited, but she seemed subdued. "You'll see your ma and your brothers and sisters soon." No reaction. Perhaps Emmey had seen through her false cheerfulness.

"Right. Where do you live, then?" Lillian asked briskly, earning Maddy's gratitude. If it were left up to her, she'd drag out these last few minutes as long as she could.

Emmey pointed to her right. "Around there."

Lillian walked in that direction and greased the palms of three beggars before they even reached the corner. Maddy had already gathered that this was the poorer area of Pinewood. She'd thought that imprisonment had removed all the meat from Emmey's bones, but the children searching for scraps were almost as emaciated as Emmey had been. "Do you think it's safe to leave the horses unattended?" she asked Lillian.

"Don't worry. Anyone who tries to touch the horses is in for a nasty surprise."

"Not a fatal one, I hope."

"No, no, no."

A loud, piercing yelp made Maddy turn in time to see a child racing away from the horses, shaking his hand.

Lillian grunted. "See? Still alive."

They turned the corner and entered a cul-de-sac ringed by dilapidated wooden shacks. "Which one is yours?" Maddy asked, keeping the horror out of her voice with effort. A home was built on love, not coin. But it was difficult not to be dismayed, especially when she'd return to the comforts of the monastery. Perhaps Salbine was trying to teach her to count her blessings and be grateful for what she had, rather than focusing on what she lacked.

Emmey pointed. "That one."

"Are you sure?" Maddy asked as they approached it. The front door stood ajar, the single front window was shattered, and the roof would no longer keep out the rain.

Lillian frowned. "It looks abandoned." She hesitantly pushed the door open and stepped inside.

Maddy followed her, still holding Emmey's hand. She raised her stump and pressed it against her nose. Rubbish lay strewn over the floor of the single room. Maddy quickly stepped aside as a rat lumbered by, then jumped at a loud shout behind her: "Oy! What are you doing in there?" She didn't need more of an excuse to leave the rank shack.

"I'm sick of you folk dumping your rubbish and pissing and shitting in there," the woman standing outside the shack yelled. "You're attracting all the vermin. They don't stay in there, you know. They end up in—" Her eyes widened; she lowered her head and backed up. "Begging your pardon, Sister. I didn't know it was you. I thought—"

"It's all right," Maddy said, gratefully sucking in fresh air. A grimacing Lillian stumbled out after her.

Emmey looked up at Maddy. "That's Mrs. Clarehill."

Clarehill straightened. "How do you know my name?" She peered at Emmey. "Emmey, is that you?"

Emmey nodded.

Clarehill's hand went to her chest. "My goodness, child, I never expected to see you again. Look at you! You're a proper little girl."

"We're hoping to return Emmey to her family," Maddy said.

Clarehill snorted. "Long gone, they are." She swept her arm toward the abandoned shack. "As you can see. She found another fella and fell in love, the stupid cow. Followed him who knows where, ready to pop another babe. She won't be back, and I doubt she expected this one to be back. How did you get out, Emmey? And why? You were probably doing better in there."

Maddy's breath caught in her throat. "You knew she was in prison?"

"Of course I did! Right ruckus, it was."

"What happened?" Lillian asked.

"You don't know? Cassy had her own little den of thieves, she did. Emmey's ma," she clarified in response to Maddy's questioning look. "Popped one out regular, she did. All with different pas, I'm sure. You don't want to know the comings and goings, Sisters, believe me. Once they were four or five, it was out to rob whoever they could." Her gaze shifted to Emmey. "But this one didn't want to. Fought fiercely with her ma, she did. Ran away so many times I lost count, but she always came back."

"How did she end up in prison?" Lillian asked impatiently.

"Oh, well, this one got it into her head that if she nicked something big, that would be it. She wouldn't have to nick again. Some noble rode into town—who was it?" She was silent for a moment, then shook her head. "I don't remember his name."

"It wasn't Conrad, Duke of Merrin, was it?"

Maddy breathed a sigh of relief when Clarehill shook her head, before nodding it toward Emmey. "This one tried to empty his purse. Well, he caught her, and he turned out to be a vindictive son of a— Oh, begging your pardon."

"Son of a bitch?" Lillian said.

Maddy inwardly sighed.

Clarehill eyed Lillian uneasily. "Yes, well, he dragged her here with his men in tow, ranting and raving that he'd burn Cassy's shack down and see that she was hanged for harbouring dirty thieves. Now, Cassy always cared more about Cassy than anyone else. So she threw her own daughter to the wolves, saved her skin by offering Emmey to him. Fortunately he wasn't inclined that way, so he said he'd throw her into prison to rot. Maybe he planned to use her when she was older. Who knows? Truth be told, I thought he'd get rid of her the moment he left town."

Maddy wasn't sure if Clarehill had expected him to dump her or kill her.

"But a few months later one of his men passed through to, uh, visit Cassy. He said the lord had dumped the child in some prison, just like he'd said he would. I never thought I'd see her again. How did you get out?" she asked Emmey. Her eyes flicked to Lillian, then to Maddy. "You got her out, didn't you?"

"Sort of." Maddy's mind raced. "Do you know where Cassy went?"

"Listen to me, Sister. I don't know where she went, and I'm not sure I'd tell you, if I did. You'd be better off leaving this one to the alleys than you would taking her to that woman. Mind my words—I wasn't lying when I said she was probably better off in prison than she'd ever been here. Her ma probably don't even remember her name. She didn't seem to miss her."

"Surely that's not true."

"You don't know what it's like out here, Sister." Clarehill gave Maddy's sewn sleeve a pitying glance. "Though your life isn't without hardship, I'm sure."

Maddy felt her face tighten. "Thank you for the information."

"No bother, Sister. There's an orphanage of sorts up in the merchants' sector, on the north road out of town. Look for a blacksmith's, it's right next door. I'd drop her off there. Anyway, I best be getting back to my sewing."

"Salbine keep you," Maddy murmured.

"Thank you, Sister." She turned away, not giving Emmey a second glance.

Maddy met Lillian's eyes, not sure what to do next. She looked down when Emmey tugged on her robe, then dropped to her knee at the sight of Emmey's trembling chin. "I'm sorry your ma isn't here."

Emmey blinked rapidly. A tear rolled down her cheek. "Can I keep my clothes?" she asked in a quavering voice.

It took Maddy a second to understand the implication of Emmey's question. "We're not leaving you here!" Though she had no idea what they were going to do.

"You kept your promise, Miss." Emmey wiped away the tear, but she was clearly fighting more. Maddy reached for her, but Emmey stiffened. "You have to go home," she said solemnly. "You kept your promise."

"I may have kept my promise, but that doesn't mean I don't care about what happens to you."

"I got nowhere else to go now." Emmey's lips quivered. "I just want my clothes, Miss."

Why was Emmey being so stubborn? She couldn't possibly believe they'd just walk away and not give her a second's thought. Then again, if what Clarehill had told them about Cassy was true . . .

"Emmey, we need your help," Lillian said. "I want to sleep in a proper bed tonight, so I'm well-rested when we begin our journey back to Merrin. You know the types of inns we like—quiet, where the bards pack up early. Do you think you can help us find one? You know Pinewood better than we do."

"Yes, help us!" Maddy said, seizing the opening Lillian had thrown her.

Emmey screwed up her face. "There won't be one like that around here, Miss."

"Well, let's go back to the horses and try to find one, all right?"

"And then I can have my clothes?"

"Yes, you can have your clothes." Maddy straightened and caught Emmey's hand.

It took them a couple of hours to find an inn that suited their needs. "Can I have my clothes now?" Emmey asked after they'd booked a room and were gathering a few items from Ticky's saddlebags.

Maddy glanced at Lillian. "I'll tell you what. It's almost supper time now, isn't it? Why don't you have supper with us? It would be silly for you to go on an empty belly." She dropped to one knee. "To be honest, I wish you'd stay with us until we know you'll be all right."

Emmey stuck her fingers in her mouth. "I got nowhere."

"That's why I think we should stay together until we find you somewhere. What do you think?"

"You kept your promise, Miss."

"I promised I'd take you home to your ma. But things didn't work out quite the way we expected, did they?"

Emmey shook her head. "I didn't think my ma would want to see me, but I didn't think she'd be gone."

"I see." Maddy digested this new information. Was that why Emmey hadn't been excited? But she'd wanted Maddy to take her home. After the prison fire, Emmey had reminded Maddy of her promise. "Since your ma's not here, why don't we stay together a while longer? If I don't know you're safe, I'll worry about you."

"Would you, Miss?" Emmey asked, her eyes bright.

"Of course I would. So will you stay with us, then?"

"Can I have stew?"

Maddy smiled. "We'll see what's on offer. Come on." She looked around for Lillian, who seemed awfully quiet. Lillian wasn't there.

"She went into the inn," Emmey said.

"She must be hungry. Here, do you think you can carry this paper? We should practice our letters tonight."

A boy who looked to be about fourteen sauntered into the stables. "Sister inside says I'm to bring a roll in for the lass."

"Thank you." Guessing that Emmey would stay with them wouldn't have been a stretch. Maddy had only pretended that Emmey had a choice; she never would have let her disappear into Pinewood alone and coinless. They waited while the boy hoisted a roll onto his shoulder, then followed him into the inn.

Supper was a subdued affair. For once, Maddy and Lillian did most of the talking, with Emmey throwing in a word here and there. "Can I go to the room?" Emmey asked the moment she'd spooned the last of her stew into her mouth.

"Are you sure?" Maddy said. "The bard's singing isn't that bad."

"I'm tired."

Maddy frowned. "You're not ill, are you? Perhaps I should go—" She felt Lillian's hand on her arm. "You go on. I'll be up soon."

Emmey scampered up the stairs.

"We need to chat," Lillian said. "And give her some time on her own. She's a proud little thing. Let her have a cry in private."

"She's cried in front of me before. She sobbed her heart out when we said good-bye at the prison."

"That was different. She hadn't been rejected by her own ma. And I suspect that's not all she's crying about."

Maddy dropped her spoon into the bowl. "I feel so stupid. I pictured her and her ma hugging each other and hanging onto each other and crying . . ."

Lillian smirked. "And sunshine and rainbows and birds twittering with joy?"

"I wanted the bloody rainbows! I can't believe it—what kind of ma just abandons a child?"

"The kind of ma that sends out her children to steal while she stays home and whores herself."

"Whenever I thought of Emmey's ma, I always imagined her beside herself with worry and grief, powerless to get her daughter out of prison." Maddy slowly shook her head. "She probably doesn't even remember her name! Probably wouldn't recognize her!"

Lillian gulped down some cider. "My pa didn't pay me much attention, but I always felt safe. I always had a roof over my head, food on the table, and a pillow for my head. And Sophia." She wiped up her remaining stew with a piece of bread. "I never felt hard done by, and if I had, I'd be chiding myself for it now."

"I'm the luckiest of all." Maddy's ma and pa loved her and were probably worried sick, not having heard from her in months. The first thing she'd do when she returned to the monastery was get a letter off to them, even if her letters weren't perfect. "What are we going to do? We can't just leave her to her own defences."

"That woman mentioned an orphanage," Lillian reminded her.

"It could be another Lila's."

"We won't know until we've had a look. I thought I'd go over now. The barkeep knows of the blacksmith's on the north road. He said it's not far."

"I want to see it too," Maddy said.

"If I think it might be suitable, we can all go tomorrow."

"Why don't I go?"

Lillian patted her hand. "Because I'll be more objective. I'm not sure any orphanage will be good enough for you, not without a bit of persuasion." She hesitated. "And I can defend myself. I'd rather you stay here, with Emmey. She'll want you, not me."

Maddy sighed. "I don't know, she seems eager to get away from both of us."

"You don't believe all that rubbish, do you? Do you know why she's upset? Because she thinks you're going away now."

"No, she's upset because her ma isn't here."

"That's only a small part of it, Maddy."

Maddy vigorously shook her head. "Before she knew I was dying, she reminded me to take her home. She was upset that I wouldn't be able to."

"She reminded you because it meant you'd still be together. There was nothing stopping you from leaving the prison without her. She doesn't want you to go away." Lillian met Maddy's eyes. "Don't you see? All that talk about leaving with her clothes and releasing you because you've fulfilled your promise is her way of rejecting you before you reject her. Because that's what she's expecting. Another rejection."

Maddy swallowed. "She knows I'm a sister and that we have to go back to the monastery. She always knew we couldn't stay together forever." But Emmey was only eight. Had she truly understood? Had Maddy somehow misled her? "We were in a cell together for months. I couldn't avoid caring about her. Perhaps someone else could have remained detached, but I couldn't. I didn't even know if I'd ever get out. And when I did, I couldn't just turn my back on her." She buried her face in her hand.

"I'm not blaming you, I'm just telling you how I see things." Lillian gently pulled Maddy's hand away from her face. "We'll sort this out."

"How?"

"I don't know," Lillian said sheepishly. "But we will. Let me go see this orphanage."

"All right." But as she watched Lillian push back her chair and drain the last of her cider, Maddy felt like a liar. Emmey wasn't the only one who wished they could stay together. "Lillian?"

Lillian looked down at her. "What?"

Her eyes filled with tears. "I should hope the orphanage will be a wonderful place for Emmey. But I don't."

Lillian's face softened. "I know. That's why I'm going." After a furtive glance around the common room, she kissed Maddy on the cheek and left.

MADDY PUT HER finger to her lips when Lillian stepped into the room. Lillian tipped her head toward the door, her face grim. "Let's go down to the common room," she whispered when Maddy joined her.

Only a single fire burned, in the fireplace near the bar. Lillian sank into one of the chairs arranged around it and heaved a sigh. Maddy sat next to her. "I'm guessing the orphanage won't do?"

"That's an understatement." Lillian stared at the fire. "It's more a sick house for children. I'll drop off some herbs when we pass it on our way out, though all that will do for some of them is ease their suffering until they leave this realm. Poor things. It's fairly clean, though, and the women tending the ill seem compassionate. But it's not the place for Emmey."

Maddy wouldn't pretend to be disappointed, but what now?

"There are still a couple of towns between here and Merrin," Lillian said.

"So we'll go from town to town until we find a place to dump her?"

"I didn't say that. Do you have a better idea?"

"I might. I thought about it while you were gone. I think we should take her with us to Merrin."

Lillian turned toward Maddy, her mouth open. "We can't take her to the monastery."

"It would only be temporary."

"Maddy—"

Maddy lifted her hand. "Hear me out. Here we are, thinking of leaving her at an orphanage in some town we don't know. If we're going to do something like that, let's do it somewhere we do know and where we'll be close by. We know Merrin, we know the folk in Merrin. Even if she ends up in the alleys, at least she'll be in Merrin. I can arrange to meet her once a week, help her if need be. She won't be completely alone."

Lillian pressed her lips together.

"Well, do *you* have a better idea?" Maddy asked.

"Not right now."

"Then let's do that."

"You're assuming Sophia will let her through the gates. She has every right to turn Emmey away. Even those marked by Salbine aren't allowed through the gates until they're sixteen, and we're going to show up with an unmarked eight-year-old?"

"Emmey could be marked," Maddy said desperately.

"And she might not be. Either way, she's only eight. I know Sophia's kind and compassionate, but she's obligated to put the monastery's interests first."

"It would only be temporary, until we find her somewhere to live. She could sleep in the stables!"

Lillian fell silent. Maddy turned to the fire and forced herself to wait for Lillian to speak. Lillian hadn't said no, and pushing her wouldn't help. Seconds stretched into minutes. Was Lillian considering the idea, or deciding how best to gently turn it aside?

"I'll only agree to this because what you said about having Emmey in Merrin makes sense," Lillian finally said. "But you have to be prepared for the possibility that Sophia might turn her away at the gates. And if she does, no arguing. No pleading. Not after we've put her on the spot and asked for something we shouldn't." She raised a finger. "Sophia sometimes indulges me, but this will go well beyond being a pain in the arse."

Maddy sagged. Not the unqualified support she'd hoped for. "If you're uncomfortable with it, let's not do it."

Lillian threw up her hands. "What else are we going to do? I suppose we could leave her in Merrin before going up to the monastery, but there's no harm in trying. Sophia will forgive us. Eventually."

"I'll try to think of where we can take her if the abbess does turn her away."

"Why do you insist on calling her the abbess?"

"Because she is the abbess. She's not family to me, like she is to you."

Lillian drew breath, then apparently reconsidered and kept her own counsel. Maddy would have loved to know what she'd intended to say.

"You'll have to try to explain all this to Emmey," Lillian said. "You have to make sure she understands that she's not going to live at the monastery with you."

"I will."

"She might want to stay here. She knows Pinewood, or at least part of it."

Maddy shook her head. "She wouldn't survive. She doesn't like to steal, Lillian. Scraps will only take her so far. I'll make sure she knows the monastery won't be her home, but I'll also make sure she knows she has a better chance in Merrin."

"I think she's bright enough to figure that out for herself."

Maddy sighed. "An eight-year-old shouldn't have to face this sort of decision."

"No."

They lapsed into silence again and watched the fire, lost in thought. Maddy would never take her privileged life at the monastery for granted again. To think she'd seriously considered turning her back on it! All right, her spiritual life was a mess, but what better place to sort it out than the monastery? If she hadn't already decided it was her home and the Order her destiny, she'd certainly come around to it now.

At the prison, any lessons to be learned from her ordeal had eluded her. Not anymore. And she couldn't shake the feeling that her prison experience would remain a harsh teacher throughout her life, a prospect that excited her. It infused her wretched existence in that cell with what she sought most: meaning. And that could only come from one source: *Salbine*.

MADDY ROLLED OVER, opened her eyes, and yawned. Lillian still breathed rhythmically next to her. If they were at the monastery, she would have been up over an hour ago, if Maddy's guess at the time was right. But they'd stayed in the common room well past their usual bedtime, staring into the fire in companionable silence.

"You awake, Emmey?" she whispered, peeking over the side of the bed. Emmey's roll looked empty! "Emmey? Emmey!" Maddy sat up and nudged Lillian. "Lillian! Lillian!"

Lillian groaned and rolled toward her. "What?" she mumbled.

"Emmey's gone!" Maddy threw aside the thin blanket and grabbed her robe. "She can't have gotten very far." She stepped into her robe, pulled it over her shoulders, and tried to do up the first button. In her haste, she fumbled it. "Bloody, stupid button!" She almost stamped her foot, then remembered where she was.

"Calm down, Maddy. Let me."

She stood anxiously as Lillian did up the offending button and moved on to the next, working her way upward. When she reached the top button, Maddy fought the urge to tear out of the room.

"Go!"

Maddy needed no further encouragement. She bounded down the stairs and into the common room, frantic to get outside and start searching. After the trouble they'd had finding Emmey in Reedwick—in fact, they hadn't found her; she'd found them—Maddy feared this time would be even harder. Emmey probably didn't want to be found.

A man stood behind the bar, polishing a glass. "Sister!" he hissed as she flew past him. "Sister!"

Pretending she hadn't heard him would be rude. Maybe he could help. She backtracked. "Have you seen a little blonde girl?"

"That's what I'm wanting to talk to you about, Sister," he said quietly. He put down the glass, leaned over the bar, and pointed. Emmey sat at a table in the corner, her head bent over a bowl. "One of the boys was mucking out the stables when she came wandering in, wanting to say good-bye to your horses. He didn't think you'd want her running off, so he brought her back here. She seems determined to be on her way, but I convinced her to have a bowl of porridge first. I was going to send Dick up to knock on your door when she finished."

"Thank you," Maddy said, feeling almost dizzy with relief.

"Got one of my own, her age," the man said. "Wouldn't want her running off. Do you mind if I ask you a question?"

Despite wanting to join Emmey, she said no.

"What's a girl like her doing with two sisters?"

He wasn't the first to ask. She answered with the proverbial short version of a long story. "We're trying to find her somewhere to live."

"Oh." He nodded. "Lots of orphans around."

She understood the unspoken question: what was special about Emmey? "Emmey saved a sister's life," she said, speaking the simple truth. Without Emmey, she would have suffered much more in prison and not endured her captivity as well. But again, that wasn't the whole story, only the part everyone would easily understand.

He looked over at Emmey, renewed interest in his eyes. Maddy thanked him again and agreed that a bowl of porridge would hit the spot, then strolled over to the table and casually pulled out a chair. "Good morning."

"Morning, Miss," Emmey mumbled, her head still over the bowl.

"You're up early."

Emmey shrugged.

"Lillian and I had a chat about you last night," she said, deciding to put Emmey's attempted flight aside for now. "We were wondering if you'd like to go with us to Merrin." When Emmey didn't respond, Maddy carried on. "We have to go back to the monastery. You can't live at the monastery, but we'll try to find you somewhere to live in Merrin."

"Is Merrin close to the monastery?" Emmey asked, finally lifting her head.

"Merrin's a bit confusing, because there's County Merrin and the town of Merrin. The monastery is just outside the town of Merrin, up on a hill."

"Like the prison?"

Maddy nodded. "And the town of Merrin is in the county of Merrin. We'll enter the county in a few days, but we won't reach the town for a couple of weeks. If you come with us, we'll try to find you somewhere to live in the town of Merrin."

Emmey perked up. "If I'm in the town, you could visit me."

"That's what we thought too," Maddy said.

"I could visit you too!"

"Well, the thing is, there are no children at the monastery." She leaned back as her porridge arrived. "Thank you," she murmured, then stirred the porridge and shifted her attention back to Emmey. "We're hoping you'll be allowed to stay at the monastery until we find you somewhere to live. But I want you to listen to me very closely. You might not be allowed to stay, all right?"

"Is it big?"

"The monastery? Very big. It's almost a town itself. It's surrounded by tall walls, and it has its own roads and crops and stables, even its own catacombs. We live in buildings called towers. Not all of them are towers, but we call them that." She spooned porridge into her mouth. Its warmth spread to her belly when she swallowed it. "Some sisters hardly ever leave it. Like Lillian."

"She left it for you."

An act of love Maddy never would have expected from her. "And here she is," she said, spotting Lillian coming down the stairs. She met Lillian's eyes. "Emmey decided to have an early breakfast."

Fortunately Lillian caught on. "That porridge looks good. I wouldn't mind a bowl of that myself." She sauntered away.

"If the monastery's so big, why won't there be room for me?" Emmey asked.

"It's not a matter of there not being room. You have to be at least sixteen to live at the monastery." And marked and called by Salbine, sworn to defend the sisters, or in the employ of the monastery, details Emmey didn't need to know. "So if you decide to come with us, you have to understand that you can't live at the monastery. Even if you're allowed in when we arrive, you won't be able to stay there forever. You'll only stay there until we find you somewhere else to live. Do you understand?"

"I'll live somewhere else." Emmey lowered her head. "Not with you."

Maddy's breath caught in her throat. "That's right." And she'd make every effort to ensure that Emmey didn't live in the alleys. "I know Pinewood is your home, but there's nobody here to look out for you."

"I got nobody," Emmey agreed mournfully.

"That's not true. You have me and Lillian. If you go with us to Merrin, we'll do everything we can to make sure you're all right. I promise you that."

Emmey lifted her head. "And you keep your promises, don't you, Miss!"

"Yes, I do. So it's settled, then? You'll stay with us?"

Her head bobbed vigorously.

"Good, I'm pleased. Now, how are you feeling? It must have been disappointing, finding out your ma is gone."

Lillian returned and plunked a bowl of porridge onto the table.

"I was just saying to Emmey that it must have been disappointing, finding her ma gone," Maddy said as Lillian settled into a chair.

"I wasn't happy, Miss," Emmey said.

"At home?"

Emmey nodded. "My ma didn't like me."

"I'm sure she did."

"No. She wanted me to do things I didn't want to do, but my brothers and sisters, they'd do it, so my ma would be cross with me. I never should have nicked that purse. I didn't want to nick it, but she told me not to come home with nothing. Then I saw that fat purse."

"On an equally fat noble, I'd imagine," Lillian said, making Emmey giggle.

"And he caught you trying to steal it?" Maddy said. Poor Emmey probably hadn't known how to take a purse unnoticed; she'd just wanted to appease her ma.

"My ma said she never wanted to see me again. She gave me to that man, so I thought when she saw me with you, she'd give me to you, and then you'd have to take care of me."

Maddy marvelled at Emmey's simplistic, yet endearing, view of the world. Her pa always said that naivety and optimism often spent time together, something she could imagine Lillian saying. "Emmey, you know you can't live with me," she said primarily for Lillian's benefit.

"I know, Miss."

"We'll find a nice family for you, and I'll visit whenever I can." She turned to Lillian. "Emmey's agreed to go to Merrin with us. And we're both glad about that, aren't we?"

"Yes, we are," Lillian said, managing to sound as if she meant it.

Chapter Nineteen

Elizabeth smiled at Sophia. "This was a nice surprise, you suggesting a walk in the middle of the afternoon. You're usually shut away in your study, or meeting with a sister or Thomas or someone."

"I felt like a walk." Sophia slipped her arm through Elizabeth's. "I can't sit still these days."

"You're not sleeping well, either." Elizabeth's voice softened. "They'll be back soon."

"They should have been back already! They had to go to Garryglen, find out what happened to Maddy, and return. That's it. At this point, I'd say they're a few weeks overdue."

"If Maddy wasn't hanged, perhaps negotiations for her release are holding things up."

Sophia shook her head. "Nobody in their right mind would drag out negotiations when presented with evidence that they'd wrongly accused and convicted a sister. Where are they, Elizabeth?" She released a loud sigh and moved closer to her consort.

"Try not to fret too much. You'll only make yourself ill. Easier said than done, I know. You're almost a ma to Lillian."

Sophia chuckled. "Don't say that within her hearing. She wouldn't take too kindly to it." Even though it was true. "I should never have let her go."

"How could you have denied her?"

Sophia's silence answered the question.

Elizabeth squeezed Sophia's arm. "I'm sure they're fine. With Lillian's power and Barnabus's skills, I doubt very much they ran into a situation they couldn't handle."

"Then where are they?"

"Abbess!" came a shout from behind them. They turned as one of Thomas's men ran up to them and bowed. "Master Barnabus has returned."

Sophia's heart pounded. "And Mistress Lillian?"

"No, Abbess. He's alone. He's gone to your study."

He's alone. She couldn't speak.

"How did Barnabus seem?" Elizabeth asked.

"In good spirits, Mistress. Nothing like Master Jonathan when he rode in."

"That's promising," Elizabeth said, squeezing Sophia's arm again. "Thank you, Oliver." He nodded and left them.

Sophia swallowed. "I don't think I can bear this."

"We don't know what's happened. Let's go see Barnabus and find out."

Her mind in a whirl, Sophia relied on Elizabeth to guide her back to the study, oblivious to her surroundings.

Barnabus was waiting outside. He bowed, then met her eyes. "The mistress is fine."

Thank Salbine. Sophia led the way into her study. "Where is she, then? Why isn't she with you?" She sank into her chair and rested her shaking hands on her lap. "Forgive me, Barnabus. Please sit down. I'm pleased you've returned safely, but I had a bit of a turn when Oliver said you were alone." There was no point lying to Barnabus; he knew her too well.

"I understand, Abbess." He sat down and shifted around until he was comfortable.

Elizabeth leaned over Sophia's desk and tested the teapot with her hand. "It's still warm. Would you like a cup?"

"Please." Sophia silently thanked her. She wouldn't trust herself to pour tea at the moment. "Barnabus?"

"No, thank you." He waited while Elizabeth poured Sophia a cup of tea, then continued. "I'm pleased to tell you that Sister Maddy is alive."

"Oh, that's wonderful news!" Sophia couldn't wait to welcome her back. But . . . was that why Lillian wasn't here? Because Maddy had decided not to return to the monastery and Lillian had foolishly run away with her? "But why isn't she here? What's going on, Barnabus?"

"They are coming back, I hope," Elizabeth said, apparently thinking along the same lines.

Barnabus nodded. "Sister Maddy was imprisoned, not hanged. She shared a cell with a child."

"A child?" Sophia hadn't thought they imprisoned children.

"The sister wanted to see the child safely home. The mistress and I suggested hiring men from one of the guilds, but Sister Maddy wanted to do it herself. The girl lives in Pinewood, not far from Leaton. I expect they'll only be two weeks or so behind me."

"So the mistress has gone with the sister to take this child home?"

"Yes."

Dear, dear Lillian. If those two didn't end up as consorts, Sophia would eat her cassock.

"So you got the child out of prison too?" Elizabeth asked.

"We didn't have to get anybody out of prison." Barnabus reached inside his purse and pulled out a folded paper. "The mistress wrote you a letter, Abbess. I'm sure it explains everything."

Sophia accepted it and broke the seal. She nudged her spectacles up her nose and began to read.

Sophia,

Don't be cross. Maddy is coming back to the monastery, but she's grown fond of a girl who was in the prison with her and wants to take her home. I can't let her go alone. I tried to persuade her to hire men, but the child is important to her. If she doesn't do it herself, she'll always wonder if the child arrived home safely. She's suffered so much, I feel we owe her this one indulgence. As soon as we've dropped off the child, we'll ride for Merrin.

Don't be cross with Barnabus, either. He opposed our plan. I ordered him back to the monastery.

I hope you and Elizabeth are well. I miss you.

With love,

L

Sophia lowered the letter. "I'm afraid it doesn't tell me much beyond what you've just told me."

Barnabus frowned. "She didn't mention the prison fire, or Sister Maddy's hand?"

"No. What about the sister's hand?"

He cleared his throat. "We cut it off."

Sophia stared at him, certain she'd misheard. "Did you just say you cut off Sister Maddy's hand?"

"And part of her arm. A physician named Crandall did the actual cutting."

"But why did you do it?"

"The mistress said it was the only way to save the sister's life."

So Lillian was behind it, but hadn't thought it important enough to mention in her letter? What about the events that led up to it? Sophia pulled off her spectacles, rubbed her eyes, and drank her cup of lukewarm tea in one go. "Would you mind boiling more water, Elizabeth? I believe there's still some in the kettle, if you'd just light the fire." She put her spectacles back on and rested her elbows on her desk. "Now, Barnabus, I'd like to hear the whole story, from the beginning. What happened when you arrived in Garryglen?"

"HOLD THE REINS for a minute, Emmey," Maddy murmured. Shivering, she pulled her hood over her head and leaned over poor Emmey, who didn't have a hood. "I think we should find shelter," she shouted, taking the reins back and slowing Griffin's trot to a stop. "More rain is on the way."

When Lillian stopped Baxter and glanced over her shoulder, Ticky stopped too. "What?"

Maddy pointed toward the sky. "The rain. It's stopped, but not for long, and we're soaked. We should find somewhere sheltered to camp."

"Do you want to carry on for a bit and see if we come across an inn or a farm?" Lillian asked after surveying the sky. "I don't see anywhere to camp here. The forest is too thick."

Lillian was right. A wall of trees lined the winding path they'd navigated for the past hour. The path was muddy—Ticky had already stumbled once when he'd rounded a sharp corner—but they had no choice but to continue riding, unless they wanted to spend a chilly, damp night outside without a fire, squeezed between trees. "All right, let's go on. You all right, Emmey?"

Emmey looked up over her shoulder at Maddy and nodded, rainwater dripping from her nose.

"I like rain," Lillian said. "Though I prefer watching it through a window."

Maddy smiled, but Lillian's attention had shifted to the path ahead, and she urged Baxter and Ticky into a trot. Maddy followed, holding her breath when Lillian and Ticky disappeared around another sharp curve in the path. When she heard a shout, she rounded the curve at a careful walk and reined Griffin in next to Lillian, who'd stopped.

Lillian pointed to an overturned wagon blocking the path. "Stay as close to me as you can. I don't like this."

"Perhaps the owner couldn't right it and has gone to get help," Maddy suggested.

Lillian shook her head. "It wouldn't be in that position."

Before Maddy could respond, several men emerged from the trees, arrows nocked and bowstrings drawn. They aimed at Lillian, Maddy, and Emmey. Emmey whimpered.

"Don't worry, we'll be fine," Maddy whispered. "We're with Lillian." She couldn't sense the elements, but Lillian's rigid posture indicated that she was already drawing, ready to unleash destruction.

Another man swaggered from the trees, his thumbs looped through his belt. "Look what we've got here, boys. Three fine horses, and one packed with goods. Don't worry, ladies, we won't hurt you. Just get off your horses and continue on your way. There's an inn not far up the path. It'll only take you a couple of hours to reach it."

"Thank you for that information," Lillian said. "We were hoping we'd come across an inn soon. Now, if you could just kindly move that wagon out of the way . . ."

The leader gaped at her, then burst out laughing. "Are you hard of hearing? Get off your horses and continue up the road. Don't look back. And if you were thinking of turning around, I wouldn't. My boys are behind you, too."

"Again, thank you for the information." Lillian made a great show of peeling off her gloves. She held up her hands, palms toward her. "Now, are you sure you want to do this?"

One of the bandits dropped his bow. "Shiiiiiiiiit," he cried before disappearing into the trees.

"It's good to see one of you is intelligent," Lillian said. "A coward, mind you, but an intelligent coward. He'll see tomorrow. What about the rest of you?"

"What is it, Hank?" someone behind Maddy asked. "What's going on?"

"A Salbine Sister," a man standing near Hank replied.

"Oh, I don't know about this," another voice behind them said. "Let's leave it, Hank."

"Why, you scared?" Hank said in a high-pitched voice.

"You've heard the stories."

"Yeah, stories. My ma used to tell me the one about the big, bad wolf, too."

Several of the bandits snickered.

"I still think we should leave it," the bandit behind them insisted. "Let's go."

Hank's fists clenched when a couple of the men nodded. "Give me that bloody bow," he shouted, grabbing the weapon from the nearest man's hands. He pulled a fresh arrow from the man's quiver and nocked it. "I don't know if sisters bleed, but I know little girls do." He aimed at Emmey and released the arrow.

Emmey screamed.

The arrow flew toward her, then suddenly arched upward, changed direction, and sped to bury itself in Hank's throat. Blood gushed around the arrow. Gurgling, Hank fell to his knees, clawing at the arrow's shaft. Then he pitched forward and lay still.

The others stared in disbelief, then backed away and fled into the trees, some dropping their bows in their haste.

Maddy could feel Emmey trembling against her. "It's all right. They're gone." She glanced behind her to make sure.

"Why would they follow such an idiot?" Lillian said as she pulled on her gloves. "He shoots at Emmey? If he'd managed to hit her, that would only have made me angry. He had no chance of hitting her, but he didn't know that. Honestly." She sighed.

"How are we going to get that wagon out of the way?" Maddy asked. It looked heavy, its side and two wheels embedded in the mud. She started to dismount, but Emmey clung to her and pressed her face against Maddy's cloak. "It's all right. You're safe," Maddy said, hugging her.

"What if they come back?" Emmey asked tremulously.

"They won't. And Lillian's protecting you, so don't worry. It shouldn't take us long to move the wagon." Once they'd figured out how.

"It won't take long at all," Lillian said.

Something in her voice made Maddy look at the wagon. The ground underneath it churned, slowly lifting it. When the wagon had cleared the mud, it shot upward and burst into a white flame, then disintegrated. Ashes floated down to the path. "I'd clap, if I could," Maddy said. Unimpressed, Ticky and the other horses stood motionless.

"What happened?" Emmey asked, still hiding her face against Maddy.

"Lillian took care of the wagon for us."

"They won't use that one again to ambush travellers," Lillian said. "Sophia should send a couple of adepts out here, in case the boys haven't learned their lesson. It would be good practice for them." She turned to Maddy. "Shall we?"

"Yes. Don't look," she said to Emmey. They walked their horses past Hank's still form, then kicked them into a trot and carried on their way.

LILLIAN SHIFTED POSITION and hoped Maddy would soon announce it was Emmey's bedtime. They'd been sitting on the hard floor working on letters for over an hour, the rain pounding on the roof overhead.

"Here." Emmey handed a piece of paper to Lillian. "The Miss's is first, then mine."

She knew that. Not only had she watched them write, but their scripts were distinct. "Mmm," she murmured, examining Maddy's. "Your *b*'s and *d*'s are improving, Maddy."

"What about mine?" Emmey asked, playing with her hair.

The lamp was sitting on the floor for Maddy and Emmey's benefit. Lillian squinted at the paper, then moved it closer to the lamp. Emmey's script was a bit smaller than Maddy's. "I don't know if it would pass Mistress Averill's inspection, but it passes mine."

"Mistress Averill is the head scribe at the monastery," Maddy explained to Emmey. "She works in the library."

"We're almost at the end of this piece," Lillian said, hoping Maddy would take the hint.

"One more, please!" Emmey cried.

"Oh, all right. One more." She pondered what to have them write.

"Lillian, can I ask a question about what happened earlier?" Emmey said.

Maddy drew her legs up to her chest. "When we ran into those bandits?"

Emmey nodded. After their encounter with the bandits, she'd been unusually quiet, only perking up when they'd sat down for supper. Lillian had wondered if she'd raise the incident. "What's your question?" she asked.

"Um, you know when the arrow turned around and hit him in the throat? You didn't aim it."

"That's not a question, that's a statement," Lillian said, masking her surprise with difficulty. "Why do you think I didn't guide it?"

"Because you would have missed."

"I beg your pardon!"

"Because you can't see very well. When you read, you, um, move the paper like this." She lifted her hand and moved it back and forth in front of her eyes.

Lillian's face grew hot. "I do not!"

"Yes, you do! Until you can see. I had a friend once, and her grandma did that."

Maddy burst out laughing. "Did you hear that, Lillian? Her friend's grandma." She buried her face in her knees.

"Her grandma couldn't read!" Emmey said. "But when she sewed and things, she did what Lillian does, because she couldn't see."

Lillian pressed her lips together. "You cheeky bugger! I can see perfectly fine. It's the light," she said over Maddy's muffled laughter.

"Oh, it's the light, is it?" Maddy gasped. "I see."

"I only have problems when I read," she said through clenched teeth. And she spoke the truth. That idiot Hank had been as clear as a bell to her. But Emmey was right; she hadn't guided the arrow.

"It doesn't matter, Lillian," Emmey said. "The Miss only has one hand."

Lillian looked at Maddy, expecting her to be annoyed, but Emmey's remark sent Maddy into gales of laughter. "My belly hurts," Maddy managed to say.

Miffed, Lillian glared at Emmey. "And you lack tact and manners!"

"But she's honest," Maddy declared, tears streaming down her face.

Emmey looked from one to the other, confused.

Lillian wanted to throw the paper into the air and go to the common room. A cider would hit the spot. "I think that's enough for tonight."

"One more." Emmey clasped her hands together in front of her. "Please!"

Fine. She knew just what to write. Fortunately Maddy had buried her face in her knees again. Lillian would have to be quick. She scribbled a statement and set the paper down in front of Emmey. "Read that."

Emmey's brow furrowed. "Child-ren should be seen and—"

Maddy snatched up the paper. "Right, that's enough for tonight." She jerked it away when Emmey reached for it.

Emmey frowned. "Aw, Miss, I haven't finished."

"Yes, you have. It's time for bed."

"Aw!"

"I don't think Lillian wants to do this anymore." Maddy gave Lillian a pointed look. "She's being silly."

"Perhaps I don't like being insulted," Lillian said stiffly.

Emmey stared at her. "You saved me."

"Yes, you did." Maddy smiled at Lillian. "I'm proud of you."

A sappy grin spread across Lillian's face before she could stop it. She quickly smoothed her features. "Yes, well, I'm going to the common room."

"I'll be down in a bit," Maddy said.

Lillian pushed herself to her feet and walked to the door.

"Good night, Lillian," Emmey called.

"Good night," she said without a backward glance. But then she cursed herself and turned around—she must be growing soft! "I'll see you in the morning." Emmey smiled. Lillian ducked into the hallway when she felt the beginnings of a smile. She was losing control of her bloody face!

When she reached the common room, a bard was still plucking away on a lute and warbling some nonsense about lovers and their beating hearts. For some unfathomable reason, most of the common room's occupants had situated themselves around the colourfully clad performer. After collecting two glasses of cider from the barkeep, she claimed two empty chairs in front of a roaring fire, mercifully far away from the bard. She set Maddy's cider on the small square table that separated the two chairs, and sipped her own cider as soon as her arse hit the wood. Unless Emmey took longer than usual to fall asleep because of the excitement earlier that day, Maddy would be down in ten to fifteen minutes.

Lillian gazed into the fire and sighed contentedly. She loved this part of the day, always looked forward to it. She and Maddy had grown into the routine of sitting together after Emmey had dropped off, whether under the stars or under a roof. Lillian preferred the more private stars, so they could snuggle while they chatted. But the common room would do, especially on such a rainy night. If it was still pouring in the morning, they'd probably have to spend the day here, but one extra day wouldn't matter.

She was eager to return to the monastery and its comforts, but she'd miss her cozy evening time with Maddy. Once through the gates, monastery life would claim Maddy again, especially since she'd be busy seeking a satisfactory role for herself within the Order. How much time would she have for Lillian? An afternoon here, an overnight stay there? For a minute, Lillian visualized herself returning to her chambers after a day in the laboratory, settling into a chair in front of the fire with a cider, and recounting her day to Maddy. Then she'd listen as Maddy described hers. It would be lovely to wake up with her every morning and know that she'd see her again, if not during the day, then definitely in front of the fire before retiring for the evening. But that would mean they were consorts. Maybe Maddy would accept her. Their love had survived Maddy's ordeal. They enjoyed each other's company. And despite having spent all their days together for the past several months, they'd hardly argued.

Lillian had sometimes wished she could pass an hour or two away from Maddy and Emmey; frankly she was surprised she wasn't in a bad temper, considering she'd barely had an hour to herself for months. Yet here she was, alone for the first time today, hoping Maddy would soon plunk herself into the empty chair and lift her cider.

Could Lillian go back to how things were before she'd become involved with Maddy? Could she watch Maddy with another sister, then sit in the chapel as Maddy pledged her life to that sister? Because Maddy *would* take a consort. Most sisters did, and Lillian firmly believed that Maddy would also. She wasn't the sort to return to empty chambers at the end of a long day. She needed someone to nurture—look at her with Emmey. So why shouldn't Lillian be her consort? After Caroline, Lillian had vowed never to have another relationship again, let alone take a consort. But look at her now.

Caroline. Lillian had hardly thought of her since racing after Maddy. She hadn't raced after Caroline. She'd known exactly where Caroline was but hadn't gone after her, partly because Caroline wouldn't have wanted her to, but partly because *she* hadn't wanted to. At the time, she'd thought anger and humiliation had prevented her from making an arse of herself by riding for the Redworth monastery, but in hindsight, she'd known their relationship had been one-sided and empty. Caroline had done her a favour by leaving. Lillian's eyes blurred. She'd never thought she would reach this point. It had only taken almost twenty years and a woman who loved her.

"Are you in there, Lillian?" Maddy asked from the chair next to her. "What are you thinking about?"

She turned to Maddy to answer. Her heart sank. Maddy was grinning, her hair shining in the glow of the fire. Her skin was smooth and unblemished, not a wrinkle in evidence. Her robe accentuated the curves that wholesome food had returned to her. Her eyes were bright, kind, and usually smiling. And Lillian thought Maddy would settle for her? An older woman who felt most at home in a musty laboratory surrounded by the dead and whose robes required more wool with each passing year? If only she were younger. If only it had been Maddy, and not Caroline.

"You all right?" Maddy asked.

Lillian nodded. "Just a bit worn out."

"You've been shielding us every day, and the run-in with those bandits couldn't have helped."

Lillian grunted, not wanting to tell another fib. She forced a smile and turned back to the fire. It wasn't unusual for them to sit in silence, but tonight the silence wasn't a companionable one, at least not for her. Other nights she'd felt warm and content; tonight she felt a fool.

Chapter Twenty

MADDY COVERED EMMEY WITH A BLANKET and glanced over her shoulder at Lillian, who sat huddled near the fire.

"What do you think's wrong with her, Miss?" Emmey asked.

Surprised, she shifted her attention back to Emmey. "What do you mean?"

"She don't talk much no more."

So Emmey had noticed. "I don't know what's wrong." But she was determined to find out. Ever since the day they'd encountered the bandits, Lillian's demeanour had been different. At first Maddy had thought Emmey's teasing about her eyesight had irritated Lillian, but over a week was a long time to hold a grudge over something so trivial. Plus, Lillian didn't seem angry. She seemed subdued, depressed. It didn't make sense. They'd arrive at the monastery tomorrow. Maddy would have expected her to grow happier as they closed the distance to Merrin, but instead she was more withdrawn, and spent more time on her knees in the mornings.

"Is she mad at me?"

"No. I don't think it has anything to do with you." She touched Emmey's cheek. "Now come on, off to sleep."

"Miss, what do you think will happen tomorrow?" Emmey asked anxiously.

"I don't know." Maddy hoped her own anxiety about tomorrow didn't show. "But whatever happens, you'll still have me. If you can't stay at the monastery, I'll find you somewhere else." She had a couple of families in mind who might agree to take Emmey until she could find her somewhere permanent to live. "Now go to sleep. Sleep well."

Emmey closed her eyes. Maddy watched her drift off with a heavy heart. Even if Emmey was permitted to stay at the monastery, the time would come when they'd have to part. Maddy would visit, but those visits would probably drop in frequency as Emmey settled in with her new family. She'd no longer want or need a robed sister showing up on the doorstep to make sure she was all right.

Maddy would never forget Emmey. But considering how much she remembered of being eight, and perhaps nine, she doubted Emmey would remember much about her in a few years' time. Maybe that was how it should be. Maddy shook herself. She had a more pressing problem than what would happen tomorrow. She had to find out what was troubling Lillian before they returned to the monastery.

"How are you feeling tonight?" she asked as she sat next to Lillian and slipped her arm around her shoulders.

Lillian's eyes remained on the fire. "All right."

"Looking forward to being home tomorrow?"

Lillian nodded.

"Bet you won't miss Emmey's chatter."

Lillian shrugged.

Maddy quietly sighed. "What is it, Lillian? What's the matter?"

"Nothing."

She moved to hold Lillian's hand with the one she didn't have, then let her stump drop with a sigh. "I don't believe you. You're miserable."

Lillian's face tightened. "I'm always miserable."

"No, you're not. Not like this."

Silence.

"Is there some reason you're not looking forward to the monastery?" Maddy asked.

"Why can't you just leave it?" Lillian muttered, ducking from under Maddy's arm. She stood and left the fire, stopping a short distance away with her back to Maddy.

Maddy approached her, but didn't touch her. "I can't leave it because I care about you and something's obviously wrong." Lillian's back remained turned. After a long silence, Maddy said, "Is it me? Have I done something? Has Emmey?"

Lillian finally faced her.

"Lillian," Maddy breathed, taken aback by the worry etched across Lillian's face. "What is it? Please tell me." She stepped forward, but stopped when Lillian shook her head.

"You have to promise not to laugh. Say anything you want, just don't laugh," Lillian said.

"I promise." She couldn't imagine what Lillian would say.

"We'll be back at the monastery tomorrow."

"Yes."

"Things will go back to how they were before. I don't want that anymore."

Was that why she'd barely said a word for a week? Maddy had thought they were getting along well. Was it because she'd lost her hand? "What do you mean?" she asked quietly.

"I don't want to go back to that."

"To what?"

Lillian wrung her hands. "You in your chambers and me in mine."

Dismay turned to hope. *Could it be?*

"I shouldn't ask, because it's selfish. I'm older and set in my ways. I won't change," Lillian said firmly. "So I shouldn't ask. But if I don't ask, I'll always wonder if it could have been me, if I'd only asked."

She held her breath.

Lillian met her eyes and gulped. "Will you be my consort?"

Maddy's voice trembled with excitement and awe. "I would be honoured to be your consort."

"You—you would?"

"Yes, I would."

Lillian bit her lip, then grabbed Maddy and embraced her. She pressed her wet cheek against Maddy's. "I love you."

Maddy smiled through her tears. "And I love you. And I know you need your time alone," she said, guessing that was Lillian's main concern. "Considering how much we've been together over the past few months, I'm surprised you're not sick of me."

"Me too," Lillian murmured, making Maddy laugh.

"It's a good job we're having this part of the conversation after I've agreed to be your consort," Maddy said. "And don't worry, I won't want to spend every moment with you. I'll have plenty to occupy my time." Such as relearning to do what had come easily with two hands. "I've been thinking about my embroidery. I want to talk to the carpenters, see if they can build a frame I don't have to hold, for when I'm in my chambers."

"That's a good idea."

"I should still be able to work on tapestries. We use the large frames for those." Though she wouldn't go near a tapestry until her left hand was as skilled with the needle as her right had been, which could take months. She drew back. "Have you been building up to this all week? Is that why you've been so quiet?"

Lillian nodded. "The closer we got to the monastery, the more I knew I'd miss it."

"Miss what?" Lillian couldn't mean their relationship. They hadn't planned to end it when they reached the monastery.

"Being there for each other at the end of the day and then retiring together. I love our time around the fire."

"Oh, so do I, Lillian. So do I." She gazed at Lillian. *My future consort.* She could hardly believe it. "Until our ceremony, we won't be able to retire together every evening, but I'm sure we can manage a walk."

"I'd like that very much." Lillian looked at Maddy uncertainly. "What?"

"Do you think I'll ever see you nude again?"

"Perhaps you should have asked that question earlier on," Maddy said with a chuckle. "Of course you will. With Emmey here . . . I thought it best to put that part of our relationship on hold until we're home." Home. She'd never think of the monastery as anything other than home again. Is that why Salbine had permitted her imprisonment? So Maddy would learn what trapped really meant?

Lillian snorted. "I understand that. I wasn't suggesting we should be rolling around next to the fire. But you never want to bathe with us. Is it because you're self-conscious . . . about your arm?"

"I was in the beginning, but not now."

"Then . . ."

Maddy winked. "You're not the only one who needs time alone, though I don't need anywhere near as much as you do. The odd time you and Emmey go off to bathe is enough." She lifted her stump. "I still feel my hand, you know."

"Do you?"

"Sometimes. And I may have lost it, but I feel whole. I am whole. And so pleased that I'll be your consort, Lillian. If I look glum tomorrow, it won't be because of you."

"Emmey."

Maddy nodded.

"We'll do our best to find her a decent home."

She'd still miss her terribly and wonder about her every day. "You do realize that being my consort means you'll have no choice but to go to Heath," she said, not wanting to brood about Emmey just yet. "You won't be able to back out."

"I won't want to. I'll have a malflowed consort, which means I'll be very interested in researching the subject," Lillian said. "Purely out of curiosity, not because it makes a blind bit of difference," she quickly added.

"I know," Maddy said, glowing over the "consort" part. Lillian had more than shown that Maddy's condition didn't matter to her. She'd left the comforts of the monastery to find Maddy, saved her life, put up with Emmey, and found the courage to propose. Maddy had taken so much; now she would give. She would love and be loyal to Lillian for the rest of their lives. Lillian would come second only to Salbine and Maddy's vows.

"Shall we go sit by the fire?" Lillian asked.

"Oh, yes."

They lowered themselves next to it, looked into each other's eyes, and kissed.

MADDY FELT AS if she were dreaming as she rode up the road that led to the monastery's gates. In her squalid cell, she'd sometimes wondered if she'd ever pass through them again, and now they were just ahead. If not for worrying about Emmey, she'd gallop the rest of the way and ride through them with tears of joy. Instead her eagerness to return to her sisters warred with dread.

"There's men there, Miss," Emmey said.

The sun reflected off the breastplates of the defenders standing guard at the open gates. "Welcome back," several of them shouted as Lillian slowed and waited for Maddy so they could walk their horses through together.

"Thank you," Maddy shouted back.

The moment she was through the gates, she pulled back on the reins. Lillian did the same and dismounted. The defenders at the gates must have spotted them climbing the hill and sent word of their arrival, because a group of sisters had gathered and now rushed forward to greet them, led by the abbess. Maddy dismounted and reached for Emmey.

"Welcome back!" the beaming abbess said, a sentiment echoed by those with her.

Maddy could feel Emmey clinging to her cloak. She put a reassuring hand on her shoulder and smiled at the familiar faces behind the abbess: Rose, Nora, Mistress Averill, and Mistress Elizabeth, among others. Rose's eyes widened when she saw Emmey. Then she gave her a little wave, warming Maddy's heart.

Maddy was most interested in Abbess Sophia's reaction, but the abbess was focused on Lillian; she probably wanted to pull her into a fierce hug. Maddy suspected that would come later.

"Why have you stopped here?" the abbess asked Lillian. "You don't need permission to enter."

"We don't, but we're not alone." Lillian looked at Emmey.

The abbess followed Lillian's gaze. Something—perhaps surprise—flickered across her face. "I see." She turned to those gathered behind her. "Sister Rose, would you mind caring for our guest while I speak to the mistress and the sister? Perhaps you can accompany the horses to the stables."

"I don't mind at all." Rose leaned forward, her hands on her knees. "Would you like to come with me and the horses . . ." She threw Maddy a questioning look.

"Emmey," Maddy said.

"Emmey!" Rose smiled. "Would you like to come with me, Emmey?"

"You should go with Sister Rose," Maddy said when Emmey looked up at her.

"Is she the one you pray for?" Emmey asked.

"Yes, she is." She met Rose's eyes. "And I'm very glad to see her."

Rose's eyes were moist. "We'll talk later," she said, glancing at Maddy's sewn sleeve. "Right now, this young lady and I are going to the stables." She held out her hand.

Maddy gently nudged Emmey. "Go on."

"Will I see you again?" Emmey asked, still clinging to Maddy.

"Yes, you will," she said, certain the abbess would allow her to say good-bye. "Now go with Sister Rose and Baxter, Griffin, and Ticky."

"Come on," Rose said encouragingly, still holding out her hand. Emmey finally took it. "We'll just wait here a minute for the stable hands to arrive, and then we'll go with them, all right?"

"Let's go to my study," the abbess said.

"Will we see you after evening prayers?" Mistress Averill asked. "Everyone's eager to welcome you home."

"Yes, will we?" Nora echoed.

"You certainly will," Maddy said, looking forward to catching up with everyone, but realizing too late that someone would have to care for Emmey while she was in the chapel—if Emmey was allowed to stay.

Mistress Averill looked at Lillian. "What about you, Mistress?"

"I suppose I can spare a few minutes after the service," Lillian said.

"Splendid. That's more than I would have expected," Mistress Averill said, her mouth turning up at the corners. "Welcome home, both of you."

Maddy bobbed. "Thank you."

She and Lillian fell into step with the abbess and Mistress Elizabeth. The abbess squeezed Lillian's arm but didn't say anything. As they walked in silence, Maddy wondered if the abbess would explode in anger when they reached her study, though she'd never raised her voice before, at least not within Maddy's hearing.

The abbess pushed open her study door. "I asked Henry to bring up a bottle of our best wine." A tray sitting on the small round table between the guest chairs held a bottle and four glasses. "Good, he brought glasses as well. But before we drink, let me properly welcome you home." She finally reached for Lillian and hugged her, then stepped back and took Lillian's face in her hands. "It's so wonderful to see you again," she said, smiling. "I had quite the scare when Barnabus returned alone."

"He made it, then?" Lillian said.

"Yes, he did." The abbess moved to Maddy. "And I'm so pleased you've come back to us, Maddy." Maddy was startled when the abbess moved to embrace her, but recovered in time to hug her back.

Mistress Elizabeth let go of Lillian and hugged Maddy. "Welcome back," she murmured.

The abbess poured the wine and motioned for everyone to take a glass. She raised hers. "We thank Salbine for your safe return." Her eyes settled on Maddy. "You're now back where you belong. Salbine's will be done."

"Salbine's will be done," everyone echoed. They clinked glasses and drank.

Lillian raised her glass. "My turn."

Suspecting what Lillian was about to announce, Maddy felt herself smile.

"I never thought I'd say this," Lillian said, her cheeks suddenly red. The abbess and Mistress Elizabeth looked on curiously as Lillian turned to Maddy. "To Maddy, who's agreed to be my consort. And to the wonderful life we'll spend together, in service to Salbine. Her will be done."

"Salbine's will be done," the abbess said enthusiastically as they clinked glasses again.

"That's lovely!" Mistress Elizabeth crowed after sipping her wine.

"I'm so pleased for both of you." The abbess put down her wine glass and covered her mouth. For a moment, Maddy thought she'd burst into tears. But she merely stared at them, as if she couldn't believe it. "Well," she finally said. "We have a lot to discuss, including when the two of you will pledge. I hope it will be soon." She patted Lillian's arm.

Maddy had the feeling that if the abbess could drag them to the chapel and bind them together that moment, she would.

"You'll want time to change and sup before evening prayers, so I won't keep you long. I want you both here tomorrow, after morning prayers. You can tell me everything then. For now, we'll stick to the most pressing matter."

"Emmey," Maddy stated.

"Yes. What's she doing here?" The abbess shifted her attention to Lillian. "You said in your letter you were taking her home."

"We tried." Lillian drained her glass and set it on the table. "But her ma's a whore who pops out babes to steal for her."

The abbess winced.

"You didn't take her from her ma, did you?" Mistress Elizabeth said. "She may be a woman of poor character, but you can't take a child away because you disapprove."

"We didn't!" Lillian snapped. "Her ma wasn't there."

"She'd upped and left for another town. Emmey's home was an empty, run-down shack," Maddy said. "We didn't know what to do. We couldn't abandon her with nobody to care for her. So we thought we'd bring her to Merrin and try to find a home for her. If she ends up in the alleys, we can at least watch out for her. We couldn't do that if we left her in Pinewood."

"And you're not going to do it here," the abbess said firmly. "It's not your place. Having said that, we're not without compassion. She can stay here until we've found her somewhere else to live."

"Thank you," Maddy breathed. "I'll start making inquiries as soon as I can."

The abbess shook her head. "I'll take care of it. Because it has to be done, and it has to be done quickly."

Maddy didn't protest. If it were left to her, she'd want the perfect home that didn't exist. The abbess had to do it for the same reason Lillian had gone to the orphanage.

"Where will she sleep in the meantime?" Lillian asked.

"I don't see any harm in her staying with you, in your chambers," the abbess said to Maddy. "Someone has to watch her. But make sure her stay isn't disruptive. Use your common sense. Areas like the training rooms, the library, and the study rooms are off-limits. Perhaps we should just say that she's limited to the Initiates Tower and the grounds."

"I understand," Maddy said. "What about evening prayers? I can put her to bed beforehand, but I don't want to leave her unattended."

"I can sit with her tonight." Mistress Elizabeth turned to the abbess. "If you don't mind me missing the service. Everyone wants to see these two. They won't miss me."

"True." The abbess pursed her lips. "But what about tomorrow? I doubt we'll find somewhere that quickly."

"Maddy and I can take turns," Lillian suggested. "After tonight, it won't be a tragedy if one of us isn't present at evening prayers while Emmey is here."

"I agree," Maddy said, surprised that Lillian had volunteered to sit with Emmey.

The abbess nodded. "That's settled, then. And Maddy, since you and Lillian are to be consorts, it's time to sit together. At evening prayers, come up and sit with Lillian."

"Among the mistresses?"

"You'll be consort to a mistress. And there's no rule saying the front belongs to the mistresses. It's just a habit everyone's fallen into."

Still, she'd feel as if she were elbowing her way in where she didn't belong.

"I'll announce your news when I open the service, so everyone knows."

Lillian grimaced. "Do you have to?"

"Yes, I do," the abbess replied. "Everyone will find out eventually. They'll all be there when you pledge."

Lillian muttered something under her breath, then said, "Well, it sounds like we've decided what to do about Emmey for now, so I want to go to my laboratory, see what sort of mess it's in."

The abbess rolled her eyes. "As far as I know, Dorothy followed all your instructions to the letter."

"I'll see, won't I?" Lillian headed for the door, then turned around. "Oh. See you later, Maddy." She left.

The abbess tutted. "You sure you know what you're doing, taking her as a consort?"

Maddy knew she didn't expect an answer.

Mistress Elizabeth downed the remains of her wine. "I'll leave the two of you to have a chat then, shall I? I'll see you at the service." She patted Maddy's right arm, then reddened. "Oh! Oh dear."

Maddy stifled a chuckle. "It's fine. It's just my arm."

"It's not sore or anything?"

"No."

Mistress Elizabeth looked skeptical, but left the study without another word.

"I'm sorry about your arm and hand," the abbess said. "I was horrified when Barnabus told me of it." She motioned for Maddy to sit as she rounded her desk. "Tell me, how are you?"

How to answer that question? "Glad to be home. And terribly sorry about how arrogant I was. I'm sorry I wouldn't listen and thought I knew better than everyone else here. I've just spent months away to learn that I belong where I started. If I'd only listened."

The abbess rested her elbows on her desk. "There are things we need to discover for ourselves. It's not unusual to only appreciate what you had when you no longer have it. I just wish the lesson hadn't demanded so much from you."

"I'm not sure I would have learned it, if it hadn't," Maddy admitted. "Now I know my place is here. I belong here."

"With Lillian?" the abbess asked with a smile.

"Yes." Maddy hesitated. "I know I'm young."

The abbess shook her head. "Maddy, you love my sister. More importantly, you understand her. That's all that matters. I'm delighted that you and Lillian will pledge. I suspected you would."

She didn't try to hide her pleasure at the abbess's remark.

"And I'm pleased that you feel you belong again."

"I do, but I'd still like to go to Heath. I still don't know how I'm to serve, especially now. I still don't understand why Salbine would call me and then deny me Her gifts."

"But you accept that Salbine called you."

"Yes. I have to, otherwise my life doesn't make sense."

The abbess pondered for a moment. "I think you should take some time to rest your body and your spirit. Enjoy this time with Lillian. Take the time to adapt to your . . . arm. When you're ready—" she raised a finger, "and don't tell me you are now, because I won't believe you—we'll help you find your answers. You need to rest first, recover from your ordeal and get used to life here again."

Maddy couldn't deny that puttering about the monastery without feeling she had to grapple with unfathomable mysteries would be a welcome respite. "I'd like to see if there's a way to embroider with my one hand. I thought I'd speak to the carpenters."

"You should. Don't hesitate to ask anyone for help." The abbess met her eyes. "About the documents . . ."

Maddy shook her head. "You couldn't have known."

"But you were right about those outside and how they view us."

"It could have been the circumstances, Abbess. If not for the fire near the inn, none of it would have happened. I don't blame you. So please don't blame yourself." She changed the subject. "I'm sorry I didn't contribute to your anniversary cassock. I wanted to."

"And you will. The anniversary service is still a month away. I told Mistress Bertha to leave a few stitches for you, in case you returned in time."

She must have done so before she'd learned of Maddy's hand. "But I can't."

"Yes, you can."

"My stitches will be horrible."

"But they'll be your stitches, Maddy. That's what matters. I'm sure the mistress will help you with them, if you need her aid."

Maddy's eyes welled. She should move back to the Novices Tower until she relearned what it meant to belong to a community.

"We've spoken enough for now. You should go to the stables."

"I will." She quickly wiped her eyes and rose. "Thank you for allowing Emmey to stay. I know—"

The abbess raised her hand. "We can talk about this tomorrow."

"Thank you, Abbess."

"You'll have to learn to call me Sophia when we're together socially, which I expect will be a lot more often now."

"To be honest, I'll find that difficult."

"We'll be family, Maddy. Well, we're already family, but soon we'll be family through blood, not only through spirit. I'll see you at the service." Maddy bobbed and left.

As she crossed the courtyard, she told everyone who stopped her that she'd chat with them after evening prayers. Hopefully Mistress Elizabeth would bring something to do while she minded Emmey.

At the stables, Rose was leaning over the fence, watching Thomas lead Emmey around the yard on a white horse.

"I can see she's already charmed Thomas," Maddy said, stopping next to her.

Rose nodded. "I'm surprised she wants to ride. She must be sick of it by now."

"She's never ridden by herself. She's doing well," Maddy said proudly.

Rose pushed away from the fence and held out her arms. "I didn't think I'd see you again," she said, hugging Maddy. "We were all on tenterhooks until Barnabus came back. Every time I heard that someone was approaching the gates, I'd rush out to look. To be honest, I still rushed out, even after he was back," she said sheepishly.

Maddy hugged her tightly. "I missed you."

"And I missed you." Rose stepped back. "Are you all right?" She glanced at Maddy's arm. "I couldn't believe it when I heard."

"It was that, or Salbine's realm." Yes, Salbine's realm. She had to have faith.

"I want to hear all about it," Rose breathed. "Everything!"

"We have a lot of catching up to do."

"We do! I . . . uh, should tell you something, before someone else does."

Rose's hesitation piqued Maddy's curiosity. "What?"

"It's about me and Nora. We've grown close."

"You mean—you and Nora?"

Rose nodded. "You're sort of to blame."

"Me?"

"I was worried sick about you. Nora was always willing to listen to me fret. It's funny, she'd been across the hall from you all that time, but I never really knew her that well."

"I'm glad I was out of the way for a while, then," Maddy said, meaning it. She liked Nora.

"What about you and the mistress? Are you still together? When you left without her, I did wonder," Rose lowered her voice, "if you were trying to get away from her."

"No. I definitely wasn't." Maddy drew a deep breath. "You'll probably think me mad, but Lillian asked me to be her consort, and I agreed."

Rose's eyes widened. "No, I don't think you're mad. Perhaps in the beginning I didn't quite understand it—the two of you—but I can see she cares about you. When she went riding off after you . . . oh dear," Rose placed her hand against her chest and finished in a husky voice, "so romantic."

Maddy bit back a laugh. "I don't think she sees it that way."

"But you love her?"

"Yes, I do."

"Aw . . ." Rose's face scrunched up. "I'm happy for you."

The chapel bells pealed in the distance. Maddy turned to yell, "Thomas!" When he looked at her, she beckoned him over.

He led Emmey to the fence and inclined his head. "Good to see you back, Sister."

"And I'm pleased to see you. I'm afraid I'll have to take Emmey away from you, though. We have things to do before evening prayers."

"She's welcome to come again."

Maddy smiled as she watched Thomas lead Emmey to the gate. Emmey ran toward her and stopped a few feet away. "Do I have to go now?" she asked, her fingers in her mouth.

"No. You're going to stay with me."

Emmey's face lit up. Maddy crouched to look into her eyes. "Only until the abbess finds you somewhere to live. Remember what we talked about."

"I know, Miss," she said mournfully, then glanced around. "Where's Lillian?"

"Lillian's busy."

"Will we see her later?"

Maddy would, but Emmey wouldn't. "Probably not. You'll see her tomorrow, though."

Rose ruffled Emmey's hair. "Shall we walk to the Initiates Tower together?"

"Yes, let's," Maddy said, straightening.

"You're the Miss's friend," Emmey declared, grabbing Maddy's left hand.

Rose looked at Maddy. "Are you the Miss?"

Maddy nodded.

"Then yes, I am her friend." Rose hesitated, then gently slipped her arm through Maddy's right arm. "Glad we can still do this," she said with a smile.

A lump formed in Maddy's throat. Rose's simple gesture had put to rest any lingering doubt she may have had about reaffirming her commitment to the Order. She belonged here. If not for the little girl clutching her hand, she'd regret ever leaving.

Chapter Twenty-One

LILLIAN STOPPED AT THE DOOR TO her chambers and turned to Maddy. "Now—"

Mistress Meredith emerged from the nearest stairwell. "Oh, thought it might be you two ahead of me." She gripped Maddy and Lillian's arms. "I'm so pleased for you. And I'm glad you're back, Lillian. Dorothy's tinctures just aren't the same. Think you can prepare me another one soon?"

Fortunately for Lillian, Dorothy had anticipated Meredith's request. "I'll bring you one tomorrow."

"Oh, good. Well, I won't get in the way." She released their arms and carried on up the hall.

Lillian leaned closer to Maddy. "I bet she'll tell me how much better it is than Dorothy's, even though it'll be Dorothy's," she murmured, then smiled when Maddy smiled. She pushed the door open. "Let's get this over with, then."

Maddy raised her brows. "Should I cover my eyes?"

"No, no." Lillian entered her chambers and held her breath. "Wait a minute. Let me light the fire and a couple of lamps." Her hands trembled as she knelt in front of the fireplace and struck the flint. She had butterflies! Fortunately the amadou caught the spark. Lillian blew carefully on the dry fungus and used it to light the lamps, then the fire. She straightened and faced the door. "Come in."

Maddy stepped into the chambers and surveyed the room, her gaze homing in on the horse carving sitting on a shelf. "What's that? Can I look at it?"

Her stomach churning, Lillian nodded.

Maddy crossed to the carving and lifted it. "It's lovely," she breathed. "Such detail. And there's another one!" After carefully setting the horse down, she picked up the bird at the other end of the shelf. "It's beautiful."

"It's something to do when I'm sitting in front of the fire," Lillian said quietly.

Maddy gaped at her. "You did them! Why haven't you ever shown me one before? They're gorgeous."

Probably because she'd proudly given one to Caroline, a fox she'd lovingly slaved over until it was perfect, and received a disinterested "thank you." She'd expected it to be on display in Caroline's chambers, but had never seen it again. Caroline had probably tossed it down one of the latrines.

"And I can see you do this in front of the fire," Maddy said, eyeing the dusty shavings around the chair, then smiling when she spotted her birthday gift. She looked at Lillian. "We'll need another chair."

Lillian's throat tightened. "Yes, we will."

"Are you working on one now?" Maddy gestured toward the bird carving.

"No, I wasn't sure what to do next."

Maddy raised her arms and covered her stump with her hand, something she did when she was excited. "Can I choose?"

"I suppose that would be fitting, since these will soon be your chambers too." Something Lillian could hardly believe, though she seemed to be the only one who felt that way. Had everyone expected them to become consorts except her? Few eyebrows had risen when Maddy sat next to Lillian during evening prayers, and shocked gasps hadn't filled the chapel when Sophia announced that Mistress Lillian and Sister Maddy would pledge.

"I'll think about it," Maddy said, breaking into Lillian's thoughts. She swept her left arm through the air several times.

"What are you doing?"

"Wondering how effectively I can sweep. I wonder if a shorter handle would help. Another thing to discuss with the carpenters." Maddy glanced around. "We'll have to add a bit of colour."

"Colour?"

"It's a bit austere in here, isn't it? A few hangings will help, and perhaps new cushions, to go with the one I gave you."

She'd never thought of her chambers as drab.

"Let's have a look at the bedchamber."

"This would be yours." Lillian pushed open one of the doors on the chamber's east wall.

"Oh yes, I forgot that you mistresses have two bedchambers."

"Most of us do take consorts," Lillian mumbled.

Maddy peered into the gloomy room and sneezed. She carefully picked up one of the lamps and used it to illuminate the piles of tomes and scrolls covering every inch of the floor. "Lillian! Does Mistress Averill know you have half the library in here?"

"I wouldn't say it's half the library," Lillian said faintly.

"I can see I'll be busy," Maddy said, her tone brisk. "Can I come in when you're not here?"

"Why? What are you planning to do?"

"Sweep." Maddy waved her hand into the room. "Take all this back to the library."

"What? I need these."

Maddy sighed. "Lillian, the tomes in the back are so covered in dust, it's clear you haven't touched them in years. If you do need them, they'll be in the library. Or are you expecting me to sleep on them?"

"I'm hoping you'll be with me in my bedchamber." Lillian cleared her throat. "Most nights."

"I'll still want my own bedchamber."

"I know," she said, wincing at the resignation she heard in her voice.

"Are you sure you want to do this?" Maddy asked.

"Yes! I'm just not used to someone else . . ." She searched for a way to express herself that would be less inflammatory than "taking over my chambers" and finished triumphantly with, "Organizing my chambers!"

"Soon to be *our* chambers."

"I know, I know!"

Maddy's forehead creased. "I'll try not to charge in here like a bull. But I'd like to keep myself busy, especially after Emmey's gone."

It wouldn't work. Lillian had done the same when Maddy was away. No matter how many chores Maddy found to distract herself, the second she had a quiet moment, her thoughts would turn to Emmey. But she wouldn't be lonely. Lillian would see to that.

"What's yours like?" Maddy asked, moving to the other door but waiting for Lillian to push it open. She peered inside and grunted. "Neater than I'd expected."

"I don't spend much time in there."

Maddy waggled her eyebrows. "I wonder if that will change now."

Lillian cursed her hot cheeks. "I wish you could stay tonight."

"I don't."

"What?"

"That didn't come out right," Maddy said with a chuckle. "I do wish we could spend the night together, but not here. I want to save that until we've pledged."

Lillian's blood stopped pounding in her ears.

"I'd better get back, otherwise Mistress Elizabeth will have a fit."

"We told her we'd come here after evening prayers," Lillian reminded her.

"We said for a few minutes."

Disappointed, Lillian nodded. "So we did."

Maddy bit her lip. "Emmey was asking after you. I told her she'll see you tomorrow. Will we?"

"Yes." Going a day without seeing Maddy was now unimaginable.

"I know you'll have things to do, but perhaps you'll watch Emmey while I attend morning prayers, and then we can all go for a walk together."

"All right. If you like, I'll bring you breakfast after early morning prayers. You should be up by then, with Emmey around."

Maddy set the lamp down and pinched Lillian's cheek. "I'd like that very much." She pressed her lips against Lillian's, but pulled away when Lillian parted her lips. "No. If we start that, I won't be able to tear myself away. I'll see you tomorrow." She darted into the hall before Lillian could respond.

Lillian shook her head and pushed the door shut. She swallowed at the sight of the one chair in front of the fire. Her chambers had never felt empty before, but Maddy's absence was palpable. Lillian couldn't wait for the colourful tapestries, the new cushions, and, most especially, the second chair by the fire.

Perhaps love wasn't so bad after all.

MADDY KNOCKED AT the abbess's study door and opened it in response to the muffled, "Come in."

"Please sit, Maddy." The abbess looked more drawn than usual.

"No, thank you," Maddy said when the abbess offered her a cup of tea. The air felt heavy; holding a cup might not be a good idea. She smoothed her robe and tried to relax as the abbess poured her own tea and blew on it. Her apprehension grew when the abbess gazed at her and sighed.

"I've summoned you here to tell you that I've found a home for Emmey," the abbess said.

Already? It had only been four days.

"The Carmichaels are willing to take her."

Maddy's heart sank. She knew of the Carmichaels; a constant stream of children passed through their farm, helping with the harvests and livestock and sleeping in the barns. Still, it would be better than the alleys.

The abbess's mouth pinched in sympathy. "She'll have a full belly and a roof."

But not love.

"It's the best we can do. She's not a babe."

"I know." Expecting a family to welcome Emmey as a daughter hadn't been realistic, but Maddy had hoped for it anyway. Merrin was no different from any other town; orphans roamed its streets, searching for scraps and begging for coin. Few families could afford an extra mouth to feed, nor did they have the room for another bed and the time to nurture another tiny soul. Was it so bad that Emmey would spend her days in the fields and with farm animals? Maddy had grown up on a farm—but among those who loved and cherished her, not as someone akin to a hired farmhand. "She'll have my visits."

The abbess tensed. "No."

Maddy's breath caught in her throat. "What?"

"No, Maddy. Visiting Emmey wouldn't be a good idea."

"But . . ." Maddy pressed her lips together to stop their trembling.

"I know you care about her," the abbess said gently, "but you're a Salbine Sister. Your place is here, and you have much work to do regarding your spiritual life. I can't have half of you here and half of you out there. When we join the Order, we don't cut off our families, but we do leave them behind. You're too involved with this girl, Maddy. You have to let go now."

Knowing the abbess was right, Maddy didn't protest, but tears spilled onto her cheeks. "I'm sorry. I couldn't help but care for her," she said tremulously.

The abbess rose and rounded the desk. "I'm not criticizing you," she said, crouching next to Maddy and taking her hand. "Of course you couldn't help but care. You went through a terrible ordeal together, and you were each other's only friend for months. Only someone with a heart of stone wouldn't have cared. And you always reach out, Maddy. It's one of the things I admire about you. But you can't continue your relationship with Emmey. You have to return to your calling, find that purpose you seek." She let go of Maddy's hand to return to her desk and pull a handkerchief from a drawer.

"Thank you," Maddy murmured, accepting it and wiping her eyes. "When are the Carmichaels taking her?"

The abbess settled back into her chair. "Wednesday. I wanted to give you some time with her before she goes."

Two days away. "Thank you."

"Bring her here about eleven o'clock. I'll have one of the defenders take her to the farm."

"Yes, Abbess." On the verge of losing her composure again, she pressed the handkerchief against her mouth.

The abbess swallowed. "I am sorry."

"May I go now?" Maddy managed to say. "I'd like to tell Emmey."

"Of course. Salbine go with you."

She rose and bobbed, then fled the study. But she didn't head to the Initiates Tower, where Emmey was helping Rose sew—or probably vice versa. Instead, she went to the chapel.

Two sisters sat praying to the left of the centre aisle. Maddy chose a bench on the right, lowered her head, and pressed her left hand against her heart, her way of praying, now that she didn't have two hands to press together.

No words came, nor did she seek any. She wept, wanting to purge herself before she saw Emmey. Except for Lillian, everything was a mess. Maddy couldn't seem to do anything right and didn't know what Salbine wanted from her. She'd answered Salbine's call, only to be denied Her gifts. She'd left the monastery to seek answers, only to be thrown into prison. And she'd been placed in a situation that could only ever have led to grief and a tremendous sense of loss. She'd even lost her hand! Was there a reason behind everything that had happened to her? Would she ever understand it? Was Salbine punishing her, trying to teach her, laughing at her? Did Salbine care?

"Are you all right, Sister?" someone asked softly.

Maddy raised her head.

Sister Elouise peered at her. "Would you like me to fetch Mistress Lillian?"

"No. I'm fine, thank you." She didn't want Lillian to see her like this. "It doesn't have anything to do with the mistress," Maddy quickly added, in case Sister Elouise jumped to the conclusion that she was having second thoughts about pledging. "Thank you for your concern."

"May Salbine guide you." Sister Elouise patted her shoulder and left her alone.

After dabbing at her eyes one last time, Maddy left the chapel and returned to her chambers, hoping her grief wasn't apparent. Emmey and Rose were bent over a piece of cloth. Maddy stopped in the doorway to watch them, reluctant to spoil things with her news.

"Through there," Rose said, watching Emmey. Her tongue stuck out in concentration, Emmey guided the needle through the cloth. "That's it!" Rose said, clapping as Emmey lifted the needle back into the air. She raised her head and spotted Maddy. "Look who's here!" When she saw Maddy's face, her own fell. "Put the needle down for a minute, Emmey."

Rose pushed back her chair and went to Maddy. "What's the matter?" she said softly. "What did the abbess want?"

"She's found a home for Emmey," Maddy whispered.

Rose didn't need further explanation. She hugged Maddy. "I'll leave you be, then. If you want me to watch her again, just let me know. I'll be in my chambers."

Maddy squeezed Rose's hand. "Thank you."

"Look, Miss." Excitement lit Emmey's face as she held up the cloth. "I did these stitches!"

Maddy pushed the door shut and moved to peer at Emmey's handiwork. "You did very well."

Picking up on Maddy's lack of enthusiasm, Emmey dropped the cloth to the table, her shoulders slumped. "They're no good."

"No, no, they're fine." Maddy sat in the chair Rose had left. "We need to have a little chat."

"What's wrong, Miss?"

She tried, really tried, but her voice sounded flat. "The abbess has found somewhere for you to live."

Emmey's face grew solemn. "Oh."

"It's on a farm. You'll help with the harvest and get to be around animals, and there will be other children there too. You'll sleep in a barn, but you'll be outside all day and you'll never go hungry." It was all true, but she felt as if she were lying. "I grew up on a farm." And had lived in the house with two parents who loved her.

"Will I have to nick things?"

"No. But you will have to put in a hard day's work."

"When do I have to go?" Emmey's voice quavered, defying her brave face.

"Wednesday. So we still have some time together."

"And then you'll visit me, right?"

She couldn't say it. For the first time she wondered if it would have been better if she hadn't been thrown into Emmey's cell. Lillian's words at the inn in Pinewood came back to haunt her: *"All that talk about leaving with her clothes and releasing you because you've fulfilled your promise is her way of rejecting you before you reject her. Because that's what she's expecting. Another rejection."*

Emmey's eyes welled. "You don't want me no more."

"No! That's not it at all." Her voice was trembling; Maddy took a moment to breathe. "It's just that . . . you see, I'm a sister. I came here to serve Salbine, and that's what I have to do. I have to be here. I'd love it if you could be here too, but you can't. And that makes me very sad. Because I'll miss you very much." Salbine preserve her! She thought she'd already cried herself dry.

"Don't cry, Miss." Emmey brushed away her own tears. "You saved me."

"We saved each other." She pulled the handkerchief from her robe pocket and wiped Emmey's face, then her own. Tears threatened again when Emmey's little hand slipped into hers.

Emmey met Maddy's eyes. "I wish you were my ma."

Maddy struggled to get her words out. "Children weren't meant for me, but if they were, I'd be proud to have a daughter as bright and as brave as you." When Emmey climbed into her lap and hugged her, she didn't protest and held her tightly. "You know I love you. If I wasn't a sister . . ." She couldn't go on.

"When I'm older, I'll come visit you," Emmey said.

Maddy doubted that, but still visualized herself an older woman, greeting a younger woman named Emmey at the gates. She pushed the fantasy away. She had to let go. Absolutely. "We'll both have to be brave on Wednesday. It's something we'll do together." The last thing they'd ever do together, sadly.

Emmey drew back. "I'll miss Lillian too."

Maddy tapped Emmey's nose. "And Lillian will miss you." She wasn't fibbing. Lillian's affection for Emmey didn't run as deep as Maddy's, but she made the effort to see her every day. Maddy was certain Lillian's motives for doing so went beyond pleasing her.

"Are you all right, Miss?"

"Yes." For Emmey's sake, she wouldn't be maudlin. "Let's make the best of our time together, all right?" Her forced smile probably made her look ghoulish.

"Yes, Miss." Emmey's voice lacked conviction.

Maddy swallowed. "It's almost suppertime. Shall we see if Lillian wants to have supper with us?"

Emmey nodded.

"Down you go, then. I'll take you to Sister Rose's and then get Lillian. We'll bring supper back with us."

"I want to show Lillian my stitches," Emmey said, picking up the cloth.

"We'll have supper here, so you don't have to bring it with you."

"Maybe you should take it, in case Lillian says no."

"She won't." Maddy would tell her the abbess's news, if her face didn't do it for her. Lillian wouldn't shrug and turn away.

She'd need Lillian's shoulder a lot in the coming weeks. Who would Emmey have? The best Maddy could do was pray for her, and she would, every time she knelt. But for once, she agreed with Lillian. She'd rather do something practical. She'd rather be there for Emmey, in body as well as spirit.

MADDY BLEW HER nose and pocketed the handkerchief. They were on their fourth circuit around the Initiates Tower, the torch in Lillian's left hand illuminating the cobblestones, and the breeze nipping at their ears. Emmey had been fast asleep when Maddy had left her chambers. Rose and Nora were across the hall with Nora's door open, in case Emmey woke.

She gripped Lillian's arm. "I don't know why you haven't told me to go in. I can't stop crying."

"I've expected this ever since Pinewood," Lillian said. "And I knew Sophia would be quick." She turned to Maddy, her face gentle. "You've always known she couldn't stay. If word got around that we're taking in orphans, we'd be inundated. Folk would leave babes at the gates. That's not what we do."

"I know Emmey can't stay." Maddy drew a shaky breath. "But it's one of those things you don't let yourself believe until it actually happens. It's the only way you can bear it."

Lillian grunted.

"I told her you'll miss her. Will you?"

"It will seem odd not having her around. I've grown used to her. I suppose I will miss her, but not half as much as you will," Lillian admitted.

Maddy sighed. "I foolishly got too involved."

"You were in prison with her. And you're not the sort to hold folk at arm's length. Even if you were, you would have forged a bond with her under those conditions. Anyone would have." Lillian's tone lost its gentleness. "I'd like us to pledge soon. I'll worry about you, in your chambers on your own."

"What do you mean?" Maddy said, bristling.

"Emmey's been there for you, to help you . . . do things. Now you'll be on your own."

Maddy opened her mouth to insist that she could manage by herself, then clamped it shut. She wasn't helpless, but did require aid with a few tasks. Nora had been coming across and lighting the fire in the mornings, a task too dangerous for Emmey. Truth be told, anything involving the fire frightened Maddy. She hadn't made tea since returning, petrified of burning her remaining hand. Fortunately Lillian had dropped in on them every evening and had lit the fire while there; otherwise her and Emmey's nights would have been chillier. Maddy gave Lillian a sidelong glance. Was that the reason she'd made a point to come to see them every evening? To light the fire? Maddy had been too embarrassed to ask Nora to do it in the evenings, as well.

It wasn't just the fire; it was the myriad little things that popped up during the day. One of the shutters had always been temperamental, easy to hook closed but difficult to open. She'd always had to push it against the window while unhooking it, an impossible task now. She'd tried leaning on it, but that had meant grappling with the cord from an awkward angle that hadn't worked. In the end, Emmey had stood on a chair and done the pushing. The heavy lid on Maddy's chest was more difficult to open with one hand. She'd always needed two hands to pull open the door to the Community Tower; now she had to hang around outside until someone else came along. She'd written a letter to her parents—probably illegible!—and had made a right mess of folding and sealing the paper. The tax collector who received it would wonder if she'd been drunk.

Emmey always helped when she could, and Maddy didn't feel embarrassed or humiliated when she did, perhaps because they were dependent on each other. But now Emmey would be gone. Maddy would have to ask others for help with those tasks that absolutely required two hands, and relearn how to do those that didn't. The prospect frightened her. What if she couldn't learn how to do things for herself? Would she be like a babe, always dependent on others? "I don't want to be dependent on you, Lillian."

"I don't want you to be dependent on me, either. And you won't be. But that doesn't mean you won't need a little help every once in a while, especially in the coming weeks."

"I'll hate every minute of it."

Lillian nodded. "I would too."

"But I want to pledge soon. To be with you." Though when they pledged, guilt would temper her happiness. How could it not, with Emmey on that farm?

They reached the entrance to the Tower once again. "Another round?" Lillian asked.

"One more. I won't sleep tonight, so there's no point rushing to bed."

"I thought perhaps we could all spend the day together tomorrow, since it'll be Emmey's last full day here. Perhaps ride the horses out to the river and have a picnic lunch?"

"I'd like that, and I know she would too. Don't let me get weepy."

Lillian chuckled. "And just how am I supposed to do that?"

Maddy's silence was ample answer.

Chapter Twenty-Two

SOPHIA BREATHED A SIGH OF RELIEF when Lillian stopped on the path ahead of her and surveyed the sky. She'd been trying to catch up to her since leaving the chapel after early morning prayers.

"Looks like we might get a shower or two," Lillian said when Sophia reached her. "Maddy and I planned to take Emmey for a picnic lunch."

"The sun's trying to break through. The showers won't last long."

Elizabeth joined them. "You can shelter under the trees."

Lillian lowered her eyes. "I suppose."

"You look a bit ragged this morning." It was the reason Sophia had chased after Lillian. "Everything all right?"

"I was up late with Maddy last night."

"I see." She could guess why, and felt awful. But she'd had no choice, despite knowing that parting Maddy and Emmey would deeply hurt both of them. Sometimes she wished she wasn't the abbess. "It had to be done."

"She'll be all right," Lillian muttered. "She knew it was coming."

"Even so, I don't think you can prepare yourself for that sort of loss," Elizabeth said.

"A strange turn of events, for sure," Sophia murmured. "Normally a sister wouldn't have the opportunity to become so attached to someone outside the Order, especially a child."

"And now she has to deal with losing Emmey on top of everything else," Lillian said, her face etched with worry.

Sophia patted Lillian's arm, still marvelling that Lillian cared for Maddy so much. Yet another unexpected turn, though this one pleased her immensely. "We'll all be here for her."

Lillian changed the subject. "She's having trouble with the Community Tower's main door. I don't think she can open it on her own, because she always waits for me to do it. I don't know what she does when I'm not with her."

"That door's always been stubborn," Elizabeth said.

Sophia nodded. "I'll have one of the men look at it. Anything else?"

"Probably, but don't expect her to tell me," Lillian said.

So Maddy's pride was getting in the way. "Perhaps I'll have a chat with her next week, ask her if there's anything—"

"Abbess!" Barnabus strode up to them and bowed. "One of Merrin's guards has brought word that a noble is on his way to the monastery. Apparently he's quite angry with us, claims we're harbouring a criminal."

"Harbouring a—You don't think he means the girl, do you?" Sophia asked.

"She's not a bloody criminal!" Lillian snapped.

Sophia held up her hand. "How did the guard come by this information?"

"A couple of travellers passed the noble's camp on the way to Merrin, enjoyed the comforts of his fire for a while. Apparently he's camped a few miles from the southwest gate, or at least he was yesterday. According to the guard, he planned to break camp this morning."

"Which means he could be here in mere hours. Does he have men with him?"

Barnabus nodded. "About twenty, though that's based on the travellers' estimate and could be erroneous. I doubt they did a head count."

Sophia turned to Lillian. "Do you know anything about this noble?"

"Emmey tried to steal a noble's purse. If it's him, he's the one who threw her into prison. But you can't give her to him, Sophia. She's just a child."

"That may be true, but if he has the appropriate documents, he's right. We are harbouring a criminal, and he's legally entitled to her."

Lillian's face reddened. "You can't possibly give her to him!"

"What type of man throws an eight-year-old into prison for trying to steal his purse and then rides after her when she gets out?" Elizabeth said.

"A proud one who won't go away empty-handed," Sophia said.

Lillian frowned. "Maddy thought he'd forgotten about her."

"He probably had, until he heard about the trouble at the prison. Then it suddenly became important for him to personally ensure his little prisoner was dead, or still rotting away in a cell. As I said, he won't go away empty-handed." Sophia's mind raced.

"Do you know the man's name or from where he hails, Mistress Lillian?" Barnabus asked.

"No. Arthur seemed frightened of him, to the point that he wouldn't tell Maddy the man's name. Just said he was very powerful."

Barnabus grunted. "According to the travellers, this noble is from County Bradford."

"That's where the prison is!"

"Yes, Mistress, so it's not surprising the governor would know of him."

"And probably told him about Emmey leaving the prison and Maddy's intention to take her home," Lillian added. Arthur had always been the weak point in Maddy's hastily devised escape plan for Emmey. In truth, the success of the plan had always rested on whether anyone would come looking for the "master thief." Everyone had assumed nobody would.

"I agree," Barnabus said. "He wouldn't have held his silence when faced with the man he feared. Once this noble knew Emmey was gone, it would have been a simple matter of determining that she'd left Reedwick in the company of sisters from Merrin. Any guard would have told him."

"So he followed us to Pinewood and then here," Lillian said.

"He's probably been days behind you the entire way."

Lillian turned to Sophia. "We'll meet him at the gates and see him off."

"You won't, Lillian. I don't want you and your mouth anywhere near the gates."

"He has men with him! You need me."

"You're not the only mage here. Elizabeth and I can handle twenty men on our own, but I'll greet him with at least five mistresses. We'll end any conflict before they're off their horses, but I don't want it to come to that, especially since, strictly speaking, we're in the wrong."

"She's eight!"

"I know, and I agree that she never should have been sent to prison. But she was. And strictly speaking, she escaped."

Lillian glared at her. "Don't give her to him, Sophia. It doesn't matter what you think of Emmey, you know it would be wrong."

"Of course it would be wrong!" she shouted, then exhaled sharply when she felt Elizabeth's hand on her arm. Two passing sisters stopped to look, then bobbed and quickly moved on. Sophia took a deep breath and reminded herself that Lillian cared about Emmey, whether she'd admit it or not. She softened her voice. "You have to trust me, Lillian. I trusted you and let you go after Maddy. Now it's your turn to trust me. This is a proud man who may have documents entitling him to Emmey. As I said before, he's not the sort who'll go away empty-handed. We'll have to negotiate, give him something else."

"What else?" Lillian asked.

"I don't know." Though a seed of a plan germinated in her mind. "But when we're negotiating, one wrong word, one perceived hostile look or tone, could have him stubbornly insisting on the girl. So I don't want you anywhere near the gates or this man. When the defenders spot him coming up the hill, I want you, Maddy, and Emmey out of sight."

Lillian folded her arms.

"Watch from the top floor of the Community Tower. You'll have a good vantage point from there." Sophia raised a finger. "But do not, under any circumstances, come down and into the courtyard. I don't care if a full-fledged conflict erupts and fire is raining from the sky, you stay inside with Maddy and Emmey. Do you understand?" When Lillian's mouth set into a stubborn line, Sophia inwardly sighed and tried another tack. "Maddy and Emmey will need you to protect them."

"Fine." Lillian sighed and dropped her arms to her side. "I'd better let Maddy know what's happening." She stalked off.

"So what *are* you planning to do?" Elizabeth asked.

"I may have an idea. Barnabus, would you find the Mistresses Averill and Bertha and ask them to come to my study immediately?"

"Yes, Abbess. Who else would you like with you at the gates?"

She wasn't summoning them for that reason, but no matter. "I'm not sure yet. When I've decided, I'll find them myself."

"Would you like a company of Defenders present?"

"I suppose there's no harm in putting on a bit of a show. Have them attend in ceremonial dress. Oh, and come to my study with the mistresses. I have a task for you."

"Of course." He strode off.

Elizabeth gazed at her. "Now that we're alone, are you going to tell me?"

"Tell you what?"

"Your plan."

Sophia motioned for Elizabeth to walk with her, wanting to be in her study when the mistresses and Barnabus arrived. In a low voice, she outlined her intentions for Elizabeth. "But you're never to breathe a word of this to anyone," she said when she'd finished. "If I fail, Maddy and Lillian are never to know what was on the negotiating table. They'd be heartbroken." So she couldn't fail. Especially since she didn't have a plan B.

LILLIAN PAUSED ON the Community Tower's top floor landing to catch her breath and heard Maddy's low voice answer Emmey's high-pitched one; two other voices were also contributing to the conversation. When she left the stairwell, everyone peered at her from their stools.

Sisters Rose and Nora stood, bobbed, and said, "Mistress," in unison. Sister Rose was Maddy's closest friend, and Sister Nora was Sister Rose's lover. Lillian had given some thought to this.

"There's no need to be formal when we're alone," she told them. The pleasure on Maddy's face warmed her, but then she remembered why they were gathered. "They're coming." She expected Maddy and her friends to rush to the windows, but they remained where they were, perhaps so they wouldn't upset Emmey.

Emmey looked at Maddy. "You won't let them take me, will you, Miss?"

"It's not up to me," Maddy said. "But don't worry. The abbess will protect you."

Lillian could hear the doubt in her voice and wondered if Emmey heard it too. She crossed to one of the windows overlooking the gates and pushed it open. Defenders had formed a line on either side of the gates and stood at attention, the Salbine crest emblazoned across their breastplates shining dully in the overcast light. Sophia was striding across the courtyard with Barnabus at her side and Elizabeth, Averill, Ivy, Clarissa, and Meredith behind her. Otherwise the courtyard was deserted; everyone had been told to stay inside. Sophia's group stopped several yards away from the gates and waited. Lillian sucked in her breath as fire and air swirled around her, not through her. Every mage in that courtyard was ready.

"What's happening?" Maddy asked.

"Nothing, yet," she said hoarsely. Then the tip of a standard came into view as the noble and his men crested the hill. Lillian counted twenty-two men, a pushover for a couple of mages, let alone six and a company of Defenders, though the defenders were there to protect Sophia and the mistresses as they drew, not as aggressors.

The standard-bearer and a man with a fur cloak draped over his shoulders, presumably the noble, rode in front of the others. The company stopped just outside the gates. Lillian couldn't see Sophia's face, but could tell by her gesturing that she was speaking. Suddenly the noble and his men dismounted, and one man, presumably the company's captain, walked with the noble through the gates. They bowed to Sophia, a good sign. With Barnabus still at her side, Sophia motioned for them to follow her and led them away. The mistresses stood their ground, but started to chat among themselves; fire and air no longer assaulted Lillian's senses. When the noble's men streamed through the gates, the defenders relaxed their stances and mingled with them.

Lillian turned to Maddy and the others. "They've come through the gates. He's gone off with the abbess."

Maddy looked fearfully toward the stairwell.

"They're not coming here. They went in the other direction, probably to the abbess's study." To negotiate, but for what? Coin? She couldn't see that assuaging the noble's gargantuan pride, though he wasn't stupid. He'd quickly agreed to talk. Who wouldn't, when at the gates of a Salbine monastery backed by a paltry twenty-one men? "And everyone looks relaxed. The defenders and the noble's men are friendly. They'll probably share ale at the barracks."

"I'm going to pray for the abbess." Sister Rose abandoned her stool and knelt. Sister Nora joined her.

"I will too," Maddy said, rising. "Emmey, why don't you look out the window with Lillian?"

Emmey scurried to Lillian but was too short to see outside. After pulling the window shut, Lillian carried a stool over and helped her onto it. "All this because you tried to steal his purse," Lillian murmured to her.

"I didn't want to," Emmey said. "I only did it so my ma would stop shouting at me. She wouldn't have needed me to nick no more if I'd gotten that purse."

Lillian doubted that. The greedy were never satisfied.

"I was in the market, and I saw the purse right in front of me." If the noble had been standing, his purse would have been at Emmey's eye level. Emmey's eyes must have popped out of her head when the fat purse had appeared right in front of her. "He caught me with my hand in it," Emmey finished.

"You didn't have a knife with you?"

Emmey shook her head.

"You do know that men's purses are attached to their belts. You'd never have made off with it." Only whores and armed bandits could part a man from his purse without a knife.

"That's why I had my hand in it."

Ah, so Emmey hadn't been caught stealing a purse, but what was inside a purse. "I doubt your little hands could have carried much coin. It's unfortunate you didn't have a knife with you, or at least a bag." What was she doing, expecting a naive eight-year-old to have meticulously planned the theft of a noble's purse—and worse, offering her advice on how to improve her thieving? "But you were caught, so no matter." And sentenced to life in prison by the idiot in Sophia's study.

"The others only ever got boxed around the ears when they were caught."

"You tried to steal from the wrong person," Lillian said. "Not that I'm suggesting you should have stolen from the right one."

Emmey frowned. "I didn't want to nick."

"I know." She pointed out the window. "Look, they're bringing the horses in now." Emmey pressed her nose against the glass.

Time wore on. Maddy joined Lillian at the window when Emmey wandered away. "This isn't how I wanted to spend my last day with

Emmey," she murmured to Lillian, watching the other two sisters sitting on the floor, playing pat-a-cake with Emmey. "And it's going to end badly, isn't it? He's obviously not accepting whatever the abbess is offering."

Lillian put her arm around her. "Not necessarily," she said. Though she couldn't help but worry.

Her worry only deepened as the sun continued its journey across the sky with no word from Sophia. "It's warm in here, isn't it?" she said to nobody in particular. She pushed open a couple of the windows, just in time to hear the chapel bells announce six o'clock. They'd been waiting for over five hours, she realized as she gazed out the window, surprised that she wasn't hungry. Movement caught her eye. "Wait!" she blurted. The noble's men were leading their horses to the gates!

"What's happening?" Maddy asked, nervousness tightening her voice.

"I'm not sure. It looks like they're getting ready to—"

Footsteps echoed in the stairwell. Maddy hugged Emmey to her. Sisters Rose and Nora stood protectively next to them, their faces grim. Lillian fought the urge to draw. If Sophia had given Emmey over to the noble, striking him or any of his men down would ensnare the monastery and Merrin in a bloody conflict that could last years. They'd have to free Emmey another way.

The footsteps grew louder. All released a collective sigh of relief when Averill emerged from the stairwell. She stared at them. "Oh dear. It's only me. I've come for Emmey."

"Why?" Lillian said. Maddy tightened her grip on Emmey.

"To take her to the library." Averill frowned when everyone stood their ground. "Look out the window. They're leaving."

Lillian turned back to the window. The noble and the captain had returned to the courtyard and were mounting their horses. She looked at Maddy. "It's true."

"He's not taking her?" Maddy asked, her voice tremulous.

Averill shook her head. "So let me take her to the library. The abbess wants to see you and Mistress Lillian in her study."

Maddy's grip relaxed. "She's not allowed in the library."

"The abbess will explain everything," Averill said, her expression unreadable. "Let me take her. Please."

"All right." Maddy let go of Emmey. "Go with Mistress Averill," she said when Emmey hesitated. "Go on."

Emmey still wouldn't budge. "Will I see you again?" she asked Maddy.

Maddy looked to Averill for the answer. "Yes, you'll see her again." Averill's light voice and the smile she quickly masked gave Lillian pause. "So come with me and I'll show you the library. I'm told you can read."

"And write," Emmey said proudly.

"You can write, can you? That's very interesting. I'd like to see you write. Do you think you can show me?"

Emmey's wariness vanished. Her chattering echoed up the stairwell as she and Averill descended the stairs.

"Thank you for waiting with us, and for your prayers," Maddy said, embracing Sisters Rose and Nora in turn.

"Come tell us what the abbess says," Sister Rose said. "We'll be dying to know how she persuaded him not to take her."

Sister Nora nodded. "We'll have a quick supper and then go to my chambers."

"I'll come see you as soon as I can." Maddy turned to Lillian. "Let's go see what the abbess wants."

Lillian mumbled a good-bye to the sisters and took Maddy's clammy hand when they entered the stairwell. Now that Emmey was safe, rampant curiosity replaced her earlier apprehension. Sophia had kept Emmey out of the noble's hands, but what had she given him in exchange?

Chapter Twenty-Three

MADDY FORCED A SMILE AS SHE and Lillian crossed the court-yard. "At least she won't go back to prison," she said, trying to look on the bright side. It didn't work. Tomorrow at eleven o'clock still loomed.

"Poor mite." Lillian shook her head. "I hadn't given much thought to how she must feel until she asked if she'd see you again. Thrown into prison, then into Reedwick, then finding out she has no family in Pinewood, then brought here and almost thrown back into prison again, and tomorrow to the Carmichaels. She really has been living day to day, hour to hour, not knowing if she'll have a home and any-one who cares. And always, frightened that she won't have a chance to say good-bye to you."

"I know." Maddy was glad Lillian empathized with Emmey, but Lillian's verbal musings were further dampening her spirits. "And how long will she last at the Carmichaels'?" She couldn't see Emmey staying on their farm until she took a husband.

"At least she knew love and security for a time. Many children never do."

Lillian's attempt to make Maddy feel better had the opposite effect. With a long face, she followed Lillian into the abbess's study and tried to appear at least indifferent. Pleased was beyond her.

The abbess was hunched over a document on her desk. She looked up when they entered. "Sit down."

"So don't keep us in suspense," Lillian said as they sank into the guest chairs. She glanced at an open bottle of brandy and four drained glasses sitting on the table separating the two chairs. "What happened?"

"He agreed not to take Emmey."

"We know that!" Lillian snapped. "What did you give him?"

"A document."

"A document?"

The abbess nodded. "As I said, he's a proud man who wouldn't leave empty-handed. Considering what Emmey had already endured, most men would have shrugged when they found out she'd gone. But not this one, not when his men were looking on."

"He didn't accept the governor's assurance that Emmey had died in the prison fire?" Maddy asked.

For some reason, the abbess grimaced before answering. "Too many folk had seen her, Maddy, both inside and outside the prison."

Maddy hoped Arthur hadn't suffered any repercussions for his role in helping Emmey escape.

"Bradford needed something to save face, to show that an eight-year-old hadn't got the better of him," the abbess continued. "So he came here, and I gave it to him."

Maddy glanced at Lillian, saw the puzzlement that mirrored her own. "Did he release Emmey from her sentence?" she asked.

"No, and he did have documents that legally entitled him to take her."

But the noble had left without her. "I don't understand."

The abbess gazed at her. "We concluded negotiations over an hour ago, but Mistress Averill had to scribe the documents. Let me read our copy to you." She rested her elbows on the desk, lifted the document by its edges, and cleared her throat. "'I, Duke Richard—'"

"You mean she tried to steal from a bloody duke?" Lillian blurted.

"Yes." The abbess started again. "'I, Duke Richard Byron Sedrick Ulysses Bradford the Fifth, have entered into an agreement with the Salbine Sisters of the Merrin monastery concerning the common criminal henceforth referred to as Emmey. I sentenced Emmey to live out her days in Dunmurk Prison until she reached the age of fourteen years.'"

"Fourteen?" Maddy exclaimed. "The governor said she'd been sentenced to life, and so did Emmey."

"That's because the duke shortened her sentence today."

"Oh." Maddy felt terribly naive. She wasn't cut out for diplomacy and politicking.

"She was seven when she entered the prison," the abbess said.

"Seven?" Maddy exclaimed. "She said she was eight."

"She probably is now. And since Bradford didn't know her date of birth, we agreed that she turned eight six months ago." The abbess shifted her attention back to the document. "'When it came to my attention that an uprising had taken place at Dunmurk Prison, I travelled there myself, to ensure that the immoral thief who had callously stolen from me hadn't escaped. When I arrived, I discovered that a Salbine Sister from Merrin had taken pity on the girl. She threw herself at my feet—'"

Lillian's eyes bulged. "Threw herself at his—"

The abbess raised her hand and continued to read. "'—and begged me not to condemn the girl to another second in a cold, dark cell. I cannot pardon such a heinous crime that shows an appalling lack of respect for those of noble stature, but I am a merciful and wise man, and I honour Salbine. I could not turn a deaf ear to a sister's plea.'" She fell silent for a moment, then looked directly at Maddy. "'In my mercy, I agreed that the criminal Emmey would serve out her sentence,'" a smile spread across the abbess's face, "'under the care of the Salbine Sisters at the Merrin monastery.'"

Maddy held a trembling hand to her mouth. "Does that mean . . . Emmey will—"

"Live here?" The abbess lowered the document. "Yes, that's what it means. And Bradford left quite satisfied. He can wave this document around as proof of how merciful and wise he is, and to show that a sister asked him for Emmey."

Her cheeks wet, Maddy couldn't speak. *Thank you, Salbine! Thank you!*

"Not only that, he's now off to the royal estate to attend a party Merrin's throwing in his honour."

Lillian's brows rose. "Merrin agreed to throw him a party?"

The abbess nodded. "He was quite agreeable when Barnabus asked him to. Merrin's useless, but he does know how to throw a good soiree. And Stephen's salivating at the prospect of a trade agreement between

Merrin and Bradford. As for us, we have this document that legally entitles us to Emmey."

"But now we'll have orphans showing up at the gates," Lillian said.

"We're not taking in an orphan, Lillian. We're taking in a criminal, and only because we asked a noble to show mercy. I don't expect we'll be doing that again, and I doubt we'll have a rush of nobles at the gates asking us to show mercy to those they've had convicted." The abbess shrugged. "And if we do, we'll just tell them to sod off. Anyway, I won't bore you with the rest of the agreement. You know the interesting bits."

Lillian grunted. "Normally I'd tell you to burn such a tall tale or give it to a bard to compose a song. But not this time. You outdid yourself, Sophia."

"I do have my uses," the abbess said, clearly pleased. "And I may regret this." She turned to Maddy. "But I'm glad to see you crying joyful tears instead of sorrowful ones."

"What about the Carmichaels?" Maddy managed to say, still sniffling.

Lillian shifted in her chair. "Who cares about the bloody Carmichaels?"

"There's never a shortage of children willing to work their farm," the abbess said. "I doubt they'll care."

No, they wouldn't, because Emmey would have been just another anonymous child to them. She would have gone unloved, unnoticed, and ended up who knew where? But not now. Not now.

The abbess moved the document aside. "Let's talk about rules. We'll probably discover more over the coming weeks and months, but let's start with the obvious ones. First, I expect Emmey to properly address sisters. I don't expect her to formally address the two of you, but I do expect her to call you Maddy, not Miss. The usual rules of address apply to everyone else. Understood?"

They both nodded.

"Second, this *is* a monastery. Emmey will be living among a religious community. I expect her to respect our ways. I expect her to learn of Salbine. And I expect to see her in the chapel on a regular basis."

"Of course." Maddy looked forward to taking her to a service.

"Third, she's not allowed anywhere near the training rooms."

"Yes, Abbess."

"And then there's the matter of who will be responsible for her. Mistress Averill will draw up a lesson plan for her, and Mistress Bertha has agreed to introduce her to several artistic pursuits, to see what catches her interest. But she needs a home, one that will provide her with stability and a sense of security. Passing her from sister to sister won't do. She needs to know where she belongs, and with whom she belongs."

Maddy could relate, and wasn't surprised when the abbess looked at her.

"She needs someone to unconditionally accept and care for her, to be her guardian, if you will. That sounds like you, doesn't it, Maddy?" Maddy's vision again blurred with tears. "You wanted a purpose. Well, now you have one. I'm sure it's not what you expected, but it rarely is. You'll still want to go to Heath and investigate your condition, but perhaps the matter won't be as pressing for the next few years."

She bit her lip to stem another tide of tears, and nodded.

"You and Lillian will have to sacrifice individual bedchambers. I presume that won't be a problem."

Lillian's jaw dropped. "You mean she'll live with us, in *my* chambers?"

The abbess nodded.

"Abbess, may I have a few minutes alone with Lillian?" Maddy asked.

"Of course." When Maddy started to rise, the abbess motioned for her to sit back down. "I'll go for a walk. I've been cooped up in here all afternoon." After glancing at Lillian, she left.

Maddy turned to Lillian. "Lillian, you don't have to do this," she said quietly.

"Do what?"

"I'll understand if you don't want to pledge. When you asked me to be your consort, you didn't know it would mean taking on Emmey, as well."

Lillian rose and towered over her. "Oh, so now that you have Emmey, you don't want me, is that it?"

"No!" Maddy sighed and stood up, so she wouldn't feel at such a disadvantage. "I certainly do want you! I told you, I'm a selfish cow.

But I'll understand if you don't want to share chambers with Emmey. We can carry on as we did before."

"No, we can't—not with Emmey living with you!" Lillian's hands clenched. "I meant what I said that night at the fire. I don't want to go back to how we were before." She hugged herself, gripped her robe. "I've already put the carpenters to work on another chair, for in front of the fire."

Maddy stepped toward her. "Lillian—"

"It's not as if she'll be in my—our chambers all the time, is it?"

"No, she won't. But she'll be there every morning and will want to be tucked in every night. And she'll want to spend time with us when we're there. We can't lock her away in her bedchamber," she said lightly.

"Why not? Strictly speaking, the monastery *is* her prison," Lillian said.

Maddy could tell she was joking, but the remark humbled her. She'd once thought the monastery would become *her* prison.

Lillian's arms dropped to her sides. "I want to be with you, Maddy. If that means taking on Emmey too, then that's what it means. You're the one who seems to think I'm not capable of caring for her, not me."

"I know you're capable. And Emmey cares about you. But when the abbess said—"

"I was surprised, that's all. I don't know why, though, where else would she live? I'll get used to it." Lillian wagged a finger. "She's not allowed in my laboratory, though."

"Of course she isn't."

"And she'll have to learn to knock on our bedchamber door."

"She will."

"And she has to listen to me, not just you."

"Of course she does." Maddy reached out and grabbed Lillian's rough robe. "Because we'll guide her together. The abbess said it would be me, but she knows that means us. And I'm glad I won't be alone in this, because frankly, I'm terrified."

Lillian's brow furrowed. "Why?"

"I never expected to be responsible for a child."

Lillian gripped her shoulders. "Maddy, you've been responsible for Emmey for months. Now you'll have an entire community to support you. You'll have me, too."

"You've already been supporting me." Maddy let go of Lillian's robe. "And not just with Emmey. I don't want to be dependent on you, or her."

"You won't be. Sometimes you might have to ask for help, but that doesn't mean you're dependent. So don't be stubborn, Maddy."

"I'm not stubborn."

"Yes, you are."

"No, I'm not." Maddy pointed at Lillian. "*You're* the stubborn one."

"No, I'm not.

"Yes, you are."

"No, I'm not."

They stared at each other, then broke into laughter. "Poor Emmey, being stuck with us," Maddy said.

"Poor Emmey, my arse! That girl doesn't realize it yet, but she's just landed squarely on her feet."

Maddy couldn't wait to tell her.

A SMILE SPREAD across Maddy's face when she entered the library and saw Emmey perched on a stool, moving quill across paper.

Mistress Averill leaned over Emmey's shoulder. "All right, let's have a look."

"I'm not finished yet," Emmey protested.

"I only wanted you to write the first two lines." Mistress Averill plucked the quill from Emmey's hand, lifted the paper, and studied it. "Mmm. You might show up a couple of the novices, but there's room for improvement." She lowered the sheet and noticed Maddy and Lillian. "Oh, hello! Emmey says you've been helping her with her letters, Lillian."

"She's helped both of us," Maddy said.

"Why?" Lillian asked when the mistress's eyebrows rose.

"I'm a bit surprised, that's all. I can barely read your script." Mistress Averill looked at Maddy. "It's your turn next."

"I feel like I'm a novice again," Maddy said, remembering the first time she'd apprehensively lifted a quill and scribed an *a* under Mistress Averill's watchful eye.

Emmey scrambled off the stool and looked up at Maddy. "Do I have to go now?"

"No, you don't." Maddy crouched. "I have something to tell you. To make the noble go away, the abbess had to make him a promise." She swallowed and took a moment to collect herself.

"She promised him something bad about me," Emmey said, misinterpreting Maddy's emotional state as distress. She lowered her head. "It's all right, Miss."

"She promised him something good," Maddy said hoarsely. "At least *I* think it's good. She promised him that you'll live here, with me and Lillian."

Emmey lifted her head, her eyes filled with hope. "Until I go to that farm?"

"No, you're not going to the farm. You're staying here until you're old enough to take care of yourself."

"With you?"

Maddy nodded. "And Lillian."

Emmey stood deathly still.

Maddy's elation faded. "Emmey?"

Suddenly Emmey launched herself into Maddy, who would have fallen backward if not for Lillian standing behind her. Maddy returned Emmey's fierce hug, then smiled when Emmey struggled from her grasp, ran into Lillian's legs, and hugged them.

Lillian clumsily patted Emmey's back. "Yes, well, I'm glad everyone's happy."

Mistress Averill dabbed at one eye with her fingertip. "Perhaps you can come back later and scribe for me," she said to Maddy.

"I will, Mistress. Right now, we're going to show Emmey Lillian's chambers. That's where we'll be living," she explained to Emmey as she straightened and bobbed at Mistress Averill, who nodded.

"My—my chambers," Lillian said. "All right. But don't touch anything."

Maddy took Emmey's hand. "Maybe you'll help me carry some books to the library so we can start setting up your bedchamber."

"I get my own bedchamber, Miss?" Emmey said as they left the library.

"Yes, you do. Now, you have to follow the rules we set out for you, all right?"

Emmey nodded vigorously. "I don't want you to make me go, Miss."

"We won't, Emmey." Maddy stopped and let go of Emmey's hand to cup her chin. "This is your home now. Nobody will tell you to leave." Catching Emmey's hand, she started to walk again. "But you do have to follow the rules, so listen closely to the first one. You can't call me Miss anymore. You have to call me Maddy. And when you talk to other sisters, you have to call them Sister or Mistress. You'll learn who's what."

"How come people call Lillian Mistress and you Sister?"

Lillian spoke up. "Because I'm a mistress and Maddy isn't."

Emmey frowned at Lillian. "But why are you a mistress?"

"Because I'm very good at drawing the elements."

"Why are you good at drawing the elements?"

Lillian opened her mouth to reply, then closed it.

"We don't know," Maddy said. "She just is. She's probably the most powerful mage alive."

Emmey's brow furrowed. "What's a mage?"

"Salbine preserve us," Lillian muttered, rubbing her temples.

Maddy stifled a grin. "Do you want to go to your laboratory, Lillian? I can show Emmey your chambers alone."

"No! No, no, no. I want to be there, to make sure she doesn't get into anything she shouldn't."

Maddy inwardly sighed.

"And when we're finished, I'll go see the carpenters, tell them we'll need another chair."

Maddy cursed her lack of a free hand, wanting to take Lillian's hand and squeeze it. The abbess was right. Heath could wait. Salbine had taken away, and Salbine had generously given. Maddy would never doubt Her again.

Chapter Twenty-Four

Sophia leaned back in her chair and contentedly sipped her tea. The roaring fire popped and crackled, lulling her into an almost hypnotic state. She jumped when the door to her chambers swung open, grateful there wasn't enough tea remaining in her cup to spill onto her robe.

Elizabeth bounded in. "You look comfy." She lifted the bottle of cider she held.

"No, thank you. I've already had a brandy today."

"I thought you might want a mug anyway, to celebrate. You did well."

"Yes, I did, didn't I?" Sophia murmured.

Elizabeth poured herself a mug of cider and sat next to Sophia. "What's wrong? I thought you'd be pleased with yourself."

"I am. But I can't help but wonder whether I'm just a pawn in all of this."

"All of what?"

Sophia set her cup and saucer down on the table next to her chair and gazed at Elizabeth. "Lillian, probably the most powerful mage we've seen this century, will soon pledge her life to Maddy, a sister who went to prison because she can't light a candle, and in their care will be Emmey, a child Salbine has gone to great lengths to bring to us. I can't help but think that pieces are being positioned on a board I can't see."

Elizabeth stood and lifted Sophia's teacup to sniff its contents.

Sophia leaned away from her. "What are you doing?"

"Checking to see if you turned down the cider because you've already added a couple of dollops of brandy to your tea."

"I did no such thing!" Sophia snatched up her cup and saucer the moment Elizabeth set the cup down. "But perhaps I am seeing something that isn't there," she added at Elizabeth's smirk.

Elizabeth shrugged as she returned to her chair. "It's just happenstance."

"Or me."

"What do you mean?"

"Being sentimental. Here I am, in front of the fire with a nice cup of tea, thinking about my sister and how she'll pledge next week. I never thought I'd see it, Elizabeth."

"You're pleased, I hope."

"Very pleased. She and Maddy will do well together." Sophia sipped her tea. "And that's another thing. Out of all the initiates Lillian could have ended up with for fire training, she ended up with Maddy."

Elizabeth rolled her eyes. "Doesn't it make more sense that they became involved because Maddy was assigned to Lillian, rather than believing that Maddy was assigned to Lillian because they were supposed to become involved?"

"I suppose so." But she still couldn't shake the feeling that Salbine, or one of the other gods, was orchestrating events. After arranging for Emmey to stay at the Carmichaels, she'd envisioned her at the monastery and felt uneasy. Now she felt as if Emmey was where she belonged, and with whom she belonged. Sophia looked down at her tea. Or perhaps she was a sentimental fool who hadn't wanted to tear a child away from the sister who loved her, and was now trying to justify her weakness. Time would tell. "I hope Lillian and Emmey get on all right. It might be a bit difficult for them at first, poor things."

"I think Maddy deserves our sympathy more than they do. She'll always be caught in the middle."

Sophia chuckled. "Perhaps you're right. And she'll be a splendid guardian. Emmey couldn't have asked for a better influence as she grows into a young woman."

Elizabeth stared at her. "Aren't you forgetting something?"

"What?"

"That Maddy won't be Emmey's only influence. Her other primary influence will be Lillian."

"Oh, you're right." Visions of a young woman hunched over a tome, muttering bloody this and bloody that, flitted through her mind. "You know, I think I'll have that cider after all."

Elizabeth arched a brow. "I thought you might."

MADDY WAS DYING to give Lillian a sidelong glance, but since the abbess's right hand was resting on the top of her head, she restrained herself. "Mistress Lillian and Sister Maddy," the abbess said. "You have pledged your lives to each other in the presence of Salbine." She lifted her hands and stepped back. "Rise, and greet each other as consorts."

Maddy pushed herself to her feet and kissed Lillian on both cheeks, then embraced her. The assembled sisters' voices swelled in song.

"We've gone and done it now," Lillian murmured.

And Maddy couldn't be happier. From the platform at the front of the chapel, she smiled at Emmey, who was sitting on the front bench with Rose and Nora. Emmey had better remember not to run.

When the voices faded, the abbess stepped forward. "And now, would Emmey come here, please."

Don't run.

Emmey sprang from the bench and started to run, then suddenly stopped and slowly walked to the steps, looking solemn in the pretty blue dress the seamstresses had delighted in making for her. Maddy wanted to give her an encouraging look, but Emmey's eyes were on the abbess. Last night they'd reviewed what the abbess would say. Emmey only had to respond with one word.

The abbess leaned forward. "Emmey, you've just seen Mistress Lillian and Sister Maddy pledge their lives to each other. Now it's your turn to make a pledge. Do you pledge to respect Mistress Lillian, Sister Maddy, and all the Salbine Sisters, Defenders, and workers who belong to our community?"

Emmey vigorously nodded.

Maddy grinned at the same time the abbess smiled. "Do you think you can say yes, so everyone can hear you?" the abbess said.

Emmey clapped her hands. "Yes!"

Laughter rippled through the assembly.

"Thank you." The abbess straightened. "Please welcome Emmey to our community."

"Welcome, Emmey!" numerous voices called.

Maddy motioned for Emmey to join her and Lillian, and rested her hand on Emmey's shoulder when she stood in front of them.

The abbess raised her hands, palms up. "Sisters." Robes rustled as everyone stood. "Do you pledge to support Mistress Lillian, Sister Maddy, and Emmey as they grow together?"

"We do," they responded as one.

Abbess Sophia nodded in satisfaction and turned to Maddy, Lillian, and Emmey. "May Salbine bless you in your lives together."

"Salbine's will be done," Maddy murmured along with Lillian.

The abbess faced the assembly, closed her eyes, and stretched out her arms. "May Salbine guide you. May Salbine provide for you. May Salbine keep you."

"Salbine's will be done," Maddy said again.

"Please congratulate our newest family, then proceed to the dining hall for the sumptuous meal the cooks have prepared for us," the abbess called as chapel bells pealed in celebration.

Not surprisingly, Lillian hung back as Maddy and Emmey descended the steps and sisters rushed forward to hug them. Maddy turned to beckon to her, but Lillian was in the arms of her sister. "Congratulations!" Rose cried, reaching for Maddy. The next ten minutes were a blur. Maddy lost count of the number of sisters who embraced and congratulated her, and would have been hard-pressed to identify them all later. Lillian eventually stood at her side, acknowledging congratulations with a nod, and accepting hugs from those brave enough to offer one.

The attention seemed to bewilder Emmey, but not frighten her. At one point Maddy lost sight of her, but could hear her chattering away with someone.

Finally the throng around them thinned. Maddy faced Lillian, intending to say something memorable and poignant, but words would ruin the moment. They beamed at each other.

"I'm hungry!" a little voice piped up.

Lillian didn't roll her eyes, but Maddy could tell she wanted to. "I guess we should go to the dining hall, then," Maddy said. When Emmey reached for her hand, she crouched to meet the little girl's eye. "Would you mind if I hold Lillian's hand, just this once?"

"Here, hold mine." Rose offered her hand to Emmey, who willingly grasped it.

"Thank you for taking her tonight and tomorrow morning," Maddy said to Rose. "We really appreciate it."

"It's no bother," Rose said, slipping her other hand into Nora's. "I enjoy her company."

"So can we expect you at morning prayers tomorrow, Maddy?" Nora ended her question with a giggle.

Maddy gave her an indulgent smile as she took Lillian's hand and fell into step with everyone.

"Are you sure you don't want me to stay with you tonight, Mi—Maddy?" Emmey said. "I promise I'll be quiet."

"We've already talked about this. Lillian and I want some time alone together. You'll sleep in your new bedchamber tomorrow."

"Don't you want to stay with me?" Rose teased.

"No, I do, but they'll miss me," Emmey said.

Rose smiled. "Oh, I see." Nora covered her mouth. Maddy dared not look at Lillian, whose face would be a picture.

Emmey gasped. "I know, I'll come see you as soon as I wake up!"

"No, you bloody-well won't!" Lillian bellowed. "Wait for us to come for you."

"Aw . . ."

"I don't want to see you anywhere near my—our chambers, all right?"

"But what if I have to talk to you?"

Lillian's face reddened. "You can wait!"

"But—"

"Emmey, do what Lillian says and wait for us to come for you tomorrow," Maddy said firmly.

Emmey's shoulders slumped. "All right." She brightened when Maddy slowed down to peck her on the cheek. "You and Lillian are consorts! Now we'll all be together!"

"Yes, we will." Maddy's cheeks hurt. "It's a very happy day."

"Are you happy, Lillian?" Emmey asked.

"Oh, yes, I certainly am." Lillian cleared her throat.

Maddy met Lillian's eyes and squeezed her hand. As she surveyed the sisters in front of her streaming to the Community Tower, their robes forming a kaleidoscope of colours, she thanked Salbine for not giving up on her and for bringing her home. She was in for an interesting few years, filled with love and laughter, bickering and exasperation. During the trying times, she might doubt her love for Lillian and question her worthiness as Emmey's guardian, but she'd never again doubt that she belonged to the Salbine Order. She was, and always would be, Sister Maddy, of Merrin.

Author's Note

Thank you for reading *The Salbine Sisters*. If you enjoyed it, you might like Rymellan Fiction, a short story series about two women who live in a society that selects mates for its citizens. For more information, visit www.RymellanFiction.com

For more information about me, visit www.SarahEttritch.com

May Salbine guide you. May Salbine provide for you. May Salbine keep you.

~ Sarah Ettritch